Praise for *The Quilter's Apprentice*

"An involving story of strong women who sustain
and nourish each other."
—Charlotte Holmes, author of *Gifts and Other Stories*

"Heartwarming. You'll discover friendship here, and
you'll learn a thing or two about quilting."
—Sandra Dallas, author of *The Persian Pickle Club*

"Glows with the love of quilts, the importance of family,
and the value of friends to share our joys and sorrows with."
—Kathryn Smith, *Anderson* (South Carolina) *Independent-Mail*

"I enjoyed the way Chiaverini deftly stitches the lives of these two
women together. Tell Sarah and Sylvia I'd quilt with them any day."
—Ami Simms, author of
*How to Improve Your Quilting Style* and *Invisible Appliqué*

"Like the quilts described, the novel is carefully pieced together,
and each piece feels, sounds, and *is* fat with history and
meaning. This is a quiet, beautiful novel, full of
gentle wisdom and genuine humility."
—Percival Everett, author of *Frenzy* and *Watershed*

A former writing instructor at Pennsylvania State University,
**Jennifer Chiaverini** lives in Madison, Wisconsin, where she is at
work on her third novel, *Cross Country Quilters*. Her first novel,
*The Quilter's Apprentice*, is available in a Plume edition.

# ROUND ROBIN

## AN ELM CREEK QUILTS NOVEL

## Jennifer Chiaverini

A PLUME BOOK

PLUME
Published by the Penguin Group
Penguin Putnam Inc., 375 Hudson Street, New York, New York 10014, U.S.A.
Penguin Books Ltd, 27 Wrights Lane, London W8 5TZ, England
Penguin Books Australia Ltd, Ringwood, Victoria, Australia
Penguin Books Canada Ltd, 10 Alcorn Avenue, Toronto, Ontario, Canada M4V 3B2
Penguin Books (N.Z.) Ltd, 182–190 Wairau Road, Auckland 10, New Zealand

Penguin Books Ltd, Registered Offices: Harmondsworth, Middlesex, England

Published by Plume, a member of Penguin Putnam Inc.
This is an authorized reprint of a hardcover edition published by Simon & Schuster.
For information address Simon & Schuster, 1230 Avenue of the Americas,
New York, New York 10020.

First Plume Printing, April 2001
10 9

Ⓟ REGISTERED TRADEMARK—MARCA REGISTRADA

The Library of Congress has catalogued the hardcover edition as follows:
Chiaverini, Jennifer.
    Round robin : an Elm Creek Quilts novel / Jennifer Chiaverini.
      p.   cm.
    ISBN 0-684-86892-X (hc.)
        0-452-28227-6 (pbk.)
    I. Title.
PS3553.H473    R68 2000
813'.54—dc21    99-045743

Printed in the United States of America
Original hardcover design by Jill Weber

PUBLISHER'S NOTE
This is a work of fiction. Names, characters, places, and incidents are either the product of
the author's imagination or are used fictitiously, and any resemblance to actual persons,
living or dead, business establishments, events, or locales is entirely coincidental.

# Acknowledgments

My heartfelt thanks go out to:

My agent, Maria Massie.

The people at Simon & Schuster who worked on this project, especially my gifted editor, Denise Roy; her assistant, Brenda Copeland; and publicists Elizabeth Hayes and Rebecca Davis.

My online quilting friends, especially the members of R.C.T.Q., QuiltNet, and QuiltersBee.

Carol Coski and Terry Grant, who shared their experiences of a quilt shop owner's life.

The members of the Internet Writing Workshop, especially Christine Johnson, Candace Byers, Dave Swinford, Jody Ewing, and everyone in the Lounge.

Geraldine, Nic, and Heather Neidenbach; Virginia and Edward Riechman; and Leonard and Marlene Chiaverini; and my extended family in Cincinnati and elsewhere.

Most of all, I wish to thank my beloved husband, Marty, whose love and faith sustain me.

For

Martin Chiaverini,

Geraldine Neidenbach,

Nic Neidenbach,

and

Heather Neidenbach,

*with all my love*

# ROUND ROBIN

# Chapter One

In a few months, spring would turn the land surrounding Elm Creek Manor into a green patchwork quilt of dark forested hills and lighter farmers' fields and grassy lawns. After last night's snowstorm, however, the view from the kitchen window resembled a white whole cloth quilt, stitched with the winding gravel road to Waterford, the bare, brown tree limbs, and a thin trace of blue where the creek cut through the woods. The barn stood out in the distance, a cheerful splash of red against the snow.

So much about Elm Creek Manor had changed, but not the view from the window over the sink. If not for the stiffness in her hands and the way the winter chill had seeped into her bones, Sylvia could convince herself that the past fifty years had never happened. She could imagine herself a young woman again, as if any moment she would hear her younger brother whistling as he came downstairs for breakfast. She would look up and see her elder sister entering the kitchen, tying on an apron. Sylvia would gaze through the window and see a lone figure trudging through the snow from the barn, returning to his home and his bride after completing the morning chores. She would leave her work and hurry to the back door to meet him, her footsteps quick and light, her heart full. Her husband was there and alive again, as was her brother, as was her sister, and together they would laugh at the grief of their long separation.

Sylvia squeezed her eyes shut and listened.

She heard a clock ticking in the west sitting room off the kitchen, and then, distantly, the sound of someone descending the grand staircase in the front foyer. For a moment her breath caught in her throat, and she almost believed she had accomplished the impossible. She had willed herself back in time, and now, armed with the wisdom of hindsight and regret, she could set everything to rights. All the years that had been stolen from them were restored, and they would live them out together. Not a single moment would be wasted.

"Sylvia?" someone called out from down the hall.

It was a woman's voice, one she had come to know well over the past two years. Sylvia opened her eyes, and the ghosts receded to the past, to memory. In another moment Sarah appeared in the kitchen doorway, smiling.

"The Elm Creek Quilters are here," Sarah said. "I saw their cars coming up the back drive."

Sylvia rinsed the last coffee cup and placed it in the dishwasher. "It's about time. They'd be very disappointed if they missed the show." She caught the smile Sarah tried to hide. Sarah often teased Sylvia for her insistence on punctuality, but Sylvia had no intention of changing her opinion. She knew, even if Sarah and the six other Elm Creek Quilters didn't, the value of a minute.

Sarah gave Sylvia a look of affectionate amusement. "The show won't start for twenty minutes, at least," she said as they went to the back door to greet their friends. They had called themselves the Tangled Web Quilters when Sylvia and Sarah had joined the bee nearly two years before, but together they adopted the new name to symbolize the creation of a new group and to celebrate the beginning of their business, Elm Creek Quilts.

Gwen and Summer entered first, laughing together like no mother and daughter Sylvia had ever known. Bonnie followed close behind, carrying a large cardboard box. "I cleared out a storage room at the shop last night," Bonnie told them. "I've got scraps, leftover ribbon, and some thread that's been discontinued. I thought we could use it when classes start up again in March."

Sarah thanked her, took the box, and placed it on the floor out of the way. Bonnie owned Grandma's Attic, Waterford's only quilt shop. Elm Creek Quilts ordered material and notions through her, and in return Bonnie gave them any leftovers or irregulars that couldn't be sold. Sylvia admired Bonnie's generosity, which had not lessened even after the new chain fabric store on the outskirts of town opened and began steadily siphoning away her income.

Diane entered just in time to overhear Bonnie's words. "You should let us root through that box first," she said, holding the door open for Agnes. "I can always use a bit of extra fabric, especially if it's free."

"Did you hear that?" Gwen asked Bonnie, as Judy entered, holding the hand of her three-year-old daughter, Emily. "Better turn on the security cameras next time you let Diane help in the shop."

Diane looked puzzled. "You have security cameras? I never noticed any." When the others began to chuckle, she grew indignant. "Not that I had any reason to look."

Gwen's eyebrows rose. "Sounds to me like you have a guilty conscience."

The hallway rang with laughter, and Sylvia's heart soared as she looked around the circle of women. She had welcomed them into her home, first as friends and later as business colleagues. In her heart, though, she would always consider them family. Not that they could replace the family she had lost more than fifty years before—no one could do that—but they were a great comfort, nonetheless.

The new arrivals were breathless with excitement and red-cheeked from the cold. They put their coats away in the hall closet and soon were settling into the formal parlor. Sarah took a seat on the sofa beside Sylvia's chair. "Didn't I promise you someday you'd be glad we got cable?" she said as she turned on the television.

"Indeed you did," Sylvia said. "But I'll reserve judgment until after the show."

"Sarah's going to drag you kicking and screaming into the twenty-first century if it's the last thing she does," Gwen said.

"She most certainly will not," Sylvia retorted. "I have more dignity than that. I'll move along calmly and quietly, thank you."

Emily squirmed on Judy's lap. "I want to sit by Sarah."

"Sarah wants to see this show," Judy told her. "Maybe later she can play."

"That's okay. Emily can sit here if she likes." Sarah slid over and patted the seat beside her. "I haven't seen her in two days. We have lots to talk about."

Emily jumped down from her mother's lap and ran across the room to Sarah, who laughed and helped her climb onto the sofa.

"When are you going to have one of your own?" Diane asked.

Sarah rolled her eyes. "You sound like my mother."

"You can't wait forever, you know."

"I realize that." Sarah shot Diane a quick frown before putting her arm around Emily. Emily giggled and smiled up at her. Sylvia caught the fragrance of baby shampoo and something else, something sweet and fresh beneath it, and she wondered why Sarah, who used to speak confidently about having children someday, had not said a word on the subject in months. Perhaps the couple had decided against having children, or perhaps they had no choice. Sylvia didn't want to pry, but her heart was troubled for Sarah and Matt, and she wished she knew how to help them.

"Where is Matthew, anyway?" Sylvia wondered aloud.

"He's inspecting the orchards for storm damage," Sarah said. "He said he'd try to make it back in time for the show, but . . ." She shrugged.

"He can't miss this," Judy protested.

"He won't. There's a new tape in the VCR." Sarah smiled, tight-lipped. "You know how he is about those trees. Besides, he was here for the filming last fall, and that was the exciting part, right?"

Nonsense, Sylvia wanted to say, but she kept quiet.

"The show's starting," Summer announced, taking the remote from

Sarah. Sylvia saw their eyes meet, and something passed between them. Whatever it was, it made Sarah relax, and so Sylvia did as well. Summer was an exceptional young woman—optimistic and empathetic, and more thoughtful than most people her age. Sylvia would miss her when she went off to graduate school in the fall. The young couldn't help growing up and wanting to make their own ways through life, but Summer would be the first Elm Creek Quilter to leave their circle, and they would not feel whole without her.

Sylvia pushed the thoughts to the back of her mind, choosing instead to focus on the television. As the theme music played, a familiar man with graying hair and a red-and-black flannel coat appeared on the screen and walked across a gravel road toward the camera, a snowy cornfield in the background.

"Good morning, friends," the man said. "I'm Grant Richards."

"He looks better on TV than in person," Diane said.

Grant Richards smiled out at them. "Welcome to *America's Back Roads*, the show that takes you down the road less traveled to the heart of America, to the small towns where old-fashioned values still endure, where life goes on at a slower pace, where friends are friends for life, where the frantic clamor of the city ventures no closer than the evening news."

Gwen grinned. "Apparently he's never seen campus during Freshman Orientation."

"He's right about one thing, though," Judy said. "Around here, friends are friends for life."

"Hmph." Sylvia frowned at the screen. "I don't care for his folksy posturing. He makes it sound like we're a bunch of hayseeds out in the middle of nowhere."

"We are in the middle of nowhere," Agnes pointed out, and no one contradicted her.

Grant continued. "This Sunday morning we're traveling through the snow-covered hills of Pennsylvania, where you'll meet a man who makes musical instruments out of old auto parts, a Tony Award–winning actress who abandoned the bright lights of Broadway to become a high school drama teacher, and a group of quilters dedicated to passing on their craft, warming toes and hearts alike in a place called Elm Creek Manor."

The Elm Creek Quilters burst into cheers and applause.

Emily looked up at Sarah, puzzled. "We're last?"

"Probably," Sarah told her. "We won't have to wait too long, though." Emily's face fell anyway, and Sarah laughed and kissed her on the top of her head.

The excitement in the room built through the first two segments. The weeks between the arrival of the producer's first letter and the final wrap had passed swiftly compared to the months they had waited for this moment. Sylvia could hardly keep still. If she were almost three years old like Emily, she, too, would be bouncing up and down in her seat, but she settled for drumming her fingers on the arm of her chair.

Then, finally, it was time.

"There's Elm Creek Manor," Agnes said, just as the rest of them saw it. Grant Richards was walking up the front drive as he told the audience about Elm Creek Quilts, the business founded by Sylvia Compson and Sarah McClure, two women from Waterford.

"Sarah isn't really from Waterford," Diane said. "She moved here."

The others shushed her.

"After months of preparation, Elm Creek Quilts welcomed their first guests." Grant's voice-over kept pace with a montage of scenes: quilters arriving at the manor, moving into their rooms, attending quilt classes, laughing and chatting as they strolled through the grounds.

Then Sylvia appeared on-screen, Sarah by her side. "We wanted to create a place where quilters of all backgrounds and skill levels could come to quilt, to make new friends, to practice old skills and learn new ones," Sylvia explained. "Quilters can come for a weekly quilt camp or they can rent a room for as long as they like and work independently. Beginning and intermediate quilters usually prefer the former; advanced quilters, the latter."

Unconsciously, Sylvia sat up straight and touched her hair, pleased.

She did look very smart there on the television in that nice blue skirt and blazer Sarah had insisted she purchase for the occasion. Her friends looked very nice, too, she thought, watching as the camera showed the Elm Creek Quilters sitting around a quilt frame, answering Grant's questions as they worked. Sylvia couldn't help smiling at the sight. They all looked so cheerful, so companionable.

On-screen, Grant admired Judy's red-and-white Feathered Star quilt in the frame. "I guess you finish a quilt much faster when you all work on it together, right?"

"That's exactly so," Agnes said.

"That's not what's most important about working around the quilting frame, however," Gwen said to the camera.

"Get ready, everyone," Diane said, watching. "The professor is about to expound." The real-life Gwen threw a pillow at her.

On-screen, Gwen's expression had grown serious. "The quilting frame speaks to something deep within the woman's soul. Too often, work in the modern society isolates us in offices or cubicles. We speak to people on the phone or through the computer rather than face-to-face. The essential element of human contact has been lost. The quilting frame, on the other hand, draws us back together, back into a community."

Gwen wrinkled her nose at the television. "Do I really sound that pompous when I talk?"

"Yes," Diane said, throwing the pillow back at her.

Sylvia held up a hand. "That is a throw pillow, but let's not take the name quite so literally, shall we?"

Gwen's speech played on. "Women's work used to be much more communal, as when the entire village would gather food together, as when the women would all go down to the river together and do the laundry by pounding the clothes on rocks."

Summer looked up from her quilting, her eyes wide and innocent. "That's how they did it when you were a girl, right, Mom?"

Both on-screen and off, the Elm Creek Quilters laughed.

Even Grant chuckled before resuming the interview. "But what about you? How did you learn to quilt? There were no Elm Creek Quilters around to teach you as you now teach others."

"My mother taught me," Sylvia responded.

"And Sylvia, in turn, taught me." Agnes gave her a sidelong glance. "Or at least she tried to."

"My mom taught me," Summer said.

Grant looked around the circle. "So most of you learned from your mothers, is that it?"

All but Sarah nodded. "Not me," she declared. "I mean, please. The idea of my mother quilting. . . ." She laughed and shook her head. "I don't even think she knows which end of the needle to thread."

On-screen, the Elm Creek Quilters smiled, but in the parlor, they didn't.

"Oh, dear," Agnes said.

"It seemed funnier at the time," Bonnie said, looking from the television to Sarah, who sat rigid and still on the edge of the sofa.

"I didn't know they filmed that part," she said.

Diane shot her a look of disbelief. "That little red light on the camera didn't clue you in?"

"I thought they had stopped filming by then. Really." Her eyes met Sylvia's. "Really," she insisted, as if something in Sylvia's expression conveyed doubt.

"I believe you," Sylvia said, although she wondered.

"What'll your mom say when she sees this?" Summer asked.

"Maybe she won't see it," Sarah said.

"Of course she'll see it," Agnes said. "No mother would miss her daughter on national television."

Sarah said nothing, but her expression was resolute, as if she had seized a thin thread of hope and had no intention of letting go.

Then the phone rang.

Agnes was closest, so she answered. "Good morning, Elm Creek Quilts." A pause. "No, I'm Sylvia's sister-in-law, Agnes. Would you like to speak to her?" A longer pause. "Sarah? Yes, Sarah's here." Her eyes went wide. "Oh, yes, hello. I've heard so much about you." She threw Sarah a helpless look. "Why, yes, I'll get her. Hold on, please." She held out the phone to Sarah. "It's your mother."

Sarah dragged herself out of her seat, took the phone and the receiver, and carried them as far toward the doorway as the cord would permit. Watching her, Summer fingered the remote as if unsure whether to lower the volume so that Sarah could hear her mother better or turn up the sound to give Sarah some semblance of privacy.

Sylvia turned back to the television and pretended to concentrate on the show. The other Elm Creek Quilters followed suit, but Sylvia doubted they were paying any more attention than she herself was.

"Hi, Mother. . . . Yes. I know. I know. I'm sorry, but—" Sarah winced and held the receiver away from her ear for a moment. "Look, I said I was sorry. . . . I didn't know the camera was on. . . . Of course that makes a difference." A pause. "Well, so what? I didn't mention you by name or anything. . . . It's not an excuse. It's the truth." Silence. "I said I was sorry. It was just a joke. Summer told a joke about her mom, and so I—" Sarah's mouth tightened. "I do not. That's unfair, Mother." Her face went scarlet. "He would not. Dad would never say such a thing. I'm sorry, okay? I'm sorry. What else do I have to do? . . . I can't apologize on national television and you know it." Silence. "Fine. If that's the way you feel, have it your way." She slammed down the phone and stormed across the room to return it to the table.

"How did it go?" Diane asked.

Sarah shot her a dark glare and flung herself onto the sofa. "How do you think?"

Emily didn't recognize the sarcasm. "Bad?" she guessed, looking up at Sarah with wide eyes.

Sarah softened and snuggled her close. "Not so bad," she assured her, but she gave the others a look that told them otherwise. "She'll never let this one go. Never. She's convinced I made her look like a fool."

"Well . . ." Summer hesitated. "You kind of did."

"Not intentionally," Sarah protested. "She thinks I did it on purpose, just to humiliate her. Honestly. She's so self-absorbed. She thinks everything's about her."

"Hmph," Sylvia said, thinking.

Sarah turned to her. "For goodness sake, Sylvia, what's 'Hmph' supposed to mean?"

Sylvia refused to be baited. "Don't lash out at me, young lady. I'm not the one you're angry at, and neither is your mother." To her satisfaction, Sarah's anger wavered. "You know your words were thoughtless and silly, just as you know your mother's feelings are justified. You're embarrassed and ashamed, and rightfully so. If I were your mother, I would have given you an earful, too."

Sarah sank back into the sofa, defeated. "If you were my mother, none of this would have happened."

"Now, now," Sylvia said. "You'll put things right. Take an hour or so to cool down, then get back on that phone and apologize."

"I did apologize."

"I mean apologize sincerely."

Sarah shook her head. "I can't. You don't know her like I do. There's no use talking to her when she's this upset."

"Call her tomorrow, then."

"I can't." Sarah rose. "You don't understand."

"Explain it to us," Gwen said. "We'll listen. We want to understand."

But Sarah just shook her head and left the room.

"What should we do?" Judy asked.

"Nothing," Diane said. "We should stay out of it."

"There must be some way we can help." Summer looked around the circle of friends anxiously. "Isn't there?"

No one could answer her.

The show had ended, though no one had seen the last half of their segment. Sylvia considered rewinding the tape they had made for Matt and playing the last part, but decided against it. Already the Elm Creek Quilters were getting to their feet, preparing to leave. She would save the tape for another day.

Later, when she was alone, Sylvia mulled over the morning's events as she quilted in the west sitting room. She thought of a promise Sarah had made to her nearly two years before as they sat on the front veranda negotiating their agreement to launch a new business together.

"I don't know what kind of conflict stands between you and your mother," Sylvia had said, "but you must promise me you'll talk to her and do your best to resolve it. Don't be a stubborn fool like me and let grudges smolder and relationships die."

The unexpected request had clearly caught Sarah by surprise. "I don't think you know how difficult that will be."

"I don't pretend to know, but I can guess. I don't expect miracles. All I ask is that you learn from my mistakes and try."

Sarah had given her a long, steady look, and for a moment Sylvia had been certain that she would refuse and that their agreement to create Elm Creek Quilts would founder on this one point. Sylvia had been tempted to tell Sarah she would take back the condition, but she held fast, determined to see to it that Sarah would learn from her older friend's mistakes and not have to endure the hard lessons of a lifetime, if she could be spared them.

Her patience had been rewarded.

"All right," Sarah had said at last. "If that's one of your conditions, I'll try. I can't promise you that anything will come of it, but I'll try."

Nearly two years had come and gone since Sarah had spoken those words, and what had she to show for it? Sylvia let her hands fall to her lap, still holding her quilting. She sat there for a long while, lost in thought.

So many things could go wrong, she knew. But life carried no guarantees for anyone. That couldn't keep one paralyzed, fearing to act. That was no way to live.

Once Sylvia made up her mind, she saw no reason to wait. She put her quilting aside and went to the parlor, where she eased the door shut so she could make her call in privacy.

# Chapter Two

Spring came to the hills of central Pennsylvania early that year. By mid-March, buds had formed on the stately elm trees lining the road to Elm Creek Manor, where Sarah, Sylvia, and the other Elm Creek Quilters waited for the first group of campers of the season to arrive. Sarah was pleased that Sylvia had agreed to direct their guests to the front entrance rather than the back.

"But parking is behind the manor," Sylvia had argued at first. "They'll only have to move their cars later."

"We'll do it for them, like valet parking. This way they won't have to carry their luggage all the way from the back door to the foyer for registration." Sarah didn't tell Sylvia she was more concerned about the first impression the quilters formed of Elm Creek Manor. She knew how they would feel as they approached in their cars, in groups and alone: first the gray stone manor itself would strike them, strong and serene in a sea of green grass. Then they would notice the wide veranda running the length of the building, lined with tall columns supporting a roof that bathed the veranda in cool shade. As they drew closer, they would see the two stone staircases that arced away from each other as they descended from the veranda. Their cars would come to a stop at the foot of those stairs in the driveway, which encircled a fountain in the shape of a rearing horse, the symbol of the Bergstrom family, the founders of Elm Creek Manor.

But Sarah didn't tell Sylvia this. Sylvia was pragmatic, not sentimental. Fortunately, Sarah's argument about carrying luggage through the house convinced her. Sarah could hardly keep from grinning as one quilter after another stepped out of her car, awestruck and thrilled that she would be able to spend a week in such a grand place.

"That makes eight," Judy said as the latest arrival took her room key and followed Matt upstairs. As caretaker of Elm Creek Manor, he spent most of his time maintaining the grounds and the building, but on check-in days, he carried bags and parked cars. The Elm Creek Quilters took turns sitting behind the registration desk and directing cars up the driveway. There wasn't really enough work to keep them all busy, but they thought it better, friendlier, to have everyone there on the first day to welcome their guests.

Sylvia checked her clipboard. "Four more to go, unless we have a cancellation." Her gaze returned to the wall opposite the front doors.

"What are you thinking about?" Sarah asked her. Sylvia had been uncharacteristically quiet that day, and she had been studying the wall above the entrance to the banquet hall off and on throughout registration.

Sylvia walked to the center of the foyer. "It occurred to me that this wall is the first thing our guests see when they enter the manor, as they look up to climb the stairs." She gestured, showing them the straight line from the twelve-foot double doors to the wall just beneath the balcony. "Our guests ought to see something a trifle more attractive than a bare wall when they arrive. We ought to have a quilt hanging there." She tapped her chin with a finger. "Perhaps one of my old quilts will do."

Summer joined Sylvia in the center of the room and contemplated the wall. "We could hang Sarah's sampler there, if she's willing to give it up. That's the quilt that brought us together."

"You'd have to fight Matt for it," Sarah said. She had given him her first quilt as an anniversary present nearly two years before, and he treasured it. She wondered if he knew how much that pleased her.

Sylvia shook her head. "We can't rob Matthew of his quilt. We'll have to think of something else."

"You know what else we need? A motto." Gwen held up her hands as if framing a sign. "Elm Creek Quilts: Where something something some-thing."

Diane's eyebrows rose. "What kind of motto is 'Something something something'?"

"That's not the motto. That's just an example."

Judy spoke up. "How about 'Elm Creek Quilts: Where you can quilt till you wilt.' "

The others chuckled, but Agnes shook her head. "I don't think it quite fits. We want people to rejuvenate their spirits here, not work themselves into exhaustion."

"I've got one," Diane said. "Elm Creek Quilts: Where hand-quilting is celebrated and machine-quilting tolerated—sort of."

"That's your motto, not Elm Creek Quilts'," Bonnie said, laughing.

"Oh, yeah? Well, I have a motto for you. 'Bonnie Markham, whose phone is busy twenty-four hours a day, especially when friends are trying to call to see if she needs a ride to Elm Creek Manor.' "

"That's rather cumbersome for a motto," Sylvia remarked.

"My phone isn't busy twenty-four hours a day," Bonnie protested. "Just when Craig's on the Internet."

"Exactly," Diane said. "Twenty-four hours a day."

Bonnie sighed and shook her head.

Gwen grinned. "My motto is 'When God made men, it was to prove She had a sense of humor.' "

Summer rolled her eyes. "Then mine will be 'Forgive our mothers, for they know not what they say.' "

Sarah figured that Summer's motto would be a good one for herself, except for that part about forgiveness.

"What about—" Bonnie said, just as the front door swung open and a new guest entered. Before they finished with her registration, two more arrived, and they forgot about bare walls and mottoes in the bustle of activity.

It wasn't until Sylvia was engrossed in conversation with one of the last guests that Agnes beckoned the other Elm Creek Quilters. "I think we should make Sylvia a round robin quilt for that wall," she said, keeping her voice low so that Sylvia wouldn't overhear.

"What's a round robin quilt?" Sarah asked, picturing a circular quilt with birds appliquéd in the center.

"It's a quilt made by a group of friends," Bonnie explained. "Each quilter makes a center block and passes the block along to a friend, who passes her own block along to the next person in line, all the way around the circle. Then each quilter pieces a border and attaches it to the block she received."

"Then the blocks are passed on to the next person," Judy said. "Everyone adds another border and passes on the blocks, and so on, until everyone in the group has added something to each person's center block and everyone has her own quilt top back."

Diane looked dubious. "If we work on only one center block, it won't be a true round robin."

"Who died and made you the quilt police?" Gwen retorted.

"True round robin or not, I think it's a great idea." Bonnie glanced at Sylvia, who was calling Matt over to help a guest with her bags. "Are we going to try to make it a surprise? That won't be easy."

"We'll keep it a secret until the top is finished," Agnes decided. "Sylvia would want to quilt it with us. I'll volunteer to make the center. Who else wants to help?"

"I do," Sarah said.

The others chimed in their agreement, all but Summer, who shook her head. "I'll have to sit this one out. With finals coming up, and graduation, I don't see how I'd have the time. I'll help you quilt and bind it, though."

"And baste," Diane added. "Don't even think about sneaking out of that."

The women laughed, but they quickly smothered their mirth when Sylvia broke into the circle. "What are you all giggling about over here?" she asked.

"Nothing," Summer said, her eyes wide and innocent.

"Supper," Sarah said at the same time.

"You know us," Gwen quickly added. "Always thinking about our next meal."

"Hmph. That's true enough." Sylvia checked her clipboard. "After our last guest arrives, we'll get supper started."

"Did someone mention food? Is supper ready?" Matt said, returning from his latest trip upstairs, where all but one of their guests were settling into their rooms. He usually wore a baseball cap over his curly blond hair, a habit against which Sylvia fought a tireless campaign. Today, apparently, she had won.

"No, supper isn't ready yet." A smile played at the corners of Sylvia's mouth. "If we aren't moving quickly enough for you, you're welcome to go to the kitchen and get started."

She said it so comically that everyone laughed, and as Sarah joined in, she felt her heart glowing with a warmth and happiness she once only dreamed of possessing. She and Matt had struggled so long to find their way, first as newlyweds in State College, and then even after the move to Waterford, where getting settled had been more difficult than they had anticipated. How fortunate it was that she had accepted that temporary job helping Sylvia prepare her estate for auction. She never could have imagined how that simple decision would open up her life to new friends and new challenges. It was as if she had finally found her way home after a long journey.

Over the sound of her friends' laughter, Sarah heard the door open. "That makes twelve," she said, turning to greet the last new camper.

A middle-aged woman stood just inside the doorway, a suitcase in her hands. "Hello, Sarah." As the door closed behind her, she shifted her weight from one foot to the other and broke into a hesitant smile.

Sarah stared at her, unable to speak.

"Do you know her?" Summer murmured.

"Yes." Though sometimes Sarah felt she didn't know her at all. "She's my mother."

As one, the Elm Creek Quilters gasped—all but Sylvia, who deliberately avoided looking in Sarah's direction.

"Mom." Matt bounded across the marble floor and down the stairs leading to the front door. "How nice to see you." He took her suitcase and leaned forward to kiss her cheek.

She laughed self-consciously and endured the kiss. "Please, call me Carol."

Matt beamed, unaware of the slight, or ignoring it. Sarah felt a smoldering in her chest—astonishment, dismay, and the tiniest flicker of anger. "What are you doing here, Mother?"

Carol's smile faltered. "I came for a visit, of course. And for quilt camp."

"Quilt camp? You don't quilt."

Sylvia gave Sarah a sharp look. "Then there's no better place for her to learn."

"That's what I thought when I saw Elm Creek Quilts on *America's Back Roads.*" Carol followed Matt to the registration desk, where Bonnie helped her sign in and gave her a room key. "You remember *America's Back Roads,* don't you, Sarah?"

Sarah nodded, unsure how to interpret her mother's nonchalance. Her mother looked thinner than she remembered, and her reddish brown hair hung past her shoulders. All the other campers had worn casual, comfortable clothing, but Carol had shown up in her usual conservative skirt and blouse.

Then Sarah noticed that Summer was giving her an odd look. "Aren't you going to go say hi or something?" she whispered.

Sarah nodded and forced herself to cross the foyer. Naturally, Summer would think it odd that she hadn't wrapped her mother in a great big welcoming hug the instant she crossed the threshold. Summer and Gwen liked each other, shared interests, were friends as well as mother and daughter. Sarah could only imagine what that felt like.

"Welcome to Elm Creek Manor, Mother," she said, her words as stiff and formal as the hug they exchanged. Perhaps it was her imagination, but it seemed her mother clung to her a moment longer than she used to, and held her tighter. Over the top of her mother's head, Sarah glimpsed Matt grinning broadly as he watched the embrace.

As Sarah pulled away, her mother took her hands. "You look good," she said, holding her daughter at arm's length. After further appraisal, she added, "I suppose if you'd known I was coming, you would have gotten a haircut."

Sarah gave her a tight smile. "I got my hair cut last week. Why didn't you tell me you were coming?" She almost said "warn" instead of "tell," but her friends' presence urged restraint.

"I thought it would be a nice surprise." Carol's smile mirrored Sarah's own. "Besides, if you'd known I was coming, you might have found some reason to leave town for the week."

"That's ridiculous. How can you say that?"

"Here, Mom—Carol." Matt touched his mother-in-law on the shoulder and picked up her suitcase. "Let me show you to your room. You'll love it."

Carol gave Sarah one last inscrutable look before following Matt upstairs. Sarah watched them go, Matt gesturing with his free hand as he described her room, her mother listening and nodding. Only when they disappeared down the second-floor hallway did Sarah relax.

"Well," Sylvia said. "I suppose I'll get supper started."

"Not so fast." Sarah caught her by the arm before she could escape down the hallway. "So this is why you so generously offered to take care of the registration sheets this time."

Sylvia brushed her hand away. "There's no need to get angry."

"There is so. Why didn't you tell me she was coming?"

"Why? So you could cut your hair?"

"Of course not. So I could prepare."

"We did prepare, when we made the manor ready for our quilt campers."

"I mean prepare mentally." Sarah looked around the circle of friends. "I can't believe you didn't tell me. Were you all in on this?"

Summer's eyes widened and she shook her head. "I sure wasn't."

"We're just as surprised as you are," Judy said.

"Sarah, you know very well I kept this to myself." Sylvia's voice was brisk. "If I had told one Elm Creek Quilter, I would have been obligated to tell the others, and we all know Diane can't keep a secret."

"Hey," Diane protested.

"Now, we'll have no more of this pouting." Sylvia held Sarah by the shoulders and looked her squarely in the eye. "Your mother's here, and I expect you to treat her with respect befitting the woman who raised you."

"You have no idea how difficult this is going to be. We don't get along."

"So you've said, and so I've just seen for myself. That's no excuse. You made a promise to me, don't forget, a promise that you'd reconcile with your mother."

"I've tried." Sarah wanted to squirm out of Sylvia's grasp. Her gaze was too knowing, too determined. "We talk on the phone, and Matt and I visited her last Christmas—"

"For a mere three days, as I recall, and you speak on the phone once a month at best. That's hardly enough time to rebuild your relationship." Her voice softened. "Nearly two years since you made that promise, dear, and so little to show for it. After that television fiasco, I had to invite her. Don't you see? If she had waited for you to ask, she would be waiting forever."

"I'm sure you mean well, but you should have told me."

"Next time, I shall." Sylvia gave Sarah's arms an affectionate squeeze. "I promise."

Sarah nodded, hoping there wouldn't be a next time. Her stomach wrenched when she thought of what the week would bring—a constant stream of criticism about her hair, her clothes, her speech, her attitude, and anything else that caught her mother's attention. No matter how well Sarah lived her life, Carol seemed to think she herself would have done much better in her daughter's place. Sarah sensed but had never understood the urgency behind the criticism, as if Carol was preparing her daughter for some impending disaster she alone could foresee. Carol was so unlike Sarah's easygoing, indulgent father that Sarah often marveled that they had ever considered themselves compatible enough to marry.

Sarah knew her father would have liked Matt as much as Carol disliked him. If only he were there to keep Carol's criticism in check as he used to when Sarah was younger. If Carol got started on Matt—"that gardener," as she used to call him, and perhaps still did—she could aggravate Matt's growing concerns about his job at Elm Creek Manor. He loved the grounds, the gardens, the orchards, but recently he had begun to wonder if he should have stayed at his old firm instead of coming to work for Sylvia.

"But Exterior Architects assigned you to Elm Creek," Sarah had reminded him when he first brought it up. "You're doing the same work at the same place. What's the difference?"

"The difference is the source of my paycheck. Exterior Architects used to pay me. Now Sylvia does."

Sarah had stared at him, perplexed. A year ago he had been all too eager to have Sylvia buy out his contract. "What's wrong with that?"

"I don't feel comfortable investing our entire future in one place, that's all."

"Why not? Lots of people who own their own businesses do."

"That's my point. We don't own our own business. Sylvia owns it."

"Of course she owns it. It's her estate. But so what? You know she'd never fire us."

"Yeah, I know." He walked away, saying that he had to check on the orchards, or the north gardens, or the new greenhouse. Sarah didn't remember which excuse he had used that time.

Now he was escorting Carol to her room, where her litany of complaints would surely begin. The room would be too small, or too shabby, or too far from the bathroom, or too near. Matt would nod to be agreeable, and her words would strengthen his own misgivings about living in Elm Creek Manor.

At that thought, the joy Sarah usually felt at the beginning of quilt camp went out of the day.

She could hear the new guests talking and laughing upstairs as they went from room to room getting acquainted. It was time for the other Elm Creek Quilters to leave for the evening, to return to their homes and their other responsibilities. Sarah and Sylvia walked them to the back door, then went to the kitchen to prepare the evening meal.

Sylvia wanted to discuss the week's schedule as they worked, but Sarah found her mind wandering. Her thoughts drifted back to the day she told Carol she was dating Matt McClure. "What about Dave?" Carol asked, referring to Sarah's previous boyfriend, whom she had dated for more than a year.

Sarah wrapped the phone cord around her finger and took a deep breath to steel herself. "Actually, we kind of broke up."

"What?"

"We're still friends," Sarah hastened to say, though she knew that wouldn't appease her mother. In truth, Sarah hadn't seen him in weeks. She had put off telling Carol about the breakup, knowing how much her mother adored him. Dave had charmed Carol just as he did everyone else.

"Maybe if you apologize, he'll take you back."

"I don't want him back. And why do you assume that he broke up with me?"

"Because I know you're a smart young woman and you wouldn't let a great catch like Dave swim away."

"He isn't a fish, Mother." And he didn't get away; it had been all Sarah could do to send him away. It had been a struggle to convince him that she didn't want to see him anymore. "You'll like Matt. Just give him a chance."

"We'll see." Carol's voice was flat, and Sarah realized Carol was determined to despise him and wouldn't give him any opportunity to change her mind.

Sarah hung up the phone with a sigh. She couldn't really blame Carol for not seeing through Dave; after all, it had taken Sarah fourteen months to figure him out. But now she could see that he was all style, no substance. As a freshman she had been dazzled by his popularity, his expensive car, the luxurious lifestyle his parents had provided him—but in the weeks preceding the breakup, she had grown restless. Dave was charming and witty, handsome and athletic, but something was missing.

He wouldn't allow anyone to bring him down with bad news or serious conversation, not even Sarah. With him she had to feign perpetual cheerfulness or lose his interest. Once when she needed to talk about a frustrating argument with her mother, she watched as his face went blank and he began to look over her shoulder for someone more pleasant to talk to. That was when Sarah understood that Dave kept her around not because he loved her—although perhaps he thought he did—but because she worked so hard to amuse him. She had learned early in their relationship that there were plenty of other women on campus who would pretend anything, hide anything, if it meant having his warm smile directed at them. But Sarah was tired of acting, of being onstage every moment they were together. She wanted someone who could love the real Sarah, with all her bad moods and faults.

After knowing Matt only a short while, she realized she had found that someone in him. He was kind and sensible, and though he didn't have Dave's charisma, he was handsome in a strong, unpolished kind of way, and he made Sarah feel valued. The first time they kissed, she learned that what she thought was love with Dave had not been love at all, or even a close approximation. Infatuation, yes; admiration, definitely. But not until Matt came into her life did Sarah truly know what it meant to love someone and be loved in return.

It would have been pointless to explain this to her mother. She was convinced that Sarah had traded in a pre-med student from a good family for a man whose ambition in life was to mow lawns and prune bushes. Even after she met him, Carol never saw Matt's solid core of strength and kindness, and never sensed how much he truly cared for Sarah. Those qualities made Matt worth two of Dave, with his roving eye and his refusal to plan anything more than a week in advance. Sarah saw this, but Carol couldn't, or refused to.

Carol evidently never gave up hoping that Sarah would change her mind, not even when Sarah told her she and Matt were getting married. Then Carol grew frantic. She warned Sarah that she would never be happy if she settled for a man like Matt. She begged Sarah to wait, to date other men, if only to be certain that she wasn't making a hasty decision.

She offered Sarah a check—enough for a more lavish wedding than Sarah could afford or even wanted—if only Sarah would cancel the ceremony.

Sarah managed to hold her fury in check long enough to point out that Carol herself had chosen a man much like Matt. "Did you settle for Dad?" Sarah demanded. "Would you have let your parents buy your affection?"

"I didn't have your choices," Carol said.

"I've made my choice," Sarah said, and as far as she was concerned the matter was settled. But Carol wasn't willing to give up, and her appeals continued throughout the engagement.

Sarah had torn up and discarded the letters long ago, but she could still see them in her mind, page after page of her mother's small, neat handwriting on the letterhead stationery from Susquehanna Presbyterian Hospital, where Carol worked as a nurse. "Marriage will change your life, and not for the better," Carol had written. "Twenty-three is too young. You should have a life of your own first. You could go anywhere, do anything, and you ought to do it now, while you're young. If you marry that gardener, you'll be stuck in some little town forever, and everything you ever wanted for yourself will be swallowed up in what you do for him." Marriage was expensive, she argued in letter after letter. Sarah could forget about the little luxuries that made life bearable. If she took a job in an exciting city, she would come into contact with all sorts of eligible men, lawyers and doctors rather than overgrown boys who liked to dig around in the dirt. After a few years, while she was still young enough to look pretty in a wedding gown and bear children, she should consider marriage. But not now, and not to that gardener.

"I understand why you find him attractive," her mother had written. "But young people today don't have to be married to have sex. You can do that, if you must, and get it out of your system without ruining your chances with someone better. Besides, if you marry him, the sexual attraction will fade once the novelty wears off, and then where will you be?"

Carol's signature followed, as if anyone else could have written such a hateful letter. There was a postscript, but Sarah's hands trembled, rattling the paper so that the words blurred and she could barely make them out: "Please know that my feelings are specifically about you and your friend. They are not a reflection of my relationship with your father. We had a happy, loving marriage that ended too soon."

At once, Sarah snatched up the phone and dialed her mother's number. When she answered, Sarah didn't return her greeting. "Don't you ever, ever spew such filth about Matt again," she snapped. "Do you hear me? Do you understand?"

She slammed down the phone without waiting for a reply.

The letters halted, and despite her earlier threats, a few months later Carol came to the small wedding in Eisenhower Chapel on the Penn State campus. She spoke politely with Matt's father, posed for pictures as the photographer instructed, and wept no more than was appropriate. Sarah could hardly look at her, could hardly bear to be in the presence of someone so spiteful to the man she loved. She knew Matt sensed the tension that sparkled and crackled between them, and hoped he attributed it to the inherent stress of the occasion.

The memory of those letters stung as sharply as if she had received them only yesterday.

"What do you think, Sarah?" Sylvia asked, startling her out of her reverie.

"Oh." Sarah carried a bunch of carrots to the sink to wash them. "Whatever you want to do is fine with me."

"You haven't heard a word I've said, have you?"

Sarah shook the water from the carrots. "No. I'm sorry." She avoided meeting Sylvia's eyes as she returned to the counter. "I've been thinking about our newest camper." She picked up a knife, lined up a carrot on the cutting board, and chopped off its top with a sharp whack.

Sylvia's eyebrows rose as she watched the cutting board. "I see." She wiped her hands on her apron. "Tell me. What brought about this estrangement? Did your mother abuse you? Neglect you?"

Sarah dispatched another carrot with a few strong chops of the knife. "No." As angry as she was at her mother, it wouldn't be fair to accuse her of that.

"What was it, then? It must have been something truly horrible, the way you two act around each other."

"It's hard to explain." Sarah divided the carrot slices among four large salad bowls and began cutting up the rest of the bunch. "Sometimes I wish she had done something bad enough to justify cutting her out of my life altogether. As a mother, I'm afraid she was all too typical. Lots of mothers constantly criticize their daughters, right?"

Sylvia shrugged.

"That's what my mother did. Does. Nothing I do is ever good enough for her. For most of my life I've been knocking myself out trying to please her, but it's useless. It's like she thinks I'm not living up to my potential just to spite her."

"I'm sure your mother is proud of you, even if she doesn't always show it."

"I wish I could be so sure."

Sylvia opened the oven door to check on the chickens. "You do love her, though, don't you?"

"Of course I love her." Sarah hesitated, then forced herself to say the rest. "I just don't like her very much. Believe me, the feeling is mutual."

"Sylvia, Sarah, would you two like some help?"

Quickly, Sarah looked up to find Carol standing in the kitchen doorway. Two other quilters stood behind her, smiling eagerly. Sarah's heart sank. How much had her mother overheard?

"We're fine, thank you," Sylvia said, as she always did. Quilters were generous people who knew that many hands could make even a dull, slow job pleasant and quick. Sylvia often had to remind her guests to enjoy their vacations and let others wait on them for a change, but there were always a few who brushed off her protests.

This time was no different. "Preparing a meal for twelve is too much work for only the two of you," Carol said, motioning for her companions to follow her into the kitchen. She had changed into a dark blue warm-up suit but somehow still managed to look dressed up.

"We can handle it," Sarah said. Her voice came out sharper than she intended. "And there's fifteen, including me and Sylvia and Matt."

Carol pursed her lips in a semblance of a smile. "Fifteen. I stand corrected." She went to the sink, tucked a dish towel into her waistband, and began washing a bundle of celery while Sylvia found tasks for the others.

Sarah forced herself to breathe deeply and evenly until the edge of her annoyance softened. "I see you've made some new friends," she said as her mother joined her at the cutting board.

"They're my nearest neighbors upstairs." Carol pulled open drawers until she found a knife. "Linda's a physician's assistant in Erie and Renée is a cardiac specialist at Hershey Medical Center. We have a lot in common."

"That's nice." Sarah watched as a puddle collected beneath the bundle of celery on her mother's side of the cutting board. Carol had neglected to shake the water off, as usual, and now the salad would be soaked. Sarah held back a complaint and concentrated on the carrots.

They worked without speaking. Sarah tried to concentrate on Sylvia's conversation with Renée and Linda, but she was conscious of how Carol kept glancing from her celery to Sarah's carrots. Finally her mother's scrutiny became too much. "All right. What is it?" Sarah asked, setting down the knife.

Her mother feigned innocence. "What?"

"What's the problem?"

"Nothing." Carol's brow furrowed in concentration as she chopped away at the celery. Water droplets flew.

"You might as well tell me."

Carol paused. "I was just wondering why you were cutting the carrots like that."

"Like what?" Sarah fought to keep her voice even. "You mean, with a knife?"

"No, I mean cutting straight down like that. Your slices are round and chunky. If you cut at an angle, the slices will be tapered and have a more attractive oval shape." Carol took a carrot and demonstrated. "See? Isn't that pretty?"

"Lovely." Sarah snatched the carrot and resumed cutting straight, round slices. First the hair, now this—artistic differences over carrot slices. It was going to be a long week.

When the meal was ready, Sarah, Sylvia, and their helpers carried plates, glasses, and silverware across the hallway through the servants' entrance to the banquet hall. The other guests soon joined them, entering through the main entrance off the front foyer. Sarah steeled herself and took a seat at Carol's table just as Matt hurried in from the kitchen, where he had scrubbed his hands and face. He smiled at Sarah as he pulled up a chair beside her, smelling of soap and fresh air.

"How's everything going with your mom?" he murmured.

Sarah shrugged, not sure how to answer. They hadn't fought, but that same old tension was still there. She swallowed a bite of chicken and forced herself to smile across the table at her mother. One week. Surely she could manage to be civil for one week.

After supper, everyone helped clear the tables and clean up the kitchen, so the work was finished in no time at all. The quilters went their separate ways for a time, outside to stroll through the gardens, to the library to read or write in journals, to new friends' rooms to chat. As evening fell, Sarah and Sylvia returned to the kitchen to prepare a snack of tea and cookies, which they carried outside to the place Sylvia's mother had named the cornerstone patio.

Sarah summoned their guests. It was time for her favorite part of quilt camp, when the week still lay before them, promising friendship and fun, and their eventual parting could be forgotten for a while.

The quilters who had remained indoors put on jackets or sweaters and followed Sarah across the foyer toward the west wing of the manor. Instead of turning toward the kitchen as the guests expected, Sarah continued straight ahead to a door at the end of the hall. She held it open and allowed the others to precede her outside into the cool evening, to a gray stone patio surrounded by evergreens, crocuses, and lilac bushes not yet in bloom. After gathering the other guests there, Sylvia had arranged the wooden furniture into a circle and had placed the tea and cookies on a table, where she waited, hands clasped and smiling.

Sarah caught Sylvia's eye and smiled as she closed the door behind her. Soon, she knew, one of the quilters was bound to ask why this place was called the cornerstone patio. Sylvia or Sarah, whoever was nearer, would hold back the tree branches where the patio touched the northeast corner of the manor. The quilter who had asked the question would read aloud the engraving on a large stone at the base of the structure: BERGSTROM 1858. Sylvia would tell them about her great-grandfather, Hans Bergstrom, who had placed that cornerstone with the help of his wife, Anneke, and sister Gerda, and built the west wing of the manor upon it.

When everyone had helped themselves to refreshments, Sylvia asked them to take seats in the circle. "If you'll indulge us, we'd like to end this first evening with a simple ceremony we call a Candlelight." The quilters' voices hushed as Sylvia lit a candle, placed it in a crystal votive holder, and went to the center of the circle. The dancing flame in her hands cast light and shadow on her features, making her seem at once young and old, wise and joyful.

"Elm Creek Manor is full of stories," she told them. "Everyone who has ever lived here has added to those stories. Now your stories will join them, and those of us who call this place home will be richer for it."

She explained the ceremony. She would hand the candle to the first woman in the circle, who would tell the others why she had come to Elm Creek Manor and what she hoped the week would bring her. When she finished, she would pass the candle to the woman on her left, who would tell her story.

There was a moment's silence broken only by nervous laughter when Sylvia asked for a volunteer to begin.

Finally, Renée, one of the women Carol had befriended, raised her hand. "I will."

Sylvia gave her the candle and sat down beside Sarah.

Renée studied the flame in her hands for a long moment without speaking. "My name is Renée Hoffman," she finally said, looking up. "I'm a cardiac specialist at Hershey Medical Center. I was married for a while, but not anymore. I have no children." She paused. "I've never quilted before. I came to Elm Creek Manor because I want to learn how. Two years ago—" She took a deep breath and let it out, slowly. "Two years ago my brother died of AIDS. Two years ago this month. I came to Elm Creek Manor so that I could learn how to make a panel for him for the AIDS quilt." She shook her head and lowered her gaze to the flickering candle. "But that's why I want to learn to quilt, not why I came here. I guess I could have taken lessons in Hershey, but I didn't want any distractions. I want to be able to focus on what my brother meant to me, and for some reason I couldn't do that at home."

The woman beside her put an arm around Renée's shoulders. Renée gave her the briefest flicker of a smile. "When I walked around the gardens earlier today, I thought I could feel him there with me. I started thinking about the time when we were kids, when he taught me how to ride a two-wheeled bike." Her expression grew distant. "I told him once, near the end, that I wished I had gone into AIDS research instead of cardiac surgery so that I could fight against this thing that was killing him. He took my hand and said, 'You save lives. Don't ever regret the choices that brought you to the place you are now.' " She stared straight ahead for a long, silent moment. "Anyway, that's why I'm here." She passed the candle to the woman on her left.

The candle went around the circle, to a woman who was going through a painful divorce and needed to get away from it all, to the young mother whose husband had given her the week at quilt camp as a birthday present, to the elderly sisters who spent every year vacationing together while their husbands went on a fishing trip—"Separate vacations, that's why we've been able to stay married so long," the eldest declared, evoking laughter from the others—to the woman who had come with two of her friends to celebrate her doctor's confirmation that her breast cancer was in remission.

Sarah had heard stories like these in other weeks, from other women, and yet each story was unique. One common thread joined all the women who came to Elm Creek Manor. Those who had given so much of themselves and their lives caring for others—children, husbands, aging parents—were now taking time to care for themselves, to nourish their own souls. As the night darkened around them, the cornerstone patio was silent but for the murmuring of quiet voices and the song of crickets, the only illumination the flickering candle and the light of stars burning above them, so brilliant but so far away.

Carol was one of the last to speak, and she kept her story brief. "I came to Elm Creek Manor because of my daughter." Her eyes met Sarah's. "I want to be a part of her life again. For too long we've let our differences divide us. I don't want us to be that way anymore. I don't want either of us to have regrets someday, when it's too late to reconcile." She ducked her head as if embarrassed, then quickly passed the candle as if it had burned her hands.

Sarah's heart softened as she watched her mother accept a quick hug from the woman at her side. They exchanged a few words Sarah couldn't make out, then listened as the next woman told her story.

I will try harder, Sarah resolved. They would have a week together to sort things out. She wouldn't let the time go to waste.

But as the days went by, she learned that promises were more easily made than kept.

The quilt camp schedule was designed to give the guests as much independence as possible to work on their own projects or do as they pleased. After an early breakfast, Sylvia led an introductory piecing class, lectured on the history of quilting, or displayed the many antique quilts in Elm Creek Manor's collection. After some free time, the quilters gathered at noon for lunch. On rainy days they met in the banquet hall, but when the sun shone they picnicked outdoors, in the north gardens, near the orchard, on blankets spread on the sweeping front lawn, or on the veranda. Requests to lunch on the cornerstone patio received polite refusals and the promise that they would gather there once more before camp ended. No other explanation was given, no matter how the guests wheedled and teased.

After lunch one of the other Elm Creek Quilters would teach a class—Gwen on Monday, Judy on Tuesday, Summer on Wednesday, Bonnie on Thursday, and Agnes on Friday. Diane didn't feel ready to lead a class of her own, so instead she assisted at each class. The arrangement pleased everyone. Sylvia was spared the task of teaching two classes a day, the other Elm Creek Quilters could keep their involvement at a level that didn't interfere with their jobs and other responsibilities, and the guests could enjoy a variety of teaching styles and techniques.

More free time followed the afternoon classes until the evening meal. Afterward, Sylvia and Sarah usually planned some sort of entertainment, a talent show or a game or an outing. All activities were voluntary, at Sylvia's insistence. "Our guests are here to enjoy themselves," she said. "This is their time. If they want to do cartwheels on the veranda all morning instead of taking a class, more power to them."

Despite all the free time available to the quilters, Sarah rarely found any for herself. She spent the days working behind the scenes—balancing accounts, designing marketing plans, ordering supplies, making schedules—to keep Elm Creek Quilts operating smoothly. Her hours were busy and productive, and she had never been happier in her work, perhaps because could see the result of her labors in the smiling faces of their guests, feel it in the quilts created there, hear it in the laughter that rang through the halls.

Elm Creek Manor was alive once more, just as Sarah had predicted, just as Sylvia had wished.

This week Sarah's work load kept her even busier than usual. Each day she promised herself she would spend time with her mother, but she always found more work to do, more tasks that simply couldn't wait. Sarah felt guilty for repeatedly turning down her mother's invitations to go for a walk or sit on the veranda and chat during free time, so she was relieved when her mother stopped asking. They did spend some time together, at meals and in the evenings, but always in the company of the other guests.

"I was hoping we'd have some nice quiet time together," Carol told her on Thursday evening as they went out the back door to the parking lot. That evening Gwen had arranged for everyone to attend a play on the Waterford College campus.

"We will," Sarah promised. "We still have another whole day left, and half of Saturday." As if to apologize for her absence, she made sure they rode in the same car and sat next to each other in the theater. She knew it wasn't what her mother had hoped for, but she couldn't ignore her responsibilities.

Later that night, as the quilters went off to their separate rooms to prepare for bed, Sylvia asked Sarah to join her in the library. "You haven't been spending as much time with your mother as I had hoped," she said, easing herself into a chair by the fireplace. No fire burned there now, and probably none would until autumn.

Sarah shrugged helplessly. "I know. I've been swamped with work."

Sylvia folded her arms and regarded her. "Is that so?"

"Well, yes." Sarah ran through the list of tasks she'd accomplished over the past three days.

Sylvia shook her head as she listened. "You know very well that most of that work could have been put off for at least another week. You had no pressing deadlines preventing you from enjoying your mother's visit."

"But—"

"But nothing. You went looking for all that extra work, and so naturally you found it. You piled it up all around yourself—big, solid stacks of paperwork to keep your mother from coming near. I know you, Sarah McClure, and I know what you're doing, even if you don't."

Sarah stared at her. "Is that really what I've been doing?" As Sylvia's words sank in, she recognized the truth in them. "I didn't mean to. At least I don't think so."

"Why are you distancing yourself from her, and after she said such nice things about you at the Candlelight?"

"But that's precisely why it's so difficult to talk to her." Sarah went to the window and drew back the curtain. Through the diamond-shaped panes of glass she could see the roof of the barn on the other side of Elm Creek. "Every time we're together, we bicker. That's been our way for years. Right now we've left things on a good note. I wouldn't want another silly argument to spoil that."

"Perhaps I should have told you about her visit after all, so that you could have planned what to say to her." Sylvia sighed. "It seems the element of surprise didn't work as well for you and your mother as it did for me and Agnes."

Sarah whirled around to face her. "Is that what you were trying to do?"

Sylvia nodded, no doubt thinking, as Sarah was, about that day almost two years before when Sarah had arranged for Sylvia to meet her long-estranged sister-in-law in the north gardens. Their reconciliation had encouraged Sylvia to remain at Elm Creek Manor instead of continuing her search for a buyer; if not for that, Elm Creek Quilts never would have existed.

"But that day in the garden was only the beginning," Sarah said. "You and Agnes didn't rebuild your relationship all in that one day. You grew closer over time, over all those months planning Elm Creek Quilts."

Sylvia nodded. "You're right, of course. I was foolish to believe your difficulties with your mother could be sorted out in a single week."

"Not foolish." Sarah tried to smile. "Overly optimistic, maybe, but not foolish."

"Hmph." Sylvia returned Sarah's smile, but her heart didn't seem to be in it.

Matt was already asleep when Sarah climbed into bed beside him. She closed her eyes, but sleep wouldn't come. Sylvia was so disappointed that she had not been able to return Sarah's gift in kind. She shouldn't be. Sylvia and Agnes had been ready to reconcile. So many years of loss and regret had cleared their vision, had taught them how foolish the old squabbles were. In hindsight, it had been easy to bring them together, since they both ached for a reunion.

If Sarah felt anything of that longing, it was buried deep enough to ignore. How many decades of estrangement would pass before she cared enough about reconciliation to give her whole heart to it?

To those troubling thoughts, Sarah finally drifted off to sleep.

The next day she forced herself to avoid the office. She sat by her mother's side at breakfast, walked with her and Matt in the gardens during free time, and pushed two Adirondack chairs together on the veranda so that they could chat undisturbed during lunch. The time passed pleasantly enough, but Sarah felt restrained, as if at any moment she might say the words that would dredge up all those old animosities. Once, fleetingly, she wondered if that wasn't exactly what they ought to do—bring out all those old hurts and subject them to unflinching scrutiny. But just as quickly Sarah decided against it. She couldn't risk an enormous blowup that could take a long time to settle, not when Carol would be leaving the next day.

To make the most of their time together, Sarah joined her mother for Agnes's workshop that afternoon. At first Carol struggled to learn the appliqué techniques, but Sarah and Diane helped her. "I'm the expert on finding an easier way to do things," Diane said as she demonstrated a different way to hold the needle. "I've never met a shortcut I didn't like."

Carol laughed and assured Diane that she understood what to do now.

As they worked, Agnes strolled through the room checking on her students' progress and offering advice. When she reached Sarah's table, she took Diane and Sarah aside to talk to them about the round robin quilt. So much had happened since Sunday's registration that Sarah had nearly forgotten it.

"The center motif will take me a while to complete," Agnes said. "I think the rest of you should get started on the borders."

Diane looked dubious. "How can we add borders to something that isn't there?"

Agnes laughed and patted her arm. "Sarah can cut a piece of background fabric eighteen inches square and add her border to that. The rest of you can proceed as usual. When I'm finished, I'll appliqué my section onto the center square."

Sarah nodded, but she was still uncertain. "But what about colors? We won't want the borders to clash with the center. How can we pick coordinating colors if we can't see what fabric you're going to use?"

A quilter on the other side of the room signaled to Agnes for help. "Use the colors of Elm Creek Manor," Agnes called over her shoulder as she went to assist the student. "That's what I'm going to do."

Diane made a face. "She could have been a little more specific."

Sarah laughed in agreement, but she thought she understood what Agnes meant.

That evening the mood at Elm Creek Manor was nostalgic and subdued. It had been a special week for all, and though they had arrived mostly strangers, the quilters now felt they would be friends for life. In the midst of the many tearful hugs and promises to keep in touch, Sylvia whispered to Sarah that they ought to consider hiring a comedian to entertain them on future closing nights. "Anything to prevent such melancholy," she said, hugging her arms to her chest as if to ward off a draft.

The next morning their guests' spirits seemed to have brightened with the sunrise. As Sylvia and Sarah had promised, they gathered on the cornerstone patio for their last meal together. Sarah and Sylvia covered the table with a bright yellow cloth and loaded it with trays of pastries, breads, fruit, pots of coffee, and pitchers of juice. After breakfast, they took their places around the circle once again, this time for Show and Tell. Each quilter took a turn showing off something she had made that week and telling her new friends what favorite memory she would take with her when she left Elm Creek Manor.

Everyone proudly showed their new creations, from the AIDS quilt segment Renée had begun to the simplest pieced blocks the beginning quilters had stitched. The Candlelight on their first evening together was remembered fondly, as were the late-night chats in their cozy suites and the private moments spent strolling through the beautiful grounds.

Then it was Carol's turn.

She held up her first pieced block, a Sawtooth Star, and said that she'd like to start a baby quilt, if her daughter would cooperate by providing the baby.

Everyone chuckled, except for Sylvia, who let out a quiet sigh only Sarah heard, and Sarah herself, who clenched her jaw to hold back a blistering retort that the decision to have children was hers alone—hers and Matt's.

"As for my favorite memory, I'm not sure yet." Carol looked around the circle, everywhere but at Sarah. "My favorite memory might still be ahead of me. I've decided to stay on a while longer."

The other guests let out exclamations of surprise and delight, but Sarah hardly heard them over the roaring in her ears. "But—but—what about work?" she managed to say.

"I called the hospital. I told them it was a family emergency, and they agreed to let me have four months' leave."

Four months. Sarah nodded, numb. A family emergency. It wasn't exactly a lie.

The woman beside her patted Sarah on the back and congratulated her for the good news. She managed a weak smile in return. Four months. Time enough to patch things up, or to rend them beyond repair forever.

🔯 🔯 🔯

Sarah cut an eighteen-inch square from a piece of cream fabric. She chose green for the stately elms lining the back road to Elm Creek Manor, her home, which felt less like home with her mother in it. She picked lighter greens for the sweeping front lawn, and darker shades for the leaves on the rosebushes Matt nurtured with such care in the north gardens. She added clear blue for the skies over Waterford, though she felt they should be gray with gathering storms. Last of all she found a richer, darker blue for Elm Creek, which danced along as it always had, murmuring and rushing regardless of the joy or tragedy unfolding on its banks.

Using the same cream for her background fabric, Sarah created a border of blue and green squares set on point, touching tip to tip. Squares for the solidity and balance of the manor, for the dividing walls she and Carol had built over the years, for the blocks they had stumbled over on their journey toward each other, for the way Carol's news had left her feeling imprisoned and boxed in, forced to face the inevitable confrontation that somehow she had always known was coming.

# Chapter Three

**D**iane received the quilt top from Sarah after class Monday afternoon. "You must have worked on this all weekend," she remarked, unfolding the quilt top and holding it up for inspection. "How'd you find the time? I thought your mother was still here."

"She is."

An odd note in Sarah's voice pulled Diane's attention away from the quilt. Sarah had shadows under her eyes and she kept glancing warily over her shoulder.

"Are you okay?" Diane asked. Usually, Sarah was calm and self-assured, but she had been snappish and edgy all day.

"I'm fine." Sarah snatched the quilt top and began folding it. "I just don't want Sylvia to see this. It's supposed to be a surprise, remember? Keep it out of sight."

"Okay, okay. Relax. She's in the kitchen. She can't see through walls." Diane took back the folded quilt top and tucked it into her bag. Honestly. More and more Sarah reminded Diane of her eldest son, Michael, but he was a teenager and such behavior was expected. What was Sarah's excuse?

Diane waved good-bye to Gwen, who had led that afternoon's workshop, and left the classroom. It had been a ballroom once. The dance floor remained, but quilters now practiced on the orchestra dais, where work tables had replaced risers and music stands. She had never seen an orchestra there, but Sylvia and Agnes had, and their stories were so vivid that Diane sometimes felt as if she had witnessed the manor's grand parties herself.

On her way to the back door, she stopped by the kitchen to bid Sylvia good-bye. Sarah's mother was helping Sylvia prepare supper, and they were laughing and chatting like old friends. Maybe that explained Sarah's moodiness. Maybe she wanted Sylvia all to herself and thought Carol was getting in the way.

Diane drove home to the neighborhood a few blocks south of the Waterford College campus where professors, administrators, and their families lived. Sarah had once told her that the gray stone houses with their carefully landscaped front yards reminded her of Elm Creek Manor, but Diane didn't see the similarity. The houses on that oak tree–lined street were large, but not nearly as grand as Elm Creek Manor, or as old—or as secluded, to her regret. Diane willingly would have parted with a neighbor or two—namely, Mary Beth from next door, who had perfect hair and perfect children and had been president of the Waterford Quilting Guild for nearly a decade.

Diane parked in the driveway and walked up the red-brick herringbone path to the front porch, to the door with its brass knocker and beveled glass. The house was quiet, but she couldn't enjoy the peace and solitude, not when she was due to pick up Todd from band practice in fifteen minutes. Diane dropped her bag on the floor of the foyer, draped her coat over it, and yanked off her ankle boots. They used to call her a stay-at-home mom before she began working for Elm Creek Quilts, but a stay-in-car mom was more like it.

She padded to the kitchen in her stocking feet to check the answering machine. There was one message—Tim, she supposed, as she waited for the tape to rewind. He usually called her in the afternoons from his office in the chemistry building on campus to let her know what time he'd be home from work.

But the voice on the tape, though much like her husband's, was years younger.

"Mom?" Michael said. "Uh, don't be mad."

An ominous beginning. Diane closed her eyes and sighed.

"Um, I kinda need you to come pick me up." He hesitated. "They won't let me go until you pay the fine."

"Pick you up from where?" she asked the machine—an instant before his words sank in. Pay a fine?

"I'm at the police station. Don't tell Dad, okay?" Without a word of explanation, he hung up.

Diane shrieked. She ran to the foyer, threw on her coat, and stuffed her feet into her boots. She dashed outside to her car and raced downtown, her heart pounding. What had he done? What on earth had he gotten himself into this time? After the vandalism at the junior high last fall, she and Tim had put such a scare into him that he vowed never to get into trouble again. Their family counselor had warned them to expect ups and downs, but this— She felt faint just thinking about the possibilities. He must have done something horrible, just horrible, for the police to lock up a fifteen-year-old until his parents came to bail him out.

Sarah was wise to avoid having children, Diane thought grimly as she pulled into the parking lot behind the police headquarters.

Diane hurried inside, her heart pounding. Michael could be injured, ignored by the busy police officers as he slowly and quietly bled to death in a lonely cell. She gave the first officer she saw Michael's name. "Is he all right?" she asked, breathless. "Is he hurt?"

"He's just fine, ma'am." The officer looked sympathetic. Maybe he was a parent, too. "He's just in a little bit of trouble."

"Can I see him? What kind of trouble? How little? How long has he been here?" She took a deep breath to stem the flow of questions. She had gone to Elm Creek Manor at noon; Michael could have left the message any time after that. He could have been locked up for hours with violent offenders. The last thing Michael needed was that kind of influence.

The officer raised his hands to calm her. "He's been here less than an hour. He's waiting in an interrogation room."

"What exactly did he do?"

"He was skateboarding in a marked zone. We wouldn't have held him except he didn't have the money for the fine."

Diane gaped at him. "Skateboarding?" Her voice grew shrill. "You locked up my child for skateboarding?"

The officer squirmed. "In a marked zone, yes."

"Why didn't you call me at Elm Creek Manor? Why didn't you call my husband?"

"Your son insisted. He wanted you to get the news rather than his father, and he didn't want to interrupt your class."

Diane smothered a groan. Of all the times for Michael to get considerate. "I can't believe this." She rooted around in her purse for her wallet. "Well, it certainly does my heart good to know that the citizens of Waterford are being protected so heroically from skateboarders. Now, if only you could do something about all those thieves and murderers and terrorists running loose, well, then I'd really be impressed."

"We don't get many murderers and terrorists around here, ma'am."

"How much is the fine?" she snapped.

"Fifty dollars."

Diane counted out the bills, gritting her teeth to hold back the tirade she was aching to release. She'd save it for Michael. Oh, would he ever rue this day! "Here's your ransom," she said, sliding the bills across the desk. "May I have my son back, please?"

A few minutes later, the officer brought out her son. As usual, his skinny frame was enveloped in oversized clothes, so large and baggy that they could have been his father's, except Tim never wore black jeans and Aerosmith T-shirts. He carried his jacket wadded up in a ball under his arm, and his baseball cap was turned backward.

"Is that my earring?" Diane gasped when she saw the flash of gold in his earlobe.

He nodded.

"Where's the other one?"

"In your jewelry box." He paused. "You never said I couldn't wear your earrings."

"I didn't know I had to." She hadn't wanted him to get his ear pierced in the first place, but Tim had pointed out that they ought to reward him for asking permission, to encourage him to do so more often. Besides, it was only one ear he wanted, thank God, not his nose or his eyebrow or his tongue. "I also never said you couldn't set the house on fire or run a counterfeiting ring out of the basement, but you knew you weren't allowed, right?"

"Yeah," he muttered. "I guess so."

"You guess so?" Then Diane remembered the officers watching them. "Let's go, Michael," she said briskly, placing a hand on his shoulder and steering him toward the door.

They drove in silence to Todd's middle school. Michael sat in the back seat staring out the window. Diane was so angry and embarrassed that for the first time in her life she didn't know how to begin the lecture.

"Does Dad know?" Michael finally asked as they sat at a long red light.

"Not yet."

"Are you gonna tell him?"

"Of course I'm going to tell him. A father has a right to know when his eldest son, his heir, his pride and joy, has earned himself a criminal record."

In the rearview mirror, she saw him roll his eyes. "You don't have to make such a big thing out of it."

The light changed, and Diane sped the car forward. "Mister, you have no idea how big this is already."

They drove on without speaking.

When she pulled into the school's circular driveway, Todd was waiting out front alone, banging his trumpet case against his knee and looking up at the sky. The sight of his woebegone face prompted a twinge of guilt.

"You're late," he said as he climbed into the back seat beside his brother, as mournful as if he had been waiting hours, days, long enough to be certain that she had abandoned him forever.

"I'm sorry," she said as she drove on. "I would have been on time, except I had to swing by the slammer to bail out Michael here."

"You were in jail?" Todd asked his brother, his tone at once shocked and admiring.

"Shut up."

"I don't have to."

From the back seat came a dull thump of a fist against cloth and flesh. "Hey," Diane snapped, glancing from the road to the rearview mirror and back, trying to figure out who had thrown the punch. "No hitting. You know better than that." She heard Todd mutter something about one of them knowing better than to wind up behind bars, too, and then another dull thump. "I said, knock it off!"

When they got home, she promptly sent them to their rooms. Michael went upstairs without a word, shoulders slumped, hands thrust into the pockets of his enormous jeans, but Todd's mouth fell open in astonishment. "Why do I have to?" he protested. "I didn't do anything."

Because your mother needs a few minutes to herself or she'll go completely berserk, Diane wanted to say, but instead she folded her arms and looked her youngest son squarely in the eye. "Your room is not a gulag. You've got homework, books, TV, and about half a million computer games. Just until supper, so I can have some peace and quiet, so I can figure out what I'm going to tell your father, okay?"

"I don't see why I get punished when he screws up," Todd muttered, his mouth tugging into a sullen frown.

An unexpected wave of sympathy came over her, sympathy for Michael. Todd had always been the good kid, and he couldn't understand why his older brother did the things he did. None of them understood, not really, but it saddened her that Todd seemed to feel so little empathy for Michael, so little solidarity. Sometimes she wished Todd would side with Michael, forming the typical united front of kids versus adults. More than anyone else Diane knew, Michael needed an ally.

She wrapped Todd in a hug. "Please?"

"All right," he said, resigned. As he dragged himself upstairs, Diane was tempted to remind him that he always went straight to his room after band practice, to put away his trumpet and get his homework done so that he could play basketball with the neighbor kids after supper. She was tempted, but she said nothing.

The phone rang as she was preparing supper.

"Hi, honey," Tim said. "How was your day?"

"Oh, you know, the usual." She wiped her hands on a dish towel and switched the phone to her other ear. "Your son gave me another dozen gray hairs, that's all."

She pictured him leaning back in his chair, removing his glasses, and rubbing his eyes. "What did he do now?" After she explained, Tim sighed, heavy and deep. "I suppose it could have been worse."

"Are you kidding?" It was his standard reply, but somehow Diane hadn't expected to hear it. "What's worse than being hauled in by the police?"

"Being hauled in by the police for something worth being hauled in for."

He was right, of course. "What are we going to do?"

"Try to take it easy until I get home. We'll have supper and talk. We'll figure out what to do." His voice was comforting. "It'll be all right. You'll see."

"Maybe." Diane wasn't so sure. In a few years she could be receiving Mother's Day cards from Death Row, not that Michael had given her a Mother's Day card since the sixth grade.

Supper was a strained affair, with Michael scowling at the table and waiting for the punishment to be levied. Diane concentrated on moving her food around on her plate with her fork because she knew that one look at Michael would have her snapping at him to sit up straight, take off his ball cap, get his elbows off the table, and for the love of all that was good in the world, stay out of prison. Only Todd treated the evening as any other, chattering on about new band uniforms and the swim team's upcoming candy bar sale. Diane wondered if he really was unaware of the tension blanketing the room or if he was trying to lighten the mood so that his parents would go easy on his brother. She hoped it was the latter, not that it would work.

After supper, Todd went outside to join his friends; Michael trudged back upstairs without waiting to be told. As Tim and Diane cleaned up the kitchen, they discussed their options. Michael had lost so many privileges already for past transgressions that there weren't many left to revoke. Grounding him wouldn't do any good because he spent most of his time in his room anyway. They could take away his skateboard, but to Diane that seemed like a slap on the wrist compared to the fright and embarrassment he had given her.

"Why does he do these things?" she asked.

"I don't know," Tim said, a thoughtful look crossing his face. "Why don't we ask him?"

They called him into the living room. He slumped into an armchair and studied the floor as they seated themselves on the sofa facing him.

"Michael," Tim said, "your mother and I have been trying to figure out why you got yourself into this situation today." Diane admired the way he kept his voice so calm, so reasonable, without a trace of the worry she knew he was feeling.

In reply, Michael shrugged.

"Come on, son. You must have some reason. Didn't you see the sign?"

"No, I didn't see it," Michael muttered. "But I knew I wasn't allowed to skate there."

"Then why did you?" Diane demanded. When Michael shrugged, she fought off the urge to shake him out of pure frustration.

Tim looked puzzled. "If you didn't see a sign, how did you know you weren't allowed to skate there?"

Finally, Michael looked up. "Because we aren't allowed to skate anywhere. Every single place is off-limits. The sidewalks, the parking lots, the campus—everywhere. It's not fair. I bought my skateboard with my own money and I can't even use it."

"Why not use it in the driveway?" Diane asked.

Michael rolled his eyes. " 'Cause I don't just want to go back and forth, back and forth all day like a five-year-old idiot."

"Don't talk to your mother that way," Tim said. Michael scowled and slumped farther into his chair. If he kept it up, Diane figured he would be

horizontal before the conversation ended. He muttered something in-
audible that could have been an apology.

Tim left the sofa and took a seat on the ottoman close to Michael's
chair. "Look, we're trying to understand things from your point of view,
but you have to help us, okay? If you knew you weren't allowed to skate
there, why did you do it?"

"Because it's skate where I'm not allowed to or not skate at all."

Diane modeled her tone after Tim's. "Why not do something else?"

"Because I don't have anything else," he burst out. "Don't you get it?
Todd has band and swimming and about a billion friends, Dad has his job
and his workshop, you have all that quilting stuff—all I have is my skateboard. I suck at school, I can't play sports, the popular kids don't know I'm
alive, but I can skate. I'm good at it. It's the only thing I'm good at."

"That's not true," Diane said, astonished by the bitterness in his tone.
"You're good at lots of things."

He shook his head. "No, I'm not. You think I am because you're my
mom, but it's not true. I'm not good at anything. Except for this. I'm one
of the best skateboarders in Waterford, and the other skateboarders
know that. I have friends when I skate. I'm important. I'm not just Todd's
loser older brother for a change."

Diane didn't know what to say. She and Tim exchanged a long look—
enough for her to see that he wouldn't be able to take away Michael's
skateboard, either.

They sent him back to his room. He eyed them as if not quite believing that they meant for him to go without being yelled at first, but eventually he shuffled out of the room. They heard his footsteps as he went
upstairs, slow, despairing, like a man on his way to the gallows.

Diane and Tim talked until it grew dark outside and Todd came in
from shooting hoops in the driveway. He greeted them and continued on
to the kitchen, but on the spur of the moment Diane called him back.
She would ask him, she decided. She would ask him if what Michael said
about himself was true.

"What's up?" Todd asked, tossing the basketball from hand to hand.
He stood in the doorway, red-cheeked and glowing from exercise, grin-

ning as if recalling a great shot he had made minutes before or a joke a friend had told. He had inherited Diane's beauty and his father's temperament, and as Diane admired him it occurred to her that he would always have an edge in life his brother lacked, his brother who had inherited his mother's temper and smart mouth along with his father's slight stature and narrow shoulders. Michael was two years older, but in the past few months Todd had almost caught up to him in height and weight, and threatened to leave him far behind soon.

"Mom?" Todd said after a long moment passed in silence. "You wanted to talk to me?"

"No." Diane shook her head and forced herself to smile. "That's all right."

He gave her a bemused grin and continued on to the kitchen.

"There must be someplace in this town where a kid can ride a skateboard in peace." Diane bit at her lower lip, thinking. "Todd has his basketball courts, the swimming pools, the band practice rooms—we have to find a place for Michael. What does a skateboarder need, anyway?"

Tim didn't know, either, but he promised to find out. Tomorrow he would let his graduate students fend for themselves while he helped Michael find a place to skate. He kissed Diane, squeezed her arm in a gesture both affectionate and comforting, and went upstairs to talk to their son.

The next afternoon, as she assisted Judy with her workshop at Elm Creek Manor, Diane's thoughts wandered from the quilt campers to her husband and son. The search could take them days or weeks, and as they looked, they would have time alone to talk. Maybe Michael would lower his shields for a while and allow Tim the chance to become closer to him, close the way Gwen and Summer were close.

That evening at supper, Tim and Michael took turns describing their search. They hadn't found anything yet, but Tim was learning a great deal about skateboarding. Right before coming home, they had checked out a parking lot behind a medical office.

"There was this paved ditch next to it that I liked," Michael began.

"And I liked the fact that there were so many doctors nearby, just in case," his father finished. They looked at each other and laughed.

Diane blinked at them, speechless. Since becoming a teenager Michael had scowled instead of smiled, but now here he was, laughing.

On Wednesday, Tim and Michael investigated the edges of town, and this time they took along Troy, Brandon, and Kelly, who, Diane learned at supper, were Michael's best friends.

"How nice," Diane said, thinking, Michael has friends?

"Aren't those the geeks from computer club?" Todd wanted to know.

Michael's scowl returned. "Shut up."

Diane ignored the outburst. "Were you thinking about joining computer club with your friends?"

"I dunno." Michael shrugged and took a drink of milk. "Maybe. They said they could help me make a skateboarding website. Sometimes they go on trips, like, to computer companies to see how they run. Next month some movie animator guy's coming in to talk. He got, like, an Oscar or something for special effects." He took a bite of casserole and chewed thoughtfully. "That would be a way cool job."

Diane pretended not to be thrilled. "Hmm. I don't know. I don't think you'd have enough time for something like that. When would you get your homework done?"

"After school. After meetings." His alarm was unmistakable. "It wouldn't take too much time. I could do both."

She bit her lower lip. "Well . . ."

Tim was shooting her frantic looks across the table, clearly convinced she'd lost her mind.

"Please?" Michael looked almost desperate. "I'll get my homework done, no problem. I'll even show it to you."

She feigned reluctance and said, "We'll see." Michael nodded, but his brow furrowed in determination, as if his mind was already working on how to change that "We'll see" to "Yes." For years she'd urged him to get involved in school activities, and he had countered every effort with resistance. Now he would do everything short of begging to be permitted to join, and since he'd had to work for the privilege, he would become the computer club's most enthusiastic member. Maybe he would even become their president, and wouldn't that be something to mention to

Mary Beth from next door, who practically sent out daily press releases about her kids' achievements.

She gave Tim the tiniest flicker of a triumphant smile when she was certain Michael wouldn't notice. Tim hid his grin, but he couldn't mask the admiration in his eyes.

On Thursday evening the mood shifted. Tim and Michael had exhausted the local possibilities and weren't sure where to look next. "You'll think of something," Diane told them, disguising her concern behind a cheerful smile. Without skateboarding, there would be no friends, no computer club, no motivation to do homework, no inside jokes with his dad. Michael would revert back to his old, practiced ways, she was sure of it.

The next afternoon, the Elm Creek Quilters held a business meeting during the campers' free time after Agnes's workshop, so Diane headed home later than usual. Todd would be finishing his homework already, and Tim and Michael would be continuing their search. She hoped their luck would change, and soon.

To her surprise, Tim's car was in the garage when she got home. She pulled in beside it, wondering. Had they found a place for Michael, and was he even now spinning around and popping wheelies or whatever those tricks were called? Had they been forced to admit failure, and was Michael sulking up in his room while Tim paced around the house trying to figure out how to tell her? She got out of the car and leaned up against the door to close it, nervousness twisting in her stomach. She couldn't stay out there forever, she told herself, but she could delay the bad news a while.

Then she heard strange sounds coming from somewhere outside the garage. She walked down the driveway, listening, until she realized the noise was coming from behind her own house. It almost sounded as if the woods abutting their property had been turned into a construction site. She went around the side of the house and found Tim and Michael at the far edge of the backyard with all manner of building supplies and tools piled up on the grass around them.

She was almost afraid to know, but she approached them and asked what they were doing. They looked up from their work with nearly identical happy grins. "Dad's building me a ramp," Michael exclaimed. "Isn't this cool?"

"That's one way to describe it." She folded her arms and surveyed the damage to the lawn. They had enough material there for a small house. "Are you sure you don't need a building permit?"

Michael laughed and returned to his work.

She fixed her gaze on Tim, who was kneeling on the grass and sanding a board. "You know, for some reason I can't remember the conversation where you told me you were going to build a skateboard ramp in our backyard. I must have forgotten it, because I know you wouldn't begin a project like this without talking to me first."

He gave her a look that was both pleading and sheepish. "Honey, we looked everywhere. Every suitable place was off-limits. The only solution was to build our own place."

"Maybe I would have come to the same conclusion, if I had been asked, if we could have discussed this the way normal, rational, sane people usually discuss these things."

"It couldn't wait," he said simply, and Diane knew that he, too, had sensed something last night, some unspoken, unintended signal that this could be their last chance to reach their son, to convince him they were interested in his life, that despite their greatly advanced age and their abhorrence of all things fun, they didn't want his teen years to be entirely miserable.

She sighed and shook her head, and when Tim's face brightened she knew he understood that she was granting permission for the project to continue. What else could she do, really? They had installed a basketball hoop for Todd; was a skateboard ramp for Michael any different? Aside from its size, of course, and the expense, and the loss of a good portion of their backyard.

She turned and walked back to the house so that she wouldn't have to think about just how large the skateboard ramp would be if it required so much material. Their backyard was big enough; all of the backyards on this side of the street were, because they bordered the Waterford College Arboretum. The yards were separated by fences and mature trees, so they wouldn't disturb the neighbors. Really, she couldn't complain.

Tim and Michael worked until supper, then headed back outside as soon as the meal was over. After clearing away the dishes, Diane took her sewing basket and the round robin quilt out to the balcony off the master bedroom, so that she could keep an eye on the construction as she planned her border. But the quilt rested in her lap unnoticed. Tim and Michael worked until it grew too dark to see, and all the while Diane watched them, thinking.

The skateboard ramp took shape that weekend. By Saturday afternoon they had erected a structure of crossbeams that supported a U-shaped curve resembling the cross section of a pipe. It was higher than Diane had expected, and longer, but she clamped her mouth shut and vowed that instead of complaining, she'd buy Michael a helmet.

That evening some of Todd's friends came over to watch videos. From the family room where she was loading piles of folded laundry into her basket, she heard them raiding the refrigerator and arguing about which movie to watch first.

Then one of the boys interrupted the debate with a cry of astonishment. "What the hell is that?"

Todd's reply was barely audible, and she had to strain to catch it. "Something for my brother."

"But what is it?" another boy asked.

"It looks like a skateboard ramp." This voice was lower; it belonged to Mary Beth's son, Brent.

"Great theory, Einstein," Todd retorted. "It only took you one guess."

Brent laughed. "I didn't know you were a skateboard geek."

"I'm not."

"Your brother is."

"So? That doesn't mean I am. I mean, look at him. He's a total loser. I'm nothing like him."

Diane's grip tightened on the handles of the laundry basket.

"You better watch out," the first boy drawled. "You have the same genes, right? It might show up later."

The boys snickered.

Diane sailed into the room and slammed the laundry basket down on the kitchen table. Todd and his friends jumped at the sound. "Well, hello, boys," she declared, nailing a grin to her face. "Getting yourselves a snack?"

They muttered hellos and sneaked furtive glances at Todd, all but Brent, who had the nerve to look her straight in the eye and smile. "We were just checking out the skateboard ramp," he said. "It's really cool. Do you think Michael would let us try it when it's ready?"

Insolent little weasel. "You could ask him," she said, still grinning.

"Maybe later," Todd said, shoving his friends out of the kitchen. "Mom, I didn't mean that the way it sounded."

She would have been more impressed by his apology if he hadn't waited until his friends were out of earshot. "You have no idea how much it hurts me to know you score points with your friends by ridiculing your brother. You, of all people, should defend him." She snatched up the laundry basket and stormed from the room.

Tim and Michael worked until dusk, and the next morning Diane woke to the sounds of hammers and saws outside her window. They worked all day, taking breaks only for meals and church. Michael tried to convince her to let them skip mass just that once, and Tim looked like he might agree, but Diane would have none of it. "With this thing in the backyard we're going to need all the divine assistance we can get," she said, herding father and son inside with orders to clean up and change within twenty minutes or she'd cancel construction for the day.

Tim and Michael got back to work after church, and when Diane returned from welcoming a new group of quilt campers to Elm Creek Manor, they were still at it. By Sunday evening the skateboard ramp was finished. Diane and Todd joined Tim and Michael outside for the final inspection.

Michael was holding his skateboard and grinning. "What do you think?"

"Unbelievable," Todd said, eyeing the structure, and Diane agreed. The U-shaped half-pipe nearly spanned the width of the yard and looked at least twelve feet high.

"It's safe," Michael assured her. "Really."

Diane circled the ramp, looking it over. When the supporting beams hid her from view, she seized the nearest one and threw her weight against it. It didn't budge.

"Dad already tried that," Michael called. "It's sturdy."

Diane joined them in front. "It seems to be," she admitted.

Michael apparently took that as the signal to begin the test run, because he put on his helmet. He climbed up a ladder built into one side of the structure and moved onto a platform at the top of the U. He placed his skateboard at the edge, stepped on it, and scanned the length of the ramp.

"I can't watch," Diane murmured, but she couldn't look away, either.

Then Michael launched himself forward, over the edge and down the slope. His momentum carried him up the opposite side, where he turned at the edge and raced back down again. He shot up the first slope, but this time he soared above the U, crouching down to grab the skateboard with one hand as he turned.

"Big air," Tim whooped as Michael rode down the slope again. "That's what the kids say," he added in an undertone.

Diane nodded, her anxiety giving way to amazement as she watched Michael swoop down one side of the U and up the other. He was positively graceful.

Finally he slowed and came to a stop at the bottom of the U. "What did you think?" he called, smiling with triumph and breathing hard from exertion. Somehow he tossed the skateboard into the air with his feet and caught it.

Diane couldn't speak for a moment. He looked so proud and happy. "I'm impressed," she said. "I'm also terrified you're going to break your neck."

Michael laughed. "It's not as dangerous as it looks."

"Thank God for that."

Michael rode a while longer, until Diane told him he had to go inside and do his homework. To her amazement, he obeyed without protest.

"What happened to our kid?" she whispered to Tim.

"I don't know, but I'm not complaining." He put an arm around her shoulders and they crossed the lawn side by side.

The next day, Diane went to the manor earlier than usual to have lunch with the new campers and some of the Elm Creek Quilters. She had the whole group laughing with the story of how she and Tim had punished their wayward son by building him his own skateboard ramp.

"Why does Waterford have such a problem with skateboarding?" Summer asked. "There aren't any laws against in-line skates. How are skateboards any different?"

"I suppose it's because skateboarders tend to be teenage boys who dress a certain way and listen to a certain kind of music," Gwen mused. "They might be the nicest kids in the world, but they project an image which makes some people uncomfortable."

Diane was forced to agree. Michael was a basically good kid, but he looked like the stereotypical punk teenager. If he dressed differently, cut his hair, and lost the earring, adults would treat him with more respect. Unfortunately, despite her many attempts to explain, he didn't see the connection.

When she brought Todd home from band practice later that day, Michael was in the backyard with three other boys—no, two other boys and a girl. "Kelly, I suppose," Diane mused. She had assumed Kelly was a boy, since Tim had not indicated otherwise. She watched them through the kitchen window as they took turns zooming up and down the ramp. When it was Kelly's turn, Michael called out something that made her laugh. One of the boys nudged him and Michael grinned.

Well. That was certainly interesting.

Just then, Michael and his friends put down their skateboards and began walking toward the house. Diane let the curtain fall back across the window and busied herself emptying the dishwasher. They came into the kitchen laughing and talking and looking for food.

"We have apples and grapes in the fruit bin," Diane suggested, not surprised when they grimaced. She found them a package of cookies instead, and Michael took four glasses from the cupboard and filled them with milk. Kelly helped him carry them to the kitchen table and paused to thank Diane for the cookies. She was a pretty, dark-haired girl, and Diane decided she liked her.

When they finished their snack, Diane took the round robin quilt outside to the deck so that she could plan her border and watch the kids skate. She swung back and forth on the porch swing in the shade of her favorite oak tree and held up the quilt top. Sarah's border of squares on point used a cream background and varying shades of blue and green, so Diane decided to use similar colors. But what pattern should she choose? She had never participated in a round robin before, and she wished Agnes had given more specific instructions. Should she use squares, too, since Sarah had, or was the point to make each border completely different?

"Yoo hoo. Diane, yoo hoo."

Diane smothered a groan and tried to hide the quilt on her lap. "Hello, Mary Beth," she said to the woman peering over the fence. "How are you?" It was an automatic question. She couldn't care less how Mary Beth was that day or any other day. They had never been friends, and Mary Beth had never forgiven Diane for challenging her for the office of president of the Waterford Quilting Guild. Diane would have won, too, if Mary Beth hadn't made an impassioned speech to the guild the night before the election, asking them if they were willing to hand over the responsibilities of the Waterford Summer Quilt Festival to someone who had never won a ribbon. After Mary Beth's reelection, Diane and her friends were so fed up with the silly politics that they left the guild to form their own bee.

For years Diane had resented Mary Beth, but suddenly she realized she ought to thank her. If not for Mary Beth, she and her friends wouldn't have formed their own bee, so they couldn't have invited Sarah to join it, and then Elm Creek Quilts might not have existed.

But Mary Beth's phony smile pushed all gratitude out of Diane's mind. "What do you have there?" Mary Beth asked, craning her neck to see what was in Diane's lap.

Reluctantly, Diane held up the quilt top. "It's a round robin quilt I'm making with the Elm Creek Quilters. One person makes a center block and the others take turns adding borders to it."

"Oh, I know. I've made dozens of them." Mary Beth squinted as she studied the quilt. "You do realize you're supposed to put something in the middle? Not just leave it a big blank square?"

"Oh, really? My goodness. I had no idea. I thought it looked strange, and now I know why. Thank you for clearing that up."

Mary Beth eyed her, as if trying to gauge her sincerity. "You're welcome," she finally said. She nodded to the skateboard ramp as if seeing it for the first time. "What on earth is that?"

"It's a skateboard ramp."

"It looks like an accident waiting to happen." Mary Beth shook her head and made tsking noises with her tongue. "Do their parents know how high it is?"

Diane felt a pang of worry, but she refused to let Mary Beth see it. "Of course. In fact, some of them think it's not high enough."

Mary Beth's eyes widened. "No kidding? Well, I guess that's fine, then. I wish I were as brave as you. If that thing were in my backyard, I'd never have a moment's peace. I'd be too worried about liability."

Diane felt a twinge of nervousness. "We've taken care of all that."

"Of course. Tim is so practical."

Diane nodded and turned her attention to the quilt, hoping that Mary Beth would take the hint and go away.

"Aren't you worried that a skateboard ramp will attract—how can I put this—a certain undesirable element?"

Diane's head jerked up, and when she spoke, her voice was cold. "That undesirable element you're talking about is my son and his friends. They're under my supervision, and they aren't bothering you, so why don't you just leave them alone?"

For a moment Mary Beth just gaped at her—stunned, for once in her life, into silence. "You don't have to snap at me. I was just trying to help, in case you haven't thought it through."

"Thanks all the same, but we have thought it through, and if I wanted your advice, I'd ask for it."

"Fine." Mary Beth sniffed and set her jaw. "You're wrong, you know, about one thing. This monstrosity *is* bothering me, and it's probably bothering a lot of other people, too."

"No one else has complained."

"Not yet, maybe, but we do have rules in this neighborhood, you know, ordinances and things." Mary Beth gave her one last glare and marched back into her house.

Diane tried to return her attention to the quilt, but Mary Beth's remarks nagged at her. Eventually she put the quilt away and crossed the lawn to speak to Michael's friends. Their faces fell when she told them there would be no more skating until their parents came by and inspected the ramp for themselves. Brandon said his mom could be there in five minutes, but Kelly and Troy said their parents were working and couldn't come over until that evening, at the earliest.

"I'm sorry," Diane told Michael, and she meant it with all her heart.

Michael scowled, humiliated. "You said we could skate."

"It's okay," Kelly said, sparing a quick glance for Diane before turning back to Michael. "We can watch a video or something. We can skate tomorrow when everyone's allowed."

Michael muttered something, gave Diane a dark look, and motioned for his friends to follow him inside.

Diane went inside, too, after stopping by the deck to retrieve the quilt and glare at Mary Beth's house. If Mary Beth thought she could scare Diane into taking down that ramp, she was more foolish than Diane had given her credit for, and Diane had never been stingy when it came to estimating Mary Beth's faults.

By Tuesday evening, the parents of Michael's friends had inspected the ramp and had given their children permission to skate there. Diane enjoyed meeting them, especially Kelly's mother. "For weeks it's been Michael this and Michael that around our place," Kelly's mother said, shaking her head and smiling. "Kelly says Michael's the first boy she ever met who doesn't think it's odd for a girl to skate. He told her that boys who say girls can't skate are just worried about the competition."

"Really?" Diane was pleased. Somehow she'd raised a feminist. Gwen would be proud of her.

On the following night Diane joined the other Elm Creek Quilters for a staff meeting at the manor. Afterward, she updated her friends on the saga of the skating ramp. "I used to think like Mary Beth," she admitted. "But when I look at Michael now, it's hard for me to imagine why I ever disliked skateboarding. He hasn't seemed this well adjusted since the second grade."

"It isn't the skateboarding per se," Gwen said. "It's the attention you and Tim have been paying him lately."

"Thank you, Dr. Spock, but Michael's never lacked parental attention."

"But this is positive attention for an activity he enjoys. He's probably thrilled that you finally support one of his pastimes."

"You expect me to encourage his usual hobbies?" Diane shot back, thinking of the heavy metal music, the vandalism at the middle school, the fights with Todd. "Besides, it's not like you have any experience dealing with this sort of mess. Summer never gave you a moment's trouble."

Gwen held up her hands, apologetic. "You're right. I'm sorry."

"I used to get in trouble a lot when I was Michael's age," Judy said. "Talking back to the teachers, skipping classes, fistfights, you name it."

"Fistfights?" Bonnie said. "You? I can't believe it."

"It's true." Judy smiled wryly. "I got picked on a lot at school. The other kids would go like this"—she put her fingers to the outer corners of her eyes and stretched the lids into slits—"and tell me to go back to China."

"Their grasp of geography is depressing," Gwen said.

"You try explaining the difference between China and Vietnam to a bunch of obnoxious adolescents. They'd do Bruce Lee imitations and steal my lunch, saying I couldn't eat it anyway since I didn't have any chopsticks." Judy shook her head. "It sounds silly and stupid now, but at the time it was very painful. I guess I acted out because I didn't have any friends, anyone to support me. I didn't want to complain at home, because my mom had already been through so much."

"So what happened?" Diane asked. "You obviously straightened out somehow."

Judy shrugged, and her long, dark hair slipped over one shoulder. "My dad figured out what was going on and had me transferred to another school. No one teased me there, so I didn't need to cause trouble anymore."

"Do you think I should have Michael transferred to another school?"

"That's probably not necessary," Bonnie said. "Wait and see. It sounds like things may be turning around already."

"And making him leave his friends might make everything worse," Carol said. "The more advice you give your children, the more you try to help them do what's right, the more they insist on going their own way."

Sarah gave her a sharp look. "Sometimes parents try to help too much when no help is needed."

"Sometimes children don't know what's best for them. Sometimes they'd be wise to learn from their parents' mistakes instead of fumbling around on their own."

"Who's fumbling?" Sarah asked.

Carol said nothing, and an awkward silence descended on the foyer until a group of new campers arrived, sending the Elm Creek Quilters back to work.

The next day's classes kept Diane so busy that she had no chance to ask any of the Elm Creek Quilters about the strange exchange between mother and daughter, so she put it out of her mind. On the way home, she stopped at the grocery for a few things for supper and more cookies. The night before, Todd had complained that Michael and his friends had eaten all the snacks in the house, leaving nothing for Todd's friends.

"There's fruit," Diane had said, but Todd had scowled and muttered something about how things sure had changed around there. It was obvious he did not mean they had changed for the better. Diane hoped that an ample supply of snacks would appease him, if only temporarily.

As she pulled into the driveway, Diane saw the curtain in Mary Beth's living room window move aside. Her eyes met Mary Beth's before the curtain fell between them. Diane frowned and parked the car. Didn't Mary Beth have anything better to do all day than to spy on her neighbors? She carried the bag of groceries into the kitchen, then returned outside to check the mail. In her peripheral vision she saw Mary Beth's curtain draw back again, but she ignored it. That woman really needed a hobby.

Diane collected a handful of envelopes from the mailbox and leafed through them as she walked up the driveway. Credit card application, bill, bill, credit card application—and a thick envelope with a return address of the Waterford Municipal Building. She stopped in the middle of the driveway and opened the envelope, dreading the news. Rumor had it that the property taxes in their historic neighborhood were going to be reassessed, despite residents' complaints to the Zoning Commission.

The first line made it clear that the letter was not about taxes, but her relief soon turned to dismay. The Waterford Zoning Commission had received complaints that the Sonnenberg family had erected a skateboard ramp in their backyard. Since that structure met the definition of an Attractive Nuisance, and since they had not applied for the proper building permits, it must be razed within forty-eight hours.

"Is this some kind of a joke?" Diane exclaimed, gaping at the letter. The ramp was on private property. The Zoning Commission couldn't force them to tear it down, could they?

Diane looked up, her mind racing—and saw Mary Beth watching her through her living room window.

She crumpled the letter in her fist and marched across the lawn to Mary Beth's house. She could see the panic in her neighbor's face—before Mary Beth quickly hid behind the curtain. Diane stormed up the porch stairs and pounded on the front door. "Mary Beth," she shouted. "Get out here, you vicious little troll! I know you're responsible for this." She paused, but there was no response. She hammered on the door with her fist. "I know you're in there. Come on out!"

Mary Beth wisely remained inside. Eventually, Diane gave up and returned to her own house, seething. The nerve of Mary Beth, to turn Diane's family in to the Waterford Zoning Commission! "May her fabric bleed, her rotary cutter rust, and all of her borders be crooked," Diane muttered, slamming the door behind her and storming to the kitchen to call Bonnie. Diane was reluctant to interrupt her at Grandma's Attic, but this couldn't wait, and she wasn't going to risk getting a busy signal later that evening because of Craig's constant web surfing. Bonnie had served on the commission in the past as a representative from the Downtown Business Association. If the Sonnenbergs had any options, Bonnie would know what they were.

Quickly, Diane explained what had happened, then asked, "I know there are certain restrictions because this is a historic neighborhood, but is there anything I can do?" She steeled herself. "If I crawl over there on my hands and knees and beg Mary Beth to withdraw the complaint, and if by some miracle I manage to persuade her, would the Zoning Commission let us keep the ramp?"

"That's not how it works," Bonnie said. "Once the commission has made a ruling, the original complaint no longer matters. You have two options at this point. You can either comply with their request and tear down the ramp, or you can file for an exemption. That means you'll have to present your case to the commission at a public hearing."

Diane couldn't believe it. "You mean the kind of hearings they hold when someone wants to build a new mall or a new road?"

"I'm afraid so. According to their bureaucratic way of looking at things, your ramp is no different than a major construction site. You'll have to convince the commission that the skateboard ramp isn't a hazard to local residents, doesn't create unnecessary noise or traffic problems, and doesn't destroy the aesthetics of the neighborhood."

Diane groaned. "I know. I remember that part."

"I don't understand why Mary Beth went to the authorities instead of trying to work things out with you personally. Maybe you two aren't friends, but you are neighbors." Then Bonnie paused. "What do you mean, you remember?"

"Look, I have to go. Michael's going to be home from school any minute, and I have to figure out what I'm going to tell him."

"Oh, no, you don't. You're not hanging up until you tell me what you meant by 'I remember.' "

"Mary Beth has been a thorn in my side for too long." Diane sank into a chair, propped her elbows on the kitchen table, and let her head rest in her palm. "She never would have known about that ordinance if not for those stupid wind chimes."

"What?"

Diane's anger faded into chagrin. "Two years ago, Mary Beth hung some wind chimes outside her kitchen window. I swear to God, they were the wind chimes from hell, clanking and banging with the slightest breeze. They must have had amplifiers or something. They scared away every bird for miles—"

"Miles?"

"Well, yards, anyway. And they kept me and Tim awake all night. The only way we could escape the noise was to shut every window facing the backyard, and that wasn't fair. So I asked her very nicely to take them down—"

"Oh, I bet you did."

"I did, I swear. Whose side are you on? Naturally she refused, so I called the municipal building and asked them about noise ordinances."

"And when you found one, you called Mary Beth and threatened to turn her in, didn't you?"

"Of course not." Diane paused. "I went over and told her in person."

Bonnie burst out laughing.

"But I only threatened to turn her in," Diane protested. "I wouldn't have done it."

"Either way, you're the one who started it, and now it's come back to haunt you."

Bonnie's amusement was exasperating, mostly because Diane knew she was right. "I'm glad you find this so humorous, but you're not help-ing. My son's going to lose his skateboard ramp, remember?"

"I'm sorry. You're right." Bonnie made a strangling sound as if fighting to contain her laughter. She promised to help Diane file for the exemption and prepare for the hearing, if that's what she and Tim decided to do.

When Diane called him with the news, he came right home. They talked about it as they made supper, while outside Michael and his friends zoomed up and down the skateboard ramp, unaware that their fun could be short-lived. Diane and Tim considered the time and effort it would take to file for an exemption, the stress and publicity the hearing would generate—but most of all, they thought of Michael and how he would be affected by the loss of his skateboard ramp and by the knowledge that his parents had meekly submitted to the Zoning Commission's first and only letter.

"If we want to keep the skateboard ramp, we'll have to fight for it," Tim eventually said, and Diane agreed, but she had an additional motive. She wanted to fight because she refused to let Mary Beth win so easily. She'd give up quilting before she'd hand that woman an uncontested victory.

During supper, they told the boys about the letter and what they were prepared to do to keep the skateboard ramp. Michael's expression changed from alarm to relief when he realized they weren't going to give in, at least not until they had to. "Is there anything I can do?" he asked.

"I'll let you know what Bonnie suggests," Diane said. "It'll be a lot of work, but with all four of us helping out, we'll take care of it." Michael nodded, but Todd muttered something, nudged his plate away, and put his elbows on the table. He had hardly touched his supper, and suddenly Diane realized that he hadn't said a word since she brought up the letter. "Is something wrong, Todd?"

"Why do you just assume that everyone wants to help? Maybe I don't care about this stupid skateboard ramp. Did you ever think about that?"

Startled, Diane turned to Tim, who looked back at her with the same surprised helplessness she was feeling. "But—but Michael is your brother," she stammered.

"So?"

"So?" Diane stared at him, disbelieving. "So we help each other. That's part of what makes us a family."

"What about helping me? How come nobody thinks about me?"

Diane was at a loss, so Tim stepped in. "What do you mean, son?"

"Did you ever think about what it's gonna be like at school?" Todd's voice was high and thin. "Why does she have to fight with Brent's mom all the time? I'm not gonna have any friends left thanks to her."

Tim's mild voice grew stern. "Don't talk about your mother that way. Apologize this minute."

"But it's true. She's gonna ruin everything."

"I said, apologize."

Todd glared at the table and clamped his mouth shut as if afraid an apology might slip out by force of habit.

Tim's eyes sparked with anger. "Go to your room. Now."

Todd shoved his chair back from the table and stormed away.

"I'm sorry," Michael said when Todd was gone.

"Why?" Diane said briskly, picking up her fork. "You didn't do anything wrong." For once it was true. In a matter of weeks, her sons had traded personalities.

The next morning, Diane went downtown to Bonnie's quilt shop, where the red sign with the words GRANDMA'S ATTIC printed in gold seemed to welcome her. The quilt hanging beneath it in the shop window comforted her, too, since she had often seen Judy working on it at the Elm Creek Quilters' meetings. Everything about Bonnie's shop—from the folk music playing in the background to the shelves filled with fabric and notions—was familiar to her, a reminder of her friends and the good times they had shared throughout the years. Her friends would support her no matter what happened, she knew, and that knowledge strengthened her.

Bonnie was at the large cutting table in the middle of the room helping a customer when Diane entered. The bell attached to the door jingled, and Bonnie looked up and smiled. "Pull up a stool," she called out, motioning for Diane to join them at the cutting table. Diane did and waited for the customer to pay for her purchases and leave.

When they were alone, Bonnie showed Diane some papers she had picked up from the municipal building. She explained how to fill them out and described the exemption hearing process, and as she did, Diane began to feel better. She and Tim had a lot of work ahead of them, but not nearly as much as she had feared. With Bonnie there to reassure her, the task didn't seem as hopeless and overwhelming as it had the night before.

As Diane turned to go, she thanked Bonnie wholeheartedly. Bonnie waved off her thanks with an easy laugh and said, "You would have done the same for me. Now, try not to worry, okay? Work on the round robin quilt; that'll relax you."

"Oh." Diane had forgotten all about it. "That's a good idea."

Bonnie's eyebrows rose, and she gave Diane a look of amused exasperation. "You do know you're supposed to have it done by the end of this week, right?" Then her expression softened. "Look, why don't you just give it to me? You have enough on your mind already."

"No, I can do it," Diane said, heading for the door.

"Are you sure?" Bonnie called after her. "We can extend the deadline."

"That's not necessary. I'll get it done." Diane thanked her again for all her help and left the shop. There was no way Diane was going to let Mary Beth prevent her from participating in the round robin. Mary Beth had already interfered too much in Diane's life; she wasn't going to ruin this quilt, too.

That weekend, Diane and Tim collected documents on local privacy laws supporting their right to keep the skateboard ramp. The Elm Creek Quilters did their part, too. Summer researched possible precedents in the Waterford College library; Judy's husband, Steve, wrote a feature article on the conflict for the local newspaper; and everyone joined in to keep Diane's spirits up.

On the same morning Steve's article appeared in the *Waterford Register,* Agnes stopped by the Sonnenberg home with unsettling news. The boys were scrambling to get ready for school, but they hovered around the kitchen as Agnes told their parents about Mary Beth's weekend activities.

"She went to every house in the neighborhood with a petition supporting the commission's decision," Agnes said, her blue eyes solemn behind pink-tinted glasses.

The news made Diane uneasy, though she wasn't surprised. "How many signatures has she collected?"

"I didn't get a good look at the petition because naturally I didn't sign it, but I believe she had almost one page filled." Agnes pursed her lips and shook her head. "The nerve of her, bringing that petition to my door."

Diane hugged the older woman. Mary Beth knew very well that Diane and Agnes were friends. Agnes had baby-sat Diane when she was a child, and they were both Elm Creek Quilters. Mary Beth had to have known that Agnes would tell Diane about the petition. Was this a message, a boast that Mary Beth didn't care if Diane knew what she was up to because she knew Diane was powerless to stop her?

One page filled, Agnes had said, an entire page covered with signatures demanding the destruction of the skateboard ramp. The thought of it made Diane dizzy with apprehension. How could it be that so many of their neighbors had sided against them?

The phone rang as soon as Agnes left; it was Gwen, calling to gloat over Steve's article. "It's perfect," she crowed. "You'll have every parent and private property hawk in Waterford on your side."

"I haven't had a chance to read it yet," Diane said, pinning the receiver to her ear with her shoulder so her hands would be free to pack the boys' lunches. Tim sped through the kitchen and planted a kiss on her cheek on his way out. "Bye, honey," she called after him.

"Honey?" Gwen echoed. "Hanging up so soon?"

"That was for Tim, but yes, I do have to go." Had Gwen forgotten what school mornings were like in a family with teenagers? "First, though, does the article say anything about Mary Beth's petition?"

"No. What petition?"

"I'll tell you after your workshop. See you at Elm Creek Manor." Diane hung up and called out to her sons. "Lunches are ready. Hurry up or you'll be late."

Michael snatched his from the counter and ran out the door, but Todd hesitated, his brows drawn together in disbelief. "Brent's mom made a petition against us?"

The phone rang again.

Diane glanced from her son to the phone, to the clock over the kitchen table, and back to her son in the amount of time for the phone to pause between rings. "Not against us, honey, not against you. We're just having a difference of opinion. This is the way adults settle these things. We shouldn't take it personally. We can talk about this later, okay? You'd better hurry or you'll miss your bus."

He nodded, put his lunch bag in his backpack, and left, but he didn't look convinced. Why should he? Diane knew her explanation was a half-truth at best. Neither she nor Mary Beth was demonstrating textbook adult behavior, and Diane herself was taking this matter all too personally. She snatched up the phone a second before the answering machine would have clicked on. "Hello?"

It was a neighbor, calling to apologize for signing Mary Beth's petition. She never would have signed it, she said, if she had known the whole story, but now that she'd read the newspaper article, the Sonnenbergs had her support. Diane thanked her, but as soon as they hung up, the phone rang again.

"Hello?" she said, glancing at the clock.

"Tear that damn thing down or we'll tear it down for you," a voice growled in her ear, low, gruff, a man's voice. Then there was a click and the dial tone.

Stunned, Diane slowly replaced the receiver—and the phone rang again. Heart pounding, she unplugged the cord from the jack.

After Gwen's workshop, while the campers were enjoying their free time, Diane told Gwen, Sarah, Carol, and Sylvia about the call. All but Sylvia listened with wide eyes, stunned by the story. Sylvia looked concerned, but somehow she didn't seemed surprised.

"Did you use star sixty-nine to trace the call?" Gwen asked.

Diane shook her head. "I didn't think of it." Her heart sank as they all urged her to do so next time. Why were they so certain that there would be a next time?

"I must say I'm amazed by all this," Carol said. "This seemed like such a nice little town."

Sarah gave her a slight frown. "It almost always is. This is an anomaly."

"I hope you're right," Carol said, but she looked dubious. "It doesn't seem like a very nice place to raise children."

Sarah gave her a disapproving look but said nothing more.

Diane dreaded to go home, but eventually she could think of no more excuses to stay, and she wanted to be there when the boys arrived. Before she left, Sylvia took her aside and placed her hands on Diane's shoulders.

"Promise me you won't let those fools scare you," Sylvia said.

"I won't," Diane said. Though she was taller, she felt young and small beneath the older woman's knowing gaze. "I'm not scared, just angry."

"Good." Sylvia squeezed Diane's shoulders. "I want to believe in the good in people, I do, but I've seen how the people in this town can turn on a person. I know how it feels to have a whole town against you. Don't let them make you afraid. Don't let them make you feel ashamed when you've done nothing wrong." And with that, she strode away, back to her sewing room.

Diane watched her go, wondering.

When she got home, the house was quiet, but instead of the restful peace she usually sensed there at that time of day, the silence seemed strange and watchful. She chided herself for her nerves and told herself she was being silly, but still, she walked through the house checking every room to see what was amiss. She felt alert, wary. Something wasn't right.

When she returned to the kitchen and drew back the curtain to peer outside, she saw it.

Paint as red as blood stained the skateboard ramp; angry splashes and hateful words marred the smooth curves. Diane found herself running outside, strangling a scream of rage as she drew closer, close enough to see shattered eggs and mud and broken glass. She stopped at the base of the U, clenching and unclenching her fists, fighting to breathe. Her eyes darted around the yard, though she knew the culprits were long gone. The paint was dry; the dark patches of mud were cracked on the surface; the eggs had hardened into yellowish, foul-smelling streaks.

Michael. She couldn't let him see this.

She raced to the back of the garage for the garden hose, unwinding it like a thick green snake on the lawn. Most of the mud surrendered to the force of the spray, but the eggs were more stubborn and the paint glared scarlet through the droplets. She brought out buckets and soap and brushes and scrubbed at the stains with all her strength. She scrubbed harder, faster, until her muscles burned, sweat trickled down her forehead, and all she could do was scrub and scrub and scrub and spit out curses through clenched teeth.

"Mom?"

She gasped and turned so quickly that she upset the bucket, sending a stream of pink, soapy water running down the base of the ramp to the lawn. Michael and Todd were staring at her, too stunned to get out of the way.

Diane couldn't think of what to say. She sat back on her heels and drew the back of her hand across her brow, pushing the sweaty blond curls aside.

"What the hell happened?" Michael said. Openmouthed, he climbed onto the ramp and slowly spun around, taking it all in.

Diane watched him until she caught her breath, then she picked up her brush and got back to work. Her fury was spent; she worked slowly now, deliberately. A few moments later, she heard Michael set the bucket upright and fill it with water and soap. Soon he was on his knees beside her, plunging a second brush into the bucket and scrubbing furiously.

Five minutes passed, and then ten, and then Todd joined them. Unnoticed, he had gone back inside to change out of his nice school clothes. It was such a typical Todd thing to do that Diane almost burst out laughing, but she didn't let herself, because she knew if she did, tears would soon follow.

They worked until Tim came home. Diane had forgotten to make supper, so they ordered pizza. When they sat down to eat, Diane yanked the curtains shut so they couldn't see into the backyard.

"We need a guard dog," Todd said, chewing thoughtfully on a long string of mozzarella. "A huge, mean dog. A Doberman pinscher or a rottweiler."

"Or a pit bull," Michael said. "Or a couple of pit bulls."

"Or a velociraptor on crack," Tim suggested, reaching for a second piece.

It was so ridiculous that Diane had to laugh—deep, aching, whole-body laughs that soon had the entire family joining in. They laughed completely out of proportion to the humor in Tim's remark, and that awareness was what finally helped Diane stop laughing long enough to finish her supper. But for the rest of the evening, as the four of them tried to remove the signs of the vandalism, all anyone had to do was snarl and claw the air like a dinosaur after prey and they were all helpless with laughter again.

The next day, Diane left for Elm Creek Manor as late as possible and rushed home as soon as Judy's workshop ended. To her relief, no additional vandalism had occurred during her absence. Perhaps the culprits thought none was needed; traces of paint were still plainly visible on the smooth curve of the ramp, spelling out words she liked to fool herself into thinking her sons didn't know.

She was sitting on the swing on the deck, the round robin quilt untouched in her lap, when Todd came home. "I skipped band practice," he said by way of greeting, but she hardly heard him. His shirt was torn, the collar stained with blood that probably came from his split lip. His left eye was puffy and bruised.

"What on earth?" Diane jumped up, letting the quilt fall, and raced to him. She checked him all over for more serious injuries before marching him inside to patch him up.

"Brent," he said, though she had already guessed. "He got mad because I was passing around a petition after school."

"A what?"

He reached for his backpack, wincing in pain, and took out a crumpled sheet of paper. "I figured if they could have a petition, we could, too."

Diane skimmed the page, taking in about two dozen children's signatures below a paragraph asking the commission to let Michael Sonnenberg keep his skateboard ramp.

Her heart was too full for words. She wrapped Todd in a hug and held on tight.

"Mom," he said in a strained voice, "that kind of hurts."

Immediately, she released him. "Sorry." Then movement in the family room doorway caught her eye. It was a young man with hair neatly trimmed and nary an earring to be seen.

Diane stared. "Who are you and what have you done with my son?"

"Funny, Mom," Michael said, but he grinned, pleased.

Todd looked astounded. "Dude, what did you do to your hair?"

"I got it cut." Michael flopped into a chair. "I don't want to give those guys any ammunition."

A month ago, Diane never could have imagined she'd ever say the words she was about to speak. "I wish you wouldn't have. You don't need to change for them."

But Michael merely shrugged. "It's just my hair. It's not me." His eyes met hers, and for a moment Diane felt that they understood each other.

🪷 🪷 🪷

Her heart full of sorrowful pride, Diane took up the round robin quilt that had been so often studied and too long neglected. She chose fabric in a deeper shade of cream than what Sarah had used, for Sarah's fabric was too bright for this new feeling, for this not-yet-comprehensible sense that in fighting for her son's happiness she had done exactly what they needed her to do, so that regardless of the hearing's outcome, she would know she had not failed them.

She cut four large triangles from the cloth, knowing that although they came from the same fabric, and looked alike, and might even seem identical to an outsider, there were subtle differences among them—a more crooked line here, a sharper point there, an edge not quite as long as it should be. Some quilters would call them mistakes, these variations that made each piece unique, but now Diane knew better.

She sewed the longest side of each triangle to an edge of the round robin quilt, setting the design on point, forcing a new perspective. One triangle for Tim, one for Michael, one for Todd, and the last for herself. The two smaller tips of each triangle met the analogous angles of the triangles on its left and its right, like four members of a family holding hands in a circle, united at last.

# Chapter Four

He had thought about Sylvia often since that Sunday morning weeks ago when he had seen her on television. It was a shock, at first, to see the short gray hair where once there had been long, dark curls, but her spirit was the same, there was no doubt about that. The young woman who had spent so much of the program at Sylvia's elbow, though, the one who had made that joke about her mother—she was a mystery. She and Sylvia seemed close. Could she be a granddaughter? Had Sylvia married again after all? He didn't think so. He hoped not. If he'd had any idea that Sylvia would ever consider taking another husband, he would have stuck around.

A pang of guilt went through him. "I didn't mean that the way it sounded, Katy-girl," he said aloud. He could picture her wagging a finger at him in mock reproach, and he grinned. No, Katy knew he wouldn't trade anything for the more than fifty years they had spent together. Those years had given him two children, a home, and a peace he had never dreamed he could possess. Katy never minded his limp, or his background, or the way he needed to be by himself every once in a while. When he woke in the darkness shaking and sweating from the nightmares, she had held him and shushed him and stroked his head until he could sleep again. In the mornings she would say nothing of his terror, leaving him his dignity.

He missed her. Sometimes he wished he had been the one to pass on first. Katy would have managed fine without him, better than he had done without her. Then again, he wouldn't wish this loneliness on anyone, least of all his wife.

It sure would be nice to have her in the passenger seat, riding along beside him as they crisscrossed the country. Of course, if Katy were still alive, he wouldn't have sold the house and bought this motor home. She loved that little house. Over the years, as their nest egg had grown, he'd often suggested they find a bigger place, but she wouldn't hear of it. "Why move now, just when I have my garden the way I like it?" she had asked. Another time it was because the kids were in school, and then it was because all their friends lived in the neighborhood. But one by one their friends retired and moved to condos in Florida or rooms in their children's homes. His buddies at the VFW grew fewer and fewer. Some died, and all too soon Katy joined them.

The house was an empty shell without Katy, and he couldn't bear to remain. The kids agreed that selling the house was a good idea—and they both assumed he would be moving in with one of them. Bob's wife, Cathy, tempted him with descriptions of the California sunshine, while his daughter, Amy, promised him his own apartment over the garage and plenty of New England fishing trips with her husband. He had waited until after the sale to tell them he had other plans. They thought he'd lost his mind when he bought the motor home, and they tried to talk him out of it. They didn't succeed. Oh, he knew if he lived long enough there would come a time when he would no longer be able to look after himself, and then he'd be grateful for the kids' help. But not yet. He had much to do before then.

"They're great kids, Katy, but they think anyone over seventy is ready for the old folks' home," he said. Still, although he wished he didn't seem so old and helpless in their eyes, he was glad that they wanted him. That proved he must have done something right all those years. He hadn't learned much from his own father about how to be a good parent, but he must have done all right in the end.

His philosophy about raising children had been simple: Do nothing that his own parents had done, and everything they had not.

The day Katy told him she was carrying their first, he had broken out in a cold sweat. He had been thrilled at the prospect of being a father, of welcoming a new life when he had seen so much death, but there had been fear enough to match his happiness. He worried about Katy, of course; he knew women could die in childbirth. But Katy was strong and healthy, and deep down he knew she'd be fine. What made him tremble from fear was the image of himself beating his son, of touching his daughter until she cried, of bludgeoning his wife's soul until she became a pale shadow of the vibrant woman he had married. He had seen this happen. Except for the few brief glimpses of the Bergstroms, this was the only family life he knew.

"You are not your father," Katy had told him passionately. "You are the kindest and most loving man I've ever known. I wouldn't have married you if I didn't know this with my whole heart."

He had wanted so much to believe her, but still he had feared the monster that might lurk within himself, cruelty passed to him along with his father's build and sandy hair.

When he held his daughter for the first time, so much love coursed through him that he knew he could never hurt a child of his and Katy's. But he would take no chances. He could not discipline his children the way the other parents in the neighborhood did; even when they had earned themselves a spanking he couldn't bear to raise a hand against them, or even to scold them. He would send them to their rooms instead, and go for long walks until his anger eased. When the children needed a scolding, it was up to Katy to provide it. "I always have to be the villain," she would grumble, glaring at him as she marched upstairs to face a disobedient child. He and Katy had been able to resolve each and every disagreement that ever came between them, except for this one. He hoped that despite her exasperation she understood somehow, and if not, that she forgave him anyway.

When he came to a wayside, he pulled off the freeway and fixed himself a sandwich. He carried it and a can of soda outside to a picnic table near a patch of trees. There he sat, thinking, eating his lunch and watching the cars speed past.

He would be the first to admit that Katy and Sylvia were a lot alike. That's what had attracted him to Katy the first time he saw her at that dance. He had been struck by the dark hair, the confident way she had thrown back her head and laughed just from the pleasure of the evening. He was instantly transported back to the moment he had first seen Sylvia on horseback on the Bergstrom estate, riding around the ring, oblivious to her young brother's playmate, who had climbed the corral fence to watch.

"She's like a lady from a story," he had said to Richard, awestruck.

"Who, Sylvia?"

"She's like—" Only seven, he fumbled for the words. "She's like a princess."

This had sent Richard into hysterics, and he fell to the ground, where he rolled from side to side on his back, laughing.

His face went hot, and he quickly joined in the laughter so Richard wouldn't think him a sissy. Richard was his only friend. Everyone else at school shied away from him, frightened by his bruises or by something in his eyes, something his father had put there.

He knew Richard was wrong. Sylvia was a princess, and Elm Creek Manor was a paradise. He would do anything to live there with them, away from the shouts, away from his father's stick and his mother's weeping. He would bring his sister, and Mr. Bergstrom would adopt them and they would be safe. Even when he grew up he would never have to leave, never.

He had invited himself to live with them the day he turned eight. It had been the worst birthday ever. His parents had forgotten about it, and he had known better than to remind them. The teacher scolded him for forgetting to bring cookies for the class to share, and everyone but Richard had laughed at him. In truth, he hadn't forgotten the cookies. They didn't have a single cookie in the house or anything to make them with, but he wouldn't tell the teacher that, not with everyone watching and laughing.

That evening he stayed for supper at Richard's house, knowing those few pleasant hours would be well worth the licking they would surely cost him. The Bergstrom house seemed so full of light and laughter. Sylvia quarreled with her elder sister, Claudia, sometimes, but that was nothing, nothing compared to what he saw at home.

After the meal he offered to help Sylvia clean up.

She thanked him and raised her eyebrows at her brother. "It's nice to know someone around here is a gentleman. We can't get Richard to lift a finger."

For a moment he feared Sylvia's chiding would work and Richard would join them. But Richard must have been accustomed to Sylvia's teasing, for he stuck out his tongue at her and remained in his seat. And Sylvia merely laughed. She didn't strike him across the face or scream at him or anything. She *was* like a lady from a story, no matter what Richard said.

When they were alone in the kitchen, she washed the dishes and he dried them. As they worked, she talked to him as if he were a grown-up. It more than made up for the awful birthday.

He wiped the dishes slowly to make the moment last, and soon she finished washing and picked up another towel to help him. "I wish I were a boy," she muttered, as if she had forgotten he was there. "The girls have to do all the work but the boys get to play."

He nodded, thinking of what his sister suffered at their father's hands. He wouldn't want to be a girl, either. "I would always help you," he said instead.

"No, you wouldn't. You'd be like all the rest of them."

"I wouldn't," he insisted, his heart pounding as he screwed up his courage. "If I could live here, I'd help you with the work every day, I promise. I'd do all the work myself so you could go play. If I could live here, please, I promise—"

Sylvia was staring at him.

It was all wrong, and he knew it. "It's just a joke," he blurted out. "Richard dared me to say it. I didn't mean it. I'd hate to live here. Really."

She watched him, bemused. "I see."

"No, I don't really hate it here—I mean—" He didn't know what he meant. He felt a prickling in his eyes that warned him he might cry, and it sickened him. He couldn't cry like a baby in front of Sylvia, he couldn't.

But Sylvia didn't seem to notice. "What did you win?" she asked, turning back to the dishes.

"Wh-what?"

"The dare. What did you win for the dare?"

"Oh." He thought quickly. "Richard—he has to give me his lunch tomorrow at school."

"I see." She sounded impressed. "That's quite a prize. I'll have to make him an extra-big lunch tomorrow, won't I? Do you think maybe you could share it with him, so that he doesn't get too hungry to learn his lessons?"

"Oh, sure, sure." He nodded so vigorously that his head hurt.

"Thanks." She gave him a quick smile, then looked out the window. When she spoke again, her voice was casual. "It's too bad it was only a joke. We like having you around. You're always welcome here."

He felt so pleased and proud he couldn't speak. He kept wiping that one dish until Sylvia laughed and took it from him, saying that if he kept it up he'd rub a hole through the china.

After that, Richard's lunches contained twice as much food as even a hungry growing boy could eat. And Richard always shared everything with him, split right down the middle.

Richard would have been a good man, if he had lived.

Sighing, he wadded up his trash and carried it to a garbage can. In a few minutes he was back on the road, heading east to his daughter's place in Connecticut.

As he pulled onto the Indiana Toll Road, he wondered if Sylvia remembered him. Probably not. He wrote to invite her to the wedding, but she didn't come. She didn't even write back. Claudia had, though, to tell him that Sylvia had left Elm Creek Manor but that Claudia would send his invitation to Sylvia's in-laws in Maryland. They would know how to reach her.

Claudia added a postscript informing him that she was Claudia Midden now and had been ever since she married Harold.

He went cold at the news. Yes, he had known that Claudia and Harold were engaged, but he never thought she'd go through with it. Hadn't Sylvia told her how Harold had let Richard and Sylvia's husband, James, die?

The four men had enlisted within hours of each other—he and Richard first, thinking World War Two would bring them adventure and glory; James and Harold later, when they learned of the younger men's actions. James went to watch over Richard for Sylvia's sake, but if Harold shared James's intentions, his courage failed him at the crucial moment.

He could never forget the view from that high bluff, the droning of planes overhead, the relief that turned to terror as their own boys fired upon them, the tank on the beach below exploding in flames. James, climbing out of the other tank and racing to help, as he himself had done, sprinting straight down the steep bluff to the beach, knowing he would never make it in time. In his nightmares he was forever running toward that tank, knowing Richard was inside, running with his feet sinking into the soft, wet sand, never gaining any ground. In the night-mares he could see James struggling to open the hatch, desperately trying to free his wife's beloved brother, calling out to Harold to help him.

But Harold ducked back inside his own tank. The planes made an-other pass, and the world exploded in flames.

Harold's cowardice had saved him, but the cost was great—Richard's life, and James's, and Mr. Bergstrom's, and that of the child Sylvia was carrying. Richard and James died in the second explosion; the shock of the news killed Mr. Bergstrom and caused Sylvia to miscarry James's child. Tragedy piled upon tragedy drove a wedge into the family, estrang-ing the grieving sisters when they needed each other most. And now Harold had maneuvered his way into the family he had so devastated.

The outrage, the injustice of it all, nearly drove him mad. He fright-ened Katy with his fury, and only the shock in her eyes allowed him to re-gain control of himself. For an instant the part of him that was so like his father had escaped. He sealed it up again, eventually, but his anger never completely died. He couldn't bear it. He had longed to be a part of the

Bergstrom family ever since he was a young boy playing with Richard on the banks of Elm Creek—but that honor had gone to Harold, the one who least deserved it.

That was why he had stayed away so long. Why return to Elm Creek Manor when Richard was dead, when James was dead, when Mr. Bergstrom was dead, when Sylvia had left for good? The place once so full of light and laughter must surely have become as cold and silent as a tomb. He could not go back. There was no point to it.

At least, there hadn't been for many years.

Shaken by memories, he pulled the motor home onto the shoulder of the road. He set the parking brake and turned on his hazard lights, then sat motionless, gripping the steering wheel, staring ahead through the windshield. The motor home trembled whenever a car sped past, but he barely noticed.

Later—it could have been ten minutes or several times that—he took out his wallet and held it for a moment before retrieving the old photo he knew was there. He had carried it all those years, ever since he and Richard were young men in Philadelphia.

He had seen the black-and-white snapshot in Richard's room, where his friend was boarding as he attended school. In the photo, Sylvia was standing beside a horse, one of the last Bergstrom Thoroughbreds, though of course no one knew that then. She wore close-fitting pants and carried a rider's helmet and crop in one hand; the other arm was draped around the horse's neck. She was smiling at the photographer with perfect joy, as if she had never known sorrow and never would.

"James took that picture," Richard had told him, seeing how he admired it.

He had nodded, his heart sinking a little. Of course, it had been nonsense to think that she would have waited for him. He was a child to her and always would be. He had not seen her in years, not since the social workers had taken him and his sister from their parents and sent them to live with an aunt in Philadelphia. He consoled himself with the knowledge that James was a good man—Richard had nothing but praise for him—and that Sylvia was happy.

"Can I have it?" he heard himself asking.

Richard grinned, removed the photo from the frame, and gave it to him. He'd carried it ever since, and it showed. He should have taken better care of it.

He studied the smiling face in the photo.

He could do it; there was no reason not to. He could take the Pennsylvania Turnpike to the road that led to Waterford. He would recall the way to Elm Creek Manor once he got closer. Sylvia might not remember him, but that wouldn't bother him too much. He just wanted to see her, to talk about old times and see for himself that she was all right. Now, when the past sometimes seemed more vivid to him than the present, it would be good to talk to someone who remembered the old days.

He put the photo away and turned the key in the ignition.

He'd do it. First, though, he had to get something better to wear. He had to be presentable when he saw Sylvia again, not worn and shabby in his old fishing clothes. For the first time he wished he'd given in to Cathy's urging to let her take him shopping.

"An hour at the mall won't kill you, Dad," she'd admonished him.

"You never know, it just might," he'd retorted, enjoying her teasing and delighted, as he always was, that his son's wife called him "Dad."

He smiled as he pulled back onto the road and headed east.

# Chapter Five

Sarah knew Matt hated to hear her grumble about her mother, but one evening as they got ready for bed, she forgot herself. The more she told him about the annoying things her mother had done and said that day, the more irritable she became. She didn't realize that she had been rambling on for ten minutes, her voice increasing in volume and pitch with each sentence, until Matt cut her off.

"Sarah, I'm tired," he said, climbing into bed. "Can you just pull the plug, please?"

"Pull the plug? You mean, tell her to go home?"

"No, I mean stop playing this broken record." He lay down and drew the covers over himself. "Your mother says the wrong things, she embarrasses you, she doesn't understand you—I get the idea. We all get the idea."

Sarah stared at him. "Since when do we not talk to each other about our problems?"

"If you want to talk, we can talk. You're just ranting and raving." He rolled over on his side, ending the discussion.

Sarah watched him, speechless, before she finally finished undressing and got into bed. She lay down on her side with her back to him. She waited, but he didn't mold his body around hers as he usually did. She felt cold and alone, and it was an increasingly familiar feeling. She missed their old closeness and wondered what had become of it.

Sometimes she felt like she couldn't talk to Matt about anything anymore. She would have turned to Sylvia, but the older woman already had enough misgivings about bringing mother and daughter together; Sarah couldn't bear to add to them. She would have confided in the Elm Creek Quilters, but they had already accepted Carol as one of their own. Two years ago the Elm Creek Quilters had welcomed Sarah without judgment, without conditions, with no other wish than to offer her their friendship. In spite of everything, Sarah couldn't bring herself to insist that they deny that gift to another newcomer, even when that newcomer had her so crazy she often thought she'd rather fling herself into Elm Creek than spend another minute in her presence.

As the spring days grew longer and warmer, Sarah put her energy into counting the days until her mother's departure. If Diane could tolerate the skateboard ramp fiasco, Sarah could surely endure the rest of her mother's visit.

On a Thursday afternoon, Sarah left the office and went downstairs to the ballroom, where Diane was assisting Bonnie with her workshop. Sarah watched as Diane moved briskly and confidently from table to table, assisting the campers. If Diane was worried about the upcoming exemption hearing, she hid it well. There was a new determination in her eyes, an awareness and confidence Sarah hadn't seen there before.

When the class was over and the students had gone off to enjoy their free time, Diane took a folded bundle out of her bag. "I finished adding my border," she said. "Do you want it next, Bonnie?"

Bonnie agreed, took the quilt, and held it up. Sarah took one look at it and began to laugh.

"What?" Diane asked. "What's the problem now?"

"All you did was add four triangles and set it on point," Sarah exclaimed.

"So? No one said we couldn't set it on point."

"Setting it on point isn't the problem."

Bonnie shook her head. "No piecing, no appliqué—I consider that cheating."

"At least I got it done on time," Diane said, then she paused. "Almost on time. I'm only a little late."

They all laughed, but Sarah felt a wave of sympathy for Diane, who had been much too distracted lately to enjoy working on the quilt. Diane's piecing had improved so much over the past two years, and she had probably been eager to show off her new skills. Once again Mary Beth had forced Diane to modify her goals.

A similar thought must have crossed Bonnie's mind, for she folded up the quilt top and packed it carefully in her tote bag. "Your border's just fine," she said. "In fact, I think it was an excellent choice. An unbroken space for hand quilting will set off the center block perfectly."

Diane was so pleased by the compliment that she couldn't speak.

Suddenly, Sarah heard an odd rumbling coming from outside. "Do you hear that?" she asked her friends.

They all listened.

"Thunder?" Bonnie guessed.

"I don't think so," Sarah said. They went to a window on the west-facing wall, where they could hear the sound more plainly as they looked out on the back of the manor. Elm trees obscured most of the view, but in the distance Sarah could see a cloud of dust rising along the back road, near the barn and moving closer.

"What is it, a cattle drive?" Diane asked.

"I don't know, but I'm going to find out." Sarah left the ballroom and headed for the west wing, Bonnie and Diane close behind. Sylvia met them at the kitchen doorway as they passed.

"What on earth is that noise?" she asked them. Without waiting for an answer, she tossed her dish towel onto the kitchen table and followed her friends to the back door.

Sarah opened it and led the three women outside, where they shaded their eyes with their hands and looked down the back road. A motor home was crossing the narrow bridge over Elm Creek.

Sylvia sucked in a breath. "Watch the trees, watch the trees," she called out as the vehicle scraped through the stately elms lining the back road. Sarah was glad Matt hadn't seen it.

The motor home slowed as it entered the clearing behind the manor and circled the small parking lot, carefully making its way past the campers' cars. When it reached the far end of the lot, it maneuvered into a block of open spaces and halted.

A moment later, the door opened and a man got out. Sarah guessed from his gray hair and the slight stiffness to his movements that he was in his early seventies, a few years younger than Sylvia. He wore tan slacks and a striped golf shirt—the uniform of the leisure set—but the hard knots of muscle in his forearms suggested years of demanding physical labor.

"Someone's husband?" Bonnie murmured.

"Maybe." Sarah watched the man approach. They had a few campers around his age. Alarm pricked her. What emergency would require a man to come pick up his wife from quilt camp without phoning first?

Sylvia brushed past Sarah as she descended the steps to welcome their unexpected guest. "Hello," she greeted him from a few yards away. "Welcome to Elm Creek Manor. May I help you?"

A grin broke over the man's face, and Sarah found herself smiling, too. He looked almost bashful, and his brown eyes were warm and kind. "Hello, Sylvia," he said.

He knew her. Sarah, Bonnie, and Diane exchanged surprised glances, and Sarah could tell by their expressions that they didn't recognize the man, either. She wished she could see Sylvia's face, but the older woman's back was to her.

There was a long moment of silence.

Then Sylvia's hand flew to her throat. "Good gracious me, it couldn't be."

The man's grin deepened, and he nodded.

"Andrew Cooper, as I live and breathe," Sylvia exclaimed. It happened too suddenly for Sarah to detect who stepped forward first, but in an instant the distance between Sylvia and the man had been closed and they were embracing. Then Sylvia placed her hands on his shoulders and stepped back to see him better. "How are you? Better yet, what on earth are you doing here?"

"I saw your program on television," he explained. His voice had a rough edge to it, the sound of a man who spoke only when he had something important to say. "I was traveling east to visit my daughter, and I figured I'd pull off the turnpike and see the old hometown."

"I'm glad you did, but you could have told me you were coming," Sylvia scolded him. "You certainly know how to give a body a shock."

"Sorry." He smiled, and suddenly Sarah realized he'd been looking forward to that scolding for miles. As if sensing her thoughts, he looked up at her.

Sylvia followed his line of sight and started as if she had forgotten her friends were there. "Oh, dear. Andrew, you surprised the manners right out of me. These are my friends and colleagues—Bonnie Markham, Diane Sonnenberg, and Sarah McClure. Ladies, this is Andrew Cooper, a dear old friend of the family. He and my brother Richard were once as thick as thieves."

Andrew. With a jolt, Sarah realized who the man was, who he had been—the child who had hidden from his abusive father in Richard's little red playhouse so many years before; the young man who had shared Richard's excitement and naive bravery as they went off to war; the veteran of so much horror who had told Sylvia how her brother-in-law's cowardice had led to the deaths of Richard and her beloved husband, James. That figure from the past was greeting her and taking her hand in his callused, work-hardened one. She was as stunned as if Hans and Anneke Bergstrom themselves had suddenly appeared and waved at her as they strolled arm-in-arm across the lawn.

"We have so much catching up to do," Sylvia was saying to Andrew. "But surely you didn't travel all this way alone. I'll be terribly disappointed if you didn't bring your wife with you."

Andrew's smile wavered. "My wife passed on three years ago."

"I'm so sorry. I didn't know."

"How would you have?" He shrugged apologetically. "I've never been very good about writing letters. The last time I wrote was to invite you to the wedding."

"I wish I had come," Sylvia said. There was an ache in her voice Sarah hadn't heard in a long time. "I wish I had known her."

"You would have liked her."

"I'm certain I would have." Sylvia took Andrew by the arm. "Come inside and tell me all about her." She led him into the manor.

That evening, after the campers had turned in for the night, Sarah, Matt, and Carol joined Sylvia and Andrew in the parlor to hear more of Andrew's story. The day Andrew broke the tragic news to Sylvia had been his last in Waterford, and from there he had gone to Detroit for a job on the line in a factory that was being returned to auto production since tanks were no longer in such demand. Within a few years he had worked his way up to shift supervisor, and soon after he became foreman he married a young widow whose husband had died in Normandy, a beautiful young schoolteacher with dark hair, a ready laugh, and a quick temper that was appeased as quickly as it flared up. They had a daughter and a son, the most perfect grandchildren in the world, and almost fifty years together. She had died of an extended illness, but Andrew so couched this part of his story in euphemism that Sarah wasn't exactly sure what had taken her life. After his retirement, Andrew had bought the motor home and spent most of his time traveling between his son's home, on the West Coast, and his daughter's home, in the East. His many years of hard work had earned him the freedom to come and go as he pleased, and he'd made the most of it—and he planned to keep doing so as long as he and the motor home held up.

"I'm glad you finally decided to take the road home to Waterford," Sylvia said.

He smiled at her. "So am I."

They held each other's gaze for a moment. Sarah would have sworn Sylvia's cheeks colored before she looked away.

Then Andrew turned to Matt. "Is Elm Creek still good for trout?"

"One of the best streams in the state," Matt said. "They stock it every year."

"In the old days they didn't need to," Andrew said, shaking his head. "Domestic fish. Bet they train them to swim right up to your hook and take the bait. Where's the challenge in that?"

Matt grinned. "Think of it this way. They stock upstream, and that's where most people fish. The trout that make it down here have to be pretty smart to run that gauntlet. It might be harder to catch them than you think."

"Good. It's more fun that way."

"We can go out tomorrow morning if you like."

"I would," Andrew said, pleased. "We'll have trout for you and all your campers for lunch, Sylvia."

"Thank you, but I think I'll go ahead with my original menu, just in case."

Andrew smiled and turned to Sarah. "How about you? Do you fish?"

"Not much," Sarah admitted, making a face at the thought of putting a worm on a hook.

"I'll teach you so you'll like it," Andrew promised. "I taught a young woman to fish once. She caught her first fish with her bare hands. Well, actually, it was with her foot, and she didn't mean to catch it, but it wasn't bad for a first try."

"What on earth?" Sylvia asked.

He shrugged and waved the question off. "It's a long story. You don't want to hear it."

"Yes, we do," Sarah said. "You're just keeping us in suspense so we'll beg you to tell us."

The twinkle in his eye told Sarah she had guessed correctly. "My wife and I used to have a cabin up north near Charlevoix," he began. "We used to talk about retiring there, but when Katy fell ill, we went less and less, until I finally decided to sell it. No sense in owning a cabin you never use. But when my son was in college, we still had the place, and the whole family used to go up there all the time and go fishing.

"His third year in school over in Ann Arbor, my son met a real sweet girl and he wanted to bring her home to meet us. We had already planned a trip to the cabin, so we told them to come on up and join us. Cathy was a pretty little thing, but she was a city girl. Sweet and smart, but not much for the outdoors." He indicated Sylvia with a jerk of his head. "Not like this one, here. Never saw an animal she couldn't tame."

"Nonsense," Sylvia said, but she looked pleased.

"So one afternoon, me and Bob—that's my son—and Cathy were out in the rowboat. Cathy didn't want to fish, though. She said she just wanted to watch. Pretty soon she started to get bored, or hot, or something, because she took off her shoes and socks so she could dangle her feet over the side of the boat to cool off."

Matt grinned. "I think I can see where this is heading."

"Well, she couldn't, and we did try to warn her. 'Better not,' my son said. 'There's muskie in this lake.' "

" 'What's a muskie?' she asked. I told her it was a big, mean, ugly fish with sharp teeth, a sour temper, and curiosity to spare. 'You put your foot over the side, and a muskie might think it's lunch,' I warned her, but she didn't listen. She thought we were just making it up to tease her." He looked abashed. "She had good reason. We'd been teasing her a lot already."

"So what happened?" Sarah asked.

"She put her feet over the side, and for the first half hour or so she was fine. 'See, I knew you were making it up,' she said, and then she let out a shriek that would curl your hair. She yanked her feet back into the boat—and she brought a fourteen-inch muskie with her."

Carol gasped. "You're kidding."

"I wish I was. That ugly thing had its teeth clamped around the heel of her foot, and it wouldn't let go no matter how hard she waved her leg around. Bob wrestled with it and managed to get it off, but it wasn't easy, what with Cathy clutching him and sobbing and carrying on."

"I would have been sobbing, too, if it had been me," Sylvia declared.

Andrew smiled at her. "No, not you, Sylvia. I've seen you break horses. You wouldn't be scared by a little fish."

"I never broke horses," Sylvia said, smiling back. "I gentled them. There's a difference."

"Fourteen inches doesn't sound so little to me," Sarah said. "Was Cathy all right?"

"She was fine. She needed a few stitches, and she hobbled around for a while with a bandage around her foot, but she was okay. She was a good sport about it afterward, too."

"What happened to the fish?" Matt asked.

The others laughed, but Andrew seemed to consider it a logical question. "I told Cathy and Bob that I threw it back. It was too small. Wouldn't have been legal to keep it. But I didn't really. I kept it, then went to the DNR, turned myself in, told them the story, paid a fee, and took the fella home." He grinned. "I had it mounted and gave it to Cathy and Bob two years later as a wedding present."

His listeners burst out laughing.

"Now, that's a fish story," Sylvia said. "You two aren't allowed to get into any trouble like that tomorrow, understand?"

"Yes, ma'am," Matt said meekly, but Andrew only grinned at her.

"I'll never look at filet of sole the same way," Carol said, laughing. "You just scared me away from fishing forever."

Andrew chuckled. "If you change your mind, you're welcome to join us."

"No thanks." Carol shuddered.

Andrew turned to Sylvia. "You run a quilt camp. Why don't you run a trout camp, too?"

Sylvia's eyebrows arched. "A trout camp?"

"Sure. Maybe once in a while you could have a weekend for couples. The ladies could quilt during the day while the men go fishing. At night you could play records in the ballroom and have a dance."

Sarah and Sylvia looked at each other.

"That's a lovely idea," Sylvia said.

Sarah agreed, wondering why they hadn't thought of it first. They could have fishing for the men, or golf—there were so many possibilities they hadn't even considered.

"Andrew, between your story and your suggestion, you've earned your keep," Sylvia said. "Sarah, would you mind fixing up a room for our newest guest?"

Sarah nodded and rose, but Andrew shook his head. "I brought my bed with me."

"You can't mean it," Sylvia said. "Surely you don't want to stay in the parking lot when you can have a nice, comfortable room indoors?"

"The motor home's comfortable enough for me," he said, and in his mild way proceeded to deflect all of Sylvia's arguments to the contrary. To Sarah's amazement, Sylvia eventually gave up. She almost never backed down from a position once she had made up her mind.

The next morning, Sylvia phoned Agnes and told her to come to Elm Creek Manor earlier than usual, because Sylvia wanted to show her something before her appliqué workshop. Agnes arrived while Sarah, Sylvia, and Carol were preparing lunch and Andrew was entertaining them with stories of his travels. When Andrew identified himself, Agnes shrieked, burst into tears, and threw her arms around him, and for a moment Sarah could see the girl she had been, the impulsive, emotional young woman Sylvia had nicknamed "the Puzzle." If Sylvia had been surprised to see Andrew, Agnes looked positively astounded. Agnes, Andrew, and Richard had been great friends those few years in Philadelphia before the men went off to war. Sarah could only imagine how Agnes felt at seeing this figure from the past sitting so casually at the kitchen table.

Agnes insisted Andrew tell her everything that had happened to him since she had last seen him. He laughed and complied. She clasped one of his hands in both of hers and hardly took her eyes off him as he spoke.

"She's the one he really came to see," Sylvia told Sarah and Carol in an undertone. "It makes sense. They were friends in their youth, they're both alone again, and she was his best friend's widow."

Watching the pair, Sarah wasn't so sure. Andrew was looking at Agnes with genuine affection, but it seemed to be the love of friends or of family. There had been something different, something more, in his expression when he first spoke to Sylvia, she was sure of it.

On Saturday, after the campers had departed, Sylvia and Andrew took a picnic lunch out to the north gardens. They had asked Sarah and Matt to join them, but Sarah begged off, claiming too much work. What she really wanted was to give Sylvia and Andrew some time alone. They had so much to talk about, and they could do so more easily without the younger couple present.

After Sylvia and Andrew left, the manor was quiet for the first time all week. On Sunday morning they would need to prepare for the arrival of the next group of quilters, but Sylvia insisted they keep Saturday afternoons for themselves, to recover from the previous week and rest up for the one to come. Sarah considered spending some time with Carol, but the sight of Sylvia and Andrew strolling arm in arm with their picnic basket reminded her of picnics she and Matt used to go on when they were first married. They would pick up bagel sandwiches and bottles of iced tea from a deli on College Avenue, and hold hands as they crossed the campus to President's House. Behind it was a secluded garden with a wooden gazebo where they would sit and eat and talk about everything—their hopes for the future, their worries, their plans. Sometimes Sarah would pretend that President's House was theirs and that they were sitting in their own backyard, though she kept this dream to herself. She never could have imagined that one day she and Matt would live in a house many times larger and grander than the one on the Penn State campus.

Sarah went upstairs to their suite, but Matt wasn't there. She searched the manor for him, planning their picnic menu as she looked. Before long she found him alone on the veranda, sitting in an Adirondack chair and reading the newspaper.

"Are you hungry for lunch?" she asked him. "I thought we could go on a picnic." It would be like old times. They would talk and laugh and kiss and Matt would be content again.

But Matt didn't even look up. "I'm kind of busy right now." He turned the page of the newspaper.

Sarah's happiness dimmed. "Can't the paper wait?" She playfully snatched at the pages until she realized what section he held. "The classifieds? Are you looking for another job?"

"No." Matt set the paper down. "If I want another job, Tony said I can come back to work for Exterior Architects any time I want."

"Why would you want to go back to your old job?" Then his words fully registered. "Tony said you could come back. So you've already talked to him about it? Without discussing it with me?"

Matt frowned. "I knew you'd react like this."

"Like what? How am I reacting?"

"Like a nag." He stood up. "Like a control freak."

"How can you say that?" Stung, Sarah felt tears spring into her eyes. "That's not fair. All I did was ask you a simple question and you snap at me like I'm your worst enemy instead of your best friend."

Her eyes met Matt's as she fought back the tears. He must have seen how she struggled, how he had wounded her, because he took her in his arms. "You're right." He kissed her on the top of the head. "I'm sorry. I didn't mean it."

But Sarah was not comforted. "I don't know what's been going on lately. You're just not nice to me anymore."

"I'm sorry," he said. "It's not you."

Sarah pulled away so she could see his face. "Then what is it? Can you tell me what's wrong? Is it my mom? Is it something I've done—or haven't done?"

"No. Of course not." He drew her close again, and held her so tightly that the buttons of his shirt pressed into her cheek. "I'm just being a jerk. I'll stop it. I promise."

His voice was gentle and loving in a way that it hadn't been for far too long, but Sarah's heart ached. She didn't know why he was so unhappy, but if he disguised his feelings rather than risk hurting her by sharing them, their troubles were sure to continue.

As Matt gave her one last kiss and released her, she recognized the same aching worry she had felt throughout those long months of his unemployment in State College. Matt's recent behavior, too, reminded her of that bleak time; his impatience with her, his restlessness, his hurtful words like lightning strikes on her soul. Back then, the smoldering emotions had too often erupted into arguments that left them hoarse from shouting and exhausted from the endless, circular quarreling over imagined slights and old resentments. Matt had blamed their fights on the strain of his unsuccessful job search, and usually Sarah had agreed with him, since it seemed the obvious culprit. After the worst fights, however, when the peace between them strained like new skin over burns, Sarah had wondered aloud if his unemployment was really the problem. Maybe it was their marriage. Maybe it was their life together that evoked his dark moods.

"Don't say that," Matt would respond. "You're the best thing that ever happened to me. It's being out of work, I swear. Once I get a job, everything will be different. Everything will be fine."

She had believed him then because she wanted it to be true, because the alternative was unthinkable. And when he finally found the job that brought them to Waterford, it seemed that she had been right to believe him. For a long time after the move, their marriage had been happier and stronger than ever. Matt seemed to think so; he couldn't have faked contentment for such a long time. Why had things changed in the past few months, when she thought all those old dark times had been left behind in the move, when Matt had a job doing what he loved for a kind and generous employer?

She couldn't bury her worries, not this time, even though she and Matt went on their picnic after all and had a pleasant, if subdued, afternoon together. She had to talk to someone, but definitely not her mother. Not Sylvia, either; the older woman had been so happy ever since Andrew had arrived, and Sarah didn't want to spoil it. Summer was kind and sympathetic, but she had no experience with marriage; Gwen had been divorced for so long that she had little more marital experience than her daughter. Diane would probably give her a few wisecracks before blabbing her story to anyone who would listen, and Judy was so happily married that Sarah's problems would no doubt baffle her.

Bonnie. She had been married a long time. Maybe she could help.

Sarah managed to take her aside on Sunday afternoon during new camper registration. She grew tearful as she told Bonnie about Matt's behavior and her own helplessness in the face of his growing dissatisfaction. When she finished, Bonnie was silent for a while, her expression a mixture of concern and compassion. Sarah watched her and waited for her to speak, hoping for a solution—or at least a course of action—and dreading that instead she'd receive a confirmation of her worst fears, that all signs pointed to a marriage in jeopardy.

"The first thing you need to do is stop agonizing over this," Bonnie finally told her. "Matt loves you—that much is obvious. Even if you have hit a rough patch, you'll work it out."

Sarah took a deep breath, relieved. That was what she had been telling herself, too, but it meant more coming from someone else, someone more objective.

Bonnie placed a hand on her shoulder and gave her an encouraging smile. "All marriages go through ups and downs. It's not like a movie, where everyone lives happily ever after. You're going to have times where you feel so close and loving that you'll think your marriage is invulnerable. Then you'll enter another cycle where everything you say is the wrong thing and the happy times seem over for good. But they won't be; they'll come back. You'll see."

"But I don't want ups and downs. I just want the ups."

"The only way to stay that consistently happy over a lifetime is for both of you to be heavily medicated," Bonnie said dryly. "And that approach brings problems of its own. As a relationship grows, it changes. Sometimes those changes can create tension, maybe even pain, but that doesn't mean you love each other any less. The only way to avoid those growing pains is to stagnate, and that's far worse."

Sarah nodded. Bonnie hadn't given her the panacea she'd hoped for, but she had given her hope. "Is there anything I can do to get us out of this bad cycle more quickly?"

"You could ask him to talk about how he feels. You might not have the answers he needs, but it sometimes helps to talk."

Sarah smiled. "That's true." She herself felt better after talking things out with Bonnie. Describing the problem helped her to better understand it, and putting it into words somehow gave it borders, made it finite. "Thanks, Bonnie."

"Anytime. I mean that. Whenever you need to talk—"

"Talk about what?" Carol said.

They looked up, startled. They had been so intent on their conversation that they hadn't seen her approach, but there she stood, looking from one to the other, eager to be included.

"Nothing," Sarah said automatically.

Carol's smile evaporated. "You must have been talking about something. You've been whispering in this huddle for at least twenty minutes."

"Oh, you know," Bonnie said easily. "The usual lover's quarrels. She just needed to sound off."

Carol fixed her gaze on Sarah. "Are you and Matt having problems? Why didn't you tell me?"

Because you'd say you told me so, Sarah thought; you'd say you warned me about him and you'd gloat that you had been right all along. "We're not having problems. Everything's fine."

"It doesn't sound fine." The familiar worry lines appeared around Carol's mouth. "I would think this was something a daughter would want to discuss with her mother." She glanced at Bonnie as if to say that Bonnie's intrusion pained her as much as Sarah's neglect.

If Bonnie noticed, she didn't show it. "You'd think that, wouldn't you?" she said, shaking her head and casting her gaze to heaven. "That's never how it works, though. Sarah's willing to talk to me, but my own kids would run screaming from the room rather than listen to my opinion."

Carol gave her a tight smile. "I see we have a lot in common." Her eyes met Sarah's briefly as she turned to rejoin the others, long enough for Sarah to see she had been deeply hurt.

"Mom, wait," Sarah called after her, but Carol kept walking.

Bonnie put her arm around Sarah's shoulders as they watched Carol return to the registration table. "Don't worry. She won't stay angry. You can talk to her later."

Sarah nodded, but she felt as if at any moment she'd collapse beneath the growing pile of worries. It was as if the stitches holding the scraps of her life together were unraveling faster than she could put them in, and if she didn't work quickly enough, a gust of wind would send the unsewn pieces scattering in all directions, whirling in the air around her, just beyond her grasp.

# Chapter Six

Bonnie woke to find Craig's side of the bed empty. She listened for the sound of the shower, but instead she heard the faint clattering of fingers on the computer keyboard in the family room. He had risen early to check his E-mail before work again. It was becoming a habit with him. She preferred his old habit—lying in bed with her as they held each other and planned their day—but as she had told Sarah the day before, relationships changed.

She kicked off the covers, drew on her robe, and padded into the family room in her slippers. Craig was sitting at the computer, his back to her, a cup of coffee and a doughnut within easy reach on the desk. He had already dressed for work.

"Morning," Bonnie greeted him.

He jerked upright as if she had sent an electric current through his chair. "You startled me."

"Sorry." She hid a smile and joined him at the computer just as he quit the application. "Any interesting mail?"

"Not really." He shut down the computer. "The usual memos, you know, reminders about meetings, things like that." He picked up his breakfast and carried it into the kitchen.

Bonnie followed. "Doesn't sound like anything worth getting up early for."

"Just wanted to get it out of the way." He poured the rest of his coffee into the sink and left the mug on the counter. "I'd better get going."

"So early?" It was only seven o'clock.

He nodded and wrapped his doughnut in a napkin. "Bob called an emergency meeting about graduation."

"Oh, dear. What is it this time?" Bonnie went to the sink, rinsed the coffee down the drain, and placed the mug in the dishwasher. "Not the floor again, I hope?"

Three years before, heavy rains had flooded the auditorium only days before commencement, warping the wood parquet floor into a series of small hills. The Office of the Physical Plant staff had to scramble to re-arrange stages, seating, and enough microphones and speakers for a modest rock concert. It had made for several exhausting days and late nights, but they'd pulled it off in time for the ceremony.

"No, nothing like that, fortunately," Craig said. "Just the usual logistical snarls. You know how it is."

"Will you have to change your plans for the weekend?"

He shot her a quick look. "What?"

"Your trip to Penn State. Don't tell me you forgot."

"Oh." His features relaxed. "No, I didn't forget. And no, it won't be a problem. We'll have everything sorted out by then." He took his sack lunch out of the refrigerator and kissed her on the cheek on his way out of the kitchen. "I'll see you tonight."

She trailed after him. "Craig?"

He paused at the door. "What?" He had picked up his briefcase and was waiting for her to speak, his hand on the doorknob.

Suddenly she felt tired, as if it were the end of the day rather than the beginning. "Nothing. Never mind. Have a good day."

"Sure, honey. You, too." He hurried out the door. She heard him lock it behind him, then the faint sound of his footsteps going downstairs. She felt rather than heard the heavy door to the back parking lot slam shut, and then silence, broken only by the hum of the refrigerator and the odd clicking noises of their automatic drip coffeemaker as it cooled.

Bonnie sighed.

She threw out the used grounds and filled the coffeemaker with fresh grounds and water, then went to take a shower while she waited for the pot to fill. As she showered, she thought about the advice she had given Sarah the previous day. Was it sound advice, and was Bonnie the right person to give it? She had never considered herself an expert on relationships, but then again, she and Craig had been married for nearly twenty-eight years. That had to count for something.

Their marriage fit the usual pattern, she supposed. Newlywed joy, followed in turn by the challenges of raising kids, the relief when they went off to college, and the pride mixed with loneliness when they found jobs and spouses and lives of their own. Bonnie hoped that their youngest son, still a junior at Lock Haven University, would find a job close to home after he graduated, unlike his brother, who now lived in Pittsburgh, and his sister, who had moved to Chicago.

Their home seemed so quiet now, even though it was over a store downtown and right across the street from the Waterford College campus. Bonnie used to fear that without the daily business of raising their children, she and Craig wouldn't be able to find anything to talk about for the rest of their lives. Fortunately, that hadn't been the case. Craig talked about his job and Penn State football, Bonnie talked about Grandma's Attic and Elm Creek Quilts, and they both wondered aloud when they would have their first grandchild. Maybe they weren't as romantic as they used to be, but they were both so busy, too busy to carry on like love-struck teenagers. Craig had never been the love poetry and red roses type of man, anyway, and Bonnie liked him too much to demand that he change. What was most important was that they were comfortable together. Over the years they had settled into an easy friendship illuminated by increasingly rare but intense flashes of passion, reminding them why they had come together in the first place and why they had remained together so long.

After breakfast, Bonnie dressed in a comfortable pair of slacks and a quilted vest she had finished over the weekend. The pattern had come from a new book she was stocking in the shop; if customers complimented her on her attire, she could direct them to the book so they could make vests of their own. Then she finished reading the newspaper, tidied up the kitchen, and began her two-minute commute to work.

She smiled to herself as she went downstairs to the shop, remembering a joke she and the kids used to share. "This is the only house in town where you go downstairs to get to the attic," Tammy would say.

On cue, Craig Jr. would chime in, "You should have called it Grandma's Basement." Then they would all laugh.

It was a silly joke, but it was theirs, and they enjoyed it. How noisy and cluttered and bustling the house used to be, and how quiet and tidy it was now. Craig didn't seem to mind, but Bonnie missed the mess.

At least the shop was the same—as cozy and friendly as ever. Grandma's Attic was the only quilt shop in Waterford, and over the years its steady and loyal customers had become her friends. The business had not made her rich—in fact, some years it was all she could do to break even—but it meant the world to her. She was her own boss, and her success depended entirely upon her own efforts. She also knew that in addition to selling fabric and notions and pattern books, she was providing Waterford's quilters with a gathering place, a sense of community. How many other people could say that about their jobs?

Her only disappointment was that none of her children had ever wanted to work at Grandma's Attic; not even the promise that they would own the shop someday had tempted them. Summer Sullivan enjoyed her part-time job there so much that Bonnie once thought she might want to go full-time after graduation and eventually take over the entire business, but when Summer was accepted into graduate school at Penn, Bonnie decided not to bother asking her. Summer was a bright young woman with a promising future, one she wasn't likely to abandon for a small-town business. Bonnie had put her heart and soul into Grandma's Attic, but when the time came for her to retire, she would have to close it down or sell it to a stranger. Neither option appealed to her, but fortunately she wouldn't have to think about that for a while. Sylvia's energy inspired her; if Sylvia could start up a new business in her golden years, Bonnie could certainly keep hers going for another few decades.

At least that's what she'd thought before the chain fabric store opened a branch on the outskirts of Waterford six months ago. They didn't carry the specialty quilting fabrics found in Grandma's Attic, but they sold calicoes and other cotton prints at nearly wholesale prices. They could afford to; their buyer ordered bolts of fabric for the entire national chain, winning enormous discounts because of the bulk orders. Bonnie couldn't match their prices without going into the red—but as the months passed, she slipped gradually nearer to that mark anyway.

At first she had told herself that once the novelty of the new store wore off, her sales would bounce back, but that didn't seem to be happening. "Maybe it's time to close the shop," Craig suggested when she mentioned the problem as she fixed his breakfast. "You could always find a job somewhere else."

The very idea of closing Grandma's Attic had horrified her. The quilt shop wasn't just a job; it was her passion, her calling, and her inspiration. She had broken down in tears that afternoon as she counted the week's receipts. Fortunately, Summer was there to console and encourage her. Better yet, the younger woman offered to help. Bonnie accepted, more grateful for the compassion than hopeful anything would come of the offer, but to her surprise and delight, Summer returned the next week with page after page of ideas. "Once I started brainstorming, I couldn't stop," Summer had said, so excited she could hardly stand still long enough to hand Bonnie the papers. "Grandma's Attic isn't beaten yet, and won't ever be, if I can help it."

Summer's master plan included putting the shop on-line so that quilters from all over the world could purchase their fabric, notions, and books. They also created Grandma's Attic Friends, a club offering discounts to frequent shoppers. As the shop's losses gradually declined, Bonnie decided to implement more of Summer's ideas. Still, as much as she appreciated the help, Bonnie worried that Summer was sacrificing too much of her study time to what was really only a part-time job.

"Are you kidding?" Summer had replied when Bonnie tentatively approached the subject. "I'd much rather help Grandma's Attic than study. Besides, classes will be over in a few weeks."

"But doesn't that mean you have finals coming up? And won't you need to prepare for graduate school?"

Summer laughed and told her not to worry. Bonnie tried, but she still had misgivings. Gwen would never forgive her if her brilliant daughter got less than straight A's because Grandma's Attic was monopolizing her time.

Smiling, Bonnie let herself in through the back door and locked it behind her. She flicked on the lights and chose a CD to play in the background. Simple Gifts, a folk group from Lemont, suited her mood that morning, and soon the sounds of hammered dulcimer, guitar, violin, and flute were coming through the speakers over the main sales floor. Humming along with the music, she went through the aisles straightening bolts of fabric and tidying shelves. The bathroom was clean, but she gave it a quick going-over anyway before vacuuming the carpet in the main room, her office, and the small classroom in the back. She taught fewer classes there than in the days before Elm Creek Quilts, and now the room was more often used as a playroom for customers' children. Bonnie lingered over the toy box. The stuffed animals were store samples she had made to help promote pattern sales, but the other toys had belonged to her own children. It pleased her to have an excuse to hold on to them long after her own kids had put them aside.

After retrieving her money bag from its locked hiding place in her desk, filling her cash drawer, and dusting the items in the display window, Bonnie unlocked the front door and turned the sign in the glass so that passersby could see the shop was open. It was exactly half past eight o'clock, and another workday had begun like so many others before it—and, God willing, like many more to come.

Since the morning hours were traditionally slow, Bonnie went to her office to take care of bills and prepare deposits. The bell on the door would ring if any customers entered, and she could see the entire sales floor through the large window beside her desk.

Even pausing to help a customer or two, Bonnie was able to finish her paperwork within an hour. Then, with her inventory checklist in hand, she turned on her computer and logged onto the Internet. Some of her suppliers accepted orders by E-mail, which shaved at least a day or two off delivery time. Summer had shown her how even a business based on something as traditional as quilting could benefit from technology.

But not today, apparently. To her exasperation, her server was down for the second time in less than a week. "That does it," she said. Before the week was over, she would find a new service provider. It was bad enough that she couldn't place her fabric order, but how many sales had she lost because customers couldn't log on to her web page?

A second attempt and a third were equally unsuccessful. Bonnie realized it was useless and chewed on her lower lip, thinking. What now? She could fax the order, but that would delay the shipment. Regular mail would take even longer.

She could log on using Craig's account; his E-mail used Waterford College's server, and she knew his password—JoePa, the nickname of Penn State's famous football coach. Craig had been so proud of his clever choice that he hadn't been able to keep it a secret.

"I'll be able to hack into your account now," Craig Jr. had warned.

"Do it and I'll disinherit you," his father had retorted, with a grin to show he was only teasing.

Bonnie wondered if Craig would mind if she used his account, and decided that if he had, he wouldn't have announced his password to the entire family. If their places were reversed, she would let him use her account without a second thought. Besides, as long as she sent just one message and didn't download anything, he would never know.

It took only a moment to change the settings on her E-mail software, and soon she was connected to the Internet. Breathing a sigh of relief, she typed in her fabric order and sent it off with a click of the mouse. Then, by force of habit, she checked for incoming messages.

"Oh, no, no, no," she exclaimed, frantically tapping the sequence of keys to cancel the request. But it was too late. A message was downloading. With growing chagrin, Bonnie watched the indicator bar showing the transmission's progress. Now she'd have to print out the message and give it to Craig when he got home or forward it back to his account so that he would receive it the next time he checked his E-mail. Either way, he'd know she had been using his account. He might not mind, but what if he did?

She should have just used the fax machine and damn the delay.

The computer beeped cheerfully and flashed an announcement on the screen: "You have new mail!"

"No kidding," Bonnie muttered. The question was, what should she do with it? She could just delete it. Eventually the sender would ask Craig why he hadn't written back, and they would attribute the message's disappearance to the vagaries of cyberspace.

But what if the message was important?

Bonnie resigned herself to reading the note. If it was important, she'd fess up; if it was just another piece of spam, she'd delete it, breathe a huge sigh of relief, and never again use Craig's E-mail account without permission.

She double-clicked the message—and with the first few words, her sheepish embarrassment was driven away by wave after dizzying wave of shock and disbelief.

"My dearest Craig," the letter began. What followed was a jumbled muddle of words and phrases that were incomprehensible and yet all too clear. A strange roaring filled her ears; she read the note over and over again, her body flashing hot and cold as the words sank in.

Her hands trembled as she clicked the mouse—first, to send the message back through cyberspace to her own account, and a second time, to print it. When the sheet of paper emerged from the laser printer, she deleted all traces of the message from Craig's account. Then she shut down the computer, shaking.

Craig was carrying on some kind of relationship—no, she ordered herself, say it—an affair. An affair over the Internet. A passionate affair, if this message was any indication, with a woman named Terri.

Woodenly, Bonnie rose from her chair, and before she was entirely sure of her purpose, she locked the shop door and flipped the Open sign to Closed, then set the plastic hands of the display clock to indicate that she would return in ten minutes.

That's all she would need, she thought as she went upstairs to the home she and Craig had shared for most of their marriage. Ten minutes to see how far it had gone. Unless he had erased all the other messages, because surely there had been others. One didn't write "I can't wait to meet you in person" in a first message. She prayed that he had erased the evidence of his infidelity.

But he hadn't. When she called up the E-mail software on Craig's computer, she found a file of messages from Terri dating back to the previous November. A second file contained messages Craig had sent to her; Bonnie choked out a sob when she saw that he had written to Terri on their wedding anniversary. And on New Year's Eve he had sent a special note: "It's nearly midnight, my darling, and I'm standing beside you ready to give you the first kiss of the New Year." On the stroke of twelve, Terri had responded, "Happy New Year, Sweetie! My arms are around you and I'm kissing you!"

Bonnie had been in bed by then. She had given Craig his kiss at ten o'clock and had gone off to bed, still weary from the previous weeks of holiday sales and entertaining, but glowing from the joy of the kids' visit home.

She read all the messages, every one, and pieced the story together. Craig and Terri had met on some kind of Internet mailing list for fans of Penn State football. Eventually they began exchanging private notes, first about the Nittany Lions and then about themselves. Bonnie learned that Craig's wife was so wrapped up in her two jobs and her friends that she couldn't carry on a conversation without mentioning them. Terri was divorced, with two preteen girls.

Bonnie calculated the approximate difference in their ages, not that it mattered. Terri was significantly younger.

Craig's wife didn't share his interests; she didn't know former Lion KiJana Carter from President Jimmy Carter. Terri found that enormously funny, and confessed that her ex was an Ohio State grad. Messages had flown back and forth regarding rumors that Notre Dame might join the Big Ten; they eventually agreed to disagree whether this would be good for the Penn State team or disastrous.

And then the messages grew more serious, more longing. There was a brief discussion of Craig's guilty feelings regarding the wife; Terri wrote that what the wife didn't know wouldn't hurt her, and no more was said on that subject. They wrote of how much they looked forward to each new message, and how they ached when none arrived. From the sheer volume of messages, Bonnie figured they weren't aching very often.

Finally she shut down the computer. She sat very still for a long time, staring at the dark screen, numb and dazed.

Her life had been eroding for months, and she had been entirely unaware. All the while she was doing her best to be a loving wife and partner, Craig and this woman were joking about her. They called her "the wife" like she was a pet or a piece of furniture—"the dog" or "the chair."

A wave of nausea swept over her. She bolted to the bathroom and leaned over the sink, retching and gasping, but nothing came up. Eventually the heaves subsided, and she clutched the basin to steady herself until she caught her breath. Then she turned on the tap full blast, cupped her hands beneath the icy spray, and splashed her face, over and over again, until her hands were red from the cold and her stomach had settled.

As she turned off the water, she glimpsed her face in the mirror and was frozen in place by what she saw there. Eyes shadowed and haunted. Skin pale and dripping wet. She looked like she'd seen a ghost. No, she looked like the ghost itself—the ghost of a suicide by drowning.

She leaned closer to the mirror, close enough to see the fine lines around eyes and mouth and the deeper grooves crossing neck and brow. Gray had returned unnoticed to her hair, though she'd dyed it after seeing herself on *America's Back Roads*. She had never been slender, though she wasn't heavy, either, and the weight in her face made her look puffy and drawn. Or maybe it wasn't the weight. Maybe it was the shock, the betrayal.

She wondered what Terri looked like. She wondered if Craig knew.

"You must confront him," she told the ghost woman in the mirror. When he came home from work that evening, she would be waiting for him. She would tell him she knew that "Terry," the fraternity brother he planned to meet at Penn State that weekend, was actually "Terri," single mother and potential homewrecker. She would remain calm and grave as she spoke, giving him no sign that he had torn her heart out. And then Craig would—

Would what?

Would he break down and beg forgiveness? Would he become angry and claim ignorance so she would have to drag him over to the computer and point to the incriminating evidence? Would he grow silent and distant and disappear into the bedroom, emerging with suitcase in hand? In any event, a confrontation would ruin everything. There would be no salvaging their relationship if they openly acknowledged Craig's betrayal. Her pride and his shame would be too great to overcome. If she wanted them to stay together, she would have to think of something else.

But *did* she want them to stay together after what he had done?

Yes. Yes. He was her husband, and she loved him. She did not want her marriage to end.

He had betrayed her, but he had not yet committed adultery, something she would not have been able to forgive. Her only hope was to keep him from doing so and to have him decide on his own that he wanted no woman but herself. He had to choose her of his own free will, without any tears or threats or begging from her. It was the only way.

"It's the only way," she explained to the ghost woman, and left the bathroom in a daze. She returned to the shop downstairs, her movements stiff and requiring great effort, as if her joints had locked up after years of inactivity, or as if she had slipped inside someone else's body and had not yet learned all the connections between brain and nerve and muscle.

As soon as she entered through the back door of the shop, she heard rapping on the front door. It was Judy, knocking frantically and peering through the glass.

"Where were you?" she exclaimed after Bonnie unlocked the door and pushed it open. "You're always here this time of day, and the sign says you were going to be back fifteen minutes ago. When you didn't answer my knock, I got worried."

"I'm sorry. I was upstairs." Bonnie's voice sounded distant, artificial.

She held open the door so Judy could enter. "Emily's not with you today?"

"I'm between classes. She stays home with Steve when I work. You know that." Judy looked concerned. "What's wrong? You look terrible."

That was not what Bonnie needed to hear at that moment. "That sounds like something Diane would say."

"I don't mean you look bad, but—" Judy hesitated. "No, I do mean it. You look awful. Are you ill?"

Bonnie clasped a hand to her forehead. "Now that you mention it, I think I am coming down with something." A small touch of adultery, to be exact. She felt hysterical laughter bubbling up inside her, but she choked it down.

"Is Summer working today? If it's not too busy, maybe she could handle things on her own and you could get some rest."

"She won't be in until this afternoon." Bonnie forced a smile onto her face. "Do you have time for a visit? I could brew a fresh pot of coffee, or we have tea . . ." And by the time their beverages were ready, Bonnie would be able to tell Judy what was really wrong.

But Judy had already been waiting a long time, and she had to leave right away or she'd be late for her class. After urging her once again to take it easy, Judy left. Except for the occasional customer, Bonnie spent the next few hours alone with her thoughts, which was the last thing she needed or wanted.

Somehow she managed to get through the rest of the morning. When Summer arrived in the middle of the afternoon, Bonnie asked her if she would mind working on her own for a few hours. "I'll be back in time for closing," she promised.

"Go ahead and play hooky for the rest of the day if you want," Summer said, laughing, and Bonnie gratefully agreed.

She drove to Elm Creek Manor, where Gwen and Diane were finishing the afternoon workshop. Bonnie helped them clean up the classroom, trying to figure out how to tell them what had happened and how to ask for their help without making Craig look bad. But it was no use. No matter how she explained it, Craig would look like a heel.

So finally she just took a deep breath and told them.

As she spoke, Gwen and Diane stared at her in disbelief. The Markham marriage was one of the constants in the Elm Creek Quilters' lives, and now Bonnie was telling them that it was in jeopardy. When she finished, they tried to comfort her by telling her that everything would be all right, but Bonnie didn't believe them. Nothing would be all right ever again unless she did something about it.

"Diane," she asked, "do you think you could give me a makeover? Hair, clothes, makeup—the works?"

"Of course." Diane looked Bonnie up and down and played with her hair. "I think you should go a bit shorter, you know, a bit more modern. I'll introduce you to Henri. He does wonders."

Bonnie turned to Gwen. "I want to start an exercise program, too. Do I need special shoes if I want to start running?"

Gwen looked dubious, but said, "If you're serious about this, we can go shopping as soon as we're finished here."

"And then we'll visit Henri," Diane broke in.

"And then Henri," Gwen agreed. "You should start out by walking briskly, and gradually build up to a run, if you like. Walking is just as good for your cardiovascular system, and it's easier on the joints." Gwen paused. "And don't expect to look like Christie Brinkley by Saturday. These things take time. I've been running for years and I'm bigger than you are."

"That's because you eat anything that isn't glued to the table," Diane said.

"But Gwen's in good shape," Bonnie said. "I'm flabby and jiggly."

Diane shrugged. "Some men like a little jiggle in a woman. Don't worry about it."

Bonnie gave her a wan look. "That's easy for you to say." Diane never exercised, as far as Bonnie knew, but she hadn't gained an ounce in all the years Bonnie had known her. It wasn't fair that a woman with two children should have such a flat stomach.

Gwen looked uncomfortable. "Bonnie, I hope you'll forgive me for saying this, but someone has to." She hesitated. "Are you sure he's worth it? After what he did, are you sure you still want him?"

"Is that what this is all about?" Diane exclaimed. "I thought the point was to get you ready to play the field."

"No," Bonnie said softly. "I want Craig back."

Gwen shook her head. "I know I'm the last person in the world you'd want for a marriage counselor, but have you given this enough thought? If you're doing this for the sake of the kids, well, they're old enough to handle divorce."

"And even if they weren't old enough, kids can adapt to anything," Diane added. "It's far better for kids to be in a loving, peaceful, single-parent household than to witness a messed-up marriage every day."

Bonnie winced. She had never thought of herself as someone with a messed-up marriage, but she supposed she was.

"Nice, Diane." Gwen glared at her.

"What?" Diane protested. "Would you stay with someone who did to you what Craig did to Bonnie? If Tim pulled this crap with me, I'd kick him out the door and throw his computer after him, and I'd do my best to bean him on the head with it. Let little miss homewrecker have him if she wants him. Anyone who would do something like this is no prize, as far as I'm concerned. If I were Bonnie—"

"But you're not me," Bonnie said.

They looked at her, silent and surprised, as if they had forgotten she was there.

They didn't know what they would do, not for certain, Bonnie wanted to tell them. No woman would ever know what she would do until she was faced with the situation herself. Gwen could advise her to put Craig out of her life because Gwen loved her independence and didn't know what it was like to build a life with a partner and to see that life threatened. Diane could say she'd kick Tim out if he did what Craig had done, because she knew Tim never would. Of course, six hours ago, Bonnie would have sworn the same thing about Craig.

"You're right," Gwen said. "We're not you. If this is what you want, we'll help you."

"Of course we will," Diane said. "You can count on us."

"Thank you."

"But—" Gwen hesitated. "Craig knows what you look like. A makeover won't keep him if he wants to go."

"Maybe," Diane said. She frowned in concentration and toyed with Bonnie's hair again. "But it can't hurt."

They went downtown to an athletic shoe store, where Gwen advised, "Find the most comfortable ones and worry about the price later."

Bonnie complied, but when she finally did look at the tag, the price nearly sent her reeling. "Is this for the shoes or the entire store?" she called out to a passing salesman, who ignored her.

Beside her, Diane was trying on pair after pair. "I'm getting some, too, so you don't have to go through this alone."

"The price will keep you motivated," Gwen said. "You'll walk every day because you'll want to get your money's worth."

"I'll walk with you," Diane promised. She stood up and took a few practice steps, then paused to examine her feet in the mirror. "Do you think these shoes make me look fat?"

Gwen burst out laughing, and Bonnie forced herself to join in. They were trying to cheer her up. The least she could do was let them think it was working.

After they made their purchases, Gwen had to return to campus, but she promised to phone later that evening. Diane took Bonnie by the arm and led her down the street to Henri's salon. Henri himself bounded over to welcome them. When Diane told him Bonnie needed "emergency resuscitation," Henri shook his head and made tsking noises. "It is a man, no?"

"No—I mean, yes," Bonnie said. "How did you know?"

He raised his eyebrows. "I know," he said significantly, and led her off to wash her hair.

Diane had been correct; Henri did work miracles. When Bonnie left the salon she looked a good five years younger—"Ten if you were not so very sad," Henri said. He had enhanced her best features with a wonderful haircut and clever makeup techniques. As she watched the transformation, Bonnie tried to rein in her delight with the sobering thought that this makeover was costing her a small fortune. Craig is worth it, she told herself firmly, and stopped calculating the bill for the long list of products Henri insisted were essential for re-creating her new look. But she needn't have worried. "Put it on my account, Henri," Diane sang out as they left the salon.

"But of course, *ma cherie,*" Henri called after them, waving cheerfully.

"I'm a very good customer," Diane confided as she took Bonnie next door to a fashionable boutique. Bonnie had often admired the expensive dresses displayed in the front window, but this was the first time she had actually gone inside. She felt out of place, but Diane breezed through the shop as if it were her own closet.

The dress Diane chose for her was light blue, and the flattering style seemed to take five pounds off her hips. With the new hair and makeup, the dress dangerously out of her price range, Bonnie looked amazing.

"You have to get it," Diane insisted.

"I can't." Bonnie fingered the price tag, gazed at herself in the dressing room mirror, and sighed. "It's out of the question."

"It would be a crime to let anyone else wear this dress," Diane grumbled, but she didn't pursue it. When Bonnie slipped back inside the stall to change, Diane offered to return the dress to the rack. Bonnie gave it to her reluctantly. She had wanted to admire herself in the mirror a few moments longer.

When Bonnie left the dressing room, Diane was waiting by the cash register, a shopping bag in her hand and a mischievous grin on her face. "You didn't," Bonnie said.

"I did." Diane handed Bonnie the bag.

"Thank you. I'm very grateful, but where on earth would I wear a dress like this?"

"L'Arc du Ciel, when you take Craig there for a romantic dinner and dancing Saturday night. Craig does like to dance, doesn't he?"

"Well, yes, but at L'Arc du Ciel?" Bonnie protested as Diane steered her from the shop. "I could feed the whole family for the price of one of their entrées. We've never eaten there before."

"Maybe you should start."

"But Craig will be at Penn State on Saturday," Bonnie said without thinking. She shook her head. "You're right. L'Arc du Ciel it is."

They parted at the corner. Bonnie hurried home to drop off her packages and returned to Grandma's Attic just in time for closing. Summer's delight at her new appearance made Bonnie blush. As she counted the day's receipts, locked the front door, and flipped the sign to Closed, she planned what she would say to Craig that evening. As she walked two blocks to the bank to drop off the deposit, she wondered if he would even notice her new appearance. She didn't expect him to match Summer's enthusiasm, but she hoped he'd show some appreciation, at least. Maybe she should put on a negligee and drape herself over his computer; he would have to notice her then.

She was preparing supper when he came home from work. He stopped by the kitchen to give her a quick kiss, then headed straight to the computer.

"Supper will be ready soon," she told him. "I don't think you have time—"

"It won't take long." He didn't bother to look at her as he spoke. "I have some important business to take care of."

"I bet you do," she muttered, too low for him to hear.

The table was set and Bonnie was in her usual chair waiting for him when he finally slunk into the dining room. "Sorry," he said. "I didn't mean for that to take so long."

"That's no problem," Bonnie said cheerfully. "I know how work can get away from you sometimes." So many evenings lately she had waited for him to drag himself away from the computer to come to supper or to bed, all the while feeling sympathy—sympathy!—for her poor, overworked husband. She'd been such a fool.

He gave her a quick smile as he took his seat, then did a double take. "You look different."

"Do I?" Bonnie rose and began serving him.

He nodded. "Did you get your hair cut?"

"Yes, I did." She could hardly get the words out, so pleased and relieved was she that he had noticed, and so angry at herself for feeling that way. She forced herself to smile. "What do you think?"

"You look very nice."

"Thank you, honey." She smiled at him, wondering if he detected the undercurrent of anger. She filled her own plate, taking smaller portions than usual.

Craig glanced at her plate. "Is that all you're having?"

"Oh, I decided to take off a few pounds." She said it breezily so he wouldn't think she was going to start obsessing about food, or worse yet, put him on a diet as well. Women who constantly criticized their figures annoyed him; he considered them self-absorbed and desperate for attention. Bonnie took an enthusiastic bite of chicken to show him she still had an appetite. "I'm going to start walking every day, too."

"Really." He eyed her with mild surprise.

She nodded. "That's right. There's going to be a whole new Bonnie around here soon." Not by Saturday, but soon. "Don't worry; I'm only changing my appearance, not the things that really matter. I know how fond you are of the old Bonnie." She heard herself speaking and wondered how she could sound so cheerful, so confident, so affectionate, when her heart was splintering into jagged pieces in her chest.

"I am fond of you," he said, holding her gaze for a moment before returning his attention to his food.

She jumped at the opening. "I know that, but it's nice to hear you say it," she said. "And while you're being so sweet . . . I was thinking, why don't we plan a special evening out soon? It's been a while since we've done something special, just the two of us."

"It's been just the two of us every day and every night since Barry started college."

"You know what I mean." She reached for his hand. "I mean going out, having fun."

He looked dubious. "What did you have in mind?"

"I thought we could go out for dinner and dancing at L'Arc du Ciel." She steeled herself. "I went ahead and made reservations for Saturday night."

"Saturday?" He set down his fork. "This Saturday?"

She nodded, her heart sinking as his frown deepened.

"But you know I have plans for this Saturday."

"I thought maybe you'd be willing to change them."

He shook his head and helped himself to more mashed potatoes. "We can go out to dinner any night. The Blue-White Game is only once a year."

"But it'll just be one half of the team playing the other half, right? Wouldn't it just be like watching a practice?"

"It's much more than a practice and you know it. It's the first time we get to see next year's starting lineup in action."

"Can't you tape it?"

"No, I can't tape it." His voice was rising, growing more agitated. "They might show it on local TV in State College, but we won't get it around here. It's not a Big Ten game."

Bonnie heard herself speak, and her voice sounded as if it were coming from someplace very far away. "Please don't go to Penn State this weekend. Please stay here and go dancing with me instead."

His face was hard. "I've already paid for my ticket, and I've been planning this a long time. We'll go out next weekend, all right?"

He was adamant, and she knew it. All the nervous energy drained from her. "All right."

She watched him eat, cutting into the tender chicken with his fork, chewing angrily on a slice of buttered bread. She was seized, suddenly, by the urge to dump the bowl of corn over his head. "I think I left the oven on," she said, and rushed back to the kitchen, where she waited for the urge to subside before returning to the table.

She slept poorly that night and woke, numb and confused, to the sound of the keyboard clattering in the other room.

Gwen was right.

A new hairstyle and makeup wouldn't keep him. The promise of a trim, healthier Bonnie wouldn't keep him. Neither would a romantic night on the town or a lovely new light blue dress that seemed to take five pounds off her hips.

If she wanted to win him back, it would have to be with her brain. She was over fifty, and although she had treated her body kindly throughout the years, it could do only so much for her. But although her beauty wasn't as great as it had been when she and Craig first met, her mind was better than ever. Years of managing a household, running her business, interacting with her wonderful, creative, intelligent friends had sharpened her mind and developed her soul. She had accomplished so much in her life; she was a partner worthy of any man. She would make Craig remember that.

Filled with new resolve, Bonnie kicked off the covers and started her day. By the time she had showered and had styled her newly cut hair, she knew what she had to do. She dressed in her favorite blue slacks and the quilted jacket she had made over the course of many months at meetings of the Elm Creek Quilters. Wearing it now, she felt as if her friends were with her, silent but encouraging, supportive, lending her their strength. She took a deep breath and strode into the family room to announce her intentions.

Craig was still at the computer, naturally, sipping coffee and munching buttered toast. On any other morning she would have scolded him gently and warned him about cholesterol, but today she was tempted to load the toast with as much butter as it would hold and force-feed it to him, along with a few slices of bacon and a cup of lard.

"I have a great idea," she declared.

Craig jumped in his chair. "Oh? What's that?" With a swift movement of the mouse, he turned on the screen saver. A school of fish appeared where an E-mail message had been.

"Since you can't change your plans for Saturday, I'll change mine." Bonnie smiled brightly as he swiveled around to face her. "I'll come with you to Penn State."

Craig's face went from furious red to queasy pale more swiftly than she would have imagined possible. "What? What do you mean? You can't."

She deliberately misunderstood him. "Well, sure I can, honey. I'm not too busy."

"But—you have—" He gulped air. "What about the shop? Saturday's your busiest day. You can't afford to close on a Saturday, not when business has been so bad."

"Summer's working, and Diane offered to help her." Bonnie hadn't asked her yet, but she knew she would agree.

"What about quilt camp? I won't be back until Sunday afternoon. You'll miss registration."

"They can manage without me just this once."

Craig's mouth worked silently for a moment. "Ticket," he said, relief replacing his sickly cast. "You don't have a ticket to the game. You can't go."

"Oh, that." Bonnie dismissed that with a wave of her hand. "You and your friend can watch from Beaver Stadium, as you planned, and I'll find a nice sports bar downtown and watch the game on TV. You said it would be broadcast locally, right?" He nodded weakly. "Then it's all settled. I don't know why I didn't think of this earlier. It's been so long since I've seen campus."

"We could go together some other weekend—"

"And have you miss the Blue-White Game? I wouldn't dream of it." She crossed the room to where he sat limp and dazed before his computer, then squeezed his shoulders affectionately and kissed him. "Do you think we'll run into any of our friends? I'm sure we will. I bet if you had gone by yourself, you would have run into everyone from the old gang. They would have been asking where I was and promising to call me as soon as they got home." His eyes widened slightly; that had not occurred to him. She kissed him again, this time to say good-bye. "I'll see you tonight. I'm going to work."

"So early?" he asked in a hollow voice.

"Diane's coming by to plan for the exemption hearing," she lied. She shrugged helplessly and hurried out the door.

In the stairwell, her legs felt so weak that she had to clutch the handrail and lean against the wall. She had done it. She had never been more nervous in her life, but she had done it. She had not backed down, and he had not suspected a thing.

When she had composed herself, she continued down the stairs to Grandma's Attic.

All that week she planned and prepared, enlisting the help of her friends. Diane came over one afternoon and helped her choose an outfit for the day of the game. Bonnie had planned to wear jeans, thinking they would make her look younger, but Diane convinced her to wear a more flattering pair of casual slacks instead. She would also wear a white knit top under the blue Penn State cardigan Craig had given her for her birthday. She modeled the outfit, relieved to see Diane nod in satisfaction. "You look great," Diane said. "I just hope little Miss Terri asks you where you got the sweater."

Bonnie managed a smile as she pictured Terri's jealousy. She hoped Craig had never given Terri any gifts.

Judy had her husband, Steve, look up articles on Penn State football, and he also collected amusing anecdotes from his sportswriter friends, stories that had not made it into print. Every evening Bonnie doted on Craig as if they were newlyweds. He seemed perpetually bewildered, as if he didn't know what to make of her. On Friday evening he asked her if she still meant to accompany him; when she assured him she did, his shoulders slumped and he went off to his computer, dejected.

Bonnie's heart leapt in alarm. He was going to tell Terri not to come, and that would ruin everything. They would make arrangements for another time, another place, an occasion when it might be impossible for Bonnie to intervene.

As night fell, Bonnie lay in bed in the dark, unable to sleep. Finally, Craig climbed in beside her. When she was certain he had drifted off, she stole from the bed, tiptoed into the family room, and switched on the computer. It let out a chord when it started up, and the melodic chime shattered the silence. Bonnie held her breath, listening, but not a sound came from the bedroom. Slowly she let out the breath. She would have to hurry.

After turning the volume all the way down, she opened the E-mail program. A quick check of Craig's most recent outgoing messages confirmed her fears. He had written to Terri to tell her not to come to Penn State the next day.

"I don't understand," Terri had written back. "Are you having second thoughts or what?"

"Just don't come," he had responded.

Barely a minute had passed between his message and Terri's reply. "I'm not your wife. You can't tell me what to do. I have my own ticket and a baby-sitter and I'm going to this game with you or without you."

It was the last message they had exchanged.

Bonnie chewed on her lower lip, staring at the screen and wondering what to do.

She typed in Craig's password and double-clicked the mouse. Her heart pounded as the computer announced the results of her query: two new messages were downloading into the computer. Terri had sent them both.

The first said, "Are you still there?"

The second had been sent ten minutes later. "I'm sorry I got mad," Terri had written. "I just don't understand why you're backing out like this. If you would just tell me why, I could accept it. What's wrong? Please write back."

Bonnie took a deep breath and slowly, slowly reached for the keyboard.

"I'm sorry," she wrote. "I guess I just got nervous. Forget I said anything. Let's meet at the Corner Room at ten as we had planned. I'll see you then."

She signed Craig's name and sent the message on its way. Then she erased the note from the outgoing messages file and disabled the internal modem. She shut down the computer and returned to bed.

The alarm woke her early Saturday morning. She shut it off quickly—Craig stirred but didn't open his eyes. She bounded out of bed and raced to the shower, but she didn't finish as quickly as she had hoped. By the time she had fixed her hair and dressed, Craig was out of bed and at the computer. He did not look pleased.

"Is something wrong with the computer?" she asked.

"Something is, but I'll be damned if I know what," he said. "I can't get on-line."

"Do you want to try the one downstairs?" She hoped with all her heart he'd say no.

He glanced at the clock on the screen. "No, I don't have time." Still scowling, he shut down the computer and stomped off to the shower. Bonnie hid her satisfaction. If there were any new messages from Terri telling him how pleased she was that he had changed his mind, Craig wouldn't see them.

She put on a pot of coffee and made him his favorite breakfast—cinnamon apple waffles. When he returned to the kitchen, his anger had faded and he seemed his usual self again. "Do I smell cinnamon?" he asked.

"You certainly do, so sit down and eat before it gets cold." She gave him a warm smile and carried their plates to the table.

After breakfast, they locked up the house and carried their overnight bags to the car. At first Craig responded to her attempts at conversation with brief phrases or shrugs, but as the two-hour drive progressed, he relaxed and began to chat comfortably with her. They talked about the NFL draft that had taken place earlier that month; Bonnie knew from the articles Steve had given her that the graduating Nittany Lions had had an excellent year. The conversation turned to their kids, and then to their favorite memories from their student years at Penn State. By the time they turned off Route 322 and were driving down Atherton Street toward campus, they were chatting and laughing and enjoying themselves.

At a quarter to ten, they checked into the Hotel State College on the corner of Allen Street, right across College Avenue from the main gates to the campus. They were given a pleasant room with a queen-size bed and a large window overlooking Allen Street. As Craig unpacked, Bonnie went to the bathroom to freshen up. She scrutinized herself in the mirror. Her eyes were bright with excitement, and the new hairstyle looked fresh and pretty. She was ready to face the enemy.

She summoned up her courage and put the next stage of her plan into motion.

In the other room, Craig was sitting on the edge of the bed flipping through the local newspaper. "So, when and where are we meeting your friend?" Bonnie asked him.

"Oh. There's been a change of plans. My friend isn't coming."

"Why not?" she asked, putting all the disappointment she could muster into her voice.

"Something came up." He set the paper aside and rose. "Do you feel like a cup of coffee before the game?"

"I'd love one." Bonnie smiled at him. "Why don't we go to the Corner Room?"

Craig agreed—and why not? It had been their favorite restaurant when they were students. As they went downstairs to the lobby, Bonnie slipped her hand into his, her thoughts racing. Since the restaurant was affiliated with the hotel, she and Craig could reach it without going outside—but what about Terri? Would she wait inside or outside? Terri expected to share Craig's room, so she had not needed to enter the hotel to register. Bonnie cursed herself for not being more specific. Even if Terri were waiting just outside, they wouldn't run into her, not that Bonnie would recognize her if they did. All Bonnie had was the description Terri had sent Craig months ago, and how accurate would that be?

She needn't have worried.

The restaurant foyer was filled with other Penn State fans. A smiling hostess with a clipboard was walking down the line taking customers' names and apologizing for the wait. When she reached Craig, he said, "Markham, two, nonsmoking, please."

The hostess smiled in recognition. "Craig Markham?"

"Why, yes."

"The other member of your party is already here." The hostess took them out of line, picked up two menus, and motioned for them to follow her. "I thought she said table for two, but I guess she meant she was waiting for two. That's okay, though; you have a booth, so there's plenty of room." And with that, she placed their menus in a booth already occupied by a wide-eyed woman with shoulder-length blond hair held back in a barrette.

"Craig?" the woman said. Her eyes flicked from Craig to Bonnie.

"Enjoy your meal," the hostess chirped, and left.

"Well, hello," Bonnie declared, sliding into the high-backed seat. "You must be Terri. Craig told me you had to cancel. I'm so delighted you came after all."

Terri's mouth opened and shut.

"I'm Bonnie, of course." She extended her hand, and Terri limply shook it. Craig stood rooted in place. "Well, come on, honey, sit down." She grabbed his arm and pulled him into the booth, then smiled again at Terri. "It's so nice to finally meet you."

"It's . . . it's nice to meet you, too." Terri held out her hand for Craig to shake and shot him a look of pained bewilderment, which Bonnie pretended not to see.

"I thought Craig told me he would be meeting a friend from his old fraternity, but obviously I misunderstood." Bonnie interlaced her fingers and rested them on the table. "So tell me—how do you two know each other?"

Terri swallowed. "Um, well—" She looked to Craig for help. "Why don't you tell her?"

"No, no, you go ahead." Craig sounded as if he were being strangled. "I'm not much of a storyteller."

Betrayal and annoyance flashed in Terri's eyes. Craig didn't see them since he had buried his face in the menu, but Bonnie did.

"We met on the Internet," Terri said.

"Oh, well, that explains it," Bonnie said. "No wonder I got mixed up. It's so hard to keep track of all Craig's Internet friends. He has so many."

Terri's mouth pinched into a hard line. "Is that so?"

"Oh, yes. He writes to people all over the world—men, women—"

"Not so many women," Craig interrupted. Terri just looked at him.

They ordered coffee, and while they waited, Bonnie summoned up all that was good and loving in herself so that she could stop hating the woman on the other side of the table, this woman who was trying to steal her husband and ruin her life. She imagined they were in Grandma's Attic and that Terri was a newcomer to Waterford, charmed inside by a bright quilt hanging in the shop window, unsure and uncomfortable, hovering nearby and listening wistfully to the laughter of the Elm Creek

Quilters. There had to be something, something in this woman that Bonnie could love.

The shape of her face reminded her of Sarah. Her hair was the same shade of blond as Diane's. Her husband had left her for another woman and she was raising two children alone.

There. That did it. Her hatred faded.

This time when she smiled at Terri, she felt genuine kindness. "So tell me about yourself," she said.

Terri glanced at Craig, but he had not yet recovered his wits and was clearly of no use to anyone. So she began. When she mentioned her children, Bonnie asked if she had any photos. Hesitantly, Terri took a small album from her purse and passed it to her. Bonnie admired each picture and begged for the story behind them, and soon Terri was smiling shyly and talking almost as if they were friends. Craig looked on; by the time the server came by to refill their coffee cups, he had composed himself enough to join in the conversation, which shifted from family to work. Terri was working as an office manager in Harrisburg, but she dreamed of owning her own business someday.

Bonnie knew this; she had read the E-mail. "I run my own business," she said.

Again Terri glanced at Craig. "I thought you worked in a fabric store."

Bonnie burst out laughing. "Oh, don't I often wish it were that simple. No, I own a quilt shop, a place for specialty fabrics and notions and books, and just about everything else a quilter needs. I also teach quilting classes there, though I've cut back since I started teaching for Elm Creek Quilts."

"That name sounds familiar," Terri said. "Weren't you on *America's Back Roads* a few months ago?"

"That's right."

"I remember it now." Terri's eyes grew misty and she sighed. "That manor is so beautiful. You really get to work there? That must be so great. And the people seemed so nice."

"They're the best people I've ever known," Bonnie said, and she meant it. "You should come to quilt camp sometime."

"Oh, no, not me." Terri flashed her a quick smile and shook her head. "I don't know how to quilt."

"What better reason to come to quilt camp? We'll teach you."

"It looks so hard—"

"If she doesn't want to come, she doesn't have to," Craig broke in. Bonnie and Terri looked at him. Terri frowned. Bonnie tried to hide her amusement. She sighed, looked at Terri, and rolled her eyes. Terri giggled.

"So tell me about your idea for your business," Bonnie said. "I'd be happy to share my experience with you."

Eagerly, Terri told her about her idea to open a computer software and supply store with products of interest to women and children. Bonnie had to admit it was an interesting idea, full of possibilities. She answered Terri's questions about start-up capital and location and marketing; together they brainstormed and debated. They talked through a few more refills of coffee until Craig finally cleared his throat and reminded them about the game.

"He's right," Bonnie said. "You two better get going or you won't make it to the stadium in time."

"What about you?" Terri asked, climbing out of the booth.

"I'm going to watch it from the club down the street." Bonnie explained that she didn't have a ticket because she had decided to come at the last minute. She saw Craig and Terri exchange a long look. Now Bonnie's presence had finally been explained, and now Terri finally understood why Craig had canceled the date. But Craig still didn't know why Terri had shown up after he had told her not to, and Terri had no idea why Craig had changed his mind and why on earth he had brought his wife along.

They would have plenty of time to talk at the game.

Craig and Terri walked with her to the bar, two blocks away. They arranged to meet outside the stadium after the game. Bonnie waited until Craig and Terri climbed onto the Campus Loop bus that would take them to the stadium, and then she went inside the bar.

She was exhausted. Everything was going well so far, but the effort had drained her.

The layout of the bar had not changed since her last visit years ago; the dining room was empty, but the bar was nearly full. One wall was lined with big-screen TVs, all tuned to the same station. Bonnie took the last available table and ordered a drink.

Her eyes were fixed on the screen, but her mind was with Craig and Terri. There was no reason for them to go to the game, not with "the wife" safely out of the way. They could be in the hotel room that very minute. After they wore themselves out with lovemaking, they would turn on the game and watch it as they cuddled, so later they could describe plays and statistics to her as if they had been in the stadium. At the last possible moment they would race hand in hand across campus to the meeting place outside the stadium, still glowing from their encounter and from the glee of deceiving her.

Bonnie shook her head to force the thoughts away. She couldn't think like that. Surely by now they were too worked up and anxious and guilty to even contemplate having sex. Besides, they knew she had a key to the hotel room. They wouldn't risk it.

She kept reassuring herself until she almost believed it.

She nursed her drink through the first quarter, then switched to soft drinks for the rest of the game. It seemed hours until the fourth quarter, but finally it was time for her to leave if she wanted to meet Craig and Terri promptly. But Bonnie didn't budge. Her heart began to pound as the game ended, but still she didn't leave. Instead, she struck up a conversation with some of the other customers and focused her attention on an interview with Joe Paterno.

Suddenly she spotted Craig and Terri making their way through the crowd toward her, unsmiling, carefully apart from each other. She pretended not to see them until they reached the table and Craig spoke her name.

Bonnie feigned astonishment. "Is it that time already?"

"We waited for you for twenty minutes," Craig said, almost woebegone.

"I lost all track of time." Bonnie rose and forced out a cheerful smile. "You two must have enjoyed the game even more than I did, since you were in the stadium."

"It was all right," Craig said, but neither he nor Terri looked as if they'd had much fun.

They were ready for supper, so they walked several blocks east to an Italian restaurant. Craig and Terri seemed ill at ease with each other and grateful for Bonnie's conversation, which was nearly a monologue, the others spoke so infrequently. Soon she had them grinning in spite of themselves with the anecdotes from Steve's sportswriter friends. Bonnie could almost forget what had brought them together in that place.

They left the restaurant at dusk.

"Where are you staying?" Bonnie asked Terri as they strolled down College Avenue toward the Hotel State College. The three walked side-by-side, with Bonnie in the middle.

"I'm going home."

"Oh, do you have to? I was looking forward to hearing more about your computer store over breakfast."

Terri fidgeted with the straps of her purse. "No, I'd better get home. It's only an hour away. No sense in paying for the sitter if I don't have to." She shook Bonnie's hand. "Thanks so much for all your advice."

"Don't mention it. Any time. You have my number."

Terri nodded. Then her mouth tightened and she extended her hand to Craig. "Good-bye," she told him, and her words carried a ring of finality.

Craig shook her hand and nodded, but said nothing. Terri flashed them a quick, tight smile and walked away.

Bonnie and Craig watched her until she rounded the corner, then they continued on to the hotel.

"Terri seems very nice," Bonnie said.

"She thinks you're nice, too." He paused. "Actually, she thinks you're wonderful. She said you were 'an inspiration.'"

"No kidding. I don't think anyone's ever called me that before." Bonnie kept her voice casual. "The next time you write to her, why don't you invite her to visit us in Waterford?"

"I don't think we'll be writing to each other anymore."

"Oh."

A moment passed in silence as they walked on.

"Bonnie—" Craig hesitated. "There's something I need to tell you about this trip."

"No, you don't."

"Yes, I—"

"Craig, I already know."

Silence.

"Oh." His voice was leaden. "I guess I knew that."

She glanced at him, and saw to her amazement that his face was contorted, as if he were fighting back tears. His pace slowed until he came to a stop in the middle of the sidewalk.

"Bonnie—" His voice broke. "I'm so sorry—"

Her first instinct was to comfort him, to tell him everything would be all right, that they could slip back into their comfortable, routine married life as if he had not set out to betray her. She had won, and in her victory she could afford to be generous. But the words stuck in her throat. She had won him back, but watching him fight off tears, she couldn't imagine ever trusting him again.

"I don't think I can go through this again," she heard herself say.

"You won't have to. I promise."

She tried, but she couldn't believe him. She would never know when the next Terri would come along, and she couldn't bear to spend every waking moment suspecting him, watching him, waiting for the ground beneath her feet to shift and crumble again. She deserved better than a lifetime of suspicion and mistrust. She deserved better.

"Bonnie?" Craig pleaded. "Please say you forgive me."

"Of course I do," she said, thinking, *I don't know if I can.*

They walked on.

✿ ✿ ✿

When they arrived home on Sunday, Bonnie unpacked her suitcase with barely a word for her husband. Then she went to her sewing room, where she took out the round robin quilt.

She chose green and blue for the colors of Elm Creek Manor. She chose blue for truth and green for new beginnings. She followed Diane's lead and chose a darker shade of cream for her background; Diane had given her such good advice lately that it seemed reasonable to accept her guidance this time, too.

She pieced a border of pinwheel blocks—pinwheels for her wind-blown life, which with faith and perseverance she tried to stitch into or-der. The pattern was a four patch, a square divided into four smaller squares, which were in turn divided into two equal triangles, one light, one dark, like the darkness of the past week and the light hope of the fu-ture. She wanted to believe in hope.

One side of each triangle was for Craig, one for Terri, and one for herself, but as the border took shape, the triangles melted into the pin-wheel pattern, and all she could see was the motion spinning ever for-ward, but to what destination, she did not know.

# Chapter Seven

Sylvia traced around the template, careful to keep the points of the diamond clear and distinct as she drew on the wrong side of the dark blue paisley fabric. She would hand-piece this quilt, she decided, to insure the accuracy of the piecing and the sharpness of the points. She had made other Broken Star quilts before, but this one was special. When it was complete, it would hang in the front foyer to welcome their guests to Elm Creek Manor.

A twinge of pain shot through her hand, so sharp that she dropped the scissors. She massaged her right hand with her left, waiting for the ache to subside. More and more frequently these days, aches and pains interrupted her work. Sarah told her she ought to see a doctor, but Sylvia put it off. She loathed doctors. They never kept their appointments promptly, and she had much better things to do than sit in an uncomfortable waiting room chair paging through outdated magazines. When the doctors finally condescended to see her, they would immediately trot her over to the scale and urge her to put on some weight. A few minutes later, they would draw some blood and order her to watch her cholesterol. How on earth was she supposed to watch her cholesterol and put on weight at the same time? Honestly. She was seventy-seven years old and didn't need some child a fraction of her age telling her how to feed herself.

After all, nothing was wrong with her. Even her little scare a few months ago had turned out to be nothing. Fortunately, Sylvia had kept it to herself or Sarah would have rushed her to the emergency room. The headache had come out of nowhere, and it was more severe than any Sylvia had ever felt. When she stood up to get an aspirin, she couldn't keep her balance. When she tried to call for help, the words came out in the wrong order, startling her into silence. She was on the verge of asking Sarah to call the doctor, but when the sensations faded after only a few minutes, she decided there was no sense in complaining. Later she heard Gwen describing a migraine, and she realized that was what she had experienced. It was a relief, but annoying, too, to learn she had suddenly developed migraines at her age.

When the pain in her hand had faded, Sylvia began to arrange the pieces she had already cut, dozens of diamonds in blue, green, and purple jewel tones. Claudia preferred—had preferred—pastels, but Sylvia liked the intensity of the darker hues. If Claudia were to walk in on her now, she would surely work herself into a good pout. "Can't you choose something more cheerful for once?" she would say.

"You're the cheerful one, little Miss Sunshine. You make the happy quilts if you want them so badly."

Claudia would scowl at the nickname, but it wouldn't prevent her from carrying on. "And what's this—another Lone Star?"

"No."

"It looks like a Lone Star to me."

"It's not." Sylvia would pause and hide a smile. "It's a Broken Star."

"Well, close enough," Claudia would retort, exasperated.

Claudia was right; Sylvia did make many Lone Stars and Lone Star variations. And why not? It was her favorite pattern, after all, and there were so many ways to arrange the colors and values to create the appearance of depth and movement. And perhaps just a tiny part of her found a smug satisfaction in choosing a pattern that Claudia struggled with. Even with the far simpler LeMoyne Star block, Claudia would chop off the tips of her diamonds, line up seams improperly, and distort the fabric so that the star bulged in the center. Meanwhile, Sylvia would hum pleasantly as she worked and would pretend not to notice Claudia's jealousy as one Lone Star diamond after another fell into place swiftly and precisely, as if it were no effort at all.

Only Sylvia knew the truth: although she made it look easy, it was difficult to piece those blocks so perfectly. If she were alone, she might have relaxed and allowed herself a slight misalignment, the tiniest bulge. But not with Claudia hovering around, watching and waiting for her to make a mistake.

She caught herself. Claudia wasn't watching anymore. She knew that.

Suddenly she felt overcome by shame. Of course her sister had been jealous of her all those years. Sylvia had done everything within her power to encourage that jealousy. She knew she was the better quilter and made certain everyone else knew it, too. She had been an arrogant show-off since the day she first picked up a needle. She could have helped Claudia become a better quilter; she could have been modest about her own successes; she could have admitted that Claudia's quilts were as warm and comfortable as her own. She could have ignored the minuscule errors that no one else saw until she pointed them out.

But at the time, Claudia had always seemed the one at fault. How could Sylvia have been so wrong and not have sensed it?

Sylvia closed her eyes for a moment and forced the thoughts away. Her right hand shook as she reached for the scissors again. The pain returned like an electric shock from her knuckles to the elbow. She gasped and tried to drop the scissors, but her hand had frozen up, tightening with the pain. She used her left hand to open the clenched fingers, and the scissors fell to the table.

"Are you all right?"

She looked up to find Andrew in the doorway of the sitting room. He looked concerned as he approached, and she wondered how long he had been standing there.

"I'm fine," she said. "Just some aches and pains."

"Are you sure?"

She followed his line of sight and saw that he was studying her hands. Without realizing it, she had resumed the massaging motions. She forced herself to stop and let her hands fall to her sides. "It's nothing."

Andrew nodded, but he reached for her right hand anyway. "Let me see if I can help."

"No, really, you don't—" But he had already taken her hand in both of his, gently working it with his thumbs. His hands felt sure around hers, gentle but toughened from work. She approved. Soft hands didn't belong on a man.

She watched him, but his eyes were intent on her hand. Suddenly he looked up and smiled. "How's that? Feel better?"

To her surprise, she did. "Why, yes, I do." There was no pain at all. "How did you do that?"

"I just showed those pains who's boss." He smiled and held her gaze, and as he did, she felt the strangest sensation, a stirring—and then she realized he had finished rubbing her hand but was still holding it clasped in his own.

She pulled her hand away. "Thank you."

"Any time."

He smiled at her again, so easy and comfortable, and the faint sensation—whatever it was—returned. What on earth was wrong with her? Perhaps Sarah was right and a trip to the doctor was in order.

She checked her watch, hoping the gesture wasn't too artificial. "I'd better find Sarah. It's about time to leave for Diane's Zoning Commission hearing. Carol agreed to look after our guests while we're gone." Her voice was brisk, and so was her stride as she turned away from Andrew and went into the kitchen.

He followed. "Anything I can do to help?"

"No, thank you. You've been such a big help already. You've earned yourself a rest."

"You sound like my kids," he said. "They're always trying to push me into a rocking chair. There'll be plenty of time to rest when I'm old."

Sylvia couldn't help smiling. Sarah and Matt used to give her that kind of talk, until she insisted they stop. "You're a man after my own heart, Andrew."

He caught her eye and grinned, but made no reply. She looked away, embarrassed. Somehow her words had come out differently than she had intended, almost flirtatious.

It was because she had grown so accustomed to Andrew's presence, that was all. In the few weeks since his arrival, he had found a niche for himself at Elm Creek Manor. He fit in so naturally—assisting Matthew with his caretaking duties and generally helping out around the manor—that it was hard to believe he had been away so long and that more than fifty years had passed since she had last seen him.

Carol, too, was making a place for herself, though not as smoothly as Andrew had done, nor as quickly. After that first week, Sylvia had invited Carol to stay as a personal guest, refusing her offers of payment as adamantly as Andrew declined a room in the manor in favor of his motor home. In return, Carol insisted on earning her keep. She took over lunch and supper preparations, and before long added straightening up the attic to her duties. The room stretched the entire length of the south wing of the manor and was filled with trunks, boxes, and furniture. Sylvia had long put off sorting through the attic, since even with Sarah's help it would have been a daunting task, but Carol enjoyed the challenge. Every few days she brought down a new treasure—a lamp, a vintage gown, a rocking chair—and after she or Andrew cleaned and repaired it, Carol found the perfect spot for it somewhere in the manor.

When Sylvia pointed out to Sarah that her mother was sparing them a great deal of work, Sarah said, "As long as she stays out of the way, she can keep busy however she likes." Sylvia decided to interpret her reply optimistically, though it was far from a resounding shout of gratitude.

She found Sarah and Carol seated on the veranda with their backs to the doorway. Sylvia was so pleased to see them talking instead of arguing or ignoring each other that she hung back, unwilling to interrupt.

"Your uncles took most of Grandma's quilts," Carol was saying. "But they left a few for me. I have one on my bed now, one with stars in all different colors. I wish I'd thought to bring a picture. If I send you one, could you tell me what the pattern is?"

"Sure," Sarah said, her eyes on the quilt block in her hands. "If I don't know what it is, Sylvia will."

"Thank you."

They fell silent for so long that Sylvia was about to approach them, when Sarah suddenly spoke again. "Maybe it's the same pattern Grandma used for my quilt."

"Grandma made you a quilt?"

"Yes, don't you remember? A pink-and-white Sawtooth Star quilt. She gave it to me for my eighth birthday."

"Did she? I don't recall seeing it on your bed."

"Maybe that's because you took it away from me as soon as I unwrapped it." Sarah's voice was cool. "You kept it in a box in your closet."

"Are you sure? I don't remember." When Sarah merely shrugged, Carol added, "Why would I have done a thing like that?"

"You said it was too nice for everyday and that I would ruin it."

Carol shook her head, bewildered. "I wouldn't do that."

"You did. I remember it perfectly."

Sylvia froze as Carol suddenly turned toward Sarah. She tentatively reached out a hand to her daughter, only to withdraw it when Sarah kept her attention on her sewing.

"Well," Carol said quietly. "I don't remember this, but if you say it happened, I believe you. I'm sorry." She clasped her hands on the arm of her chair and studied them. "I wasn't a perfect mother, but I did the best I could. All I ever wanted was for you to be happy."

Sarah put down her quilt block. "No, Dad wanted me to be happy. You wanted me to be perfect."

Carol recoiled as if the words had scalded her. "I wanted you to be the best you could, to do better with your life than I had with mine. I still want that."

"I've done fine, Mom. And so have you. You have your career, a child, friends, you had a great marriage to a wonderful man—"

"Sarah," her mother broke in, "there's so much you don't know. You and I are so much alike, and I'm afraid—"

"We are nothing alike," Sarah interrupted. "You and I couldn't be more different. You think we're the same, but we aren't. We aren't."

Sylvia wished she had spoken up as soon as she had stepped onto the veranda, but as the conversation deteriorated, she had felt frozen in place, transfixed by the awful scene. Now she forced herself into action. "There you two are," she said brightly, startling them as she strode forward. "It's getting late. We have to get ready to meet the others downtown." She heard the tremor in her voice and wondered if the two women detected it, if they could sense how sick she felt, disappointed and remorseful through to her very core. She'd had such good intentions for their reunion, but each day her hopes seemed more futile.

Sarah stood up. "I won't be long." Without another word or glance for Carol, she went inside.

Sylvia watched her go, her heart sinking. When she turned back to Carol, she found her still staring in the direction her daughter had taken. "Thank you for looking after the campers while we're gone, Carol."

"She's always running away from me," Carol said, her voice distant. "I fear for her. She's more like me than she'll ever admit, and I'm afraid Matt will turn out to be just like her father."

"But isn't that a good thing? Sarah has nothing but praise for your late husband."

Carol looked embarrassed, as if Sylvia had caught her thinking aloud. "No. You don't understand. She never knew my husband, not really, not the man I knew."

Too astonished to speak, Sylvia could only stare at her, until Carol rose and went inside the manor. When Carol was gone, Sylvia sank into one of the chairs.

She felt very old as she sat there waiting for Sarah, each regret weighing heavily on her heart. Nothing about Carol's visit had turned out the way Sylvia had planned. Usually it was such a joy to welcome new friends to Elm Creek Manor, to hear the foyer ringing with laughter and feel the guests' delight as they looked forward to a week of quilting together. As she had many times before, Sylvia wondered what Claudia would think about the manor's transformation. Remembering the hollow, echoing halls she had found on returning to the manor after her long absence, Sylvia knew that the change was for the better.

Sarah had brought all this about, proving that she was capable of great things. Now, if only the young woman would work a few more changes in her own heart.

Before long Sarah came downstairs dressed in a light blue suit, but Sylvia couldn't bring herself to mention the disagreement with Carol. Sarah drove them downtown to the municipal building, where they met Diane and the other Elm Creek Quilters in the hallway outside the council hearing room. Sylvia almost didn't recognize Diane's two sons, freshly scrubbed and dressed in sport coats and neatly pressed slacks. As the boys talked with their father, the Elm Creek Quilters tried to ease Diane's nervousness by chatting about anything other than the hearing. Soon the conversation turned to the upcoming end of the school year, which all but Diane eagerly welcomed. "You try looking after two teenage boys for three solid months," she said when they teased her for complaining.

"I did, plus a daughter," Bonnie said.

"That's different. You didn't have my two." Diane shot Gwen a look. "And don't you say a word. Everyone knows Summer is the world's most perfect child."

"Not really," Summer said hastily, looking embarrassed.

"Diane's right, for once." Gwen put an arm around her daughter's shoulders. "And believe me, I know how lucky I am." Her voice trembled.

"Oh, no, Mom, not again."

"I can't help it." Gwen dug in her pocket for a tissue. She wiped her eyes, laughing at herself. "My baby's growing up and going away. You can't expect me to take this calmly."

"Your baby's twenty-two," Summer pointed out. "I'm an adult, and I'm perfectly capable of looking out for myself."

"Don't tell her that," Bonnie said, too late, as Gwen began to sniffle in earnest.

"Now you've done it," Diane said to Summer. "You should never say, or even imply, that you no longer need your mother's help."

"No, no, it's okay. Summer's right." Gwen smiled through her tears and hugged her daughter, hard. "I'm proud of her independence. I want her to be able to look out for herself without me—that's always been what I wanted most for her. I'm going to be the happiest, most grateful mother on campus the day I drop her off at Penn."

Diane touched Summer on the arm. "If she's going to carry on like this, maybe you should drive."

Summer pulled away from her mother. "Mom, about that—"

"Don't worry, I was only kidding. I know you'll want to drive yourself." Gwen brushed a strand of Summer's long auburn hair out of her face and smiled. "I wouldn't embarrass you in front of all the other grad students in your department."

"It's not that. I—"

"Better quit while you're ahead, or she'll be walking you to your first class as if she were dropping you off for your first day of kindergarten," Diane advised. Gwen laughed, and after a moment's hesitation, Summer joined in.

Sylvia stole a glance at Sarah and found her watching Summer and Gwen wistfully.

Just then the court clerk opened the door and summoned them into the room. Diane, Tim, and the two boys entered first, the Elm Creek Quilters close behind. The zoning commissioners sat at a long, raised table at one end of the room, and as Sylvia took a seat with her friends in the row of chairs behind the Sonnenbergs, she caught a glimpse of Mary Beth, Diane's next-door neighbor, seating herself on the other side of the aisle. She was the rude woman responsible for stirring up all this trouble. Sylvia frowned at her, but Mary Beth didn't notice.

The exemption hearing lasted less than an hour. Diane and Tim presented their appeal, including facts such as the report Summer had found about a similar case in Sewickley, but in the end, Mary Beth's petition and the long-standing ordinances restricting recreational construction in their historic neighborhood swayed the commission's decision. They ruled against the Sonnenberg family, five votes to two, with one abstaining.

The boys were shocked by the loss, which Sylvia found heartbreaking. Diane accepted the Elm Creek Quilters' hugs and condolences, ignored Mary Beth's smug glare, and nodded when Tim murmured that it was time to go. She took each of her sons by the hand and left the municipal building with her chin up. Watching her, Sylvia felt a surge of pride for her friend. The Sonnenbergs had not won, but they had not been beaten, either.

On the drive back to the manor, Sylvia and Sarah talked about Diane's predicament and wondered if she had any other options. Sylvia was at a loss for suggestions. Besides, her meddling hadn't done anyone any good lately, so perhaps it would be best if she kept her ideas to herself.

Later that evening, Sylvia was too frustrated to sleep. Alone, she wandered outside through the back door of the manor and sat on the steps, watching the sun set through the trees. Their branches were covered with so many leaves that she could hardly make out the barn anymore, unlike that winter day several months ago when she had looked out on this same scene from the kitchen window. That was the day she had phoned Sarah's mother and put her misguided reconciliation plan into motion. How arrogant she had been to think that she could heal the rift between those two stubborn, deeply hurt women.

Gradually darkness fell over Elm Creek Manor, and a cool breeze began to stir. Sylvia wrapped her arms around herself to ward off the chill. Andrew's motor home was dark. She wondered if he was sleeping or if he was sitting awake as she was, thinking of his wife or his two children. His daughter had phoned earlier that day to ask Andrew when she should expect him. Sylvia didn't know what he had told her. Perhaps he would pack his suitcase in the morning and leave right after breakfast. Sylvia felt a pang at the thought, but she knew he had obligations to his family. Already he had stayed longer than he had intended, and surely he was running out of things to do. How many times could he go trout fishing with Matt before he tired of it? How many picnics in the north gardens could one man possibly bear? She was no charmer, she knew that. She had too many sharp corners and brittle edges, not like Claudia and Agnes, beautiful and charming in very different ways. Or at least they had been. The

Agnes of fifty years ago had merged in Sylvia's mind with the woman she knew today, but Claudia would forever remain a young woman not yet thirty, beautiful and bossy and alive, just as she had been when Sylvia last saw her.

Suddenly a faint creak broke the still night air. Sylvia glanced in the direction of the sound to find Andrew leaving his motor home. Unconsciously, she sat up straighter as he approached. He carried something in his right hand, and as he came closer, she saw that it was a sweater.

"You looked chilly," he said, draping it over her shoulders.

"Thank you." She drew the sweater around herself as he sat down beside her. She tried to think of something to say. "Beautiful night, isn't it?"

He nodded, and they sat for a moment in silence, watching the stars high above the trees along Elm Creek.

"You're not usually so quiet," Andrew eventually said.

"Yes, I am," Sylvia said. "I don't think one needs to chatter on and on unless one has something to say. You must be confusing me with Agnes."

"No, no." Andrew chuckled. "I could never do that."

Sylvia wasn't exactly sure what he meant, but his voice warmed her as much as the sweater did.

A companionable silence fell over them again.

Andrew shifted beside her, resting his elbows on his knees. "Something on your mind?"

"Why do you ask?"

"Something's keeping you up tonight. Is anything wrong?"

"Oh, no. I'm fine," Sylvia said briskly, forcing out a smile. "I'm just enjoying the night air."

"Is that so." He regarded her wryly. "I think I know you well enough to see when you're not happy. But you go right ahead and keep your secrets, Sylvia. I know better than to try to pry them from you."

Sylvia's smile faded. She did have her share of secrets—no one lived to her age without accumulating at least a few. But some secrets weighed too heavily on her heart, and the longer she kept them inside, the more they pulled her down.

She found herself telling Andrew about Sarah and Carol, how she had hoped to bring them together and how she had failed. She told him how much it pained her to see them estranged, and how she loved Sarah as if the young woman were her own child, how Sarah's joys brought her such delight, and how Sarah's sorrows pained Sylvia as if they were her own.

As she spoke, Andrew listened without interrupting. He didn't tell her that the problem wasn't as bad as she thought, in that infuriating, patronizing way so many men had. Nor did he try to solve the problem for her. All he did was listen, fold his hand around hers, and share her burden. And that, she realized, was exactly what she needed.

# Chapter Eight

As she left her office in the computer sciences building late Tuesday afternoon, Judy thought about the round robin quilt. It was already beautiful, even without Agnes's center motif, which apparently was going to remain a heavily guarded secret. Whenever Sylvia wasn't around to hear, the other Elm Creek Quilters would beg Agnes to show them her progress—but each time she refused. She wouldn't even give them a hint. "You want to be surprised, don't you?" she would ask, smiling.

"No," Diane would retort.

But Agnes merely laughed and brushed aside their questions, no matter how persistent they became. All she would reveal was that she was using appliqué rather than piecing, which they had assumed anyway. Not even Bonnie could equal Agnes in appliqué.

Maybe she should use appliqué, too, Judy thought as she crossed the Waterford College campus, heading for home. It would be easier to decide if she knew what Agnes was doing, especially since Judy was now making the fourth border rather than the last. According to their original schedule, it was Gwen's turn to work on the quilt, but Gwen had begged Judy to switch places.

"My life is in chaos right now, what with final exams coming up and Summer's graduation," Gwen had explained. "I'll owe you one."

Judy had laughed. "In that case, I'll do it." She had finals of her own to write and grade, but she didn't mind trading places with Gwen, although it meant coming up with a new design. The border she had originally planned had a scalloped edge, which made it unsuitable for its new position. She had studied the quilt that evening and had thought about it throughout the day, but try as she might, she couldn't think of what to add.

As she walked up her driveway, Judy decided that if inspiration eluded her much longer, she'd use Diane's trick and just set the quilt on point again with solid fabric triangles.

When she entered the house, she saw Steve in the living room on his knees, stuffing foam peanuts and wadded-up balls of newspaper into a trash bag. He looked up at the sound of the door, and before she could greet him, he held a finger to his lips. She nodded to show she understood. Emily was sleeping.

He crossed the room and wrapped her in a hug. "Welcome home," he murmured, as if she'd been gone for months instead of hours, and gave her a kiss that made her knees weak. It was the same welcome he'd given her every day for years, but she had never grown tired of it, and couldn't imagine she ever would.

"How long has she been napping?" Judy asked.

"About fifteen minutes." Steve kissed her again before returning to his work.

Judy inspected the mess. "What's all this?"

"My mom sent Emily a present."

Something in his tone made her wary. "What was it?"

"Well—" Steve hesitated. "There's good news and bad news." He rose, took Judy by the hand, and led her down the hall toward their bedroom.

"This must be the good news," Judy teased, but he passed their room and stopped outside Emily's.

"No, the good news is my mother finally understands that you're not Chinese."

Judy laughed. "At last. What's the bad news?"

Steve quietly pushed open the door. Emily was sleeping, tucked under the Log Cabin quilt Judy had made for her. She looked so adorable that for a moment Judy forgot her mother-in-law, so swept up was she in the fierce love she felt for her only child. Once she had feared that she loved Steve so much she couldn't possibly have enough love left over for anyone else, but her first glimpse of newborn Emily proved to her once and forever that she had been wrong, so wrong.

Then she saw the doll in Emily's arms. It was new, and it was wearing a kimono.

Judy turned to Steve and sighed. Steve grinned and closed the door.

"That does it," Judy said. "Next year for her birthday, I'm getting your mother an atlas."

"Or you could get her tickets to *Miss Saigon*."

"Oh, aren't you the funny one," she retorted, nudging him with her hip. He laughed and embraced her again, and kissed her, and after one more kiss they forgot about the mess in the living room for a little while.

As they lay in bed holding each other, Steve said, "I forgot to tell you. Your mom called."

"To give you more career advice, I presume?" Judy's mom considered writing a hobby, and she was anxious for Steve to find employment better suited for the husband of a computer science professor and the father of the most beautiful and gifted grandchild the world had ever seen. She'd been sending him advice columns and Help Wanted ads for years. Steve good-naturedly replied with thank-you notes and clips of his articles.

"Not this time." Steve stroked her shoulder. "She said you got a letter."

"At her house?"

"That's what she said."

"That's strange. I haven't lived there since college. Did she say who sent it?"

Steve shook his head and began to speak, but just then Emily called out from her bedroom. "Back to work," he said, kicking off the covers. They dressed quickly, and Judy went to see to Emily while Steve went to the kitchen to prepare supper. Steve jokingly called the routine they'd followed for nearly three years "tag-team parenting," but it worked well for them. Steve took care of Emily during the day while Judy worked; after supper, Judy minded Emily while Steve went off to the spare bedroom to write, or to the Waterford College library to do research. They spent the weekends as a family, away from their computers, away from their textbooks. The schedule didn't leave much time for Judy and Steve to spend alone as a couple, but that made the unexpected moments snatched from their busy days all the more precious.

It wasn't until after she'd given Emily her bath and put her to bed that Judy remembered to return her mother's phone call. Her mother lived alone in the house outside Philadelphia where Judy had grown up. When her mother's voice came on the line, Judy closed her eyes and imagined she was back there again, sitting at the kitchen table over a cup of tea, listening entranced to her mother's stories of the land of her birth and of Judy's, a country and time and place Judy no longer remembered. Every detail of that house was etched sharply into her heart. The sound of the winter wind in the trees, the smells of cooking, the sight of her father— young and alive in her memory, tall and strong as he mowed the lawn in summer or pushed her on the swing. One day, she knew, the big old house would become too much for her mother, and it would have to be sold. She hoped that day was a long time off, but she knew every year brought it closer.

"How is your husband, the writer?" her mother asked.

"He's fine. He has an essay coming out in the next issue of Newsweek."

"That's not bad," Tuyet said grudgingly. "I suppose that's good enough for now, until something better comes along." Judy suppressed a laugh. "And my granddaughter?"

"She's wonderful." Judy glanced down the hall to Emily's bedroom. "Except that today she told me she won't be eating any more green food."

"What? Green food—you mean, moldy food?"

"Of course not," Judy said, laughing. "I wouldn't feed her moldy food. I mean green as in peas, lettuce, broccoli."

"Oh." Tuyet was silent for a moment. "Tell her that I said she should eat whatever you serve."

Judy smiled. "Okay, I'll tell her." Not that it would make any difference. "Ma, Steve said you received a letter for me today."

Her mother went silent.

"Ma?"

"I'm still here." Her mother sighed, and Judy heard a chair scrape across the floor. "I don't know how to tell you this gently, so I'll just say it. The letter is from your father."

"What?"

"It's true. I'm holding it in my hand this moment."

Judy's heart seemed to skip a beat. The moment she had always dreaded had come. Her wonderful, vibrant mother, who had endured so much so bravely, was in decline, and more seriously and suddenly than Judy had feared. "Ma," she said carefully, "Daddy's dead."

"No, no," Tuyet said impatiently. "Not him, not your real father. Your other father."

Her other father. For a moment Judy's mind whirled as she tried to make sense of her mother's words.

Then she understood.

"Do you mean my biological father?" That had to be it, and yet it couldn't be. Judy had never heard from him, not once in all those years. His only contact with them had been through a lawyer more than thirty years ago, when he agreed to give up his parental rights so that her father could adopt her. Her father—that title belonged to the man who had raised her, who had married her mother. He had been her father in every way that mattered for as long as she could remember.

"Yes, your biological father. That is what I meant."

Judy took a deep breath and sank into a chair. "What does he want?"

"I don't know. I didn't open it. The letter is addressed to you, not me."

"Would you—" Judy swallowed. She felt ill, dizzy. "Would you open it and read it to me, please?"

"No."

"Why not?"

"If he wanted me to read this letter, he would have put my name on it, too. You can read it yourself when it arrives in Waterford. I will mail it to you in the morning."

Judy sighed, exasperated. She recognized that stubborn tone in her mother's voice. She would have to wait for the letter to arrive.

She told Steve about it as soon as she hung up the phone, but she said nothing to her friends. They knew little about her history; they knew she was the child of an American serviceman and that her mother had brought her from Vietnam to the United States when she was very young, but they knew nothing of the struggle to get here, nothing of the fear, that sense of being hunted. That was what Judy remembered most of their flight—the fear.

Since Tuyet had no money to pay for bribes and exit permits, she struck a bargain with an older woman and her family, who saw in the young Judy a ticket out of Vietnam. In exchange for gold, Tuyet claimed these people as her mother, her brother, and her niece, so they would be allowed to accompany them to America. Their money paid the way, but without Judy, they knew they had no chance of making it to the DP camps, let alone the States.

This family of convenience lasted until they were all safely in New York, when Tuyet and Judy were cast out. They took refuge in the small apartment of a distant relative, three rooms crowded with frightened, weary, bickering adults, waiting for a man Judy had never met to come rescue them. Months later, they instead received a letter denying his responsibility for Judy, his daughter, the child named after his own mother.

Judy remembered that, too, her mother crushing the letter in her fist and saying, "We do not need him. Remember that. We do not need him."

She said it with such determination that Judy believed her.

Since the man who had promised to marry her had changed his mind, Tuyet found work, first in a restaurant kitchen, where she met the woman who found her a better job in a hospital in Philadelphia. Some time later Tuyet moved them into an apartment of their own, a small place, with two rooms—a kitchen and a living room where they shared a sofa bed. Judy later realized that it must have seemed shabby and cramped compared to her grandparents' home in Saigon, the one her mother had fled in shame when the dashing army doctor's child in her womb became too obvious to ignore. But to Judy, the new place seemed bright and spacious. For the first time, she had felt safe and happy—except at night, when shadowed figures came out of the dark, spitting at her, striking her, shrieking in her native language *con lai, my lai,* names she did not understand.

Then Tuyet met John DiNardo. Like the man who had abandoned them, he, too was a tall American doctor, but this time the story ended differently. John DiNardo was kind and gentle, and Judy adored him, especially after he married her mother and adopted her as his very own child. After that, all the old fears had dissolved into the past.

What would the man who had denied her so long ago want with her now?

Tuesday night and Wednesday passed. She taught her classes at Waterford College and her workshop at Elm Creek Manor by rote. Her undergraduates were too preoccupied with their upcoming finals to notice, but the quilt campers sensed her distraction. She knew she must seem wooden and dull after Sylvia's crisp efficiency and Gwen's humor, but she couldn't snap out of it. Steve told her she had no reason to worry, but his words were no comfort. It wasn't worry she felt—in fact, she felt nothing. She was numb, as if her heart and mind had been encased in stone.

When she returned home from work on Thursday afternoon, she could tell from Steve's expression that the letter had arrived. She picked up the thick envelope from the table near the door and carried it into the kitchen. The return address was her mother's. She opened the envelope and found a second one inside.

She took a deep breath and sat down at the kitchen table. This envelope was addressed to Judy Linh Nguyen DiNardo—covering all bases, she supposed, with the first stirring of emotion she had felt since her mother's phone call. The name in the return address was Robert Scharpelsen of Madison, Wisconsin.

Wisconsin. She pictured rolling hills dotted with red barns and cows. So that's where he had been all these years. If he had married her mother, if he had come to New York for them as he had promised, she would have grown up in Wisconsin instead of Pennsylvania. She would have become a completely different person. She would not have met Steve; she would not have borne Emily.

Thank God Robert Scharpelsen had not come for them all those years ago. Thank God he had denied her. Her mother had been right. They did not need him. They had not needed him then and they did not need him now.

She sat there staring at the envelope for so long that eventually Steve spoke. "Are you going to open it?"

"Later." Judy stuffed the envelope into her purse and stood up. "Maybe." She went down the hall to Emily's room to read her a story, to play a game—anything to make herself forget.

Steve said no more about the letter that evening, and not once was Judy tempted to retrieve it from her purse and read it. Late that night, though, long after Steve had fallen asleep with his arms around her, she lay in the darkness, thinking. Robert Scharpelsen had blond hair, her mother had told her, blond hair and blue eyes. Judy saw nothing of him in her, and yet he was a part of her as much as her mother was. She pictured him, aged now, thin, the blond hair long gone to gray, sitting at a table, pen in hand, writing to the daughter he had abandoned a lifetime ago. What had he been thinking as he put the words down one by one? Why write now, when he had never needed to before? Was the letter an apology? An explanation? Was he dying, and wanted now to seek absolution? If so, he should have written to her mother. She was the one he had wronged.

She had a father. She did not need this man. She did not need his letter. She would destroy it unread—rip it up and burn the pieces. Let him wonder what had happened to her. Let him be the one abandoned. Let his words go unheard; however desperate he was to contact Judy now, her mother had been a thousand times more so as she waited for him to fulfill his promises. Let Judy's silence be his punishment, a small measure of justice seized on her mother's behalf, recompense for the many ways he had made her suffer for loving him.

She stole from bed, quietly, carefully, so Steve would not be disturbed, so he wouldn't ask her what she was doing, so he wouldn't stop her. In the kitchen, she took the letter from her purse and held it, feeling its weight, its thickness. He must have had a lot to say, and no wonder, after thirty years of silence.

Or perhaps he wanted to be sure that she would open the letter, so he had written page after page until he knew the letter would be too thick to tear. She could tear it up later, but she would have to open the envelope first. And once the envelope was open, it would take superhuman strength not to read at least one line of it.

She would read one line—just the first line—to see how he addressed her. That would tell her a great deal. There was a world of difference between "Dear Miss DiNardo" and "My dear daughter."

She took a deep breath and slipped her finger beneath the flap and opened the envelope. A single sheet of folded paper was tucked in front. Judy removed it, left the rest of the contents in place, and set the envelope on the kitchen counter.

Her hands trembled as she unfolded the paper and began to read the typed words. "Dear Judy," she read aloud, and the words seemed to stick in her throat. She forgot her resolve and read on:

*Dear Judy,*

*I put my father's name on the outside of the envelope because I wanted you to have the choice to throw this letter away unread. My father's name alone would indicate the nature of this letter, and if you wanted no part of him, or of me, you wouldn't have to read any further than the return address before tossing it in the trash. That is, as long as you know who my father is, and what he is to you.*

*You see, I wrote "my father," but I should have written "our father." I am your sister, your half sister. My father tells me you already know about him, though not about me. I hope his memory is accurate, and that this is not the first time you are hearing this news. If it is, please accept my heartfelt apologies. No one should have to receive news like that in a letter.*

*I've tried to write to you so many times. I've tried to imagine what it must be like to be you, and whether you would even want to hear from me. You have a life of your own and maybe you don't want a sister—a stranger—coming into it after all these years. I finally realized that I can never know what it's like to be you. I can't know whether you would want to hear from me. But I do know that if our places were reversed, I would want to hear from you. I would want to know I had a sister.*

*I would have written to you sooner, but I only learned of you two months ago, after my mother's death. Before then my father never spoke of you—out of respect for my mother, I guess. I'm trying to understand things from his point of view, but it's hard not to be angry at him. All my life I've had another sister and I never knew it.*

*My father has told me little of his relationship with your mother, but it is enough for me to infer that they did not part amicably. I would understand if you hate my father and do not want to see him. However, I hope you will be willing to see me. I really want to meet you.*

*Because of my father's declining health, he is unable to travel to Philadelphia and I am unable to leave him. It is my hope that you will use the enclosed voucher to purchase a plane ticket to Wisconsin. You might wonder why I sent it—I admit I wasn't sure if it was the right thing to do or if it would be offensive. I finally decided to send it to show you how much I want you to come, and so that you can do so without any cost to yourself.*

*If you can't come, I hope you will at least write back to me. I am more eager to hear from you than I can express in a letter.*

*Your sister,*
*Kirsten Scharpelsen*

*P.S. You have other family here, too. I have a brother and a sister.*

---

Steve had come into the room while she was reading, and now he stood behind her, rubbing her shoulders and waiting for her to finish. Judy read the letter again, this time aloud. Her voice shook, but whether from nervousness or anger or something else entirely, she wasn't sure.

"I have a sister," she said at last, without emotion, spreading the letter flat on the counter.

"Two sisters and a brother," Steve said. He picked up the envelope and fingered through the remaining contents.

Anger surged through her. She snatched the envelope and flung it down on the counter. "She sends me a travel voucher, like I'm—like I'm some kind of refugee."

"You were, once."

"Not anymore. I don't need her charity."

"She doesn't know that."

"That's not the point."

"Don't be angry with her. I think she means well," Steve said. "All she knows is that her father abandoned you in Vietnam. She probably feels a lot of guilt for what he did, for what he didn't do. It sounds like she's trying to make up for his mistakes."

Anger still roiled in the pit of her stomach. " 'If our places were reversed,' she says. As if she could ever understand my place. 'I can infer they did not part amicably.' What a joke. He abandoned us. We could have died for all he cared. If we hadn't got out before the VC took Saigon, I can't even imagine what would have happened to us. They weren't exactly kind to the children of the enemy and the women who bore them."

She was shaking. Hot, angry tears blinded her until she couldn't read the letter anymore. Steve put his arms around her and murmured soothingly. She clung to him, and his strength bore her up until she could calm herself. She had never been so angry, so hurt, in all her life. It bewildered and alarmed her. In the back of her mind she knew the letter should not hurt so much. She should be joyful. After all these years, she had a sister, a sister who wanted to know her.

"He couldn't even write to me himself," she whispered, stunned by how much that pained her.

"Maybe he's not able," Steve said. "He doesn't sound like he's in the best of health. If—" He hesitated. "You might not have much longer to meet him."

"Do you think I should?"

He stroked her cheek. "I think you should consider it very carefully and then do what you feel is best."

His expression was so compassionate it made her heart ache. Steve loved her so much, and yet Robert Scharpelsen could not bring himself to love her even a little.

But she had two sisters and a brother.

"I wish she would have given me more information," Judy said. She picked up the letter and scanned it, hungry for details. "I don't know how old she is, the names of her brother and sister—there's so much she doesn't say."

"My guess is she's younger than you."

"Oh. Well, of course, she would have to be. He was with my mother for two years before he went back to the States and remarried. Married," she corrected herself. Her mother had considered Robert Scharpelsen her husband, but they had never officially wed.

"You're right, but that's not why I thought so. It's her style of writing. She's obviously educated. She has a solid grasp of grammar and access to a laser printer. I'd say middle class, possibly upper middle class, or aspiring to be. She's young, though, maybe in her mid to late twenties. Notice the way she uses overly formal diction sometimes and other times she sounds like an anxious teenager?" He pointed to the fourth paragraph. " 'But it is enough for me to infer that they did not part amicably' is soon followed by 'I really want to meet you.' She's trying to be formal and dignified but her youth keeps sneaking through, probably because she's furious at her father for keeping you a secret."

Judy stared at him. "You got all that from two sentences?"

"What can I say?" He shrugged. "I'm a writer. After you and Emily, words are my life."

In spite of everything, Judy smiled. She hugged him to show him she was all right, then took his hand and led him back to their room. The sleep that had eluded her came quickly now that she knew what the letter said.

The following evening, Judy went to Elm Creek Manor. Ordinarily she would have brought Emily along, but she expected to be out past her daughter's bedtime. She felt guilty for taking up Steve's writing time when it was her turn to watch their daughter, but he assured her that he'd had a productive afternoon. "She'll be going to bed soon, anyway. I can write then. Besides," he added, smiling, "I'll be able to work better if I know you're having fun with your friends instead of worrying about the letter."

For his sake she tried to put the worries out of her mind as she drove through the woods to Elm Creek Manor. An evening with her friends was exactly what she needed. Tonight the Elm Creek Quilters had invited a group of theater arts students from Waterford College to put on three one-act plays for their guests. Judy joined the others in taking care of the last-minute tasks before the performance. Then she took a seat with a few guests she had befriended that week and settled back to enjoy the show. Before long she lost herself in the drama onstage, but all too soon the show ended. As the delighted campers showered the actors with applause, all the worries crowded in—the letter, her siblings, her father, the voucher—forcing out thoughts of the play, of her friends, of everything but the decision she had to make.

After the students left and the quilters went upstairs to their rooms, the Elm Creek Quilters and their friends returned the ballroom to its normal state. From where she was working on the dais, Judy saw Sylvia and Andrew putting away the audience's chairs. They were talking and laughing quietly, somewhat apart from the others.

It touched Judy's heart to see Sylvia and Andrew together and happy. Maybe she was imagining things, but there seemed to be more than friendship between them. Judy had never told her so, but she admired Sylvia very much and hoped that she had indeed received the blessing of new love in her golden years. If anyone deserved that, Sylvia did. She had lost so much, and yet she had never succumbed to despair. In many ways, Sylvia reminded Judy of Tuyet.

Suddenly, an image flashed into her mind—her mother and Robert Scharpelsen, both alone again, rekindling their long-dead love. A wave of nausea swept over her.

"Judy?" Matt took her by the arm to steady her. "Are you all right?"

Judy nodded, unable to speak. No, that couldn't be what Kirsten intended. Mrs. Scharpelsen's passing was too recent, Robert's health too uncertain. Either way, Judy's mother would never consider it. She had not even wanted to read Robert's letter. To do even that would dishonor the memory of her husband.

"Judy?" Gwen said, alarmed. "Are you ill?"

The others, hearing Gwen's words, looked up. "I'm fine," Judy assured them, but to her dismay, they began to gather around.

Carol brought her a chair and maneuvered her into it. "Could someone please get her a glass of water?" she asked, pressing a hand to Judy's brow and peering intently into her eyes. Summer nodded and ran off.

"Really, everyone, I'm fine," Judy insisted. She almost laughed when Carol lifted her wrist and began taking her pulse, but it came out as a sob. "It's late. I'm tired, that's all. I'm not sick."

"Let Carol be the judge of that," Diane said.

"Have you been under stress lately?" Carol asked.

That was an understatement. "Maybe a little."

"What's wrong?" Bonnie asked.

"Yesterday I—" Then Judy fell silent. She looked around at her friends' faces. They looked so worried, so concerned for her well-being. This wasn't how she had wanted to tell them, but with everyone watching her, expectant and anxious, she had no other choice.

She took a deep breath and told them about the letter, and as she shared her worries, she felt them lessening. She had almost finished when Summer came racing back with a glass of water. Judy thanked her and drank it, as grateful for the pause in which to collect her thoughts as for the water itself. Then she told them that she wasn't sure what to do next. Her thoughts were in such turmoil that she feared she'd never sort them out.

"Take all the time you need," Gwen urged. "You don't have a deadline."

"But I do," Judy said. "Kirsten hints that he's in poor health. If I don't see him soon, I might never have the chance."

"That's his loss," Summer snapped. "He had all your life to see you. You don't owe him anything."

Everyone looked at her, astonished by the sharpness in her voice. Summer, who was usually as sunny and cheerful as her name, was sparking with anger. When Gwen sighed and put an arm around her, Judy remembered that Summer, too, had never known her father.

"Summer's right," Diane said. "He had his chance, years ago. Why is he so interested in seeing you all of a sudden? He probably needs a kidney or something. Well, I say don't give it to him."

"Diane," Sylvia admonished.

"War can do strange things to a man," Andrew said. "He made some bad choices in the past; there's no denying that. Even so, maybe it's time to forgive him."

"He doesn't deserve it," Diane said.

Andrew shrugged. "I don't know if that's for us to decide."

"Forgiving him and going to see him aren't the same thing," Sarah said. "Judy could just write him a letter. If she goes to see him, that might make everything worse."

Carol made a strangling noise in her throat and sat down on the edge of the dais, her back to them. Sarah didn't seem to notice.

Matt pulled up a chair beside Judy. "I think maybe I know a little of what you're feeling. I don't know why my mom took off when I was a kid, and I probably never will, but when I got older I finally realized it wasn't because she didn't love me. It wasn't because I wasn't good enough. Something in her just told her she wasn't ready to be a mom, to have a family." He rested his elbows on his knees, thinking. "If she wrote to me tomorrow . . . I think I'd go see her. I think I'd like to give her the chance to make peace with me and with herself."

Judy nodded. Some of what he said made sense to her, but other parts simply didn't fit. Unlike Matt's mother, Robert Scharpelsen must have been ready for a family or he wouldn't have raced off to Wisconsin to start one as soon as his tour of duty was over. And unlike herself, Matt had no reason to feel as if he would be rejected simply for who and what he was. Judy was *con lai*, a half-breed. Her American blood made her an outcast in the land of her birth, and her Asian heritage could earn her the same treatment from her white relatives. She didn't know much about

Robert Scharpelsen, but what she did know suggested that he probably thought of her as diseased wood to be excised from the family tree.

She was proud of who she was, but her pride did not blind her to the fact that some people considered her beneath them because of her ethnicity. Robert Scharpelsen could be one of those people. Why should she go see him so he could fling the acid of his prejudice in her face?

"Give him a chance," Carol said, as if overhearing her thoughts. "He might surprise you. Maybe it wasn't neglect that kept him from contacting you sooner than this. Maybe it was shame. He's probably as nervous as you are, and he has just as much at stake."

"We're forgetting something," Agnes said. "This isn't about Judy's father, and how he feels, and what he deserves or doesn't deserve. He isn't the one who wrote to her." She turned to Judy. "This is about your sister. She wants to see you. Don't punish her for what your father did."

Her gaze was so imploring, so full of regret for her own missed opportunities, that Judy's anger and confusion dissipated. Her thoughts became clear for the first time all week. She knew what she had to do. It was the only possible choice and always had been.

But before she informed Kirsten that she would be accepting the invitation, she had to speak to her mother.

First she told Steve, who didn't seem surprised by her decision. "Do you want me and Emily to come with you?" he asked as they held each other in bed that night.

Judy thought of how proud she was of her family and how pleased she would be to show off her wonderful husband and her beautiful daughter. Surely, Robert would want to see his grandchild. But what if he rejected them both? Nowhere in Kirsten's letter had she written that her father looked forward to seeing Judy. Maybe he didn't want them to come.

Judy could bear his rejection; she was used to it. But she would not subject Emily to anyone's contempt.

"I think it's best if I go alone," she told Steve.

"Maybe next time." He shifted in bed and held her close to him. "Or maybe we can invite them out here."

"Sure," Judy said, though she didn't want to think about a next time. One visit, one weekend, was difficult enough. She had to survive this initial meeting before she could contemplate building a long-term relationship with her father's family. Besides, after her visit, perhaps neither side would want that.

On Saturday morning, while Emily was "helping" Steve work in the yard, Judy called her mother. Tuyet asked about Steve and Emily but said nothing of the letter. There was not even a hint of curiosity in her voice. Either she hid it well or she had truly put Robert Scharpelsen so far out of her thoughts that she honestly didn't care what he had to say.

When Judy told her who the letter's real author was, however, her mother grew excited. "I do not care about that man," she declared, "but this, this is different. This is wonderful news. I always regretted that I did not give you a brother or sister, and now you have one."

"I have more than one," Judy told her, and read her the letter.

Tuyet remained silent for a long moment after Judy finished. Then she let out a heavy sigh. "What are you going to do?"

Judy had already made up her mind, but out of respect, she asked, "What do you think I should do?"

"You should cash in the voucher and use the money to come see me, instead."

Judy erupted into peals of laughter. "Oh, Ma." It seemed ages since she had laughed, and it felt as if iron bands compressing her chest had been released. "You know I can't do that. I'm going to return the voucher to Kirsten. We can still come visit you later this summer."

"So you aren't going to Wisconsin. Good. That is the right decision."

Judy hesitated. "Actually, I . . . I think I'm going to go."

"Why would you want to do that?"

"I want to see my sister. You yourself said it's wonderful that I have a sister. What good is having a sister if I refuse to see her?"

"Write her a letter or call her on the phone."

"I'll do that, too." She would have to, she suddenly realized, in order to make arrangements for the visit. Nervousness stirred in her stomach. She wasn't ready to talk to Kirsten yet.

"I see." Her mother's voice was crisp. "So this is how you respect the memory of your father. You try to replace him."

"How can you say that?" she asked, shocked by the cutting words. Even after five years, her grief over her father's death was as tender as a new bruise on her heart. "I'm not trying to replace Daddy. No one could replace him. That's the cruelest thing you've ever said to me."

"I'm sorry," Tuyet replied, uncharacteristically meek.

"I'm not going to see him; I'm going to see Kirsten. She's the one who invited me." Agnes's words came into her mind. "I don't think it's right to punish her for what Robert did."

There was a long pause.

"Bob."

"What?"

"He called himself Bob, not Robert."

Judy took a deep breath. "Fine. Bob it is."

"Is that what you are going to call him when you see him?"

"I—I don't know." She couldn't picture calling him Father, but Mr. Scharpelsen would be too stiff and formal. The thought of calling him Bob, the name her mother had used, didn't feel right, either. Maybe if she was careful and creative she could avoid using his name altogether.

"Maybe he will tell you what to call him."

"Maybe."

"If you are going, why not use their voucher? Make them pay for the privilege of seeing you."

"I want to pay for it myself." She had to, she knew, or the Scharpelsens could never see her as their equal.

Her mother seemed to understand that, perhaps even to approve. Before she hung up, she wished Judy a safe journey. "I hope the visit goes well," she said. "If it seems appropriate, give the family my best wishes. But only if it seems appropriate. Use your best judgment."

"I will," Judy promised, relieved that her mother had given the trip her blessing. Until that moment, Judy had not realized she sought it.

She hung up and went outside to join her husband and daughter. She shoved all thoughts of Kirsten and Robert out of her mind for the rest of that day and most of the next. When she returned from welcoming the new campers to Elm Creek Manor on Sunday afternoon, she went to Steve's office to search the Internet for airline and hotel information. A far more difficult task followed: writing a response to Kirsten's letter. She struggled for hours to find the right words, the right tone. In the first draft she sounded chilly and reserved; in the second, too eager and grateful. After several revisions and a great deal of pacing, she settled on a simple, brief reply:

> *Dear Kirsten,*
>
> *Thank you for your recent letter and your kind invitation. I was pleased to learn that I have two sisters and a brother, and I look forward to meeting you soon. If it would work well with your schedule, I thought I could come the evening of Friday, May 8th, and stay until the afternoon of Sunday, May 10th. I hope the short notice will not be an inconvenience. Because of obligations at the college where I teach, my next available weekend will not be until July. If the later date would be better, please let me know.*
>
> *I appreciate the generous offer of the travel voucher, but I plan to make my own arrangements. Perhaps you could use it to visit me and my family here in Pennsylvania sometime. I know my daughter, Emily, would love to meet her new aunt.*
>
> *Yours truly,*
> *Judy DiNardo*

She tried to sign the letter "Your sister," as Kirsten had, but she couldn't do it.

Kirsten responded by return mail. "I'm so glad you decided to come!" she wrote. "I can't wait to meet you in person." Her enthusiasm pleased Judy, who wished she felt the same. She was looking forward to the visit only in the sense that she was looking forward to getting it over with.

The Elm Creek Quilters supported her without fail, as they always did—but they showed varying degrees of approval for the trip. Diane and

Sarah said nothing more about their misgivings, but their expressions revealed their reluctance. Gwen, Summer, and Bonnie told her they were certain the visit would go well. But it was Sylvia and Agnes who convinced her she had made the right decision. Privately, each told Judy that even if she never saw the Scharpelsens again, she would rest easier knowing she had made the effort. "You're right to do this now, before it's too late," Sylvia said, and Judy's heart went out to the older woman. She hoped Sylvia would find some comfort in knowing that Judy had learned from Sylvia's mistakes.

That week, Judy proctored the final exams for her two classes and turned in her course grades. She planned her wardrobe and bought film for her camera. On Thursday afternoon, she dug out her garment bag from the back of the hall closet—and that was when she realized what border she would add to the round robin quilt. When she closed her eyes she could picture it so clearly that she wondered how she ever could have considered any other pattern.

She left the garment bag in the hallway and hurried downstairs to her basement studio, where she searched through her fabric stash for the perfect shades of green and blue and gold. She traced pieces and cut cloth at a feverish pace, too busy to think, too busy to worry. Before she knew it, Steve was calling down from the top of the stairs to tell her supper was ready.

Guiltily, Judy swept the quilt pieces into her sewing kit. Steve had let her work undisturbed all afternoon, caring for Emily in Judy's place instead of writing. He had a deadline, too, but he had not complained.

She hurried to the kitchen in time to help him carry the dishes to the table. "Steve, I'm sorry," she said. "Next week, I swear—"

He stopped her with a kiss. "Don't be sorry. I understand." He grinned and gave her a tickle under her chin before turning to lift Emily into her chair.

Judy felt tears spring into her eyes as she took her seat. Steve was the kindest man she had ever known. She was more grateful for him that evening than she had ever been.

Later, Judy read Emily a story and tucked her into bed. She knelt on the floor beside her and brushed her soft, dark bangs off her forehead. "Honey, there's something I want to tell you."

"I know already."

Judy's eyebrows rose. "You do?"

Emily nodded, her dark eyes solemn. "Daddy told me."

That surprised her; they had agreed that Judy would tell her about the trip. "He did?"

Emily nodded again. "You're very busy. That's why you can't play."

Judy felt a pang. "Oh, sweetie." She stroked Emily's hair. "You're right. I've been very busy lately and I haven't paid enough attention to you, have I?"

Emily shrugged and said nothing, hugging the kimono-clad doll.

"You've been a very good girl not to complain."

"Daddy said not to," Emily confided.

Judy laughed. "Oh. Well, even so." She hesitated, wondering what to tell her. How much would she understand? She knew that Grandpa was Steve's daddy and that he lived in Ohio; she also knew that her other grandfather was Judy's daddy, who had gone to heaven before she was born. Would it confuse her to learn that she had a third grandfather? And what if the weekend visit went poorly and there was no more contact between the families?

Emily was still too young, Judy decided. Someday she would tell her everything, but not tonight.

"I'm going on a trip to see an old friend of Grandma Tuyet's," she finally said, picturing her mother tossing her head in scorn at the description. "When I get back, we'll have lots of time together, okay?"

Emily smiled. "Okay."

"You go to sleep now." Judy kissed her good-night and rose, turning off the light as she left the room and leaving the door ajar, the way Emily liked it.

The next day Steve and Emily saw her off at the regional airport. As she went to board her plane, Judy waved good-bye to her family with a sinking heart, seized with a sudden urge to cancel the trip. It was a mistake. It was too soon.

But instead she crossed the tarmac and boarded the plane.

The eighteen-seat prop plane looked like a wind-up toy. It needed a bumpy ninety minutes to carry its passengers to Pittsburgh, where Judy breathed a sigh of relief and transferred to a jet. The second leg of her journey was smooth enough for her to retrieve her sewing bag from her carry-on and piece a few seams of her round robin border. As she worked her needle through the soft fabric, the familiar motions soothed her.

There was a long layover in Chicago, but eventually she boarded another plane, the last, the one that would take her to Dane County Regional Airport and the family she dreaded meeting. This time she was too nervous to piece. For the rest of the flight she looked out the window, thinking.

When the plane descended through the scattered clouds over Wisconsin, Judy caught a glimpse of sunlight sparkling on a large lake—no, two large lakes separated by an isthmus. As they drew closer, she saw that the narrow strip of land was crowded with buildings; the most prominent, a dome-topped structure with four wings, was in the center. Judy craned her neck to watch it as they passed. When she couldn't see the building any longer, she turned her attention to the lake, a rich blue etched with the white wakes of boats.

The plane lurched suddenly. Judy faced forward and clutched the armrests of her seat, but it was not the turbulence that wrenched her stomach. She wished they could stay up there in the clear sky above the blue water, circling, drifting, eventually turning around and heading back east toward home.

The plane touched down.

Judy gathered her things and left the plane, the strap of her tote slung over one shoulder, her garment bag in her other hand. In the terminal people were shaking hands, embracing, calling out welcomes. She felt invisible, alone.

"Judy?"

She looked in the direction of the voice. A tall, slender woman was weaving toward her through the crowd. Her straight blond hair brushed gently at her jawline as she walked, and she looked to be at least five years younger than Judy.

The woman came to a stop in front of her. "Judy?" she asked hesitantly.

Judy nodded.

The woman smiled, delighted. "I'm Kirsten," she said, embracing her. "Welcome to Madison."

Judy returned the hug awkwardly. "Thanks." She wondered how Kirsten had recognized her, but after a quick glance around, she realized she was the only Asian-looking person who had gotten off the plane. She felt as if she had disembarked in the Land of Tall Blondes.

Before she could react, Kirsten took the garment bag from her. "Do you have any more luggage?"

"No, just this."

"Great, then we can get going. I'm so glad you're here. How was your flight?"

"Fine," Judy managed to say. Her sister was smiling brightly and practically skipping with delight as they made their way through the airport, while Judy felt as if her legs had turned to lead.

"My car's right outside," Kirsten said. "I'll give you the nickel tour on the way to my apartment. I live downtown, near campus. I have the spare room all made up for you."

"Oh. Um, actually, I have a reservation—" Judy fumbled for the paper in her pocket. "At the Residence Inn on, um, D'Onofrio."

Kirsten stopped short. "You're going to stay in a hotel?"

"Well, yes, I mean—"

"But D'Onofrio's all the way on the west side of town. Don't you—wouldn't you prefer to stay with me?"

Judy forced herself to smile. "I thought it would be better this way, you know, so that you can still have your privacy and we won't fight over the bathroom."

She said it so comically that Kirsten smiled, and the tension eased. Kirsten resumed walking, keeping up a steady stream of questions about Judy's trip as they left the airport. Kirsten's car was parked just outside at the curb, its hazard lights flashing. They loaded Judy's luggage into the trunk and drove off. Kirsten described the various sights they passed—the large domed structure, which turned out to be the capitol building; the University of Wisconsin; and State Street, a row of shops and restaurants between the capitol and campus.

"We'll go there tomorrow, after the Farmers' Market on the capitol square." Kirsten gave Judy a quick glance. "But we could stop by now and get something to eat if you're hungry. Or would you rather go to the hotel and rest?"

Judy hadn't eaten on the plane, and she was famished. They pulled into a parking garage—Kirsten called it a parking "ramp," which made Judy picture a large wedge jutting into the sky—and walked down the street to a small Turkish restaurant. The spicy aromas from the kitchen enticed them inside, and soon, over an appetizer of tabouli and hummus with wedges of pita bread, they were finally able to talk.

By the end of the meal, Judy felt more relaxed than she had since her mother told her about the letter. To her relief, Kirsten was friendly and talkative, accepting Judy's reserve for what it was—natural shyness, not a reluctance to be with her. For now that Judy was there, she found herself glad she had come and pleased by how well she and her sister got along. Kirsten was an intern at University Hospital, where her father had practiced before his retirement. She skimmed over their father lightly, but still Judy felt a fluttering in her chest at the mention of his name.

"What about your brother and sister?" Judy asked. "Are they still in school, too?"

"No." Kirsten took a hasty swallow of iced tea. "Daniel and Sharon both finished school a while ago."

Judy nodded. That made sense. Kirsten was twenty-eight, and Daniel and Sharon were probably only a few years behind her, beyond college age.

She had so many questions, but Kirsten was so eager to hear about Judy, her mother, and her life in Waterford with Steve and Emily that Judy barely learned anything about the other Scharpelsens. Kirsten answered questions about herself readily enough, but she evaded inquiries about Robert or her siblings. She did it so subtly and with such friendliness that it wasn't until the meal was over and they were walking back to the car that Judy realized she knew little more about her family than she had before the plane landed.

A shadow of doubt crept into her mind as they drove to her hotel, on the west side of the city. Judy gave Kirsten a hard look, but Kirsten was driving along, smiling and chatting happily, and suddenly Judy felt ashamed. She was paranoid to think Kirsten was hiding anything more than nervousness. This visit had to be as emotionally grueling for Kirsten as it was for Judy, perhaps even more so, since she had initiated the contact.

When Judy was finally alone in her hotel room, she kicked off her shoes, fell onto the bed, and closed her eyes, drained. Kirsten was as nice and as welcoming as Judy could have hoped, and yet their few hours together had wrung her dry. Tomorrow afternoon, when she would meet the rest of the family at Robert Scharpelsen's house, would be worse. She stretched out on the bed, soothed by the quiet darkness of the room, glad that she'd refused Kirsten's invitation to stay at her apartment.

Before getting ready for bed, she called Steve to tell him about her day. She spoke to Emily, too, or tried to—either her daughter had been struck by sudden shyness or she didn't quite grasp that the phone, unlike the television, allowed for two-way communication. Still, Emily's presence on the line cheered her, even if the only response was the sound of her daughter's breathing.

The next morning she woke feeling rested but jittery. Kirsten picked her up at eight-thirty, and they drove downtown for breakfast. The square around the capitol building had been closed to traffic, and the sidewalks were lined with booths and tables offering everything from fresh produce and baked goods to houseplants and cheese. Judy and Kirsten bought pastries and coffee at a stand on the corner and walked down the sloping street to a modern structure overlooking one of the lakes. They found seats on a stone bench and enjoyed the scenery as they ate and talked. Emily told her the building was the Monona Terrace, a convention center designed by Frank Lloyd Wright. Judy listened, nodding as Kirsten pointed out various sights along the lakeshore, glad for the cardigan she had worn over her long skirt and blouse. The sun shone brightly in a cloudless sky, but the breeze off the lake was cool.

When they had finished eating, they returned to the Farmers' Market and joined the orderly, steady flow of customers moving counterclockwise from stall to stall around the square. Every so often, Kirsten would stop at a stand and purchase something for the evening meal. On an impulse, Judy bought flowers to give to her father. When they had gone all the way around the square, they stowed their purchases in Kirsten's car and toured the capitol building. From the observation deck, Judy looked out over the lake and enjoyed the fresh smells of spring in the breeze, wishing that Steve and Emily had come with her. Everything was going so well that her earlier doubts seemed foolish.

Afterward, Judy and Kirsten walked down State Street window-shopping and people-watching. A little before noon they stopped at a restaurant for sandwiches, and as they ate, the conversation turned to Judy's journey from Vietnam to America. Judy told Kirsten the little she remembered; she had pieced together the rest from her mother's stories. Not wishing to offend, Judy glossed over the most difficult part of her history, in which she and her mother waited to hear from Robert Scharpelsen only to be disappointed by his cold response.

When Judy reached the part where her mother met John DiNardo, Kirsten shook her head in admiration. "Your mother sounds like an amazing person," she said. "How did she manage to land that hospital job?"

Judy shrugged. "Her experience on the army base helped, I suppose, and they were impressed by her fluency in so many languages. They really wanted someone who spoke English and Spanish, but she convinced them that someone who could speak Vietnamese, English, and French could easily pick up Spanish if she studied on her own. She did, too." Judy thought back to those nights when she and her mother would sit side by side at the kitchen table, Judy with a picture book, her mother with a Spanish text.

"I can understand why she would need English in the bar because of the GIs, but how did she happen to pick up French?"

"Vietnam was a French colony before—" Then Kirsten's words fully registered. "What do you mean, in the bar?"

"You know, the bar where your mother worked."

The skin on the back of Judy's neck prickled. "What?"

"In Saigon. Where they met. Where your mom met my dad."

"He told you they met in a bar?"

Kirsten nodded, confused.

"He said my mother was a bar girl?" Kirsten nodded again, color creeping into her cheeks. "My mother worked in the hospital on the army base with your father." Each word came out as sharp, as clear, and as cold as a splinter of ice. "She was a translator for the doctors and nurses and anyone else who needed her. My mother has never set foot in a bar except as a paying customer, and only rarely has she done that."

"But he said—" Kirsten fumbled for the words. "He told me—"

"And even if she had been a bar girl, what difference does that make? Bar girl or translator, he loved her enough to live with her."

"What are you saying? What do you mean, live with her?"

Judy stared at her, hard, the blood pounding in her head. Then she understood. "He told you she was just a one-night stand at a bar, didn't he?" This time Kirsten couldn't even nod, but Judy saw in her face that it was the truth. "He lied to you, just as he lied to my mother. They lived together for more than two years. He promised to marry her and bring her to the States. Then one day he didn't come home from work. She asked at the hospital, and you know what they told her? He had shipped out that morning. He had known about it for months, and yet he never saw fit to mention it. But she trusted him. She thought that if she could just get to America, he would take care of her—of us, because I was born a month after he left. She thought if he saw his child, if he saw me, he would marry her."

"But he couldn't," Kirsten choked out. "You don't understand. He couldn't marry her."

"Why? Because she was a bar girl?" Judy snapped. "No, you're the one who doesn't understand. He used my mother and abandoned us. Then he scurried off here and found himself a new wife, a white wife, someone he wouldn't be ashamed of at cocktail parties and neighborhood barbecues. That's the man your father is."

"No. No, you—you don't understand."

"I understand perfectly." Suddenly, Judy couldn't bear the sight of Kirsten, stricken and confused, struggling to speak, to make sense of the new information. She wanted to storm away from the table, to her hotel, to the next plane home. It would have been so easy, but something kept her in her seat, watching, listening, waiting to see what Kirsten would do next.

Suddenly, in a flash of insight, Judy realized that she was enjoying this. Seeing Robert cut down in Kirsten's eyes filled her with grim satisfaction. Let no one—least of all the daughter he had loved instead of herself—think of Robert as a good man, as a loving father. Let Kirsten know him for what he truly was.

Kirsten sat in silence, staring at the table, her face flushed, her eyes shining with tears.

Suddenly Judy was flooded by shame. "I'm sorry," she said. "I didn't mean it."

"No. You meant every word." Kirsten took a deep breath. "But you don't know the whole story."

"You're right. I don't." She thought of what Andrew had said, and reminded herself that Robert had been a young man when he knew her mother, a young man far from home in tumultuous times. Judy didn't know his side of the story, and though she doubted he could say anything to win her sympathies, she had no right to take out her anger on Kirsten. "I'm sorry."

"It's all right," Kirsten said, still not looking at her. She took another deep, shaky breath and fell silent.

They sat at the table without speaking until the server began clearing away their dishes. Then they paid the bill and left.

Judy wished she had not confronted Kirsten. She had ruined everything, just when they were getting along so well. Three times she tried to strike up a conversation as they walked back to the car, but Kirsten seemed unable to respond.

As they pulled out of the parking garage, Kirsten finally spoke. "Should I take you back to the hotel?"

Judy shot her a look. "I thought we were going to your apartment."

"I thought . . . I thought maybe you wouldn't want to anymore."

Kirsten looked very young as she stared straight ahead, her eyes fixed on the busy street crowded with cars and bikes and darting pedestrians. Judy reminded herself that she was the elder sister. She had started the argument; it was up to her to put Kirsten at ease.

"I don't want to go back to the hotel," she said. "I didn't come all this way to leave without meeting the rest of the family. We have to expect these kind of bumps along the way. We can't just give up the first time we run into difficulties."

Kirsten said nothing for a long moment. "You're right." She glanced away from the road to give Judy a pleading look. "I want you to know that I never intended to hurt you. If I could do it over . . ." She shook her head and drove on.

They went to her apartment, a small, one-bedroom flat on the third floor of a seventy-year-old building across the street from one of the lakes. Long ago, the building had been a pump station; though it had been remodeled for housing, the large steel pumps remained in the lobby. Kirsten came out of her silence to tell Judy this history, and by the time they reached her place, much of her earlier animation had returned.

Kirsten offered Judy a seat in the living room, a cozy place with a comfortable sofa, brick walls, and a sloped ceiling. They spent the afternoon talking over cups of tea. Judy finally began to hear more about life in the Scharpelsen family—their house on Lake Mendota, the misadventures of the three kids, Kirsten's mother's slow and painful death from cancer. As the hours passed, Judy finally began to feel as if she was getting to know these strangers. Sometimes, Kirsten broke off in the middle of a story as if to collect her thoughts; other times, she seemed vague or unwilling to reveal too much. Judy couldn't blame her. No wonder Kirsten was careful now, even tentative; neither one of them wanted to say anything that would spark more anger.

As evening approached, they went to the kitchen and prepared a large tossed salad using the produce they had purchased at the Farmers' Market. Then it was time to go to their father's house.

Judy's throat felt as if it were constrained by a fist, clenching ever tighter as they drove west, then north through a thickly wooded neighborhood of large homes on small lots. Through the trees, Judy could see the sun glinting off water, and she realized they were driving along the lakeshore.

They pulled into the driveway of a large, modern house on the lake. "This is it," Kirsten said, turning off the engine.

Judy fumbled with the seat belt and got out of the car. She followed Kirsten through the garage to a door leading into the house. Kirsten opened it and led her into the kitchen.

Classical music was playing on the stereo, and cooking smells floated on the air—bread, barbecue sauce, roasted corn. Judy stood frozen in the doorway, the bouquet of flowers in her hands, until Kirsten motioned for her to come forward.

A woman on the other side of the kitchen counter had her back to them as she took glasses down from a cupboard. She had blond hair like Kirsten's, only it was curly with a touch of gray.

Kirsten set the salad bowl on the counter. "Sharon?" she said. "There's someone I'd like you to meet."

Sharon turned—and as her eyes locked on Judy's, her expression went from pleasant to shocked in the instant it took for Judy to realize that this woman was not only older than Kirsten, but also surely older than herself. That was impossible, unless—

"My God," Sharon said. "I can't believe you did this."

"I had every right," Kirsten said. "She's our sister."

"How could you, after everything I said? Don't you care about Dad at all?"

"I care about Dad with all my heart. Don't you get it? That's why I had to do it."

Judy looked from one sister to the other, stunned. "You didn't know I was coming," she said to Sharon.

Sharon pressed her lips into a hard line and shook her head.

Judy turned and headed for the door.

"No, wait." Kirsten grabbed her arm. "Don't leave."

"I can't stay, not under these circumstances." Now she understood Kirsten's evasiveness.

"Please, Judy. I know now it was wrong, but at the time it seemed like the only way. Please don't go."

"Yes, now that you're here, why not stay?" Sharon yanked open a drawer and scooped up handfuls of silverware. "Why not ruin everything? Why not upset our father?"

"Stop it," Kirsten said.

"How dare you tell me to do anything after this stunt?" Sharon slammed the knives and forks onto the counter, then fixed her gaze on Judy. "How dare you show up now? Don't you realize how hard this will be for him?"

"I came because I was invited."

Sharon barked out a laugh and resumed her work, yanking open cupboards and slamming them shut. Just then, two boys bounded into the kitchen. When they saw Judy, they stopped short and eyed her with interest.

"Hi," said the eldest, a boy of around twelve. "Who are you?"

"She's your Aunt Judy," Kirsten said before Judy could reply.

The children's eyes widened. "Really?" the younger one asked.

Kirsten nodded, but Sharon rushed forward and thrust the silverware into the children's hands. "No, not really," she said. "Go set the table."

The elder boy shot Judy a look. "But Mom—"

"Now." Sharon clasped each boy by the shoulder and steered them out of the room.

When she was gone, Judy turned to Kirsten. "I'm not staying. I can't."

"Meet Daniel and Dad first," Kirsten begged. "Please. You came all this way."

All this way, and for what? To learn that one sister had deceived her and that another hated her on sight. What was worse, she now understood why Robert had never married her mother. Kirsten was right; he couldn't have. Sharon was older than Judy, and perhaps Daniel was as well. In an instant, Judy had gone from being the daughter of the wronged first wife to being the daughter of the other woman, and somehow that changed everything.

"Please," Kirsten repeated, pleading.

Judy gulped air, dazed—but she nodded. Kirsten took her hand and led her down the hallway in the direction of the music. In a front room, a man who appeared near Judy's age sat talking with another man several years older, their voices a low murmur beneath the sound of the stereo. On the other side of the room sat another man, worn and gray-haired. He stared out the window as if he were alone.

The first two broke off their conversation as Kirsten brought Judy into the room. "Daniel," she said firmly to the younger man. "This is our sister, Judy."

The color drained from the man's face. "Uh—hi, hello," he stammered, rising. He shook Judy's hand, his mouth opening and closing as if he wanted to speak but had no idea what to say. Kirsten didn't give him a chance to compose himself, but as she propelled Judy to the other side of the room, he found his voice. "Kirsten, don't," he said. "Dad's not having a good day."

Kirsten spun around to look at him. "Good day?" she echoed. "How long has it been since his last good day? You know as well as I do that they won't be getting any better." She continued on, taking Judy with her. Her pace slowed as they approached the old man, who didn't look up.

"Dad?" Kirsten said softly, kneeling down and placing a hand on his knee.

A muscle tightened and relaxed in the man's cheek, but his gaze never left the window.

Kirsten leaned to the side, interrupting his line of sight. "Dad? There's someone here to see you."

He blinked at Kirsten, who smiled and motioned to Judy. By instinct, Judy knelt beside Kirsten and tried to hand him the bouquet of flowers. He would not take it, so she placed it on his lap instead. Slowly his gaze traveled from Kirsten to the flowers to Judy, his brow furrowing in confusion. The muscles in his face worked as if he were struggling to focus on her features, fighting to recognize her.

Then he spoke. "Tuyet?"

A wave of grief, of pain, washed over her as the old man groped for her hand.

"No, Dad," Kirsten said gently. "This is Judy, Tuyet's daughter. Your daughter."

Judy saw at once that the old man didn't understand, if he even heard the words. She gave him her hand and clasped her other around them both. She felt the man's bones through his skin, which felt as dry and thin as paper.

"Tuyet," the man repeated.

Judy wanted to weep. Unable to speak, she squeezed the man's hand and got to her feet. Blinded by sudden tears, she hurried out of the room, back to the kitchen. She heard Kirsten call after her, but she couldn't stop. She raced out of the house, down the driveway, along the winding, wooded street until she reached the main road. She kept walking until she managed to hail a cab, which she took back to the hotel.

There were two messages waiting for her, one from Steve and one from Kirsten. She called Steve, but reached the answering machine. "It was a nightmare," she said. "I never should have come." Then she told him she'd see him tomorrow and not to call back, because she was taking the phone off the hook, in case Kirsten tried to reach her.

It was too early for sleep, but she pulled the heavy drapes shut until the room was dark, put on her pajamas, and crawled into bed. There she lay, thinking of how her world had shifted. She felt that she ought to be weeping, but the tears wouldn't fall.

Sleep came hours later.

She did not remember her dreams the next morning, but she woke feeling heavy and sore and as weary as if she had not shut her eyes all night. She had planned to spend the day with the Scharpelsens; since that was out of the question, she called the airline and arranged to be transferred to an earlier flight. After gathering her belongings, she checked out of the hotel and called a cab from the lobby.

When she went outside to wait, she saw Kirsten's car parked right out front. Kirsten was leaning against the passenger-side door, but she straightened at the sight of Judy. "Hi," she said.

Judy composed herself. "Hi."

"I figured you might leave early."

"I didn't see any point in staying."

Kirsten nodded in acceptance and opened the car door. "I'll take you to the airport."

"I already called a cab."

As if she hadn't heard, Kirsten went to the back of the car and opened the trunk. She didn't look at Judy as she picked up the garment bag and put it inside. Judy sighed and got in the car.

They drove in silence past the wooded neighborhood of her father's house, through the downtown, and across the isthmus. Kirsten didn't speak until they pulled up beside the airport terminal.

"I'm so sorry," she said. "I never meant for things to turn out like this."

"I know." Judy unfastened her seat belt and got out of the car.

Kirsten did the same, and came around the back to unlock the trunk. "Will I ever hear from you again?"

"I don't know." Judy grabbed her garment bag and put it on the sidewalk.

"Can I write to you?"

Judy shrugged.

"If I do, will you write back?"

Her voice was so forlorn that Judy relented. "Of course I will." The relief on Kirsten's face was so intense that Judy decided in an instant that this would not be the last time they saw each other. They were sisters. Even if the other Scharpelsens wished she would disappear forever, she and Kirsten could still be friends.

They embraced and promised to talk soon. Judy picked up her bags and entered the airport alone.

Sharon was waiting at the gate.

Judy approached, set down her bags, and eyed her unflinchingly, waiting for her to speak.

Sharon gave her a shaky smile. "I thought you would be here," she said. "It was the earliest flight. I figured you couldn't get out of here soon enough."

Judy didn't quite know how to respond to that, so she said nothing.

"I'm sorry about yesterday," Sharon said. "It wasn't your fault. None of this was your fault."

"If I had known Kirsten hadn't told you, I wouldn't have come."

"I know." Sharon looked away. "It was just such a shock, you see? I've known about you for years. My mother knew about you, too. Dad wanted to bring you and your mother to America, but my mother forbade him to have any contact with you. To her it was a matter of her husband's having an affair and flaunting his mistress in her face. She—she didn't understand, she couldn't have known what—what—"

Judy placed a hand on her arm. "It's all right. I understand."

"Will you stay? I'd like the chance to talk to you."

"I can't." Judy gestured awkwardly toward the gate. "I already changed my flight, and—"

"Of course. I see."

"But—" Judy hesitated. "Maybe we'll try again someday."

Sharon held her gaze for a moment. "I hope so." She clasped Judy's hand, then turned and walked away.

Judy watched until she disappeared around the corner, then found a seat and waited for her flight to be called.

🏠 🏠 🏠

Judy chose green for the homeland she had left behind and did not remember. She chose blue for the skies over the new homes she had made for herself with her mother and stepfather, with her husband and child, and with her friends at Elm Creek Manor. She chose gold for sunlight and illumination.

She set the block on point again, knowing that unexpected shifts could be as enlightening as they were jarring. She could not add solid triangles as Diane had done, however, not when the most fundamental assumptions of her life had been thrown into disarray. One day the pieces would settle into a pattern and she would feel whole again, but not yet.

Instead her triangles were composed of partial Mariner's Compass blocks, the diameter of the compass running along the longest side of each triangle. The compass was for all the journeys she had made in her life and all that she had yet to make. She knew that it was unfair to judge an entire journey by the first step. Often what seemed to be the right path turned out to lead in the wrong direction—but just as often, perseverance along a hard trail would lead to an important destination.

The potential rewards made the journey worthwhile.

# Chapter Nine

Carol watched as the round robin quilt took shape, admiring the Elm Creek Quilters' handiwork and wishing she could add a border of her own. Each time they brought out the quilt, she told herself it didn't matter that no one had asked her to participate. Since she didn't sew well enough yet, she would have declined rather than ruin the quilt. Still, it would have been nice if they had given her that choice. As always, she was the odd woman out, lingering just outside the circle of friends, wishing someone would invite her in.

Not that anyone other than Sarah had made her feel unwelcome. Sylvia was generous and kind, and the Elm Creek Quilters were friendly. With Sarah so hostile and eager for her to go away, though, Carol knew she would never feel wholly a part of the place her daughter called home.

This visit was not going at all the way Sylvia had assured her it would over the phone that winter morning several months before. Carol didn't blame Sylvia; the older woman had done all she could, more than anyone could have asked. Maybe it was time to give up. Carol could go home, back to her job and her empty house, and Sarah could resume her usual life. Maybe they would both be happier that way. Carol had not gotten along with her own mother; why should she expect anything different between herself and Sarah?

Sarah did not need her—not for advice, not for a shoulder to cry on, certainly not for friendship. Carol could leave Waterford with a clear conscience, knowing her daughter was in good hands. If Sarah's marriage faltered and failed, as Carol dreaded it would, the Elm Creek Quilters would bear Sarah up. Carol's presence would be unnecessary and unwelcome. She had warned Sarah against marrying Matt, and when her predictions about him came true, Sarah would hate her for it. She would never believe that Carol had hoped with all her heart that she had been wrong about him. Carol wanted to like Matt, despite his modest aspirations, despite his resemblance to her own husband, which she alone seemed able to detect. When she looked at Matt, Carol saw another man who was diligent and reliable instead of fascinating, a man who knew right from wrong—and would hold everyone to it no matter what the cost. How long could a man like that keep the interest of someone like Sarah? And what penance would he force from her if she failed him? In the years to come, would Sarah learn to accept her widowhood with some measure of relief, as Carol herself had done?

Carol could have used a group of friends like Sarah's to see her through the hard times after Kevin died, and those that had come before. But except for one brief period before she married, Carol had never had a group of girl friends, or even one best friend. She had been too bookish, too introverted, too sensitive. The discrepancy between the way things were and the way things ought to be had been very clear to her, but she had felt helpless, powerless to do anything to make up the difference. It had been easier to live in the safe, scripted world of stories than to try to change her own world.

She was the child of her parents' middle age, the baby they had neither expected nor wanted. Her mother accepted Carol's arrival with her usual resignation, but her father made it clear he wanted nothing to do with this new mouth to feed who hadn't the decency to be born a boy. He had the two sons he wanted and could afford; another boy would have been accepted grudgingly, but not this girl child who would drain him dry and contribute nothing. Well, at least when she got older she'd be able to help her mother around the house.

Since her older brothers had entered college by the time she started kindergarten, Carol grew up as an only child, but without an only child's sense of uniqueness and privilege. Her best childhood friends were Laura Ingalls, Nancy Drew, and the other smart, headstrong girls in books, girls who faced enormous challenges and always overcame them in the end. Carol longed to be like them. She wished she could melt into a novel and live there, and spend her days helping Pa harvest the wheat or solving mysteries with her friends Bess and George. At night before she drifted off to sleep, she would tell herself stories of the places and people she had read about, writing herself into the scenes. She was Nancy's younger sister, held hostage by a con man, rescued just in time by her lawyer father, Carson Drew. She was Laura's cousin visiting from western Minnesota, twisting hay into sticks to fight off the cold of the blizzards that howled around the small house in DeSmet. In her imagination she could be anything. She learned to welcome twilight.

As she grew older, she realized she could never climb inside a book and stay there, but at least she could get out of her parents' cold home. She could escape; she *must* escape. Her brothers had found jobs after college and came home only to visit. If she studied hard and earned good grades, she could do the same.

Her teachers were pleased to have such a diligent pupil, though they wished she'd smile more and play with the other children instead of spending lunchtime and recess with her nose in a book. In high school, her honors English teacher took notice of her, the quiet, brown-haired girl with the pale face and wide eyes who wrote such thoughtful essays. He recommended books to her—the classics, new works by emerging authors—and her world expanded. She confided in him as she had in no one else, and he encouraged her. He even told her he thought she could win a partial scholarship to college if she kept up her hard work.

His words left her with mixed feelings. A partial scholarship would do her no good if her parents were unwilling to pay the rest. They had sent her brothers to college, but Carol's future was never discussed. She studied even harder, determined to earn a full scholarship. If she did, perhaps she wouldn't have to tell her parents about her plans until it was too late for them to stop her.

In the summer before her senior year, she saved her baby-sitting money and the little her mother gave her for clothes until she had enough for her college application fees. She sent them off with a fervent prayer and waited.

When the news arrived months later, it both delighted her and filled her with dread. She had been accepted to Michigan State, but the scholarship they offered was even less than her most pessimistic estimates. Her tiny savings and a job on campus would help her make up some of the difference, but it was clear she would need her parents' help.

It took her a week to summon up enough courage. Her English teacher helped her plan what to say. She waited until after supper, before her father left for the living room and his evening newspaper, before her mother beckoned her to help with the dishes. Then she brought out the letter and told them she had been accepted to college.

Her mother looked surprised and pleased, but her father frowned. "Why do you want to go to college?"

"To continue my education," Carol said, as she had rehearsed. "To better myself. If I have a degree, I'll be able to make a good living."

"You mean you want to work?"

Carol nodded.

"Your mother doesn't work. She didn't go to college. You think you're better than her?"

Carol thought of her mother's life, of the endless cooking and cleaning and washing and sewing and picking up after her husband. Her parents were the same age, but her mother looked ten years older. "No. Of course not. I just want something different."

He shook his head. "You don't know what it will be like. There are smart kids in college, smart kids like your brothers. You won't be able to keep up."

His words stung, but she didn't let him see it. "I'm going to be class salutatorian, so I think I'll be able to manage. I know it won't be easy, but my teachers have confidence in me."

"College costs money."

"Not as much as you might think." She told him about the partial scholarship, too nervous to look at him as she spoke.

Before she could finish, he interrupted. "I won't waste money sending a girl to college. I'll pay all that money for a fancy education and for what? Will it make you prettier? Will it teach you to stop moping around? It's going to be hard enough for you to get a husband as it is. No man will want to marry you if he thinks you're smarter than he is."

A sour taste filled Carol's mouth.

Carol's mother reached over and touched her husband's hand. "What if she doesn't marry?" she said gently. They both turned to look at her. Carol felt herself shrinking beneath their scrutiny. She knew what they were thinking. They could not count on a man to come and take their ugly little mouse off their hands. They could not provide for her forever, and she would need to earn her keep.

Carol was torn between shame and hope as she waited for her father to speak. She knew she was plain and that no man would ever love her, but that was not why she wanted to go to college. It didn't matter. What was most important was that she got her education. It made no difference why or how.

Finally her father let out a heavy sigh. "How much will it cost again?" Wordlessly, Carol handed him the letter. He scanned it, frowning.

"There are lots of nice young men at college," her mother said.

"For all the good that'll do her." He set down the letter. "Well, I guess it wouldn't hurt. You can go."

Carol nearly burst with relief and gratitude. "Thank you," she said, her voice thick with emotion.

"What will you study? Typing? Nursing?" He grinned at his wife. "What kind of classes do they have for girls, anyway?"

"I'm going to study literature," Carol said. She wanted to be a college professor someday, and live the life her English teacher had described: hours spent exploring old libraries, discussing the great books with attentive pupils, writing and reading to her heart's content in an office full of books in an ivy-covered hall.

But her father's thick brows had drawn together. "Not with my money you won't. You'll be a nurse or a secretary, something practical."

"Literature is practical." She looked from her father to her mother and back, anxious. "I'm going to keep studying until I have my doctorate. I'm going to be a college professor."

"How many years will that take?"

"I—I don't know."

"She doesn't know," he repeated to his wife. Then he turned back to his daughter, stern. "I'll pay for the same as your brothers got, and no more."

"You won't have to pay. I'll get a scholarship—"

"Like you did this time?" He shoved his chair away from the table with such force that he knocked over the salt shaker. He rose and pointed at her. "You'll be a nurse or a secretary, and that's final."

Anger boiled up inside her. "One doesn't attend the university to become a secretary."

He slapped her across the face, hard. Her mother gasped. Carol clamped her jaw shut to hold in the cry of pain. Slowly she turned her head and met her father's gaze. He struck her again, harder, so hard he almost knocked her out of her chair.

"Then you'll be a nurse," he said. "Or you'll be nothing."

Her head was reeling, so she didn't see him leave the room. As she tried to regain her senses, she heard her mother go to the sink and turn on the tap. In another moment she was at Carol's side, holding a cool washcloth to her cheek.

"You shouldn't provoke him," her mother murmured. "You know how hard he works. He said you could go. If you had just thanked him and left it at that—"

Carol took the washcloth and shrugged her mother off, furious with her for cataloging her mistakes, for not standing up to her father. She felt her dreams of a scholarly life slipping through her fingers like the grains of salt her father had spilled on the yellow-checked tablecloth. Very well, she thought bitterly. She would be a nurse, if she had to. Anything to get out of there.

If she had been able to follow her dreams, perhaps she would have turned out like Gwen Sullivan, associate professor of American studies at Waterford College, Elm Creek Quilter, mother of a loving daughter, and woman of many friends. It could have been Carol teaching a workshop full of eager students and waiting for her turn to add a border to the round robin quilt.

Carol admired Gwen more than she envied her. Gwen's confidence and wit reminded her of the heroines from her childhood books. She attended all of Gwen's workshops, even when the lesson plan was the same as a previous week's. On that day, when Diane asked if she would mind helping some of the new quilters, Carol was so pleased that she almost forgot to say yes. She watched how Diane went from table to table assisting the campers and did the same. Fortunately, Sarah wasn't around to roll her eyes and scoff at the sight of neophyte Carol offering advice to women who had quilted for years.

Judy arrived as the workshop was ending, and she helped them straighten up the room for the next morning's class.

"How was your trip?" Diane asked. Carol wished she had thought of it first.

"I expected more cows," Judy said, trying to grin. "I didn't see a single one."

Gwen put an arm around her shoulders. "How was it really?"

Judy told them. Carol's heart went out to her as she spoke of her elder half sister's anger and her father's confusion. Carol didn't know how Judy could bear such disappointment after the hopes raised by Kirsten's invitation.

"What are you going to do now?" Gwen asked after Judy finished.

"I don't know." Judy sat down on the edge of the dais and rested her chin in her hands. "Part of me thinks I should wait for Kirsten to make the next move. Another part of me wants to block out every memory of last weekend and never think of them again."

"I can understand that," Diane said.

Judy gave her a wry half smile. Carol wished she could think of something comforting to say, but she couldn't. She settled for giving Judy a hug. Judy held on to her so tightly that Carol knew it had been the right thing to do.

Then Judy sighed and reached into her sewing bag. "The trip wasn't a complete waste," she said, producing a folded bundle of cloth. "I finished my border."

"Let's see," Gwen said, helping her unfold the quilt top. Judy had set the quilt on point as Diane had done, but not with solid triangles. Instead, a design resembling a compass or a sun radiated from each side, the longest, central points nearly reaching the corners. All of the points were split down the middle lengthwise, with dark fabric on one side and light on the other, giving the design a three-dimensional, shaded appearance. The tips were perfectly sharp, and the border lay smooth and flat.

"Your piecing is amazing," Diane said, echoing Carol's own thoughts. "Maybe this will finally convince these machine people to switch to hand work."

Gwen looked ready to retort, but before she could speak, they heard the door open on the other side of the room. It was Sylvia, carrying a purse and wearing a light blue dress and a white hat.

"Quick," Diane whispered, but Judy was already bundling up the quilt top. There wasn't enough time to return it to the bag, so she held it behind her back. They nailed nonchalant expressions to their faces and greeted Sylvia as she approached.

"You four are obviously up to something," she said, her eyes narrowing as she inspected them. "Are you going to tell me what it is, or will I have to guess?"

"We're not up to anything," Diane said. "We're just cleaning up after Gwen's workshop."

"Hmph." Sylvia looked around at the clean tables and the carefully swept floor. "You're going to have to do better than that."

Carol fidgeted beneath the woman's scrutiny. "It's—well, it's a surprise—"

"For Summer's graduation party," Gwen interrupted.

"I see. Very well, then, what is it?"

Judy gave her an apologetic look. "If we told you—"

"It wouldn't be a surprise. Yes, yes, of course. I understand." Sylvia adjusted her hat. "As a matter of fact, I have business of my own for Summer's party. That's what I stopped by to tell you. Andrew and I are driving in to town to fetch some decorations. We'll be back before supper."

Diane's eyebrows shot up. "You and Andrew, huh? Is this your official first date?"

"It is most certainly not a date. It's an errand."

"It sounds like a date to me," Gwen said.

"Why do I even bother?" Sylvia wondered aloud. "It's not you four troublemakers I wanted to talk to, anyway. I'm looking for Sarah. If I'm going to be driving downtown, I'd prefer to borrow her truck rather than ride in that enormous contraption of Andrew's."

"You can take my car," Carol offered, returning to the back table, where she had left her purse.

"Are you sure it's no trouble?"

"It's my pleasure," Carol said as she handed Sylvia her keys. The Elm Creek Quilters were always helping each other, and lending her car to Sylvia made her feel more like one of them. So did the way Sylvia went out of her way to include her. She could have said, "You three trouble-makers—and Carol." Carol didn't mind being considered a troublemaker the way Sylvia had said it, especially if that meant she was part of the group.

"Have a nice time," Judy said as Sylvia turned to go.

"Don't do anything I wouldn't do," Diane added.

Sylvia gave them a sharp look. "It's not a date." Before they could disagree, she left the room, more briskly than she had arrived.

Their mirth turned to relief as Judy brought out the quilt from behind her back.

"I swear that woman has quilt radar," Diane said. "She can sense a quilt within a hundred paces."

Gwen took the quilt from Judy. "We won't have to hide this much longer. I'll add my border, Agnes will finish the center, and we'll be ready to quilt."

Carol hoped that they would let her help.

The other women left, and as Carol went upstairs to her room near the library, she thought about Summer's party and tried to remember when she had last hosted one for Sarah. The wedding didn't count; Sarah and Matt had planned and paid for everything on their own. When Sarah graduated from Penn State, she might have had a party with her friends, but if she had, she hadn't invited Carol. Carol felt a twinge of guilt until she remembered Sarah's high school graduation. Carol had held an elaborate open house in Sarah's honor, even though Sarah had not been valedictorian or even salutatorian or even in the top tenth in her class. Carol had been disappointed. Sarah was such a bright girl; she could have been at the top of her class if she had spent as much time on her studies as she had her social life. She could have earned a full scholarship anywhere—Harvard, Yale, one of the Seven Sisters—if only she had been more industrious. But Sarah settled for the state school as indifferently as she had settled for B's when she could have earned A's, with no idea how much Carol envied her the opportunities she squandered.

No one had thrown Carol a graduation party, not her parents, who were still upset at her for wanting to go to college in the fall, and not her friends, since she had none. Her graduation from high school would have passed unnoticed if not for the ceremony itself, which her parents did attend, and her English teacher's kindness. On the last day of school he gave her three books: a dictionary, a thesaurus, and a leather-bound volume of the complete works of Shakespeare. Her heart leapt as she held the last and turned the gilt-edged pages to read the inscription. "These will take you anywhere," her teacher had written. "Congratulations, and may this be the first of many successes for you."

His kindness brought tears to her eyes. He alone knew how much it pained her to sacrifice one part of her dream so that she would not lose the whole. If only she were brave enough to defy her parents—but she was not. She would become a nurse rather than stay home until the unlikely arrival of a suitable young man bearing a marriage proposal. She would show her father that she was neither as stupid nor as useless as he thought. She would become the best nursing student in her class if it killed her.

And she did, but her father never knew it. He died of heart failure during her last semester, so he didn't see her graduate. Even if he had, he wouldn't have known how her joy was tempered as she accepted her degree; he would not have been able to detect a single regret, for life in his house had taught her how to hide her feelings. But beneath the placid surface, emotions churned. She never wished for him to die, not even when he beat her, but since it had happened, why then and not years earlier, so that she would have been free to choose her own path?

The thoughts shamed her, but she could not silence them.

She found a job in a hospital in Lansing, where almost by accident she made the first friends of her life. She and two other new nurses banded together for mutual support as they struggled with the nearly overwhelming demands of the hospital, and their need soon blossomed into friendship. At least once a week they went out in the evening together, to see a movie or to shop. Once, when they went bowling, a group of three men invited them out for a drink. After a quick whispered conference, they agreed. Boldly, Carol drank as much as the other girls and laughed nearly as loudly. It was the most fun she had ever had, and the next day, her friends insisted that one of the men had hardly been able to keep his eyes off her all night. She was pleased, but she didn't believe them. She didn't even remember Kevin's last name. She had preferred one of the others, a dark-haired lawyer who had put his arm around her as the men walked the nurses to their bus stop. He was well-read and charming, and she wished that it was he, not Kevin Mallory, who stopped by the hospital later that week and asked her out to lunch.

She accepted the invitation, and when he asked her out again, she agreed. With more surprised fascination than desire, she realized he was courting her. A year later, when he asked her to marry him, she would have laughed except he was so earnest.

"I'll be a good husband to you," he promised. "I'll take care of you. You won't have to work anymore. I love you and I want us to be together."

She stared at him, astounded. He loved her? He hardly knew her. She searched her heart and wondered if she had fallen in love with him without realizing it. She was almost certain she had not. He was a good, kind man, and she liked him, but passion didn't sweep over her when she looked at him. When he fumbled to kiss her good-night, she felt the pressure of his mouth but none of the electric warmth her friends described when confiding about their own trysts.

Still, she did like him, and she knew he would never hurt her. And a woman could not go through life alone.

"I'll need to think about it," she told him. He nodded reluctantly and told her to take all the time she needed; he would wait for her forever if he had to. Carol knew hyperbole when she heard it but decided to kiss him rather than scoff. He responded eagerly, relieved that she had not refused him outright.

Her girlfriends thought Kevin too dull for a boyfriend but perhaps just right for a husband, since he wasn't bad-looking and he earned a good living. Her mother, who had never met him, was his strongest advocate. "Say yes," she urged over the telephone from the town in northern Michigan Carol had successfully escaped. "You might never get a better offer."

Carol couldn't ignore the truth in her words. The next time she saw Kevin, she told him she would marry him. And later, when his insurance company transferred him to Pennsylvania, she gave up her job and the only friends she'd ever had and made a home for him in a three-bedroom house in Pittsburgh.

Sarah was born a few months after the move. Carol's mother stayed with them during the difficult months before the birth, when the dangerous pregnancy forced Carol to remain in bed, and afterward, when a thick cloud of despair inexplicably came over her. The bright new baby in her arms brought her little joy, and she did not know why. Sometimes she woke in the middle of the night to find she had been weeping. Other times she could not sleep at all, but paced around the living room of the darkened house, smoking one cigarette after another. She did not know why she wasn't happy, and she hated herself for it. She had all she had ever wanted—an education, a pleasant house, an adoring husband, a beautiful child who would have everything, everything that she herself had been denied. What was preventing her from enjoying such blessings?

Her beloved books were forgotten. If not for her mother, meals, laundry, housekeeping, and even Sarah herself would have been neglected, too. Carol nursed Sarah when her mother brought her the child, but otherwise she lay in bed sleeping or sat outside in a chair, alone with her thoughts. After a few weeks of this, her mother taught her how to bathe the baby, change her, dress her, care for her. Gradually, her mother's quiet but firm insistence helped her develop an interest in the child, and a thin shaft of light began to pierce the heavy fog surrounding her. Carol could not find the words to voice her gratitude, but for the first time, she realized how deeply she loved her mother.

For his part, Kevin left for the office soon after breakfast, and Carol did not see him again until evening. He would ask her about her day, although there was never anything to tell him. He would nod and kiss her gently, then talk quietly with his mother-in-law before going off to play with Sarah until suppertime. Carol considered telling her husband and mother that she didn't like them talking about her behind her back, but she couldn't summon up the energy to complain.

Then one day, when Sarah was three months old, Carol had a dream. She was sitting at the kitchen table of her father's house, unable to touch the plate her mother had set before her. It was raining outside, and thunder crashed until the walls shook. Her father scowled and said, "You don't deserve that baby. You can't even take care of her."

Suddenly, Carol heard a faint wail coming from outside. Sarah was out there in the storm, alone and frightened. Carol ran outside to find her daughter, but the wind drove rain into her eyes until she couldn't see. She tried to follow the thin cry to its source, but every time she thought she was nearly there, the cry withdrew into the distance. Frantic, she ran faster and faster, but always the sobbing child remained just out of reach, lost and helpless, dependent and abandoned.

Carol woke shaking. Kevin slept on as she climbed from bed and stumbled down the hall to Sarah's room, where she listened to her daughter's breathing and touched the tiny bundle beneath the quilt to convince herself that Sarah was not lost in a storm. Reassured, she sank to the floor and hugged her knees to her chest, rocking back and forth, weeping softly.

The next morning Carol told her mother that she thought she could manage just fine now on her own. Her mother brightened, eager to return home to her garden and her friends. Carol saw her husband and mother exchange happy glances, pleased that she had returned to her old self. Carol knew she hadn't, not yet and perhaps never, but she would be better than she had been. She would be a good mother to Sarah, if only to prove that her father had been wrong about her. She was not a failure, though he had been convinced of it and had nearly convinced her, too.

After her mother left, she made a schedule for herself just as she had back in college. Every day that she managed to complete the tasks on her list was a subdued triumph. She fought off the old listlessness by throwing herself into her role of mother and wife. This was her new venue, she decided, and she could achieve there as well as any other place.

In fair weather she took long walks, pushing Sarah in her stroller. They had lived in that town for nearly a year, but in her distraction Carol had not yet learned their neighborhood. With her daughter's pleasant company, she explored the streets near their home, and one day she chanced upon a sight that sent a stab of longing through her: a used book shop, its front window stacked with books of every size and description.

She maneuvered the stroller through the store's narrow aisles, pausing whenever a book caught her eye, hungrily devouring a chapter or more before moving on to the next delight. The hours passed in the luxury of words and the smell of old paper. Eventually, Sarah grew bored and fretful, so Carol found picture books for her, which Sarah gnawed and flung to the floor. When other customers began to stare, Carol blushed and paid for the picture books, then hurried from the store. When she was almost home, she realized that she had forgotten to buy anything for herself.

Her embarrassment kept her away the next day, but she returned the day after. Soon she began to visit several times a week, sometimes to purchase a book for herself or for Sarah, other times merely to surround herself with so many stories, so many words. The polite hush of the shop was nearly religious in its serenity, and after more than a few days away, she found herself craving it.

The elderly woman who ran the shop came to know her by name, and Carol began to recognize other frequent customers. They would nod politely at each other, but this was not a place to strike up friendships. No one would dare intrude on another visitor's quiet contemplation of the walls of books.

Only one person broke this unspoken rule of the bookshop: the owner's nephew, Jack, who had dark hair and a quick flash of a grin. He was not there every day, but when he was, he would greet Carol with a slight bow as if she were someone of great importance. At first his slightly mocking demeanor embarrassed her, but she got used to it and began to return his bows with a mocking curtsy of her own.

Sometimes he searched the stacks for children's books and set them aside for Sarah. When he detected a pattern in Carol's purchases, he began to point out books he thought she would enjoy, classics in excellent condition. She appreciated his help and often thanked him with a small homemade gift—a slice of cake from yesterday's baking, a basket of fresh rolls. When she saw the pleasure her gifts brought him, her cheeks grew warm and she hurried deeper into the store, pushing Sarah's stroller before her.

One day he left the cash register and followed.

"Thank you for the cookies," he said when he caught up to her, keeping his voice low so that he wouldn't disturb the other customers.

"Don't mention it," she told him. His dark hair was so thick that it always looked tousled. Instinctively she lifted a hand to touch her own hair.

He misunderstood the gesture and extended his hand. "I'm Jack."

"I'm Carol." She shook his hand and quickly released it. "Carol Mallory. Mrs. Kevin Mallory."

He grinned at her, then bent down to look into the stroller. "And who's this big girl?"

Sarah squealed with delight, and Carol couldn't help smiling. "My daughter, Sarah."

"Pleased to meet you, Sarah," he said, extending a finger, which she seized. Laughing, he let her hang on for a moment before he freed himself and stood up. "It's nice to finally know your name." Grinning, he turned and walked back to the front of the store.

Carol watched him go. It *was* silly that she had not learned his name before then, but names had not seemed necessary in the bookshop.

Suddenly she was grateful that she had not told Kevin about him.

The meetings in the bookshop turned into long chats over coffee at a nearby diner. They would discuss politics and literature—and themselves. Jack, she learned, traveled the country acquiring books for the shop; that explained his frequent absences. He had never married, though he had come close once, years before. "I came to my senses just in time," he said, laughing. He had not yet decided if he wanted to take over his aunt's shop after her retirement.

"Why wouldn't you?" she asked.

He shrugged. "I don't know if I want to be held in one place."

Carol understood. He wanted the pleasure of discovering a first-edition Mark Twain at an estate sale, not the drudgery of placing books on shelves and making change. That was all right every once in a while, but not day in, day out. That was no kind of life for a man like Jack. That was for a man more like—well, like Kevin.

Sometimes they went for long walks after the coffee, and Carol would have to race home as fast as the stroller would go in order to have dinner ready by the time Kevin returned from the office. She found herself thinking about Jack when she wasn't with him. More than once, when Kevin made love to her, she closed her eyes and imagined Jack inside her, her hands tangled in his dark hair, his mouth on hers. Afterward, waves of guilt would wash over her, but she would tell herself she had done nothing wrong. She was unfaithful to Kevin only in her imagination, and no one could condemn her for that.

She knew that Jack had a girlfriend, a woman he had been seeing off and on for nearly three years. As the weeks passed, Jack mentioned her less and less frequently. Once, after a long walk through the park, as they sat on the grass under a tree watching Sarah play, Carol asked about her.

"I haven't seen her in weeks," he said.

Her heart pounded, but she kept her voice steady. "Why not?"

He met her gaze. "I think you know why."

She trembled inside and couldn't speak. She wanted to rip her eyes away from his, but she couldn't. She felt as if he could see into the very heart of her and knew what she was thinking—and what she imagined as she made love to her husband.

Jack took her hand. "Carol, I want to be with you."

"We can't." She felt her eyes filling with tears. "I'm married."

"He doesn't have to know." He began to stroke her arm with his other hand, and she shivered, dizzy with arousal. "Please, Carol."

She wanted to say yes. She wanted to taste him. She wanted to open herself to him and love him until she was sated, complete.

But—"I can't."

It came out as a sob. Sarah looked up from her play, startled. Hurriedly, Carol snatched her up and placed her in the stroller. Jack had told her how he despised the manipulation of tears, and she would not let him see her cry.

"I won't ask again," he called to her as she walked away.

She hesitated. Was it a promise or a warning? She knew it made no difference. Without looking back, she continued on her way.

At home, she put Sarah down for her nap and flung herself onto the bed she and Kevin shared. Alone, she wept, mourning everything she had never had and would never feel. She wept until she was too exhausted to do anything but stare at the ceiling. She lay on the bed in silence, wondering how she would fill up her days with no more long talks over coffee to look forward to, no more meetings in the bookshop. She could never return to the store, that was certain.

The next morning, not long after Kevin left for work, the phone rang.

"I'm leaving," Jack said.

"Why?" she asked. "Where are you going?"

"I don't know. I just—I can't stay here." He paused. "I said I wouldn't ask you again—"

"Yes," she said quickly. "Yes. I'm coming. Don't go." She hung up the phone and rushed Sarah into her clothes. She left her with the next-door neighbor, a widow whose children were grown, with the excuse that she had an emergency doctor's appointment. When she reached the bookstore, Jack was waiting outside. Through the window she could see his aunt at the cash register, helping a customer.

"Are you sure?" he asked her when she reached him, breathless from running.

She nodded and gave him her hand.

He drove them to his apartment, where he began kissing her before he had even closed the door. She felt drenched and new and alive in his arms, and when they had finished making love, he held her close and stroked her hair. He held her for what seemed like a long time, and yet when he shifted to reach for his clothes, her heart broke that it was over so soon.

He drove her home—or nearly there; he pulled over to the curb a few blocks from her house. They kissed swiftly, fervently, before she got out of the car and hurried down the street to the neighbor's, where Sarah waited.

That evening as she served Kevin his pot roast and potatoes, she wondered how he could be so blind to the change in her. A warmth had come over her, a sensation that she had never known, and she knew she could never return to what she used to be.

Jack didn't leave after all, now that she had given him a reason to stay. Over the next two months they met as often as Carol could get away, as often as she could get the woman next door to care for Sarah. "She's going to think you have a terminal illness if you keep having so many doctor's appointments," Jack teased. In response, Carol hit him lightly with a pillow. Their lovemaking was joyful, playful, so unlike her perfunctory moments with Kevin, when she waited for him to finish so she could go to sleep.

The comparison was not fair, and she felt ashamed for making it. From then on, she tried her best not to think of one man when she was with the other. It was if she were two women, one demure and dutiful, the other passionate and reckless.

Sarah provided the link between those two halves of herself. She was too young to know what was going on, too young to divulge their secret, but she was a constant reminder of Kevin, and Carol felt herself withdrawing from her daughter as she drew closer to Jack.

Once, when Carol could not get a sitter, Sarah accompanied them on a picnic in the city park. They found a secluded spot in a grove of trees and spread their blanket. Carol ached for Jack, but she could not kiss him, not with Sarah there.

An elderly man walking his dog paused to watch them as they murmured to each other and watched Sarah play. He apologized for his intrusion and said, "It's nice to see such a happy family enjoying this lovely day together."

Carol flushed, but Jack merely grinned and thanked him.

Later that day, Kevin came home from work early with good news: His hard work had paid off, and he had been promoted. He kissed Carol deeply, then swung Sarah up in his arms. "Did you hear Daddy's good news? Did you, my little sweet pea?" he said, nuzzling her until she crowed with delight.

Watching them, Carol felt a pang of guilt. Kevin worked so hard to take care of them, never realizing that his happy family was a sham. What would he do if he learned the truth?

Day by day, her worries accumulated, affecting her encounters with Jack. She thought about what they had done and wondered where it was going to lead. "What are we going to do about this?" she asked him once as he drove her nearly home.

"What are we going to do about what?" he asked, genuinely puzzled.

She shot him a look. "About us, of course."

"What do you mean?" He glanced at her as he pulled the car over to the curb. They had reached her usual disembarking place, but he left the motor running.

I love you, she almost said, but something in his eyes made her hold back the words. "Nothing," she said instead. She kissed him quickly and got out of the car.

Jack didn't phone her for the rest of that week, and when she stopped by the bookstore, he wasn't there. Another week went by with no word. Finally she fought back her embarrassment and returned to the bookstore, where she casually asked his aunt why they had not seen him around the shop recently.

"He's off on another buying spree," the older woman said. "He's traveling up and down the East Coast looking for bargains. Is there anything you'd like me to hold for you when he brings back the new stock?"

"No, thank you," Carol murmured. She left the store, dazed.

When Jack finally came for her a few days later, her first question to him was, "Why didn't you tell me you were going out of town?"

"Hey, slow down," he said, laughing, holding up his palms as if to ward her off. Then he paused. "You're serious, aren't you?"

She nodded, furious, too hurt to speak.

"I go on these business trips all the time, you know that." His voice was soothing, but there was an undercurrent of warning in it. "You aren't going to get all serious on me, now, are you? I thought we both understood that we don't make those kind of demands on each other."

She went cold. They were in a dangerous place now, she could feel it. "But to go away for so long without telling me—"

"I don't ask what you and your husband do when I'm not around, do I?"

Stunned, she shook her head, and when she spoke, her voice sounded very far away. "No, of course not."

She understood then that he did not love her, not in the way she had thought. They would not be running away together to live penniless but happy in a room above a bookshop in another city where no one knew them. Jack would not become Sarah's doting stepfather, and Carol would not be his loving wife. He had no intentions of marrying her and never had.

Whose bed had he shared last week? How many other women had stood before him with lowered eyes, fighting to keep the grief and shock off their faces, pretending that they, too, had been in it just for laughs? He had never promised her anything more than what he had given, but still, somehow, she felt that she had been deceived.

When she told him she could not go home with him that day, he shrugged, unconcerned. The stroller supported her weight as she walked home, numb.

The dark clouds enveloped her again, worse than before, and this time her mother was not there to see her through. She stopped her daily trips to the bookstore. While Kevin was at work she let the phone ring unanswered, knowing it was Jack. Eventually he stopped calling. She often forgot to eat and had to remind herself to care for Sarah. Her life felt like it was happening in slow motion, and every part of her cried out silently for Jack.

Surely, she thought, this was her punishment for lying before God when she married a man she did not love.

As her condition worsened, Kevin grew worried, then alarmed. He called his mother-in-law for advice; he pleaded with Carol to see a doctor. She sat on the sofa, staring at the floor as he spoke. Then he was on his knees before her, grasping her hands. His eyes were full of tears as he begged her to get help. "I can't bear to see you like this," he said, his voice breaking. "Please, let me call the doctor."

He loved her, Carol realized, and thought the remorse would kill her.

"I don't need a doctor," she told him, and she began to cry. Hot, heavy tears fell soundlessly upon their clasped hands.

Kevin looked at her. "It's bad, isn't it?" he asked quietly.

She nodded, and then she told him.

He was furious, but he did not show his rage the way her father would have. The color drained from his face and he tore himself away from her. Her monotone confession still hung in the air between them. Now she was silent, waiting, unable to look at him.

When he finally spoke, it was with an effort. "You will not—" He broke off, glaring at her, breathing heavily. "You will not take my daughter with you when you go."

Distantly, she marveled at his restraint. Her father would have beaten her senseless by now. "I can't leave without Sarah," she heard herself say. It was a stranger's voice.

"I will not have my daughter raised by a whore," he said. "When you go, you go alone."

"I have nowhere to go." But he had stormed off to their bedroom.

Their voices had woken Sarah, who started to wail. Carol sat frozen in place, unable to go to her. Moments later Kevin returned with her suitcase, only half closed, with clothing hanging out of it. He grabbed her by the arm and yanked her to her feet. She cried out and tried to free herself as he closed her hands around the handle of the suitcase and propelled her to the door.

"Get out," he roared, wrestling her outside. She pleaded with him to stop, but he shoved her along the front walk to her car.

"Kevin, please—"

"Get out!"

"Please, don't make me go, don't make me leave my baby!"

His face was contorted in grief and rage. He was sobbing now, too, she saw, and then suddenly he crumpled. He released her, dropped the suitcase, and slid to the ground with his back against the car. He buried his face in his hands and wept in loud, aching sobs, as if she had ripped his heart out.

She threw her arms around him and kissed him, shushing him, promising that everything would be all right. He pulled her to him and held her so tightly she thought she would smother in his embrace, but she clung to him, welcoming the pain, needing it.

He did not divorce her as she had expected.

At first she was grateful and thought him the most generous of husbands. Only as the years went by did she realize that he had let her stay so that he could punish her, so that he could show her what it was like to live without love. He let her remain his wife, but after that night he never loved her again. Kevin let Carol stay with Sarah, but he never let her forget how unworthy she was to live in that house with the husband and daughter she had wronged. All the love he had once showered on his wife he now gave to their daughter, who grew up adoring her father and believing her mother critical and unfeeling. What Sarah did not know was that Kevin punished Carol every day for the rest of his life. He punished her by not forgiving her.

She tried to regain his trust. She lived a sinless life from that day forward, but nothing would soften his heart. It was as if she were a child again, desperately striving for perfection so that her father would love her. Her efforts were as futile then as they had been so long ago.

In one last, desperate attempt, she sought perfection through Sarah, pushing her, teaching her, trying to raise her to be the most perfect child a father could want. Then he would see how Carol had atoned for her betrayal, and he would let her be a part of the family again. In this, too, she failed. Kevin already loved his daughter and had always thought her perfect, flaws and all. All Carol managed to do was to nurture resentment in Sarah, who grew up thinking she would be forever inadequate in her mother's eyes. That was not what Carol had intended. Nothing had worked out the way she had intended.

There was no harder person to live with than a man who did not forgive, except for a daughter who despised her.

# Chapter Ten

Usually the end of spring semester brought Gwen a sense of deep satisfaction. Another school year completed; another batch of hungry young minds fed—although it might have been more accurate to say another batch of resistant young minds pummeled into submission. But not this year. Within a week, the day she had long dreaded and hoped for would arrive: Her daughter would be graduating, and after one last brief summer in Waterford, she would head off to graduate school at Penn. Judging by her own experience, Gwen knew that Summer wouldn't be coming home much after that. She would soon think of Waterford as her mother's home, and Philadelphia as her own. Gwen would be lucky to see her more than a few times a year. How awful that would be, after seeing her virtually every day since she was born! Summer had had her own apartment in downtown Waterford ever since she began college, but she still came home several times a week to do her laundry, quilt, or borrow something. But there would be no more long heart-to-heart talks over cups of tea when a quick errand turned into a leisurely visit. Now the house would be an empty nest, a hollow shell, a lonely outpost on the frontier of motherhood.

"Now you're getting melodramatic," Gwen muttered as she tied her running shoes and began to stretch. She went jogging every morning, rain or shine. Actually, it was more of a brisk waddle than a jog, but at least she was moving. She had a favorite two-mile circuit through the

Waterford College Arboretum that took her about forty minutes to complete. Other runners left her in their dust, but she didn't let it bother her. Everyone had to move at their own pace, whether along a running trail or through life.

A mist shrouded the woods that morning, and Gwen's breath came out in barely visible puffs as she ran. The only other sound was that of her footfalls on the wide dirt path. Spring was her favorite time of year in Pennsylvania. Other people preferred autumn, when the changing leaves covered the hills in brilliant color, but the renewal of spring soothed Gwen's spirit like nothing else. Winter had been vanquished at last, and the hot, humid days of summer were not yet upon them. The regular school year had ended, and the summer session had not yet begun. These few weeks provided her with a restful interim in which to take time for herself.

Perhaps she wouldn't go to campus at all today. She could work just as well at home as in her office. Or maybe she'd put her work aside entirely and quilt instead. She felt too nostalgic to work on her conference paper today, anyway. In the middle of the section on antebellum textiles, she was sure to go off on a weepy tangent about the clothing mothers sewed for their daughters before they parted forever. That would certainly make a fine impression on the review committee.

When she returned home, she showered and put on comfortable clothes—loose-fitting cotton pants and a long-sleeved flannel shirt, untucked. Far too many of her other clothes were getting snug around the waist. She would have to consider joining Bonnie and Diane for their evening walks. Better that than cutting back on treats such as the hazelnut biscotti she had with her tea for breakfast.

When she finished eating, she poured herself a second cup of tea and took it with her to the extra bedroom she and Summer used as a quilt studio. With a pang, Gwen realized that Summer would probably take her fabric and supplies with her when she went to school in the fall. Gwen had often wished for a more spacious workplace, but this was not how she had wanted to come by it.

She sighed and found the round robin quilt in her tote bag, where she had kept it since receiving it from Judy. She unfolded it and spread it out on the table, then stepped back to take it in. It was beautiful, no doubt about it. The blues, greens, golds, and various shades of cream harmonized well, and the assorted patterns complemented each other. Judy's Mariner's Compass border was dazzling. When Agnes finally contributed her center design, the quilt would be a masterpiece.

Gwen rested her chin in her hand and thought. What should she add? The last border had to be striking; it also had to somehow tie all the other borders together. That was no easy task, but Gwen felt up to it. The challenge would take her mind off Summer's departure.

She raided her fabric stash, selecting colors and prints that would work well with those her friends had selected. But that was the easy part. The question was, how would she stitch all those colors together? She knelt on the floor by the bookshelves, paging through pattern books, pondering her options.

Some time later, she heard the front door open and slam shut. "Mom?"

"In here," Gwen called out, rising awkwardly. She had been sitting with her legs tucked under her, and her right foot had fallen asleep. She was stomping her foot, trying to wake it up, when Summer entered.

Summer's eyebrows rose as she watched. "Summoning the muse?"

"Not this time." Gwen laughed and hobbled over to hug her. Summer seemed taller and more slender every day, but maybe on a subconscious level Gwen was comparing Summer to her ever-broadening self. "It's a hardwood floor, so I think the most I can hope for is a dryad or two." Summer smiled, but Gwen detected some tension in her expression. "What's wrong, kiddo?"

Summer threw herself into a chair. "How did you know?"

What a silly question. "I'm your mother, of course." No matter how far away Summer moved, that, at least, would never change. "I picked up a few blips on my mom sonar. What's going on?"

Summer picked up a Bear's Paw pillow from the floor and hugged it to her chest. "It's about graduation."

Finally, it was coming out. Ever since Judy received that letter from her half sister, Gwen wondered if this moment would come. She'd thought about bringing up the matter herself, but she had put it off, hoping that it would just go away. Or rather, stay away, since he hadn't been around for more than two decades. "I think I know what's bothering you."

Summer's eyes widened. "You do?"

"I think so." Gwen hesitated. "Kiddo, if you want to invite your father to your graduation, it's fine with me." They would have to find him first. The last Gwen had heard, he was running a coffeehouse and surf shop in Santa Cruz, but that has been ten years ago.

"Invite *him*?" Summer exclaimed. "Why would I want to do that? Why should he get to swoop in and snatch half the credit when you're the one who earned it?"

Pride surged through her, but Gwen decided to be modest. "In all honesty, you're the one who deserves the credit. You worked very hard. I'm very proud of you."

But Summer was not mollified. "Who needs him? He probably doesn't even know my name."

Gwen considered. "I'm almost certain he does."

"Almost certain. How wonderful," Summer retorted. "If he somehow shows up, promise me you'll pretend you don't know him. He might not recognize you, and he definitely won't recognize me."

Gwen nodded, surprised by her daughter's vehemence. "He won't show up. I'm not even sure if he knows where we live." She hoped Dennis wasn't a fan of *America's Back Roads*.

"Good." Abruptly, Summer rose and gave her mother a wry smile. "Get a load of Miss Whiner here. I'm sorry I've been such a grump lately."

"That's all right." Gwen hugged her. "You're entitled."

Summer laughed, and after admiring the round robin quilt and discussing options for Gwen's border, she was on her way, off to meet some friends for lunch.

Only after she left did Gwen realize that Summer had never explained what was bothering her.

Whatever it was, at least she wasn't gloomy over Dennis. She never

had been before, not even when she was a little girl and her teachers assigned essay topics like "My Daddy's Job" or had the students make Father's Day art projects. Dennis had never been a part of Summer's life.
She had truly never known him, since Gwen and Dennis had split up
months before Summer was born.

Once, Summer had asked her why they divorced, and Gwen told her
quite honestly that a more baffling question was why had they married in
the first place. Admittedly, much of that flower child time was a bit hazy
to her now, but one would think she'd be able to remember something as
significant as that. Maybe they had been caught up in a wave of universal
peace and love that blocked out all reason. Gwen could just picture the
expression on her daughter's face if she told Summer *that*.

Gwen liked to joke that she and Dennis had been married for about
five minutes, but it was actually closer to a year. She was taking time off
from college, intending to expand her mind by hitchhiking across the
country and engaging in other experimental behavior she now prayed
that Summer wouldn't dream of trying. She met Dennis at an antiwar
rally, and somehow found him attractive as he stood in the middle of the
Berkeley campus yelling epithets and burning Lyndon Johnson in effigy.
Later she realized she had confused agreement with his politics with admiration for him, and his passion for justice for passion for herself. At
the time, however, she thought she'd found true love.

After their barefoot ceremony—it was too cold to go barefoot in Feb-
ruary, but Dennis insisted—they traveled the country with two other
couples in a van plastered with peace signs and antiwar slogans. Gwen
wasn't sure how they had managed to support themselves, since self-
preservation had been the least of their concerns. They went where they
chose, with nothing to hold them down, nothing to bear them up but
each other.

The carefree times ended when Gwen realized she was pregnant. She
had always possessed a strong pragmatic streak, and after a long dor-
mancy it finally began to reassert itself. Suddenly she began to care about
where their next meal would come from, where they would live and how,
what kind of life she wanted for her child, what kind of mother she

would be. Dennis's drug use, which had been only a minor irritant before, began to trouble her. When she tried to get him to quit, he told her she was just jealous because the two times she'd tried grass, she'd gotten migraines. "Relax, baby," he said, blowing smoke in her face. Then he bent over to speak to her abdomen. "That goes for you, too, baby."

Something about the way he threw his head back in a fit of helpless giggling raised Gwen's ire. The next time they stopped for gas, she stuffed her few possessions into her backpack and left without saying good-bye to Dennis or her friends. How long had they waited for her, she wondered, before they realized she wasn't coming back?

She went home to her parents, who made her feel profoundly guilty by weeping when she arrived. She hadn't meant to abandon them, but it wasn't easy to write letters on the road. When Summer was a year old, Gwen returned to college; by Summer's eleventh birthday, Gwen had earned her Ph.D. and a position on the faculty of Waterford College.

Sometimes old friends passed through town, and they would talk long into the night about those days, about how they had tried to change the world and how they had indeed changed some small part of it. Some of their fellow travelers were still fighting the good fight; others had traded in their love beads for IRAs and BMWs. Occasionally these visiting friends had news of Dennis: He had remarried, he had divorced, he had opened a head shop, he was in Oregon chained to a giant sequoia to save it from loggers. He had never contacted Gwen to inquire about their child, and she had never asked anyone to pass along a message.

Should she have? Should she have insisted that he play a role in his daughter's life?

The questions plagued her, but one look at Summer assured her that she had done all right. Summer was the kind of daughter every mother wished for. She was thoughtful and smart and strong, and Gwen admired her. Yes, she must have done something right somehow, despite their rather precarious beginning as a family.

Summer insisted she didn't want Dennis at her graduation, and Gwen knew she was telling the truth. But if that wasn't what was bothering her, what was?

As the weekend approached and Summer said nothing more on the subject, Gwen decided that it must have been pregraduation jitters. By Saturday afternoon, Summer must have overcome them, because she was the picture of happiness at the graduation party the Elm Creek Quilters threw for her. Husbands were invited as well, and Judy and Diane had brought their children. While Craig and Matt supervised the grill, the others sat on the veranda and talked, or threw Frisbees on the front lawn. Michael and Todd took turns riding a skateboard around the circular driveway, and Gwen persuaded them to teach her how. She nearly broke her neck after a kick-turn went awry, so she decided to sit on the grass and watch the boys instead.

"What did you do with the skateboard ramp?' she asked them.

"We took it down and stored it in the garage," Michael said.

"Did you find a new place to ride?"

He shrugged. "You mean like other than our driveway and here? No."

"You must be disappointed."

"Wouldn't you be?" He came to a stop in front of her. He looked so dejected that Gwen was tempted to give him a comforting hug, but she wasn't sure he'd welcome it.

"Yes, I'm sure I would," she said. "So what are you going to do now?"

He shrugged again. "I dunno. I don't think there's anything I can do. I mean, they're like the city government and everything."

"They're not just 'like' the city government; they *are* the city government." She saw at once that the remark had gone over his head, but she was warming up to her subject and didn't want to pause to discuss his grammar. "They're elected officials, not gods. Law is a social construct, and in this country, at least, it's subject to the will of the people."

He sat down beside her, his brow furrowed. "You mean like voting and stuff?"

"That's right."

"But I can't vote yet."

"More's the pity," Gwen said. "We might have fewer stupid laws if you could. I bet you and your friends would shake things up around here, wouldn't you?"

He grinned. "Maybe."

"When I was a little older than you, my friends and I did more than just vote. We held demonstrations, sit-ins—anything to get our message out. We were trying to make our government get out of Vietnam."

"I know about that. We studied it in history class."

"Great," Gwen said, feeling ancient.

He regarded her seriously. "Were you a hippie?"

"Yes, I suppose I was." She was about to begin a long, nostalgic lecture about the passion for justice young people had felt in her day and how it compared to the callow selfishness of today's youth, but Matt chose that moment to announce that dinner was ready.

They ate on the veranda, seated in Adirondack chairs or on the stone staircase. Afterward, the Elm Creek Quilters gave Summer her gift, a signature wall hanging quilt they had worked on all winter. Summer gasped with delight as she opened the box and took out the beautiful quilt. Gwen had pieced a large Mariner's Compass block to symbolize Summer's life journey, and around it she had sewn solid, off-white borders on which everyone had written her congratulatory messages. Gwen became teary-eyed as Summer read the loving wishes aloud. Summer hugged each of them, even Andrew and Matt and the other Elm Creek husbands. Todd didn't want a hug, but Michael politely agreed to accept one.

The men must have sensed that their wives were about to talk quilts for a while, for they broke off into conversations of their own.

"I don't know how you managed to keep this a secret so long," Summer said as she carefully folded the quilt and returned it to its box.

Sylvia laughed. "We quilters are full of surprises."

"She has no idea," Judy murmured to Gwen.

"You have to promise to hang that in your apartment in Philadelphia," Bonnie said. "We want to make sure you never forget us."

"I could never forget any of you," Summer said with such feeling that Gwen had to reach for the tissues again.

"That's not good enough," Agnes teased. "You have to promise."

"Go on, Summer," Diane urged. "Raise your right hand and repeat after me: 'I, Summer Sullivan, being about to graduate from the esteemed institute of higher learning known as Waterford College, do hereby solemnly swear to hang this quilt in my new apartment far, far away in Philadelphia—' "

"Don't say 'far, far away,' " Gwen protested. "It's not that far."

"Now you made me lose track. Well, you get the idea, Summer. Go on, promise."

Summer looked around, flustered, as her friends began to chant, "Promise, promise, promise."

"All right," she finally called out above their voices, laughing. "I promise I'll hang this quilt in—in my apartment. And I promise I'll never forget the people who made it. Satisfied?"

"I thought my version was more eloquent," Diane said.

"You thought wrong," Gwen retorted.

The women broke into peals of laughter, but they could feel sadness creeping in. Summer would be the first of their group to leave since the founding of Elm Creek Quilts. They would have until autumn to enjoy moments like this, with all of them together and happy, but all too soon their circle would be broken.

As much as Gwen enjoyed the party, she was glad to have Summer all to herself the next day. While the other Elm Creek Quilters prepared for the arrival of a new batch of campers, Gwen and Summer got ready for the commencement ceremony. Gwen wanted Summer to wear her cap and gown as they walked through downtown Waterford to campus, but Summer begged off. "I'll be wearing them for hours," she said. "Can't I put them on in your office instead?"

Since it was Summer's day, Gwen reluctantly agreed. Gwen, too, would be wearing a cap and gown for the ceremony, since as a member of the faculty she would be marching in the procession. In her office, she helped Summer with her cap and gown first, then put on her own.

"You'll have one of these, too, someday," she said as she fastened the loop of her doctoral hood to the small button on the gown at the nape of her neck. She adjusted the hood's folds and smiled at her daughter. Summer flushed and gave her a quick smile before looking away.

The ceremony Gwen had participated in so many times took on a poignancy that she had not felt since receiving her doctorate. Afterward, they somehow found Judy in the crowd of other faculty. Gwen gave Judy her camera and had her snap a picture of Gwen and Summer, then Judy handed the camera to a physics professor and had him take a shot of the three of them together, arms intertwined. Judy and Summer smiled happily, but Gwen was sobbing and laughing at the same time.

That evening, Summer pleased Gwen by coming home instead of returning to the downtown apartment she shared with two friends. Gwen knew how to make only one baked dessert, a three-layer German chocolate cake, but she made it well, and she had prepared one that night in Summer's honor. As twilight fell, they sat on the back porch enjoying tea and cake, but most of all, each other's company.

"I'll miss you when you head off to Penn," Gwen said. "Before we know it, it will be time for fall quarter to begin."

"Actually, Mom, I've been wanting to talk to you about that."

Gwen reached out and stroked Summer's long, auburn hair. "What is it, kiddo? Are you nervous about graduate school?"

"Well, actually, no, that's one thing I'm definitely not." She hesitated. "First, though, promise me you won't get angry."

"Angry about what?"

"Just promise."

"No, I'm not going to promise, not without knowing what's going on." Suddenly she felt her stomach tighten into a knot. "Don't tell me you're pregnant."

"No, Mom," Summer exclaimed. "I don't even have a boyfriend."

"Oh." Gwen thought for a moment. "A girlfriend?"

Summer rolled her eyes. "Of course not—"

"What is it, then? Are you sick?" She sat up straight, clutching the armrests of her chair. "Did your father call?"

"No, it's not anything like that. I'm just not going to graduate school."

Silence.

Then, in a small voice, Gwen said, "You mean you've changed your mind about going to Penn?"

"I've changed my mind about graduate school altogether. I'm not going. I'm sorry."

Gwen felt dazed. "But . . . why?"

"It's just not what I want for my life." Summer reached out and took Gwen's hand. "I'm sorry about this. I know you must be very disappointed in me, but—"

"You have to go to graduate school," Gwen interrupted, confused. "It's what we've been planning for years. What—what—what else would you do?"

"That's just it, Mom. It's not what we've been planning; it's what you've planned for me." She took a deep breath. "I'm going to stay here in Waterford. I'm going to ask Sylvia for a larger role in Elm Creek Quilts and keep working for Bonnie. I want to own the business someday."

"Elm Creek Quilts? You could never afford it, you know that."

"Not Elm Creek Quilts. Grandma's Attic. Working there has been more rewarding than anything I've done in my major. I enjoy working with quilters and thinking up new ways to promote the shop. It's a challenge, and I'm never bored when I'm there. Unlike school," she added in an undertone.

Slowly the words sank in. Summer wanted to own a quilt shop. Instead of Summer Sullivan, Ph.D., she wanted to be Summer Sullivan, storekeeper. It couldn't be true. Gwen must have misunderstood.

With a sinking feeling, she realized that she hadn't.

"Mom, say something."

"What's left for me to say?" Gwen said. "It seems like you've made your decision, and since you obviously didn't want my opinion when you were making all of these secret plans, why would you want it now?"

"Don't talk like that, please," Summer begged. "I haven't made any secret plans. No one knows but me and you." She hesitated. "And the registrar at Penn."

"You mean you already declined your acceptance?"

Summer nodded.

Gwen sank back into her chair. "You turned down Penn without even checking with Bonnie and Sylvia first?" She knew from Summer's expression that it was true.

"I'm sorry," her daughter said again.

Her eyes were large and troubled. Gwen couldn't bear to look into them any longer, so she rose and began stacking up their dessert dishes. "Well, there's nothing more we can do about it now," she said briskly. "Tomorrow's Monday. You'll just have to phone Penn and tell them you made a mistake. I know people there. I can make a few calls myself if necessary. We'll get this straightened out somehow."

Summer placed a hand on her arm. "There's nothing to straighten out. I'm not going."

Gwen didn't trust herself to speak. She pulled away from Summer, snatched up the dishes, and hurried inside to the kitchen.

Summer followed. "You've always said that everyone has to choose their own path."

Gwen set the dishes in the sink with a crash. "Yes, but not *this* path."

"I can't believe you said that. That's so hypocritical."

"No, it's not. It is not hypocritical to want what's best for your daughter."

"Why do you assume that graduate school is what's best for me?"

"Because—" Because the world was an uncertain place. Because a woman had to be as prepared as possible to face its dangers. Because Gwen couldn't bear to think that her daughter would waste even a particle of her promise, her potential. Because Summer was meant for much greater things than what her mother had achieved.

"Think of it this way," Summer said. "You didn't want me to leave, and now I'm not going to."

That did it. Gwen burst into tears. Summer held her and patted her on the back, but Gwen was not comforted. Was that it? Had she made Summer feel guilty for leaving her? "I'll be all right," she said. "You don't have to stay in Waterford for me. I have my work, my friends—yes, I'll miss you, but I'll be all right. Don't stifle yourself for me. I never wanted that."

"That's not what this is about. Staying here wouldn't stifle me. I don't need a Ph.D. for what I want to do with my life." She stepped back to meet her mother's gaze. "Can you understand that, please? Can you try?"

"You don't have to rule out continuing your education entirely," Gwen said. "Maybe you want to take some time off first. I understand. I did the same thing myself. Maybe you won't go to Penn in the fall, but that doesn't mean you never will." She clutched at Summer's sleeve. "Promise me you won't rule it out completely."

"Mom—"

"Please."

Summer rolled her eyes. "Okay, I won't rule it out entirely. Maybe when I'm seventy years old and retired I'll decide I want to go back to school."

Gwen tried to smile. "I suppose that will have to do."

"Are you okay with this?"

"Sure," Gwen lied. "Never better."

Summer looked dubious, but she said nothing more. Together they rinsed the dishes and stacked them in the dishwasher. When Summer left, Gwen went to the quilt room they had shared for so many years, but not even the bright colors of her fabric stash or the pleasure of working on the round robin quilt comforted her.

The next day, Diane and Carol greeted her with alarm when she went to Elm Creek Manor to teach her workshop. She had dabbed her eyes with witch hazel, but still they were red and swollen.

"That must have been some ceremony," Diane remarked, inspecting her.

"The ceremony was fine," Gwen said, then told them about Summer's decision.

"Oh, how terrible," Carol said, stricken. "You must be heartbroken."

Gwen nodded. Carol looked like she understood completely, which Gwen had not expected.

"Just tell Summer she has to go to Penn, period," Diane said.

"I can't do that. She's a grown woman. I can't tell her what to do."

Gwen tried to calm herself. She couldn't get all worked up now, not with class about to start. "What bothers me most is that she didn't feel she could talk to me about her decision. I wonder. How much do our children conceal from us about their lives, about themselves?"

"How much do we conceal from them?" Carol said softly.

Gwen and Diane looked at her, surprised, but she did not seem aware of their scrutiny.

When she got home, Gwen thought about what Diane had said. No, she couldn't order Summer to go to graduate school, but she could make it possible for Summer to enroll, should she change her mind. Gwen could undo that mistake, at least.

She phoned the registrar's office at Penn, but they could not reinstate Summer without permission from the director of Summer's department. Fortunately, Gwen and the chair of the philosophy department were old friends. She called him at home, explained that Summer had accidentally sent in the wrong forms, and asked if he wouldn't mind sorting out the problem with the registrar. He agreed and promised to take care of it that afternoon. Gwen hung up the phone, relieved. Now she would have the rest of the summer to change her daughter's mind.

Summer did not come to see Gwen that day but on Tuesday she phoned. They spoke briefly on trivial subjects; neither mentioned graduate school. Gwen sensed that Summer was tentative, testing the waters, making sure that her mother was all right. Gwen did her best to sound cheerful, but she wasn't sure if Summer was convinced.

On Wednesday, Gwen was fixing herself lunch when she heard the front door open and slam shut. "Hey, kiddo," she sang out as her daughter entered the kitchen. "You're just in time. Want a sandwich?" Then Summer's expression registered—face pale, jaw set—and Gwen fell silent.

"I just received a very interesting phone call," Summer said in a tight voice.

Gwen's stomach flip-flopped, but she tried to sound nonchalant. "Did you?"

"Penn wants to know if I'm interested in on-campus housing." Summer folded her arms and fixed Gwen with a furious glare. "Why do you suppose they'd do that, a month after I told them I wasn't coming?"

"A month?" Gwen exclaimed. Summer had kept this secret a full month? "I—I don't know, kiddo. I guess someone must have gotten their wires crossed."

"Yes, and that someone is you. I can't believe you did this. What were you thinking?"

"Me?" Gwen tried to sound wronged, innocent, but her voice came out shrill and false. "What did I do?"

"You tell me. Did you call the registrar or did one of your professor friends take care of it for you?"

"Take care of what?" Then Gwen realized there was no point in pretending anymore. "Summer, honey, what else was I supposed to do? You can't expect me to sit idly by while you ruin your life."

"Are you out of your mind?" Summer exclaimed, incredulous. "How am I ruining my life? I'm not dropping out of high school to join the circus."

"You might as well be. What kind of job can you get with a B.A. in philosophy?"

"I've already told you my plans—"

"Yes, and then you run off and burn your bridges before getting even the smallest confirmation from Sylvia or Bonnie."

"Don't you think I considered that? Do you think this is just a whim? I'm sure they'll want me, but either way, I'm not going to Penn." Summer's voice was brittle with anger. "Listen very carefully, okay? I don't want to be a philosophy professor. I don't want to be any kind of professor. That's you. That's not me."

"But it should be you. The best and the brightest always find their way into the academy. That's where you belong. You shouldn't squander your talents—"

"That's not what I'm doing," Summer shouted. "You're so—so impossible. You can't ever see anything from anyone else's point of view.

Look, if that's how you want to see it, fine. I'm not going to try to convince you. But don't forget they're my talents to squander. It's my life to ruin. Not yours. Not yours, mine. Understand? If I'm making the biggest mistake in my life, that's my prerogative. So just stay out of it."

She turned and stormed out of the house without waiting for a reply.

Gwen sank into a chair at the kitchen table. Summer had shouted at her, had ordered her to stay out of her life. Gwen couldn't remember when they had last argued like that, if they ever had. She wanted to chase after Summer, but found herself too sick at heart, too upset to move. What could she do? What could she do?

She should apologize—yes, and quickly, anything to win back Summer's approval. Before long Gwen would forget her disappointment, and everything would be fine between them again.

But just as she reached for the phone, she knew she couldn't cave in simply to win back Summer's favor. No. She had to do what was best for Summer, and that meant getting her into Penn. Summer might not understand now, but someday she would. When she had her advanced degree and a fine job at a prestigious university, she would, and she'd be grateful. Gwen had to put Summer's interests ahead of her own need for her daughter's approval. Gwen would endure anything, anything, rather than let her daughter throw away her future.

But what could she do? Reasoning with Summer wouldn't work, not after today. Summer would have to choose Penn on her own. Gwen had to make graduate school the only logical choice, the only possible option.

The next afternoon, Gwen drove out to Elm Creek Manor to speak to Bonnie. She couldn't talk to her freely at Grandma's Attic, since Summer might be working. Besides, she wanted to speak to Sylvia, too.

Gwen managed to take them aside before Bonnie's workshop. Diane had already spread the word about Summer's decision. When Gwen told them that it broke her heart to see Summer's brilliant academic career ended so soon, they comforted her and assured her everything would be all right in the end.

"I hope so," she said. "I think with your help, everything will be fine."

She saw Sylvia and Bonnie exchange a quick glance. "What I mean is, I don't think it would be such a terrible thing if you were to realize that you couldn't give Summer the extra work she wants."

"You can't mean that," Bonnie said, appalled.

Gwen plowed ahead. "Bonnie, maybe you'll find that you don't have enough money to give Summer more hours at Grandma's Attic. And Sylvia, maybe you and Sarah don't need the extra help with Elm Creek Quilts."

"We most certainly do," Sylvia said.

"But maybe Summer doesn't need to know that."

Sylvia frowned. "Gwen Sullivan, I'm surprised at you."

Bonnie gave her a pleading look. "Please don't ask us to lie to Summer."

"It's for her own good," Gwen said. "You know sometimes we don't give our children the whole truth when it might hurt them. Summer doesn't know how irrevocable her decision is. I can't bear to sit back and watch her jeopardize her entire future. She's meant for so much more than—than—"

"Than life as a quilt shop owner?" Bonnie finished.

Gwen felt heat rising in her face. "I didn't mean it that way. You know I respect what you do."

"Apparently, you don't respect our work quite as much as you thought," Sylvia said.

Her voice was gentle, but Gwen felt it as strongly as a shout. She clasped her arms around herself, thoughts churning. She had insulted her friends by questioning their integrity and the value of their work; she had gone behind her daughter's back in an attempt to undermine her chosen career. Summer had been right to tell her to stay out of it. She had made a mess of everything.

What had happened to all her fine ideals, her sterling principles? Somewhere along the line she had become an elitist snob, believing that her daughter was above certain work, honest jobs that other mothers' children accepted gratefully. How had this happened to her? She had not raised Summer to believe that success was determined by the size of one's paycheck. She ought to be grateful that Summer had taken those lessons to heart, that she was seeking happiness and fulfillment rather than fighting her way up the ivory tower for its own sake.

She felt deeply, profoundly ashamed of herself.

Bonnie and Sylvia watched her, waiting for her to speak.

"I'm sorry," she said. "Please forgive me. Please forget that we ever had this conversation."

Immediately they embraced her. "Consider it forgotten," Sylvia said.

Gwen wished she could forget as easily, but she couldn't.

All she had ever wanted was for Summer to be happy, but now there she was, trying to drape her daughter in job titles and degrees, as if they would shield her from the hardships of life. It wasn't as if Summer had decided to become an arms smuggler or a drug dealer. Summer could do far worse than to assume a greater role with Elm Creek Quilts and prepare to take over Grandma's Attic someday.

Summer was right. Gwen was a hypocrite. Even worse, she was now estranged from her beloved daughter because of it. They weren't as widely divided as Carol and Sarah, or a dozen other mothers and daughters Gwen knew, but they had never let a disagreement linger on so long before, and it made Gwen sick with dismay. She couldn't bear to have Summer unhappy with her. Summer had said that she was sorry for disappointing her mother, but Gwen knew that she was the one who had disappointed—by not supporting Summer's decisions, by pressuring her, by keeping such a narrow focus on graduate school that Summer had never felt able to discuss other possibilities.

There was a rift between them now, and Gwen had put it there. Somehow she had to sew it up before it worsened. Words would not be enough. Gwen would have to show Summer that she accepted her daughter's choice wholeheartedly.

She would begin by visiting Grandma's Attic on Saturday while Summer was working. In front of everyone, Gwen would make a strong show of support for her daughter. That would be a start.

Though only a week had passed since Summer's graduation party, so much had changed that it felt much longer to Gwen. As she entered Grandma's Attic, she noticed the shop was nearly empty of customers.

Gwen had forgotten that the interim between graduation and summer session was traditionally slow for shops in downtown Waterford. So much for her big scene in front of crowds of onlookers. Well, at least Bonnie and Diane were there, and Diane's tendency to gossip made her the equal of a crowd or two.

Summer seemed pleased to see her. After greeting Bonnie and Diane, Gwen brought out the round robin quilt and asked Summer to help her find a blue and green print, preferably with some gold in it. As they moved through the store, Gwen made a point of complimenting the sample quilt blocks displayed at the end of each aisle. Bonnie had told her Summer had made them, but even if she hadn't, Gwen would have recognized her daughter's style and bold color choices.

Gwen tried to act normally, but she was nervous, and she was sure Summer knew it. She almost regretted coming in, for if she hadn't she wouldn't have had to realize that for the first time she felt awkward and uncomfortable in her daughter's presence. She wished she had never spoken to Bonnie and Sylvia that day in Elm Creek Manor. How could she have even considered asking them to deny Summer her well-deserved promotion? She was the worst mother in Waterford—no, the worst mother ever.

As Summer cut Gwen's fabric, the phone rang. Bonnie answered the extension at the cutting table, where she and Diane had joined the mother and daughter. "Good afternoon, Grandma's Attic," Bonnie said, then smiled. "Oh, hi, Judy." The others looked up at the mention of their friend's name. "No, it's just me, Diane, Summer, and Gwen. Oh, and Craig, in the stockroom." A pause, then a smile. "Of course I can let her off work. I'm not running a sweatshop here. What is it?" Her brows drew together in concern. "Oh, my goodness. Do you think—" She glanced up at her friends. "Hold on, Judy. I'm going to put you on speakerphone." She pressed a button and replaced the receiver. "Okay, Judy, go ahead."

"Diane, are you there?" Judy's voice sounded tinny.

"Yes," Diane shouted at the phone.

Gwen winced at the noise. "She's not on Mars, for crying out loud."

"Steve just got a call from his editor at the *Waterford Register*," Judy said. "They asked him to go check out a protest at the square. I thought you might want to know."

Gwen leaned closer to the phone, intrigued. The square was a small downtown park near Waterford's busiest intersection, a good choice for a protest. Waterford College students frequently selected it when they wished to air their complaints about the local government's various housing and noise ordinances. Then she remembered that the students had deserted Waterford after commencement. Who could be left to hold a protest?

Diane was wondering something else. "Why did you think I would want to know?"

"Because whoever it is, they're protesting against the skateboard ordinance."

"Uh oh," Gwen said.

"What?" Diane shrieked at the phone. "Are my boys there?"

"I don't know. Steve's on his way there right now."

"So am I." Diane headed for the front door, leaving Bonnie to hang up the phone.

They called out to Diane to wait, but she didn't seem to hear them.

"I'll go with her," Summer and Gwen said in unison.

"Don't even think about leaving without me," Bonnie said, turning toward the stockroom in the back. "Craig! Come out here a second. Quick!"

Craig appeared, startled. "What is it?"

"There's a big protest on the square, and we think Diane's son is involved. Will you watch the store while we go check it out?"

"Are you kidding?" He hurried toward them—then continued on to the front door. "I'm not going to miss this."

They locked the shop and raced down the street and up the hill to the square. They saw a crowd gathered near the bandstand and heard music blaring and someone shouting. They saw Diane ahead of them, working her way through the people who had come to see what all the excitement was about.

When they reached the square, they forged ahead to the front of the crowd, where they found Diane gaping at a group of children skate-boarding on the paved surface surrounding the bandstand. Gwen counted five boys and a girl—and two of the boys were Michael and Todd. The crowd stood on the grass as if held off the cement by a force field that only the skateboarders could penetrate.

Even Diane did not leave the safety of the grass to seize her children. "Michael and Todd, get over here right this minute," she yelled over the sound of hip-hop blaring on a boom box.

"We can't, Mom," Michael said as his companions continued weaving back and forth on their skateboards. "We have to stand up for our civil rights." His gaze shifted to Gwen, and he brightened. "Hi, Dr. Sullivan! Isn't this cool? We're having a skate-in!" With that, he pushed off on his skateboard and zoomed around the bandstand.

Diane glared at Gwen. "I don't know how you did it, and I don't know why, but I do know you're responsible for this somehow."

"Who, me?" Gwen tried to look innocent.

Summer stuck two fingers in her mouth and let out a piercing whis-tle. "You go, Michael," she shouted. He waved happily.

The crowd was growing, but Steve spotted them and made his way toward them, grinning. "Hey, Diane, mind giving me a quote for tomor-row's paper?"

"I'll give you a quote," she shot back. "Those clowns in the municipal building brought this on themselves. If they would have permitted my family to keep our skateboard ramp on our private property, these kids would be skating at our house right now, instead of creating a scene in a public park."

"Good, good," Steve said, writing it down.

Just then Todd turned off the music. The crowd grew quieter as Michael climbed the stairs to the bandstand. "My name's Michael, and I'm a skateboarder." His friends burst into cheers and applause. "I'm not a criminal, I'm not a troublemaker, I'm not a druggie. I just want to ride my skateboard. But because of the fascists in the city government, I'm not allowed to, not even in my own backyard."

"Where did he learn a word like *fascists*?" Bonnie wondered aloud.

"You never know what they'll pick up in the public schools," a man beside them said scornfully. They glared at him.

"My parents tried to reason with them, but they wouldn't listen," Michael went on. "They forgot that in this country, at least, elected officials are not gods. They are subject to the will of the people."

"This sounds familiar," Summer murmured, giving her mother a sidelong look.

"My friends and I can't vote yet, but we can show the city officials just what our will is. Skateboard laws affect kids more than anybody else, but kids can't vote for the people who make laws against skateboards. That's discrimination without representation."

Craig cupped his hands around his mouth. "That's un-American!"

"That's right," Michael shouted back. A smattering of applause went up from the crowd.

Diane shook her head. "I don't believe this."

Gwen couldn't, either.

"So, since we can't skate in my backyard, we're going to skate right here. It says right on that sign over there that this is a public park. We're the public, too, so we're going to skate."

Gwen let out a cheer, and Craig began to clap. More of the onlookers joined in this time.

But Michael wasn't done yet. "We have some extra skateboards here if any of you want to join us." Then he left the bandstand, turned on the music, and jumped on his skateboard. Soon he and his companions were zooming around, shouting and cheering.

"I had no idea Michael was such an orator," Bonnie told Diane.

"Neither did I." Diane stared at her sons.

"He's right, you know," Summer said. "If you believe in something, you have to be willing to stand up for it. It probably wasn't easy for him to do this, knowing how you'd feel, but he believed in it strongly enough to risk your anger. He's a brave kid."

"Brave or completely out of his mind. He's going to get in trouble, and not only from me."

"Even if he does, you have to let him make his own mistakes. You raised him well. You taught him right from wrong. Now you have to let him loose in the world to make his own way."

Diane looked dubious. "He's only fifteen."

"I didn't mean let him *that* loose," Summer said, laughing. She caught Gwen's eye. "You know what I mean?"

Diane shook her head, but Gwen nodded. Her heart lifted when Summer smiled at her.

Then, suddenly, Summer stepped onto the pavement. "What do we want? Skateboard freedom! When do we want it? Now!" she shouted, motioning for Michael to pause. The others joined in the chant as Michael gave her a skateboard, and soon, she too was circling the bandstand, her long auburn hair flying out behind her.

Suddenly Gwen knew what she had to do.

"Are you crazy?" Diane shrieked, grabbing her arm. Gwen shook her head and peeled Diane's fingers off her arm.

"What do we want? Skateboard freedom!" she shouted, climbing on the skateboard Michael offered her. She wobbled back and forth unsteadily until Summer took her by the hand and helped her steer. Hand in hand they skated around the bandstand, chanting until they were hoarse.

Craig kissed his wife on the cheek and grabbed a skateboard. Soon he was zooming past Gwen and her wonderful, strong-willed, bright star of a daughter. "Bonnie wanted to join us, but I told her I would instead," he said gallantly. "If one of us has to have a police record, we'll let it be me."

"I guess chivalry isn't dead after all," Gwen said. She and Summer looked at each other and laughed.

Every time they passed Diane, they encouraged her to join them. Every time they did, the crowd was a little larger, a lot noisier. Diane finally gave in and mounted a skateboard about five minutes before the police arrived and wound up arresting them all on charges of disturbing the peace.

"Did you really want me to go away and miss all this?" Summer shouted to her mother as they were being led away to separate police cars.

"I never wanted you to go away," Gwen shouted back. "Never." She could say nothing more because the police officer was guiding her into the back seat of the patrol car, careful not to bump her head on the door frame. Gwen was so elated, she wouldn't have felt it if he had. She and Summer were friends again, and that was all that mattered.

🏠 🏠 🏠

That was why Gwen didn't finish her border that evening as she had planned.

When she worked on it the next day, she cut a few pieces from the new fabric Summer had helped her select and added them to those she had already sewn in place. Just when she thought she had planned the pattern perfectly and that her work was nearly complete, Summer had given her something new to work with, something she had to learn to integrate with what she already had. Invariably this would alter the pattern, but perhaps that was not such a bad thing.

She chose blues and greens, golds and creams as her friends had done, for they had yet to lead her astray. If she did make a mistake, she could rely upon them to gently remind her what she was supposed to be about. All the quilt classes and quilt books in the world couldn't teach her as well as her friends did.

She pieced crazy quilt blocks to match her crazy quilt of a life, with patches going this way and that, apparently haphazard, with no discernible plan or pattern. That was what a careless glance would see—a random scattering of cloth. Only with more careful, thoughtful scrutiny could one discern the order within the chaos. For the patches of various sizes and shapes were stitched to muslin foundations, perfectly square, one block aligned with the next but not a part of it. The blocks were so very much alike but they were not the same, and she had learned to accept that.

The crazy quilt blocks encircled the round robin quilt in a wild and joyful dance, a mosaic of triangles and squares and other many-sided figures Gwen could not name. It was an embrace of blue and green and gold, unbroken.

# Chapter Eleven

Sarah drove Sylvia to the police station to bail out their friends. Before they left, Carol admonished them for laughing about their friends' plight. "I don't see what's so funny," she said. "Now they'll have criminal records. This will stay with them for the rest of their lives."

They were laughing more from astonishment and dismay than from humor, but Sarah was too annoyed to bother trying to explain. "Relax, Mother," Sarah said as she helped Sylvia into the truck. "It's not like they knocked over a liquor store." Carol gave her a sour look and returned inside the manor. Sarah wished that just once her mother would relax her impossibly high standards. She cared too much about meekly submitting to propriety and looking good to the neighbors. So a third of the Elm Creek Quilters had been arrested—so what? They had done what they thought was right, and Sarah was proud of them. She wished she had been there.

"I can't wait to hear the whole story," she said as she and Sylvia drove through the forest toward the main road leading to downtown Waterford. "I'm surprised Craig was arrested with them. This seems like the kind of thing Gwen and Summer would get involved in, and you never know what Diane's going to do next, but Craig?" Sarah shook her head. Craig seemed too stuffy, too rigid, to get involved in something so wacky. It was almost as difficult to picture Craig on a skateboard as it was to imagine Carol complimenting her daughter.

"Perhaps he was trying to redeem himself for his foolishness earlier this spring," Sylvia mused. "I believe he's done it. Gwen, too."

"Gwen?" Sarah glanced at Sylvia before returning her gaze to the road. "Why would Gwen need to redeem herself? What's she done?"

"Oh, you know the way you daughters are," Sylvia said lightly. "You always think your mothers are guilty of something."

Maybe that was true, but it didn't answer Sarah's question. Was Sylvia referring to Gwen's less-than-enthusiastic response to Summer's decision to forgo grad school? That wasn't even in the same realm as Craig's betrayal of Bonnie. Sylvia must have meant something else, but whatever Gwen had done, Sarah knew Sylvia wasn't going to tell her about it. Sylvia disliked gossip and deplored the breaking of confidences. "I know too well how the idle ramblings of vicious minds can destroy lives," she had said once, and Sarah remembered that, more than fifty years before, a handful of members of the Waterford Quilting Guild had driven Sylvia and Claudia from the group with their malicious words, unfounded rumors that the Bergstroms sympathized with the Germans during World War II. Claudia had told their brother, Richard, about the rumors, never dreaming that he would enlist to prove his family's patriotism. When Sylvia said that gossip could kill, she meant it literally.

Sarah respected her friend's feelings, so she didn't persist. Then she allowed herself a small smile, thinking that if Sylvia wouldn't talk about Gwen, maybe she'd talk about herself. "What were you and Andrew doing in the garden when I came to find you?" Sarah asked.

Out of the corner of her eye, she saw Sylvia straighten. "What do you mean, what were we doing?"

Sarah shrugged. "It's just that when I was looking toward the gazebo from the other side of the garden, it seemed like you two were sitting very close together. I thought maybe Andrew was having trouble with his hearing or something, or maybe he was helping you get something out of your eye."

"We most certainly were not sitting very close together. We were no closer than you and I are now."

"Oh. I guess it must have been an optical illusion. Maybe the spray from the fountain refracted the light rays or something."

"All right, young lady, I know what you're insinuating, and I don't appreciate it."

"What? What am I insinuating?"

"You know very well."

"I don't," Sarah insisted, then began to laugh. "Tell the truth. Were you two being naughty?"

"Honestly, Sarah, I don't know where you get these ideas."

"Well, why not? He obviously likes you, and you're always together—"

"Are we, indeed?" Sylvia looked left and right, up and down. "I don't see him now."

"Almost always, then. And you've been fixing your hair differently and wearing your best outfits. You can't tell me Andrew isn't the reason."

"I most certainly can. I've been wearing my spring clothes, not my best. You've merely forgotten them over the long winter." Sylvia patted her hair. "And I changed my hairstyle because Agnes recommended it. If I did it for anyone, I did it for her."

"Is the lipstick for Agnes, too?"

"Sarah, you try my patience. He's much younger than I am—almost seven years. He's Richard's age."

Sarah glanced at her, skeptical. "Do you really think seven years matters at this point?"

"Well—" Sylvia hesitated. "I don't suppose it does. Or rather, it wouldn't, if I cared for him the way you think I do, which I don't. Now, I must insist that you say no more about this."

"But—"

"I insist," Sylvia repeated, in a voice that would tolerate no disobedience.

So Sarah kept her curiosity to herself for the rest of the drive. Maybe Sylvia was telling the truth, or maybe she didn't yet recognize what her friends saw. Either way, Sarah hoped Andrew would postpone his trip east a little while longer. His company was good for Sylvia, so as far as Sarah was concerned, he was welcome to stay forever.

With Sarah's luck, it would be Carol who decided never to leave.

When they reached the police station, they went inside and followed signs that led to a waiting room. Bonnie was already there, talking to Judy's husband, Steve. Michael and Todd stood close by, whispering to each other and looking around with wide eyes. Bonnie spoke excitedly, gesturing in frustration as Steve nodded and wrote in a small notebook. When Bonnie spotted Sarah and Sylvia, she looked so relieved that Sarah wished she had driven faster. "Thank God you're here," Bonnie said. "Diane is raising such a stink in there, I'm afraid they're going to lock her up for good."

"They can't do that, can they?" Michael asked.

"Of course not," Sarah assured him, hoping it was true.

"We came as quickly as we could," Sylvia told Bonnie. "Naturally we couldn't refuse a request to bail our friends out of the pokey."

Bonnie almost smiled. "It's not really bail, just a fine. They're going to be released on their own recognizance once they pay. I feel so awful. I wanted to pay for everyone, but—"

"But you didn't want Sarah and me to feel left out, since we already missed most of the fun. That was kind of you."

Bonnie nodded, grateful, and Sarah knew that Sylvia was the one who had been kind, interrupting Bonnie before she had to admit that she didn't have enough for all the fines. It was no secret that the Markhams had to watch every penny, but the Elm Creek Quilters pretended not to notice. In turn, Bonnie pretended that her friends really did need two yards of an expensive fabric rather than one and that, as they insisted, as the most experienced teacher she deserved higher pay for the classes she taught for Elm Creek Quilts.

Sylvia wrote a check, and as they waited for their friends, Bonnie gave them more details about the protest. The police had shown up about a half hour after Michael's speech and had asked them to turn down the music and stop skating. When the protesters refused, the police listed several noise ordinances they were breaking, reminded them of the skateboard law, and warned them that they needed a permit to hold a public gathering in the square. Gwen began quoting from the Bill of

Rights and told the police that if the city of Waterford wanted them to stop skating, they were going to have to arrest them. The police agreed, and took her up on the suggestion. The adults were taken into custody, but despite their insistence on being arrested as well, the children were driven home to their parents. Bonnie had accepted responsibility for Todd and Michael.

"Will they have to go to trial?" Sarah asked.

Bonnie shook her head. "Not a trial, a hearing, but only if they decide to contest the fines."

"I suspect they will," Sylvia said.

Just then they heard their friends' voices floating down the hallway. "What do we want? Skateboard freedom! When do we want it? Now!" they chanted, their voices growing louder and louder. Steve burst into applause at the sight of them. Sarah joined in, noticing that the ovation was unanimous, even though most people in the room had no idea what was going on.

Michael and Todd ran over to hug their mother. "I knew they couldn't keep you locked up for long," Michael told her.

"Were you in a cell?" Todd asked. "Did you get to see solitary confinement? Do they call it 'the hole'?"

Diane embraced her sons. "No, we were all together in a conference room. This isn't Attica, Todd. Michael, where's your skateboard?"

"In Bonnie's car."

"Good," Gwen said. "You're going to need it. Come on, everyone. Back to the square."

Summer, Diane, and the boys cheered, but not Sarah. "You're not serious?"

"Of course. We can't give up now."

Sylvia placed a hand on her arm. "Perhaps discretion is the better part of valor, at least for now."

"Are you kidding? We have not yet begun to fight!"

"There are other ways to fight," Bonnie said. "Can't you pick one of them for the rest of the day?"

Gwen stared at her for a moment, then burst out laughing. "All right," she said good-naturedly. "No more public demonstrations today." The boys groaned in disappointment. "Relax. I didn't say we're giving up. We're going to start a letter-writing campaign."

Diane rolled her eyes. "Good luck with that one."

Michael looked dubious. "Writing letters?"

"That sounds like school," Todd said, uneasy.

"No, no, it'll be great," Gwen said. As they all left the building together, she placed an arm around each boy and began to explain.

Later that evening over supper, Sylvia and Sarah told Andrew, Matt, and Carol about the protest and the scene at the police station. They took turns narrating the story, laughing so hard that they had to wipe tears from their eyes. Andrew chuckled, but Matt just kept his eyes on his plate and said nothing, and Carol declared that she was ashamed of their friends. "I don't know what they hope to gain by making a spectacle of themselves," she said.

"They're hoping to draw attention to their concerns," Sarah said. She hated the thin-lipped, prissy, disapproving expression her mother had assumed. Sarah had seen too much of it over the years.

"Maybe that's true, but they're drawing attention to themselves, not to the issue. And they're bringing Elm Creek Quilts negative publicity. This will damage the reputation of everyone who works here."

Sylvia forced out a laugh. "I don't think it's as serious as all that."

"I wish I had your confidence." Carol shook her head, frowning as if she smelled something foul. "Maybe the rest of you can excuse their conduct, but I'm ashamed of them. Especially that Gwen. For a college professor, she doesn't have much sense. What kind of example is she setting for her students?"

" 'That Gwen' has more sense than some people I could mention," Sarah snapped. She barely noticed as Matt abruptly rose, carried his dishes to the sink, and left the room without a word. "More courage, too. It's not easy to stand up for something you believe in, knowing that all eyes are upon you and that you'll have to accept the consequences of your words and actions. Some people are brave in that way. Others can only write nasty letters about people behind their backs."

Carol set down her fork. "What are you talking about?"

"You know very well I'm talking about those letters you wrote about Matt." She glanced up to be sure he was out of the room, then realized that she wished he had not left. It was about time he knew how his mother-in-law had tried to prevent their marriage.

"I was concerned, and I don't deny that." Carol's voice was deliberate and calm. "Instead of writing a private letter to my daughter, should I have announced my concerns on national TV? Would that have been better?"

"You should have kept your concerns to yourself."

"I'm your mother. I wanted to help."

"Maybe you should try helping a little less. You're always trying to improve me, trying to make me better. All my life you've shoved my faults and problems in my face, and for years I tried to fix myself so I could be good enough for you. But you know what I finally realized? It's hopeless. As soon as I correct one flaw, you find another." Sarah shoved her chair away from the table and stood up. "You win, okay? You win. I'm a worthless nothing. My marriage is failing and my friends are criminals. You've been right about me all along."

Sarah turned away from them and stormed out of the room.

She sought seclusion in the library, but her thoughts were churning, making it impossible to concentrate on her work. Eventually she slipped out the back door, carefully and quietly, so that no one would know she had left. She used to wander the north gardens when troubled, but when Sylvia and Andrew starting going there so frequently, she had found herself another place, a quiet spot in the woods where a bend in Elm Creek created a still pool of deep water. The branches of a nearby willow fell like a curtain, nearly concealing a part of the pool and a large, smooth stone that overlooked it. Sarah had found the stone one day when a sudden gust of wind eased the branches aside. Resting on the cool stone with the murmur of the creek in her ears, she could feel her troubled thoughts clearing, her agitated spirits growing calm.

She wished she had not needed to visit the pool so often lately.

For the past two years, whenever she had needed sympathy or support, she had always been able to turn to the Elm Creek Quilters. Carol changed all that. Her friends still felt comfortable sharing their secrets and concerns, but Sarah couldn't confide her worries in the presence of the person most responsible for them. Sarah couldn't talk about Matt, either, not with her mother there to give her those looks, the ones that said "I knew it" and "I told you so." Instead she found herself withdrawing from the circle of friends—and Carol was only too eager to push her way into the space her daughter had vacated.

Sarah could understand why her mother wanted so badly to belong, to be a part of the group. Sarah had always managed to assemble a group of girls wherever she lived, but her mother had never done the same. Other mothers had friends, women they met for lunch, women they played bridge with in the evenings, but Carol did not, and for the longest time Sarah had not known why.

Then one day when Sarah was in the sixth grade, she had come home from a slumber party to find her mother scrubbing out the kitchen sink. Carol didn't ask about the party, but at that age Sarah still trusted her, so she began chattering away, buzzing from hours of talk and laughter and a near-overdose of sugar, replaying the party's events as much for herself as for her mother. All the while, Carol said nothing.

Suddenly, Sarah noticed her mother's odd silence, and it occurred to her that maybe her mother felt sad because she was too old for slumber parties. But even if she wasn't so old, whom would she invite over? Who would invite her?

"Mom," Sarah asked, "how come you never go out with your friends?"

"What friends?" Her mother turned on the faucet full blast to rinse the sink. "What makes you think I have friends?"

"Well . . ." Sarah hesitated. "Don't you?"

"I don't have time for friends," Carol said shortly. "Some people have friends. I have a husband, a job—and you."

Shocked into silence, Sarah mumbled an apology and slunk off to her room. Until that moment it had never occurred to her that she'd prevented her mother from having friends of her own. Maybe that was why her mother rarely smiled, why her voice was so sharp with criticism. Carol probably resented the way Sarah's needs had swallowed up every bit of her life until there was nothing left for her to call her own.

But if that was the reason, why hadn't things improved between them in recent years? Now that Carol was a widow, now that her daughter had married and moved away, she surely had plenty of time to herself. And if so much time on her own didn't suit her, she had her job and the Elm Creek Quilters' friendship to fill up the hours. But Carol might not have any friends back home, which was where she needed them. Was that why she had stuck around, even though it was surely obvious to both of them that their reconciliation wasn't going to happen?

Or, unlike Sarah, did Carol still hope that they would find a way?

Sarah lay down on her back upon the stone, her head resting on her hands. When she looked up she could see the willow branches gently moving with the wind. She watched until twilight fell, then, reluctantly, she left her hiding place and made her way carefully through the darkening woods, following Elm Creek until she reached the bridge between the barn and the manor. From there she could see the back of the manor clearly; some of the windows were aglow, including the kitchen and the west sitting room, Sylvia's favorite place to quilt. The suite Sarah and Matt shared was lit up, too.

Matt must be there. Sarah quickened her pace. She would try again to talk to him. She prayed that this time, when she needed him most, he would be willing to listen.

But when she went upstairs, she arrived just in time to see Carol turning off the light before leaving Sarah's suite. Sarah stopped short in the hallway. "Mother? What are you doing?"

Carol looked up, startled, but she said nothing as she closed the door and went down the hall to her own room.

Sarah hesitated. Should she go after her? She decided against it and went to her own room instead, glancing around to see if her mother had disturbed anything. Matt wasn't there, but there was an envelope on the bed with Sarah's name on it.

Sarah tore it open and found a letter.

*Dear Sarah,*

*Tomorrow I will be going home. It's obvious you don't want me here, and I no longer have the heart to stay when I know we'll continue to fight. I want you to know that I'm truly sorry I could never be the mother you wanted. My intentions were good, but we all know where good intentions lead you.*

*I'm sorry I wrote those letters. You're right, I should have kept my opinions to myself. If I wouldn't have objected to Matt so much, maybe you wouldn't have been so eager to marry him. You always did the opposite of what I told you to do. I should have known better.*

*You have wonderful friends and a wonderful life. They have shown you such generosity, and yet you won't share even the smallest scrap with me. I wish things were different between us. I think I should leave before they get worse. At least we tried.*

*Love,*
*Mother*

Sarah read the letter again to make sure she had understood it correctly. Yes, Carol would leave in the morning. Why wasn't Sarah relieved at the news? Instead she felt hurt—and angry. How like Carol to throw another barb at Matt in what was supposed to be an apology. How like her to heap on one last serving of criticism.

Sarah sank into a chair by the window. What should she do now? Run down the hall to her mother's room and beg her to stay? Help her pack? She felt a sting of guilt for her thoughts earlier that day, when she had sat by the creek and wished her mother would go away. She still wanted her life to go back to normal, but not if it meant having her mother leave in a huff. If Carol left now, Sarah knew that the chances for reconciliation would be more remote than ever.

Just then, she saw headlights outside the window moving past the barn, across the bridge, and toward the manor. She recognized their truck as it circled the two large elms in the center of the parking lot and stopped. Matt was home. Where had he been?

She raced downstairs and through the manor to the back door. Matt was just coming up the back steps, carrying a grocery bag. "Did you go into town?" she asked. "I didn't even know you had left."

"I would have asked if you needed me to pick up anything, but I couldn't find you."

Sarah wished he didn't sound so defensive. She tried to keep her voice light. "So, what did you buy me?" she asked, grinning and trying to peer into the bag.

"Ice cream. The real kind, as Sylvia calls it. She tried some of that fat-free stuff you bought and said it tastes like plastic. I offered to get her something better."

Ordinarily, Sarah would have reminded him that Sylvia was supposed to watch her blood pressure, but she couldn't afford to annoy him. "Matt, I need to talk to you."

"Let me put this away first before it melts."

"It will only take a minute." As soon as he got inside, he'd think of a dozen other things he had to do, anything but talk to her. "My mother's leaving in the morning."

He stared at her. "Why? Why now? Did you tell her to go?"

"No, of course not," she said, annoyed that he would think that of her. Quickly she read him the note, omitting only the part about Carol's letters.

Matt set down the bag. "Do you have any idea what brought this on? Yes, you two fight a lot, and sure, you're jealous of the time she spends with the Elm Creek Quilters, but that was true yesterday and the day before, too, and she knew it. They weren't reasons to leave then. Why are they now?"

His confirmation of Carol's complaints irked her. "If you had stuck around instead of taking off as soon as you finished eating supper, you'd know."

"I didn't want to listen to any more fights. Is that a crime?"

Sarah tried to calm herself. She had to get this conversation back on track. "I think the skateboard demonstration upset her. You know how she is. She kept going on and on about how their arrest will damage the reputation of Elm Creek Quilts."

"She has a good point."

"What?" Sarah stared at him. "Matt, these are our friends she's criticizing."

"Friends or not, they used poor judgment. You haven't thought this through. How do you think prospective campers will feel when they learn half your employees were thrown into jail for disturbing the peace?"

"My friends aren't criminals," Sarah said in a tight voice.

"Yes, they are. They broke the law. Even if they don't agree with it, it's still the law."

"I can't believe you're saying this. You sound just like my mother."

"Maybe she knows what she's talking about." Matt's voice rose until it was nearly a shout.

"Matt, calm down."

"Don't tell me to calm down. Don't you get it? We're dependent on this business for everything. Everything. What if all this crap with the police scares your customers away? What then? And what if something should happen to Sylvia? Who will get the business? Who will get the manor? Not us, that's for sure. We may live with her, but we aren't her family. She probably doesn't even have a will. She'll have heirs crawling out of the woodwork, and the first thing they'll do is close down the quilt camp and kick us out of the manor."

"That's insane," Sarah snapped. "I'm sure Sylvia's planned for that."

"You're sure?" Matt barked out an angry laugh. "You don't know that. That's not how you people run things. In any other company we'd have some security, some kind of safety net, but not here. It's too damn risky, and I'm sick of living this way."

"What are we supposed to do? What other way can we live?"

"I've been trying to figure that out for months. How am I suppose to know what to do? You're the one who got us into this mess. If not for your damn Elm Creek Quilts, we'd be a lot better off. I don't know why I ever let you talk me into leaving my old job. Now everything's in one basket and it's all about to spill over. And you won't let yourself see it!"

"No one forced you to quit your old job," Sarah shouted back. "That was your decision."

"Yeah, and it was the worst one of my life." He shot Sarah a furious glare. "Make that the second worst." He shoved past her and stormed into the house.

His words burned in her ears. She stood there, stunned, so hurt she could hardly breathe. Then, somewhere over her right shoulder, she heard a noise. She glanced up in time to see a figure move away from the kitchen window.

Oh, no. Was it Carol or Sylvia who had overheard their fight? Sarah went inside, heart sinking, praying that the figure at the window had been Andrew.

When she entered the kitchen, Sylvia stood in the center of the room, alone.

"Sylvia—" Then Sarah could go no further.

"Please forgive me for eavesdropping," Sylvia said, her voice quiet. "I should have left the window as soon as I heard you, but—"

"He didn't mean it."

"Oh, I'm quite certain he meant every word." Sylvia sighed. "The question is, what shall we do now?"

"I don't know. I don't know." Sarah felt tears gathering. She couldn't remember when she had last been so upset or so scared. She clenched her hands together to keep them from trembling.

"Don't waste a single moment." Sylvia placed her hands on Sarah's shoulders. "You'll have to go to them, to both of them, and apologize. Now, before it's too late."

Sarah froze, stunned. "Apologize?"

"Of course. It's the only thing you can do."

"I don't understand." Sarah shrugged off Sylvia's hands. Apologize? Carol was the one who had given up and was running away. Matt was the one who had become angry and insulted Sylvia and the other Elm Creek Quilters.

"What's to understand? March yourself upstairs and tell Matt you're sorry for losing your temper. Then sit down and discuss the matter rationally. When you're finished there, go speak to your mother."

Sylvia's tone was matter-of-fact, but her words sparked Sarah's anger. "Wait a minute. Hold on. Matt's the one who lost his temper. Why should I be the one to cave in? Why aren't you telling him to apologize to me?"

"Because he isn't the one who sought my advice. If he were the one standing here, I would have told him the same. Someone has to bend. What do you have to gain from being stubborn?"

"Stubborn?" Sarah gasped. "I'm stubborn? You ignore your family for fifty years after one little argument and *I'm* stubborn?"

A muscle twitched in Sylvia's cheek, but her voice was cool. "That's simplifying things a bit, wouldn't you say? And we're not talking about my mistakes now, but about yours."

Sarah felt the blood pounding in her ears as Sylvia continued, telling her how to approach Matt and Carol, what to say, how to say it. She used words like *responsibility*, and *maturity*, and *selflessness*—words that jumbled up and spun around in Sarah's mind until she thought she would explode.

Suddenly she couldn't bear one more word of criticism, one more sentence of blame. "Stop it," she burst out. "What do you know about any of this? Your mother died when you were five, so what do you know about dealing with someone like Carol? And how long were you married? I've been married three times as long as you were, so who are you to tell me what to do? You're not my mother. Sometimes you don't even act like my friend!"

All the color drained from Sylvia's face.

In an instant, Sarah was shocked and sickened by her horrible words. She started to apologize, but Sylvia cut her off. "No, no, you're quite right." Sylvia wouldn't—or couldn't—look at her. "Who am I to be giving out advice? As you pointed out, I have little experience."

"Sylvia, please. I was just upset about Matt and my mother. I didn't mean—"

"You meant every word, just as Matthew did when he spoke his piece." Sylvia sighed, and the sound wrenched Sarah's heart. "Well. This won't do. Such unhappiness won't do." Her voice was bleak. "I'll say good-night now. I've had enough of being a meddling old busybody for one day. Thank you for letting me know how you feel."

"But that's not how I feel, not really," Sarah said, but it was too late. Sylvia was already leaving the kitchen, her shoulders slumped, her footsteps slow.

Sarah called after her, but the words caught in her throat, and only sobs came out. She clung to the kitchen counter, sick with remorse and shame.

A moment later, a movement caught her eye. It was Andrew, standing in the doorway of the west sitting room. He gave her a long, steady look as he passed her on his way through the kitchen after Sylvia. He spoke not a word, but she could sense his profound disappointment in her.

Never before in her life had she found herself so deserving of anyone's censure. Never before had she been more aware of her own selfishness, her potential for cruelty. Never before had she been so alone.

# Chapter Twelve

Sylvia slept poorly. Andrew's words had been kind, but they had not comforted her. "She's just a young woman," Andrew had said. "She loves you dearly. Don't hold this one moment against her."

Sylvia promised him she wouldn't, but how could she ever forget how Sarah had lashed out at her? How could they go on as if nothing had happened? This could be the end of everything, everything, not just the hopes for a reconciliation between Sarah and Carol, but Elm Creek Quilts, the new life and joy they had restored to the manor, all of it.

Her dreams tormented her and shook her awake long before dawn.

As she lay in bed, waiting for the early morning grogginess to leave her, she felt uneasiness stirring, expanding until dread and worry filled her. Slowly she realized that there was something she had to do that morning, something urgent, something regarding Sarah and Carol. But what was it? What was it? She felt as if she had gone into a room to fetch something, only to realize she had forgotten what she had come for.

Sometimes retracing her steps helped her to remember. Yes. She would wake Sarah. As soon as Sylvia saw her, she would remember what it was that she must do. In the semidarkness, she sat up and groped for her glasses on the nightstand.

Just as her fingertips touched the fine silver chain, a searing pain shot through her skull.

She gasped.

Her left hand was numb, the left side of her face was numb, but her head was on fire.

This was wrong. The thoughts came slowly. Something was very wrong with her.

She should lie down and wait for it go away.

No. No. She couldn't.

Somehow she made herself sit upright. She tried to force her feet into her slippers, but she could not get her legs to move properly. She could see her slippers there on the floor beside her bed, and yet somehow she could not determine where they were. She tried to focus, but nothing would obey her, not her perception, not her limbs.

Afraid now, and barefoot, she forced herself to stand. She fell twice on her way to the door. She fumbled with the knob, slamming her shoulder on the frame as the door finally opened into the hallway. The blow registered, but not the pain.

Sarah, help me, she screamed, but no sound came out.

Leaning against the wall, she shuffled down the hallway toward Sarah's room. Right foot, left. Again, though she had no strength for it. Right foot. An eternity passed. Left foot.

She was nearly blind from pain.

"Sharuh," she called out.

Her mouth was frozen stiff. She took as deep a breath as she could. She would have one more chance. That, and no more.

"Sharuh!"

It was the haunted wail of a stranger. It could not have been her own voice.

It was useless, useless. She could go no farther.

Then, as if in slow motion, she saw two doors open, one on either side of the hall. Sarah and Carol stepped from their rooms. Slowly their heads turned her way. Their eyes went wide with horror.

The last thing Sylvia saw as she collapsed was the mother and daughter running toward her.

Then she fell into darkness.

# Chapter Thirteen

gnes was already awake when Sarah called from the hospital at six o'clock in the morning. The poor girl was so upset she could hardly get the words out, but the dreadful news was all too clear: Sylvia had suffered a stroke. The doctors did not yet know how serious.

"I'm coming," Agnes told her. "I need to be there."

Sarah must have anticipated this. "Matt's already on his way to pick you up."

Agnes hung up the phone, numb. They didn't need her there, getting in the doctors' way. If Sylvia was going to be fine, they would have asked Agnes to postpone her visit until the afternoon at least. This was their way of telling her she would be coming to the hospital to say good-bye.

Agnes collected her appliqué patches, carefully folded the round robin center, and placed everything into her sewing box. Hospitals meant long waits, so she would take her quilting with her to keep her thoughts focused away from her grief.

Life was just one extended series of partings. She could not bear many more. She supposed she would not have to bear many more.

She put on a sweater and went to the living room, where she could see the driveway from a chair near the window. Was Sarah calling the other Elm Creek Quilters? Someone else should do it for her—Matt, perhaps, or Carol. Diane had made the calls for Agnes when Joe died, and Agnes had not been nearly as distraught then as Sarah sounded now. It wasn't that Agnes hadn't loved Joe; she had. But he had suffered so terribly for so many months before finally succumbing to cancer that his death was, in a sense, a relief, though she wouldn't dream of telling her daughters that. And, too, no matter how much she had loved those who passed, every loss since Richard's had been diminished in comparison. No other loss could compare to that enormous, overwhelming pain, that severing—but Sylvia's passing would come close.

Suddenly she remembered Andrew, and her heart went out to him. How would he bear this? He had admired Sylvia since he was a child, and had fallen in love with her as a young man. Agnes remembered a time so long ago when Richard had teased him after the two boys returned to Philadelphia following a long weekend at Elm Creek Manor.

"Andrew here is sweet on my sister," Richard told her, nudging Andrew.

"Is that so?" Agnes asked. She had not met Richard's family yet. Secretly she envied Andrew and wished Richard had invited her to come on the trip, too. "And how does she feel about you, Andrew?"

"It doesn't matter." He shrugged, disconsolate. "She's married."

"You mean you like Sylvia?" She thought Richard had meant Claudia, the pretty one, the eldest.

Richard grinned. "At least Sylvia's closer to his age."

"Yes, but she's married," Agnes said, scandalized.

"I didn't tell her," Andrew protested. "What kind of a fellow do you take me for?"

Laughing, Richard patted him on the back and said, "We'll have to find a pretty girl to keep his mind off my sister."

"I have a few friends who might be interested," Agnes teased, and Andrew's blush deepened.

They were such good friends in those days, young and carefree, with all their days yet before them, or so it seemed. No wonder she had fallen in love with Richard. He was so handsome and confident and kind. She had never met anyone like him, not at the silly cotillions her parents forced her to attend, not at dancing school, not at any of the other society functions. The boys she met there, the boys her mother firmly steered her toward, were virtually interchangeable in their backgrounds, their educations, their interests—even their mannerisms seemed identically practiced and polished. But Richard had a wild energy about him she had never sensed in anyone else. And to her amazement, she realized that he saw something unique in her, as well. He saw a part of her she had almost forgotten, a spirited girl with a mind of her own and the confidence to follow it wherever it led. For as long as Agnes could remember, her mother had labored to shape that girl into a carefully decorated, overrehearsed debutante—like her sisters, like the women her brothers would eventually marry. But her mother's idea of what Agnes should be was imposed from without, not brought forth from within. Richard had seen through the façade, and she knew she would never be the same.

Naturally her parents hated him. They pitied Andrew, the poor scholarship student who would be educated beyond his station and relegated to a life as a tutor to rich men's sons, but they despised Richard. Not that he was anything but respectful to them during those few times they were together. In fact, his manners were impeccable—which incensed her parents all the more, and delighted Agnes. Oh, but she would have loved him even if he had not been forbidden. Something in her soul recognized his, and they both knew from the moment they met that, somehow, they completed each other.

A red pickup truck pulled into the driveway, drawing Agnes from her reverie. She didn't wait for Matt to come to the door, but met him halfway up the path. Matt's expression was grim as he helped her into the truck.

"Is there any change?" she asked when he came around the other side and took his own seat.

"Nothing yet."

Her hopes wavered, but she forced confidence into her voice for his sake. "Sylvia's a fighter. If anyone can pull through this, she can. She will."

"I hope you're right."

A roughness in his voice made her look at him. For the first time she noticed that his eyes were red.

When they reached the hospital, they found Sarah and Carol in the waiting room. Sarah was staring straight ahead and crying without making a sound, so stricken that Agnes was frightened for her. Carol was by her side, speaking to her in a low voice. Once Sarah nodded slowly, but otherwise she seemed oblivious to her surroundings.

Agnes and Matt joined them, and not long afterward the other Elm Creek Quilters began to arrive in pairs and alone. Frequently, Carol would approach the reception desk and ask about Sylvia, then return to the group, shaking her head.

"When can we see her?" Agnes asked.

"Not until she's stable. Or—" Carol's voice broke off. She tilted her head toward her daughter, indicating that she did not want to say anything about Sylvia's worsening condition in front of Sarah. Sarah was still staring straight ahead, unaware. She had stretched out the hem of her T-shirt and was twisting it into a rope.

Agnes rose, glancing toward the emergency room doors, just beyond the reception desk. She had seen how the paramedics hit that large red button on the wall to make the doors swing open. If she summoned up her confidence, perhaps no one would challenge her if she walked through them. But what good would sneaking in to see Sylvia do? The last they had heard, Sylvia was unconscious. She would not know that Agnes was there. But if Agnes held her hand and whispered to her, perhaps something would reach her. Perhaps she would be comforted.

If Sylvia were awake and alert, she wouldn't want anyone to see her in such a state, confined to a bed, doctors and nurses fussing and scolding, tubes going every which way. She'd order her friends out of the room and not let them return until she was properly dressed and standing on her own two feet. Agnes almost smiled at the thought. As long as Agnes had known her, Sylvia had possessed a regal, almost imperious air, though it had softened over the years.

When Agnes first came to Elm Creek Manor, though, Sylvia had played the lady of the manor indeed.

Agnes was fifteen then; she had known Richard for only a few months, and she liked him more than any other boy she had ever met.

Her parents' coldness toward him hurt her deeply, and she was determined to change their minds.

Every Christmas the Chevaliers threw an enormous ball, the most eagerly anticipated social event of the year in Philadelphia and beyond. Anyone who was anyone came—with the exception of a few "muckraking newspapermen" who published unflattering articles in the newspapers they owned, editorials about Mrs. Chevalier's father, the former senator, and her brothers, judges and senators all, any one of whom could become president one day. In hindsight Agnes realized she had grown up surrounded by wealth and power, but at the time, occasions such as the Yuletide Ball were merely parties, with pretty ladies and handsome gentlemen, beautiful music, delicious food—and the opportunity to wear a lovely gown as she danced with Richard.

She would ask her mother to permit Richard to attend as her guest. He would charm everyone there, she was certain of it. He had such an easy way with people, with none of her own stammering bashfulness. His secret was that he was genuinely interested in whatever his companion of the moment had to say. It was no act with him. He was fascinated with the world and everything in it. Any chance to meet someone he had never met or to try something he had never tried delighted him. Surely her parents would come to like him as much as everyone else did if they would just give themselves that chance.

"Absolutely not," her mother declared. "Agnes, how could you ask such a thing? It's simply unthinkable."

"But why? You've always allowed me to invite friends before."

"Don't be stupid. This is the Yuletide Ball. We can't have a stable boy running around smelling of horses' dirt."

"He's the heir to Bergstrom Thoroughbreds, and his family is as good as any in Philadelphia. But even if he were a stable boy, I would still want him to come. He is a very dear friend."

"Indeed," her mother said dryly. "You won't want for friends at the ball. The Johnson sisters are coming, and young Mr. Cameron will be there."

"Oh, how delightful. The young Mr. Cameron." Agnes plopped down on an overstuffed sofa in a most ungraceful fashion. "Will he spend the entire evening talking about his damned greyhounds, like he did last year?"

"Agnes," her mother gasped, shocked.

It took Agnes a moment to realize her mistake.

Her mother's face was white with fury except for two scarlet blotches in the hollows of her cheeks. "Where did you learn such a filthy word?"

From Father, Agnes almost said, but she managed to hold it back.

"I know you didn't learn that at Miss Sebastian's Academy. Did your noble stable boy teach it to you?"

Agnes's anger got the better of her. "Yes, he did," she snapped. "That, and a great many other things."

Her mother nearly fainted. Too late, Agnes realized her second mistake. She had meant that Richard had taught her other curse words—which wasn't exactly true—but her mother had understood her meaning quite differently.

"You are such a trial to me," her mother said, seizing her by the arm and marching her from the drawing room. It did not occur to Agnes to resist. "You'll stay in your room until you remember how a young lady should behave."

Mrs. Chevalier had to let Agnes out to go to school, but she was watched so carefully that she couldn't run off to meet Richard and Andrew all that week. The following Monday as she left Miss Sebastian's, she spotted Richard just outside the tall wrought iron gates. Her heart quickened with nervous pleasure as she went to meet him, hoping her father's driver was not paying attention.

"You haven't come to see us all week," Richard said, his brow furrowed in concern. "What's the matter, don't you like that café anymore? Or did Andrew say something to offend you?"

Agnes laughed at thought of Andrew's saying anything offensive—but she was thrilled. Richard had missed her. She had feared he had forgotten her.

"I wanted to come. There have been—" She hesitated, wanting to protect him. "Some complications."

Richard's eyebrows rose, but he didn't ask for more details, which was a relief. As angry as she was with her parents, she loved them and was loyal to them. She couldn't bear to disparage them before anyone, especially Richard.

"Any chance these complications will sort themselves out soon?"

Agnes tried to smile. "Anything is possible."

He nodded, then looked past her to the waiting car. Her father's driver had opened the door to the back seat and stood with his hand upon it, waiting.

"Andrew and I will be at the café as usual," Richard finally said. "Come see us when you can." He gave her one quick smile before turning and walking away.

Her heart sank to see him go.

Two weeks went by, and not once could she slip away. Richard met her once again outside Miss Sebastian's, but only once. After that, she had no word from him. Her hopes dwindled as the Christmas holidays approached. Both her school and the boys' school would be closed for a month, and Richard would be going home to Elm Creek Manor. She knew his travel schedule—which train he would take, what time he planned to leave—and as that hour approached, she realized what she had to do.

Swiftly she packed a suitcase and left a note for her parents with the butler. Then she hired a cab to take her to the train station. She bought a ticket and hurried as fast as she could to the platform, where she searched frantically for Richard.

Then she spotted him in the center of a knot of passengers waiting to board the train.

"Richard," she called to him. Her voice was swallowed up in the noise of the station. Frantic, she screamed his name. He jerked his head in her direction, his face lighting up with recognition and astonishment.

He left his place in line and made his way through the crowd to her side. "Agnes, what are you doing here?" He glanced at her suitcase, but said nothing about it.

"May I come home with you for the holidays?"

"Your parents won't mind that you'll miss their party?"

"I'm sure they will, once they find out."

He studied her for a long moment. For a while she feared he would refuse. He was offended by her gall and never wanted to see her again.

But then he picked up her suitcase and offered her his arm. "I'd be delighted to have you come. If I'd known you could, I would have asked you weeks ago."

She took his arm, too overcome with relief to speak. That, Agnes later realized, was when she first knew she loved him.

The train ride west was one of the happiest occasions of her life. Finally she and Richard had the chance to talk alone for hours. Richard truly listened when Agnes spoke, unlike all the other men she had known, who would smile indulgently and exchange looks over her head, chuckling as if she were an amusing child. Richard didn't agree with all of her opinions—especially regarding the troubles in Europe—but he never once treated her as if she was nothing more than a harmless, silly decoration. To someone who had spent her life learning how to be an ornament, this was a revelation.

When they arrived at Elm Creek Manor, Agnes was nervous and excited. She didn't regret her decision to come home with Richard, but she wished his family had expected her. Maybe then Richard's sister Sylvia wouldn't have greeted her with such obvious shock. Maybe then Agnes wouldn't have earned Sylvia's immediate and intense dislike. It was obvious that Sylvia was the queen of this household, just as Agnes's mother ruled the Chevalier home. With Sylvia against her, Agnes feared Richard would not remain hers for long—if it was, in fact, right to call him hers.

"Your sister doesn't like me," she told him that evening before they retired to separate bedrooms a respectful distance apart. Richard laughed and told her she was imagining things, which made her heart drop even lower. From that moment she knew he would be forever blind to Sylvia's barely contained malevolence.

Gradually, Agnes won over the others. She got along well with Richard's eldest sister, Claudia, and the young cousins even asked her to join in their games occasionally. Sylvia's husband, James, was a true gentleman, kind and thoughtful, much like Richard himself. Only Sylvia remained aloof and resistant.

Agnes understood the source of her resentment: Sylvia was selfish. She had a husband, a sister, a loving family—but that wasn't enough for her. She also wanted her younger brother all to herself, and no young woman from Philadelphia was going to steal him away.

How ironic it was that Sylvia was treating Agnes as Mrs. Chevalier treated Richard. If those two headstrong, jealous women ever encountered each other—Agnes giggled at the thought. She wished she could share her amusement with Richard, but she didn't want him to know how her parents felt about him. No doubt he suspected the truth, but she would spare him the insulting details.

Instead she doubled her efforts to befriend Sylvia. When she sensed how proud Sylvia was of her quilting, she made certain to praise Sylvia's needlework—the fineness of her stitches, the intricacy of the designs.

"How charming," Agnes said, admiring Sylvia's current project, an elaborate quilt with appliquéd baskets, flowers, and other intricate shapes. "What pattern is this?"

"It's a Baltimore Album quilt." Sylvia went on to explain the history of the style. Agnes listened, nodding as if fascinated. Once she glanced up and caught Claudia's eye, and she saw that Richard's elder sister was trying to hide a smile. Claudia knew what Agnes was about, even if Sylvia didn't.

When Sylvia's long-winded explanation finally drew to a close, Claudia spoke up. "Do you quilt, Agnes?"

Agnes realized she had an ally. "No, I don't know how. I wish I could, but I know I could never make anything as lovely as this." She gazed at Sylvia's quilt in admiration.

"All it takes is practice," Sylvia said briskly, but Agnes could tell that the compliment had pleased her.

"I wish that were true," Agnes said. "But I don't have your talent,

Sylvia. I suppose I'll just have to keep buying my comforters in the shops in Philadelphia."

To her surprise, Sylvia pursed her lips, offended. "Naturally you'd want to do that. Out here on the frontier, however, we don't have that luxury."

"Sylvia," Claudia warned.

Agnes quickly added, "What I meant to say was that I would prefer a handmade quilt like those you have in Elm Creek Manor, but since I can't quilt, I—"

"You'll buy something made by someone with better sense." Sylvia glanced away from her work to frown at Agnes. "I hope you remembered to pack all you'll need, or you might need to go home early. Our humble shops out here in the country are no match for those in the heavenly land of Philadelphia."

The rebuke stung. Perhaps Agnes had gone on about Philadelphia during her visit, but it was only to show the Bergstroms how wonderful she found Elm Creek Manor in comparison. If only they knew how much she longed to take the happy clamor of their family back home with her. She left the room before she burst into tears. She would not humiliate herself further by allowing Sylvia to see her cry.

It was not an auspicious beginning, Agnes thought, turning away from the window. She and Sylvia had come a long way since then. In the past two years, since Sarah had reunited them, they had become friends. Agnes never would have dreamed it.

She never would have dreamed that she would one day be able to quilt like Sylvia, either, but she had learned. Sylvia had tried to teach her, but when those lessons failed miserably, Claudia finished the job. Now Claudia was gone, and Sylvia would soon join her. Once again, Agnes would be alone.

She took a deep breath to fight off the tears. It wouldn't do to break down when Sylvia needed her friends to be strong. Then she remembered the round robin center in her sewing box. Yes, that was what she needed, something to keep her busy so she would stop glancing at the clock and wondering why the nurse hadn't been back with news of Sylvia in such a long while.

The other Elm Creek Quilters, who had been so eager to see her center design, barely noticed as she took out the round robin quilt and began to work. She had strip-pieced a background for her appliqué, with varying shades of blue for the sky and green for the grass. After trimming this piece into a large circle, she had sewn pieces of gray and white onto it, creating a portrait of Elm Creek Manor in fabric. A scrap of black cotton became the rearing horse fountain in the front of the manor, and a narrow strip of blue was the creek in the distance. Now she was adding the final touch: a grove of trees at the northeast corner of the manor, where the cornerstone patio was, where the main entrance to the manor had been before the south wing was built in Richard's father's day.

Richard had told her so much of the manor's history—how Hans Bergstrom had placed the cornerstone with the help of his sister and wife, how the manor had served as a station on the Underground Railroad, how the estate had flourished over the years, and how it had sometimes faltered. Once he mentioned that the north garden was a perfect spot for a wedding, and once that the ballroom in the south wing could accommodate several hundred guests. His hints thrilled her, but she had other ideas. When she married, it would be in a proper church, and the reception afterward would take place in her parents' home. They would insist upon it. As far as Agnes was concerned, if she did somehow manage to convince her parents to accept Richard, she would let her mother do whatever she wanted for the wedding in gratitude.

As it turned out, neither Agnes nor Richard had the wedding they had imagined.

His proposal and the ensuing ceremony took place over the span of a few short days in March of the following year, 1944. Richard had returned to Elm Creek Manor for his school holidays, but this time she did not accompany him. Instead she waved good-bye from the platform as his train pulled out of the station, then she returned home with her brother, who had accompanied them at Mrs. Chevalier's insistence.

The next time she saw Richard was several days before he was actually due back. It was mid-morning, and he had come straight to the front door instead of throwing pebbles at her window and signaling her to meet him outside. Her mother's voice was frosty as she informed Agnes she had a caller waiting in the drawing room.

Agnes's heart pounded as she went downstairs. Her mother's tone told her it was Richard waiting—but why? What was he doing back so soon? Something was terribly, terribly wrong.

When she entered the room where Richard waited, he was pacing back and forth, hair tousled, face flushed, eyes bright with excitement. She was too startled to speak, but he looked her way at the sound of the door. He crossed the room swiftly and seized her hands. "Agnes, I have something to ask you." He dropped to one knee. "I love you with all my heart, and I know you love me, too. Would you do me the honor of becoming my wife?"

Agnes stared at him. Why was he asking her now? He knew she was just sixteen. He knew he ought to ask her father first, and not for years yet. Why—

Then she understood. He and Andrew—all their bold talk about enlisting—

Her legs were suddenly too weak to support her, but Richard helped her to a chair. "Please—" she choked out. "Please—"

He smiled, but there were tears in his eyes. "You don't have to beg, darling. I've already proposed."

She wanted to strike him for joking at such a time. She hated him. She loved him so fiercely she could never let him leave her. "Please tell me you didn't enlist. Please tell me you're not asking me this because you're going off to war in the morning."

"Not in the morning." His face was close to hers. He stroked her hair gently. "I have two weeks."

Her chest tightened up with sobs, so many that she thought they would tear her throat open. But she swallowed them back and wiped her eyes with the back of her hand. Unsteadily, she rose from her chair. "Will you excuse me, please?"

"But Agnes—"

"I'm going to seek my parents' blessing." Without waiting for a reply, she left the drawing room. Her mother was in her sitting room writing letters.

Agnes took a seat beside her and waited for her mother to look up. She refused to acknowledge her daughter's presence, to punish her for the undesirable caller. Agnes wondered what punishment her mother would contrive for what she was about to say, and realized it didn't matter. Nothing could hurt her more than the thought of Richard's going off to war.

Finally her mother looked up. "Yes, dear, what is it?"

"Richard Bergstrom has asked me to marry him. I would like to have your blessing, and Father's."

Her mother's face went white in fury, but her voice was perfectly controlled. "Absolutely not." She resumed writing, and nearly tore the paper with her pen. "If you're not pleased with the young Mr. Cameron we'll find someone else suitable for you, but you shall decline Mr. Bergstrom's proposal and instruct him never again to speak of it."

Agnes felt as if she were watching the scene play out from a great distance. "No," she heard herself say. "I shall not decline."

Her mother slammed down her pen. "You shall. You have no choice. You are too young. Do you really believe any judge within two hundred miles of here would allow a Chevalier daughter to marry under such suspicious circumstances?" Her voice was high and shrill. "They value their livelihoods too dearly for that, I assure you. Not one of them has any wish to be the man who allows a disobedient child to destroy the Chevalier family's good name."

Agnes grew very still. For the first time she saw her mother clearly, without fear. Agnes held the power now, and her mother was the frightened one. No matter what happened next, Agnes would never submit to her mother again. She was free.

"Richard has enlisted. He leaves in two weeks." Each word was as cold and distinct as if it had been chiseled in marble. "I will spend every moment between now and his departure by his side—every day and every night. I would prefer to do so as his wife, but I will do so as his mistress if necessary. Since you are so concerned with the Chevalier family's good name, perhaps you should consider carefully whether you truly wish to withhold your blessing."

Her mother stared at her for a long moment, breathing rapidly, clutching the desktop. "Your father will never agree," she managed to say.

"You will convince him."

Agnes was correct; her mother did make him see reason. But he gave Agnes one condition. "If you marry that man," he roared, "you leave this house forever. You will be dead to us."

His words shocked her into silence. She could only stare at him, the man she had always admired and loved so deeply. He thought she had betrayed him, and perhaps she had.

She thought of Richard, and how he might not return from the war. She might have two weeks with him, two weeks in exchange for a lifetime with her family.

She was her father's favorite daughter, and yet he could cut her out of his life with a word.

She wanted to ask her father if he meant it, but that would have been foolish. Her father never said anything he didn't mean. She wanted to beg him to reconsider, but her father never backed down from an ultimatum.

So she spoke from the heart. "I will miss you all very much," she said. Then she returned to the drawing room to tell Richard she would be his wife.

They had a simple civil ceremony the next day. Andrew was one witness, one of Agnes's school friends the other. Agnes had wanted her sisters, but she could not ask them to defy their parents.

Later that day, James and Harold arrived, too late to stop Richard and Andrew from enlisting as James had promised Sylvia. James decided to enlist so that he would be in the same unit as his brother-in-law and be able to protect him. Harold reluctantly said he would as well.

Agnes thought it was madness. "Don't do it," she had begged them. She clung to James's arm. "Please. Think of Sylvia."

Gently, James freed himself. "I am thinking of Sylvia," he said, and then he and Harold left.

Agnes was not comforted by the knowledge that James and Harold would be looking after Richard on the battlefield. Their selflessness and courage would not stop a bullet. They should have tried to free Richard from his enlistment, not join him in it. It was madness. Utter madness. And she alone seemed to see it.

They returned to Elm Creek Manor together for a few bleak days of grievous good-byes. Harold proposed to Claudia, but they did not rush off and marry as Agnes and Richard had done, as so many other young couples had done. They wanted to wait until after the men returned so they could do it right. Agnes marveled at their certainty that they would have that chance.

And then, all too soon, the men departed.

Of the four, only Andrew and Harold returned.

Agnes's hands trembled, and she stuck herself with the needle. She dropped the quilt as soon as she felt the pain, but she was not fast enough. A small drop of blood now stained the back of the block, a smear of red leaking through the gray fabric of the manor.

She shivered.

"Let me help you," Bonnie said. She took the quilt and carried it over to the drinking fountain.

"Did you hurt yourself?" Andrew asked.

"Only a little needle prick," Agnes said, but Carol had already taken her hand and was examining her finger. There was a tiny drop of blood on the pad of her left index finger. Carol insisted on taking her to the bathroom to wash the pinprick with soap and water. Then Carol carefully applied antibiotic ointment and a bandage, all from the small first aid kit she kept in her purse.

"What do you do for a cough?" Diane asked when they returned to the waiting room. "A lung transplant?"

The Elm Creek Quilters smiled, but no one had the heart to laugh.

"It's better to be safe than sorry," Carol said.

"She's right," a voice broke in. "Hospitals are the worst places for picking up germs. I read that somewhere."

It was Sarah who had spoken. They all turned to look at her. As far as

Agnes knew, those were the first words she had spoken since arriving at the hospital.

"Then I'm fortunate Carol was here," Agnes said gently, returning to her seat.

Bonnie handed her the quilt center. "The stain came out, but I'm afraid it's a little damp."

"That's all right. I'll finish when it's dry." All that was left was a tiny bit of the last tree, and then she could stitch the design in place in the center of the round robin quilt her friends had made. She tried not to, but in the back of her mind she wondered if Sylvia would ever see the completed quilt hanging in the front foyer to welcome the new quilt campers.

The quilt campers.

"Oh, dear," she said. "It's Sunday."

Her friends exchanged looks of weary dismay, and she could tell they had forgotten, too.

Gwen said, "We'll have to call everyone and tell them camp is canceled this week."

"We can't do that," Judy said. "It's already nine o'clock. If they're driving a long distance, they might have left already."

"And those who are flying already paid for their airline tickets," Bonnie added.

"Can't you refund their costs?" Andrew asked. "If you tell them what happened, they'll understand."

"No." Sarah sat up and looked around at her friends. "We can't do that. We have to hold camp as planned."

Silence.

"Maybe you're right," Diane said. "That's what Sylvia would have wanted."

Sarah whirled on her, furious. "That's what Sylvia would *want*."

Chastened, Diane looked away.

Summer stood up. "Sarah's right. We can't let Sylvia think we'll fall apart if she doesn't watch us every minute. I'll go back to the manor and start setting up."

Gwen chimed in that she would join her daughter, and soon it was agreed: Agnes, Andrew, Sarah, Carol, and Matt would remain at the hospital; the others would return to Elm Creek Manor to await the arrival of their newest guests.

"Call us as soon as you hear anything," Judy urged, and Agnes promised they would.

A strange silence hung over the waiting room after their friends left. Matt went to the hospital cafeteria and returned with steaming cups of coffee and warm muffins. Agnes accepted a cup of coffee gratefully, but her stomach was in knots and she knew she wouldn't be able to choke down a bite of food. The heat from the cup soothed some of the chill out of her hands.

Sarah was right, Agnes knew. No matter what happened to Sylvia, they couldn't let Elm Creek Quilts fall to pieces. It would be an insult to Sylvia, a betrayal, if they let her dream die. She needed to know that the life and joy she had restored to the manor would endure.

Sylvia blamed herself for Elm Creek Manor's downfall—and the Bergstrom family's decline—as if her departure had been the one killing blow that had ended it all. But Agnes knew the end had not come with such merciful swiftness. The Bergstrom legacy had ground to a halt over time in a way that was unbearable to witness. But Agnes had witnessed it. When Sylvia was far away, living first in Maryland with James's parents and later in Pittsburgh alone, Agnes had remained behind, and she saw it all.

There had been so many arguments between the two sisters. It was only later that Agnes learned how that last argument had differed from all the others. At the time, Sylvia's departure had shaken Agnes, but neither she nor Claudia ever dreamed Sylvia would stay away so long.

It had happened shortly after Andrew's visit. He had decided not to finish school; he did not explain why. He was traveling to a new job in Detroit, and had only stayed the night. That evening after supper, Agnes saw him go to the library where Sylvia was working. They spoke privately for a long time. Finally the door banged open and Sylvia stormed out, furious, tears streaking her face. Andrew had followed her as far as the library door. His face, too, was wet from tears.

"What happened?" Agnes asked him. As soon as the words left her lips, she felt a flash of panic. She did not want to know. She had too much pain already.

But Andrew had already taken her hand. "Agnes, there's something you don't know about the way Richard and James died." He hesitated. "You should know the truth."

"No." She tore her hand away. "I don't want to know."

"But Agnes—"

"I don't want to know!" she screamed.

Andrew took her in his arms and held her. "All right," he said, trying to comfort her. "Shh. It's okay."

He did not understand, but she did not try to explain. What did it matter how Richard had died? All that mattered was that he was never coming back to her. That was burden enough for one woman. She could not bear to add to it the picture of her husband's last moments—the explosion, Richard bleeding, limbs torn off or blasted away, screams of agony ripping from his throat—she imagined too much without hearing Andrew's story.

He did not ask her again.

He left the next day. As far as Agnes could tell, he had not taken Claudia aside as he had Sylvia, as he had tried to do with her. She did not remember that until later, until years after Claudia's wedding.

For the longest time, Agnes blamed herself for the last fight between Claudia and Sylvia. Sylvia had become withdrawn, locked deeply in grief. She had tried to help Claudia with her wedding plans, but after Andrew's visit, she seemed to lose all interest. If anything, she became hostile to Harold. Often Agnes saw her staring at him, brooding. Agnes would have sworn she saw hatred in Sylvia's eyes, and she did not understand it.

Eventually, Claudia sensed something, too. "She's jealous," she told Agnes as they worked on her wedding gown. "She can't bear knowing that my man came back and hers didn't."

Agnes felt a stabbing pain in her heart. Her man had not come back, either. She could only nod as she fought to hold back her tears. Claudia hadn't meant to hurt her. She still thought of Richard as her younger brother, not Agnes's late husband.

Agnes didn't think Sylvia was jealous, but she herself was. Secretly she resented Claudia, who would be able to grow old with the man she loved, who would bear his children and be allowed to love him. Agnes would never have that life.

When Claudia asked Agnes to be her bridesmaid, Agnes accepted, unaware that Claudia had already offered the role to Sylvia. When Sylvia learned she had been displaced, she was stunned and hurt. Agnes blamed herself and fled the room in tears as their argument escalated. She heard their shouts, but from a distance she could not make out their words. She did not want to.

But something had been said in that argument, something that compelled Sylvia to leave that very day and not return.

"She'll be back," Claudia had said that day and every day for several weeks. "Where would she go? This is her home."

Agnes, who knew how certain words could prevent one from ever returning home, wasn't so sure.

Claudia's wedding day came, but to Agnes the occasion seemed shrouded in grief. First there was Sylvia's absence, then the overwhelming sense that Elm Creek Manor was not ready for a celebration, not so soon after so much death. And there was what Claudia had said to her moments before she walked up the aisle.

She was deathly pale as she turned to Agnes and asked, "Is it wrong for me to marry him? Will I regret this?"

Agnes was too shocked to speak. She could hear organ music coming from inside the church. It was almost time.

Claudia's eyes were distant. "Sylvia told me something the day she left, something about Harold—" She hesitated. "But she was always jealous of me. She never wanted me to have what she couldn't have." She turned a pleading gaze on Agnes. "Do you know any reason why I shouldn't marry Harold?"

"Only one." Agnes met her gaze solemnly. "What you're telling me right now. If you have any doubts at all about marrying Harold, then you should not walk down that aisle. Once you say those vows, it will be too late to change your mind."

Claudia's voice was barely audible. "It's too late already."

In the months that followed, Agnes came to wish she had not let Claudia leave that room.

At first, the newlyweds seemed so happy that Agnes convinced herself that Claudia's fears had been nothing more than a nervous bride's last-minute jitters. Claudia and Harold seemed suited for each other. It wasn't their marriage that Agnes worried about, but their behavior. They threw parties nearly every week, spending money enough to make up for all the restrictions of the war. They lived as if to fight off death, as if by laughing and dancing they could undo all the pain they had suffered. Agnes looked on in dismay and prayed for Sylvia's return.

Harold became the head of Bergstrom Thoroughbreds, but he neglected the business. Hungry for cash, he sold off prized horses for a fraction of their true value. He and Claudia spent the money frivolously, as if it were a game, as if Elm Creek ran green with cash instead of water. Fearing disaster, Agnes searched her memory for every bit of financial knowledge she had gleaned over the years from her father and his friends, but the couple rarely heeded her advice. Secretly, Agnes began to channel some of the money into stocks and bonds; Harold and Claudia were such poor accountants that they never noticed the missing funds.

They seemed happy, but as the first year passed, Agnes began to detect an odd note in the couple's conversations, an undercurrent of hostility and accusation in Claudia's tone, a sullen defensiveness in Harold's. Once, inexplicably, Claudia asked Agnes if Andrew had told her how Richard and James had died.

Her heart leaped into her throat. "No, he didn't," she said. "I wouldn't let him."

"Of course." Claudia laughed strangely. "Well, if it were true, if it were important, he would have insisted on telling you, right?"

Agnes did not know how to answer.

The cash reserves drained swiftly the second year. A day came when there were only three horses in the stable, and then two, and then none. Claudia dismissed the last remaining stable hands, some of whom had been with the family for decades.

Agnes saw to it that they left with enough money to tide them over for a year. Since she had no money of her own, she sold off some antique furniture to raise the funds. She picked pieces at random from the empty bedrooms, forbidding herself to wonder about their sentimental value to the Bergstrom family. The Middens, not the Bergstroms, ran Elm Creek Manor now, and they were running it into the ground.

She visited the antiques shop frequently, hating herself for selling off the Bergstrom legacy, knowing she had no choice. That was where she met Joe, a history professor at Waterford College. He occasionally appraised items for the store owner, and he admired the pieces Agnes brought in. One day he asked her if he could take her to lunch in exchange for the story of how she had come to find so many lovely pieces. She agreed. When she had told him everything, he offered to put her in touch with some of his colleagues in New York, who would be able to offer her a much better price than what she could obtain in Waterford. She was so grateful she threw her arms around him. He laughed and patted her on the back awkwardly, but he didn't seem offended.

Then Claudia and Harold began selling off the land.

Agnes fought for every acre, but each time a tract came up for auction, Claudia and Harold reminded her that they had no other source of income.

"Sell one last parcel and invest the cash," she begged them. "Live off the dividends. Economize."

They ignored her.

She pleaded with Claudia to ask Sylvia to return. Claudia flew into a rage and shouted that they did not need anyone's help, least of all her hateful sister's.

Agnes knew she had to act or there would be nothing left. She did it for Richard, and she did it for Sylvia, in case she ever came home, so she would have a home to return to.

She found as many of the remaining deeds as she could; Joe helped her find the right lawyer. With his help, Agnes transferred the deeds into Sylvia's name so that as long as Sylvia lived, no one but she could sell those properties. Agnes replaced the old deeds with the new ones, berating herself for not thinking of this earlier. As the third year began, the Middens were finally thwarted. They could not touch the area that Agnes had saved, the acres bordered by forest and gardens to the north, Elm Creek to the south and east, and the orchard to the west. They blamed Mr. Bergstrom, never suspecting Agnes's role. No one but she, Joe, and the lawyer ever knew of it.

With no more land to sell, the period of frenzied gaiety came to an abrupt halt. The last remaining servants were fired. Claudia and Harold began to argue. Agnes threw herself into the cultivation of the orchard. It was their only source of income aside from Agnes's investments, which she claimed Mr. Bergstrom had made. They didn't check her story.

Agnes had nearly forgotten Andrew's untold story when Claudia mentioned it again. She told Agnes about Sylvia's accusations, that Harold had been responsible for Richard's and James's deaths.

"Do you think it could be true?" Claudia asked, her voice distant.

"I don't know." But Agnes knew Andrew would not have invented such a horrible tale, and she doubted Sylvia would have, either. Now she understood why Sylvia had gone away, and she longed to do so herself. But she could not. She had not completed her education, so she had no way to support herself. She could not return to her parents, and her pride was too great to allow her to seek help from her Philadelphia acquaintances. She was trapped in that dying house, and she saw no way out of it.

That night she was awakened by the sound of Claudia shrieking and Harold sobbing. At last Claudia had confronted him, and he had admitted the truth. Agnes pulled the covers over her head as if she were a little girl, but she could not block out the fighting.

The next day Claudia moved to another bedroom in the west wing, as far away from Harold's room as possible. After that, they no longer lived as husband and wife. They spoke only when necessary and spent little time in each other's company. Agnes thought she would drown in their silence. After a few months, she asked Claudia why they did not simply separate.

"It is my penance," she said, and never spoke of it again.

Once again Agnes felt surrounded by madness, madness she alone could see.

When Joe asked her to marry him, she hardly dared hope that he meant it. His proposal sent a shaft of light into the dark room that was her life. She told him, honestly, cruelly, that she would never love him as she had loved Richard. Joe said he had enough love for both of them. No one had ever spoken to her so kindly or offered her so much while expecting so little in return.

Claudia begged Agnes not to abandon her, for living with Harold without Agnes there would be worse than living alone. Her pleas pained Agnes, but she proceeded to show Claudia the household budget and accounts. When Claudia saw that Agnes would not be persuaded, she resorted to threats. "If you leave, you can forget about your inheritance," she shouted. "If you betray my brother's memory, you forfeit his share of the estate!"

Agnes looked at her with genuine pity. "Oh, Claudia," she said. "Do you really think that's why I stayed so long?"

She married Joe, and not a day went by that she didn't thank God for bringing him into her life. She grew to love him sooner than she would have dreamed possible, and if she never felt the passion for him that she once had for Richard, she never regretted her decision. Joe gave her love, a home, and two beautiful children. She learned that she could love again, and she knew, somehow, that Richard was happy for her.

But Claudia and Harold lived out their days in bitterness. Agnes mourned them long before they passed away.

Now she, Andrew, and Sylvia were the only ones left from those old days. Sylvia had stayed away for more than fifty years, returning only after Claudia died. Even before their reunion, Agnes was proud that Elm Creek Manor was still there to take Sylvia in. She knew she ought to be grateful that she and Sylvia had been given the past two years to reconcile.

But she was not grateful. She was angry. Two years was not enough. God owed her a reprieve. The God who had taken Richard, who had taken James, who had taken so much from the Bergstrom family, could not, must not, take Sylvia, not yet. Not yet. It was too soon. It would always be too soon.

It was the angriest prayer she had ever made, but she meant every whispered word of it. Then, her anger spent, she sat with her friends and waited.

They all looked up when the doctor entered. They rose as one and waited for him to approach. In the seconds it took him to cross the floor, Agnes tried to read his expression, but his face gave away nothing.

Not until the very last moment, when he smiled.

# Chapter Fourteen

She pulled through," the doctor said, smiling.
"Thank God," Sarah murmured. Her knees felt
weak. If not for Matt's arm around her waist, she
would have fallen.

"When can we see her?" Andrew asked.

"In a few minutes. She'll be a little groggy for a while. Don't be alarmed
if she doesn't respond when you speak to her." The doctor hesitated. "Mrs.
Compson suffered a cerebral thrombosis. That means that a blood clot
formed in an artery carrying blood to her brain, blocking the flow."

"Did you use TPA?" Carol asked.

"Actually, yes, we did. It was a viable option in Mrs. Compson's case,
especially since we were able to treat her so soon after the onset of the attack." He turned to the others. "TPA is tissue plasminogen activator, a
drug that dissolves blood clots like the one Mrs. Compson had. TPA has
its risks, but the benefits of treatment far outweigh the dangers. Ideally,
TPA will clear the blockage and allow the blood flow to resume."

"Ideally?" Matt echoed. "Has it worked for Sylvia?"

"It looks promising at this point, but we'll have to wait and see."

It looks promising, Sarah repeated silently, relief washing over her.
Thank God.

The doctor continued. "Later we'll have to discuss her long-term care
and rehabilitation, but I'm sure you'd like to see her first."

Sarah started to follow him out of the waiting room, but then she stopped short. "Wait a minute. Long-term care? Rehabilitation?" She looked from the doctor to Carol and back, heart sinking. They looked at her with such compassion and regret that she knew at once she had felt relieved too soon. Something wasn't quite right, something they knew that she didn't.

Carol took her hands. "Honey, recovery from a stroke can be a long and difficult process."

Sarah stared at the doctor. "But—but you said she pulled through."

"She did pull through," the doctor said. His voice was kind. "She will live. However, it's too soon to tell how much damage her brain has sustained."

Carol stroked a lock of hair away from Sarah's face. "Sarah, honey, when the clot blocked the artery, it prevented blood from reaching parts of the brain. If those parts die, they don't regenerate."

"Rehabilitation can help," the doctor said, trying to reassure her. "Typically, spontaneous recovery in the first month accounts for most of a stroke patient's regained skills, but rehabilitation is still very important. It might even mean that Mrs. Compson can return home rather than be institutionalized."

"Oh, my God." Suddenly, Sarah's world went gray, and her legs buckled beneath her. She felt Matt helping her into a chair. Someone placed a paper cup of water in her hands. By instinct she clasped her fingers around it, but her hands shook so violently that she spilled the water all over herself. Her teeth chattered. Someone took the cup away and ordered her to take slow, deep breaths. She tried to cooperate, but when she closed her eyes she pictured Sylvia slumped over in a wheelchair, staring into the distance, lifeless.

"I thought—" She struggled with the words. "When you said she pulled through, I thought—" She thought that meant Sylvia would be fine. How stupid of her. Of course she knew the devastating effects of stroke. She should have prepared herself. God, she was so stupid. They were only through the most frightening part of this ordeal. The most difficult part was still before them.

What if Sylvia never fully recovered?

Carol put one arm across her daughter's shoulders and grasped Sarah's arm with her other hand. "Come on," she said. "Let's go see Sylvia."

Panic flashed through her. "I can't." She tore free from her mother's embrace. "I can't."

Andrew studied her, concerned. "Sylvia will want to see you most of all."

Sarah shook her head as hot tears began to streak her face. "I can't."

Andrew began to speak, but Carol shook her head at him. "Later, maybe," she said. "You three go ahead."

"I'll be right back, Sarah," Matt said as he followed Andrew and Agnes after the doctor. "I'll let you know how she is."

Sarah nodded and wrapped the twisted hem of her T-shirt around her right hand. This was her fault. It was all her fault.

When Matt and Sarah dropped Agnes off at home later that day, she felt as if she had aged a hundred years. Sylvia had looked so still and small in that bed that Agnes had hardly recognized her. And the way Andrew held her hand and spoke to her so gently—it was enough to break Agnes's heart.

They would not know for some time how much of Sylvia would return to them. It was too soon to tell, the doctor had said.

Agnes hadn't eaten all day, and her stomach growled with hunger. It didn't seem right that the normal processes of life should continue as if nothing had happened. Somehow, Sylvia's stroke should have brought everything to a standstill as the world waited, holding its breath, to see what would become of her.

Sylvia would not deal well with incapacity. If she could not walk, if she could not speak, if she could not quilt again, she might hate the doctors for saving her life. She might hate her friends for letting them. As long as Agnes had known her, Sylvia had hidden her weaknesses, her vulnerabilities. She had always found her identity in being the strong one of the family. Now she would have to acknowledge her weakness and let others be strong for her. Would she be able to? Would she let her doctors and her friends help her? Or would she let this stroke win?

No. That didn't sound like the Sylvia Agnes knew. Sylvia hated to lose. So often Sylvia's stubborn streak had been her undoing. This time it could be her salvation.

Agnes heated a can of vegetable soup, made some toast, and ate her supper as she read the morning headlines. More bombings, more political nonsense, more children suffering all over the world. She sighed and pushed the paper away.

She cleared away the dishes, put the leftover soup in the refrigerator, and wondered what to do next. In her heart, she longed to be at Sylvia's side. She should have stayed there with Andrew, but Carol had insisted she go home and rest. Agnes was tired, but she could not rest. She wanted to do something; she wanted to help. She should have gone to Elm Creek Manor to welcome the new campers. There would be so much work to do now, what with covering Sylvia's classes, leading the Candlelight—who would lead the Candlelight that evening? Surely not Sarah. She was so distraught she ought to be in a hospital bed herself. Thank God Carol was there to look after her.

Agnes felt the knot between her shoulder blades release for the first time all day. Yes, Carol was there. So were Matt, and Summer, and Gwen, and Judy, and Diane. She needn't worry. The Elm Creek Quilters would take care of everything. They could manage without her that night. Tomorrow she would join them and contribute whatever she could, but tonight she could rest.

She carried her sewing box out to the front porch and sat on the swing Joe had hung there so many years before. For a long while she pushed herself gently back and forth and listened to the sounds of the neighborhood. She had rocked her babies to sleep on that swing more times than she could count. After the children had been put to bed, she and Joe would return to the swing and hold hands as they talked about the day, their children, the future. It had been a good life with him, and she was grateful for it.

She took the round robin center from her sewing kit and finished piecing the last tree. She had chosen the colors of Elm Creek Manor—

blues and greens, gold for sunlight, brown for earth and the strong trunks of the elms that had given the creek its name. The gray stone walls of the manor had taken shape beneath her fingers; the cotton was so much softer than the stone it represented, and yet it could endure so much.

It was an act of courage to take the scraps life provided and stitch them together, wrestling the chaos into order, taking what had been cast off and creating something from it, something useful, beautiful, and strong, something whose true value was known only to the heart of the woman who made it.

🏠 🏠 🏠

As twilight fell, the women formed a circle on the cornerstone patio. A few who had visited the manor before knew what was coming, but most waited, unknowing, anticipating, whispering questions to the women beside them, enjoying the stillness and peace of the night.

She lit a candle, placed it in a small crystal votive holder, and held it in silence for a moment, remembering how Sylvia had held that same light at the beginning of the summer. So much had happened since then. So much had yet to happen.

She sent up a quick prayer for Sylvia, inhaled deeply to calm herself, and looked around at the faces of the newest guests of Elm Creek Manor. The dancing flame cast light and shadow over them as they watched her and waited for her to speak.

"Elm Creek Manor is full of stories," she told them. "Some of these stories are joyful; some are full of regret; all are important. I have been lucky enough to call this beautiful place home for a little while, and now, for the week at least, Elm Creek Manor is your home, too. Now your stories will join those that are already here, and all of us will be richer for it."

Carol explained the ceremony and handed the candle to the first woman in the circle.

🏠 🏠 🏠

The first week was the most difficult. Gwen had never realized how much Sylvia and Sarah did behind the scenes to keep the quilt camp running. The Elm Creek Quilters divided up Sylvia's classes and other managerial duties, but they felt as if they were running day and night, just barely keeping on top of all the work. How had Sarah and Sylvia made it look so easy?

Gwen had asked Sarah that same question, but Sarah just shrugged and made no reply, as if she hadn't really been listening. Gwen wasn't surprised; all week long, Sarah had shown little reaction to the events around her, including her work. Summer had all but taken over her role in the company.

"I'm worried about her," Summer confided late one night when she and Gwen finally went home after a long, exhausting day. "I'm trying to get her involved in camp to take her mind off things, but it's like she's on another planet."

Gwen worried about Sarah, too. She had withdrawn from her friends ever since Sylvia's attack, and the few times she did join them, she had a stricken, haunted look in her eyes. Inexplicably, she had not yet visited Sylvia in the hospital, even though the rest of them had done so several times each, and Sylvia asked for her frequently.

"Sarah will be all right," Gwen said, because she knew Summer needed to hear it. "She just needs some time. This has been a shock for her."

"For all of us." Suddenly, Summer threw her arms around her mother. "I don't ever want anything like this to happen to you, okay? You have to get regular checkups, and if there's even the slightest warning sign of anything, you have to get help, understand?"

Gwen hugged her and patted her on the back. "I hear and obey, kiddo."

She stroked Summer's hair and told her everything was going to be all right, that Sylvia would be fine, and so would Sarah. As she said the words aloud, she began to believe them.

🙝 🙝 🙝

Late Thursday afternoon, Bonnie drove home from Elm Creek Manor exhausted and drained. All of the Elm Creek Quilters were worn to a frazzle, their nerves shot. There was so much to do and never enough time to get it all done. Bonnie felt as if she had been running a marathon barefoot, with the finish line still far off in the distance at the top of a steep hill. If they could just get through this week of camp, they would have Saturday afternoon to rest and recover. Surely next week would go more smoothly, once they worked out some of the bumps.

Bonnie was now teaching four classes a week, in addition to running Grandma's Attic. Even with Summer's help, it was too much. She felt as if she were being pulled in three different directions at once. All she wanted to do was rest, go to sleep and not wake up until Sylvia was better.

She stopped by the shop to help Summer close for the day. It took them longer than usual, for they could no longer put off organizing the fabric bolts and tidying the shelves. When Bonnie finally did drag herself upstairs, she decided that they'd have to get take-out for supper. She was too weary to make even something as simple as pasta. It would be the fourth time this week they'd ordered out. She hoped Craig wouldn't mind.

When she opened the door, the delicious smells of cooking floated on the air, momentarily confusing her. Had she started dinner already and forgotten? She went to the kitchen, only to find Craig peering into the oven. The kitchen counter was littered with pans and Styrofoam meat trays and spice jars.

"What on earth?" Bonnie exclaimed, taking in the scene.

Craig jumped, startled, and shut the oven. "Hi, honey," he said, coming forward to kiss her on the cheek. "Dinner will be another fifteen minutes or so. I think. The recipe on the back of the soup can called it 'Easy Twenty-Minute Chicken,' but I think that's a typo. It's taken me forty minutes already." He shrugged and smiled. "Of course, I haven't done this in a while, so maybe it's me. The table's already set, so why don't you go change out of your work clothes and lie down for a while? I'll call you when it's ready."

Bonnie promptly burst into tears.

Craig looked alarmed. "What is it?" Then he glanced over his shoulder at the mess. "Oh. Don't worry about it, honey. I'll clean it up after we eat."

"It's not that," she managed to say. She hugged him and cried, feeling foolish and unexpectedly relieved. She had held it together throughout that difficult week, and now here she was, weeping like a crazy woman in the middle of her filthy kitchen, and all because her husband had made supper.

🪡 🪡 🪡

Sylvia was getting better—that was the one bright spot of the week. She could sit up in bed now, and she was awake and alert. There was some lingering paralysis on the left side of her body, and it was difficult for her to speak clearly. Judy had visited her earlier in the day, but had left feeling frustrated and upset. She could not understand a word Sylvia spoke, and it rattled her. Andrew understood everything and had translated Sylvia's muffled, slurred speech for her, but that only made Judy feel worse, ashamed, as if she had failed Sylvia somehow. By failing to understand Sylvia's speech, Judy had made it impossible to pretend that Sylvia was just fine. She hated herself for it.

"You'll understand more when you get used to it," Andrew had told her privately. "Sylvia's getting better every day. She's not upset with you, so don't you be upset with yourself, okay?"

She nodded, but she couldn't change her feelings like switching off a light.

She was so tired. They all were, worn out from work and from worry. Once Sylvia came home, everything would be so much easier. Even if she couldn't resume her normal activities, her presence would bring the Elm Creek Quilters much-needed comfort and reassurance.

When Judy got home, she heard voices coming from the kitchen— Steve and someone else, a woman. As she walked down the hall, Judy thought the second voice sounded familiar, but she couldn't quite place it.

When she reached the kitchen, she immediately recognized the blond woman sitting across the table from Steve. "Kirsten?"

The conversation broke off as Kirsten and Steve looked up. "Hi, Judy," Kirsten said, rising. She came over and embraced her.

Judy returned the hug, her thoughts in a whirl. "Hi. What are—what are you doing here?" Her utter bewilderment kept her words from sounding rude.

"Steve called and told me about your friend. I have a couple of weeks off before summer session begins at UW, so I decided to come and see if I could help."

"But I thought you were in pediatrics," Judy said. "How can you help take care of Sylvia?"

Kirsten smiled, her face full of understanding and sympathy. "I didn't come to take care of Sylvia. I came to take care of you."

At that moment, Judy realized that she truly did have a sister.

🏠 🏠 🏠

On Wednesday of the third week, Sylvia came home. Andrew had worried about getting her up those stairs, so he was relieved when Carol suggested they make the west sitting room into a bedroom for her. "Temporarily, of course," Carol added. "She'll be up and around in no time."

"That's a good idea," Matt said. "This way Sylvia won't feel like she's shut away in a sickroom. She'll be able to be in the center of things."

Carol didn't reply, but Andrew caught something unexpected in her gaze when she looked at Matt—surprise, or maybe even respect. This was quite a change from what Andrew had observed between them since his arrival at Elm Creek Manor. Usually, Carol pretended Matt wasn't in the room.

Matt and Andrew removed one of the sofas and replaced it with a twin bed from one of the second-floor suites. Carol took care of arranging everything else, so when they finally brought Sylvia home, the pleasant, cheery room right off the kitchen was ready for her. She seemed pleased by the surprise, but said she was tired and wanted to rest.

Andrew left the room while Carol helped Sylvia into bed. When Carol went to the kitchen to help Diane prepare lunch, Andrew returned and sat down on the edge of the bed.

Sylvia seemed agitated, and Andrew thought he knew why. "Don't get too comfortable in here," he said. "You'll be back upstairs in your old room soon." He knew he had guessed correctly when her shoulders relaxed and the strain around her eyes eased.

She wanted to sit up in bed, so he helped her arrange her pillows. She asked for something, but he couldn't quite make out the words. She patted the bedcovers, exasperated. "Quilt. Quilt." After a few more exchanges, he understood. She wanted a different quilt, one that was in her bedroom.

He went upstairs to Sylvia's room, took the quilt off the bed, and brought it back down to her. "This one?"

She shook her head. "No. Scrap quilt."

"But this is a scrap quilt." He studied it. "Isn't it?"

"Wrong one."

Andrew made two more trips up and down the stairs before he found the quilt Sylvia wanted. It was an older quilt, and it had been wrapped in a clean white sheet and tucked away in the back of her closet. "Why do I suspect you hid this quilt ahead of time just so you could enjoy watching me hunt around for it?' he said as he spread the quilt over her. He had never seen the pattern before, not that he had seen many quilts before his return to Elm Creek Manor. The design almost resembled a star, but the sewing lacked the precision he usually saw in Sylvia's work. The pieces of fabric looked like they had come from old clothing. He even thought he saw a few velvets and corduroys in there.

Sylvia stroked the quilt and sighed, comfortable at last. She thanked him with a look, then gave him another command: "Quilt scraps."

For a moment he felt a sharp sting of worry. "You have the quilt already, Sylvia. This is the last scrap quilt in your room. You know that."

The exasperation in her expression told him he was the one who was confused. "Not scrap quilt. Quilt scraps." She jerked her head toward the corner of the room, where he spotted the tackle box she used to store her sewing tools. He brought it to her and helped her open the latch. She took out a plastic bag of quilt pieces, diamonds in different shades of blue, purple, and green.

"Need any help?" Andrew asked, watching her fumble to open the bag. She shook her head and waved him off.

"Okay then." He went to the kitchen for the newspaper and brought it back into the sitting room, where he settled into a chair near the window. As he read, he kept an eye on Sylvia. Several slow minutes passed as she struggled to pin two diamonds together using only her right hand. He felt a pang, realizing that before the attack she would have completed the task in seconds without a thought.

Finally she finished. She sat back against her pillow before moving on to the next task. She didn't complain, but he could sense her frustration as she tried to thread the needle. She had stuck the point of the needle into her bedcovers and was trying to jab the end of thread into the eye. Her left arm hung by her side, forgotten. That didn't seem right. He had seen boys in the war whose paralyzed limbs grew thin and wasted from disuse. Sylvia needed to work that arm if she ever wanted to use it again.

He'd have to ask her physical therapist for advice so he didn't make things worse, but for now, he had to do something. He set the paper on the floor and stood up. Sylvia looked up at him as he returned to his seat on the edge of her bed.

"Take the end of the thread in your left hand," he instructed.

She held up the thread defiantly, firmly clasped between her right thumb and forefinger.

"What are you, a wise guy? Your other left." Andrew took the spool of thread from her and placed it on her lap, giving her a teasing smile. "Don't tell me you're chicken."

She let out a scoffing laugh and reached for the thread with her left hand. It took an effort, but before long she was holding it.

"Good." Andrew found a pair of scissors in the tackle box and snipped off the frayed end of the thread. "Now, pick up the needle in your right hand."

She did so, and by force of habit brought the end of the thread toward her lips to wet it.

"Not the thread," Andrew said. "Wet the eye of the needle." She eyed him, dubious. "Trust me." She did so. "Now, hold the thread upright and move the eye of the needle over it."

Concentrating, hands trembling, Sylvia followed his instructions. After several attempts, she slid the needle onto the thread. He was so pleased for her he thought he might shout for joy.

She looked up and caught his eye, grinning. "Men don't sew."

"That's true. And women don't run businesses."

Sylvia burst into laughter. The sound brought Carol and Diane running. "What happened? What is it?" Diane asked. The two women hovered in the doorway, concerned and anxious.

"Nothing," Sylvia said. "Go make lunch."

After a long pause, they reluctantly withdrew, whispering questions to each other as Sylvia and Andrew returned to their work.

🪡 🪡 🪡

The physical therapist agreed that quilting could be an important part of Sylvia's therapy, so she added it to the routine. As the weeks passed, Sylvia slowly pieced her quilt top, and even more slowly regained the abilities the stroke had stolen from her. At least that's how it seemed to Diane, but she was impatient. She wanted to see Sylvia walking briskly around the manor again, helping the students, running the camp, bossing them all around. It couldn't happen soon enough to suit her, and she knew Sylvia felt the same.

Eventually, Sylvia progressed from a slow shuffle around the sitting room to a careful walk around the first floor of the manor. Once she confided to Diane that as soon as she was able, she was going to run up those stairs and corner Sarah in the library, where the young woman spent virtually every waking moment these days. "She's been avoiding me," Sylvia said, with only a trace of a slur in her voice.

"Some people don't deal well with this kind of thing," Diane said, but

Sylvia made a scoffing sound and shook her head. Sylvia was right; Sarah had been behaving oddly. It was one thing not to visit Sylvia in the hospital; many people had an aversion to those places. But Sarah wouldn't even come to the west sitting room, and she made the most unbelievable excuses to dodge Sylvia at mealtimes and other occasions. Each of the Elm Creek Quilters had asked her to go talk to Sylvia, and Diane had come right out and ordered her to, but Sarah refused, and she wouldn't explain why. Diane didn't understand it.

She also didn't understand why no one else was alarmed by the news that Sylvia planned to hang her Broken Star quilt in the foyer. "But that's where we planned to hang the round robin quilt," she told Bonnie as they prepared for a workshop. "All our work will go to waste if she wants to hang some other quilt there instead."

"We'll sort it out later," Bonnie assured her, smiling. "What counts is that Sylvia is quilting again."

Diane thought about it and decided Bonnie was right. What mattered was that Sylvia was persevering despite the obstacles she faced.

That Broken Star quilt might just be the most important one ever made at Elm Creek Manor.

🏠 🏠 🏠

Matt wished he knew how to comfort Sarah, but how could he when she wouldn't tell him what was wrong? "I'm fine," she insisted, despite all evidence to the contrary, as she shut herself away in the library or set off on another solitary walk along Elm Creek. Matt longed to run after her, to take her by the hand and plead with her until she told him what was troubling her. Once there had been no secrets between them, but now it seemed that with each passing day, Sylvia grew stronger and Sarah drifted farther away from him.

Finally he couldn't bear it anymore. One evening after supper, he was standing in the kitchen when Sarah passed on her way to the back door. He followed and called to her from the back steps. She froze, but didn't turn around.

"What is it?" she asked, her voice hollow and so soft he barely heard her.

"We need to talk." He joined her on the gravel road leading to the bridge, but she wouldn't look up at him. "Can you come back inside?"

"I don't feel like talking." She looked off toward the barn. "I need to be alone."

"You're alone too much." He reached out and stroked her back. "Please. It'll only take a minute. I—I miss you."

She inhaled shakily, but said nothing.

"Will you please tell me what's wrong?" Gently, carefully, he took her in his arms. The top of her head barely reached his chin. She seemed so small and fragile as he held her that he wished he could hold her like that forever and never let anything hurt her.

"Nothing's wrong."

"Sarah, I know you too well to believe that." He kissed her on the top of the head and stroked her hair. "If nothing's wrong, why won't you go see Sylvia? She asks for you every day."

Sarah pulled away from him. "I can't."

"Why not?"

Instead of answering, she turned away and began to walk toward the bridge.

"Come on, Sarah." He took a few steps after her. "Don't leave. Talk to me."

"I'm sorry," she said over her shoulder as she broke into a run.

He was tempted to pursue her, but helplessness and worry rooted him in place. He watched as she disappeared into the trees on the other side of Elm Creek, wishing he knew what to do. He had never seen her like this before, so despairing, so alone.

As he returned to the manor, a small brown shape at the foot of the steps caught his eye. A faint memory tickled in the back of his mind as he nudged it with his foot. It was a soggy mess of brown paper and cardboard—and suddenly he recognized it. It was the carton of ice cream he had bought for Sylvia weeks ago. He had forgotten it there after the fight with Sarah.

Guilt stung him as he remembered what he had said to her. No wonder she wouldn't confide in him now. Sarah deserved better than what he'd given her that night—and not just that night. All spring he had been sulky and irritable, snapping at her and stalking off whenever things didn't go his way. Why should she trust him now, when he had let her down so many times in the past few months? Why should she ever forgive him?

Sarah deserved better.

Self-loathing and anger flooded him as he cleaned up the mess.

🏠 🏠 🏠

On a rainy Saturday afternoon in mid-June, Carol sat in her room writing a letter to her supervisor at Allegheny Presbyterian to explain that she planned to use the entire four months of her leave after all. She was tempted to ask for even more time, but she didn't want to push her luck.

She looked up at the sound of a knock on the door. "Come in," she called, hoping it was Sarah. To her surprise, Matt opened the door.

"May I speak with you?" he asked.

"Of course." She set down her pen and gestured to a nearby chair.

"I'm worried about Sarah," Matt said as he sat down. "She hasn't been sleeping well, she's lost weight, she talks about Sylvia all the time but never goes to see her. Do you think something's wrong, something serious?"

He looked so distressed that Carol's heart went out to him. "She loves Sylvia very much," she said gently. "This ordeal has upset her."

"If that's all it is, shouldn't Sarah be getting better now that Sylvia's made so much progress? There's something else wrong, I just know it." He shook his head, his brow furrowed. "I want to help, but she won't tell me what's wrong. I thought since you're her mom, she might be willing to talk to you."

Carol felt a flicker of pride beneath her worry. Matt actually thought she and Sarah were close enough to have heart-to-heart talks, that Sarah would confide in her mother what she wouldn't tell her husband. "I'll talk to her," she promised, and watched as relief came over her son-in-law's face.

Matt thanked her and left. For a long while Carol sat in silence, her gaze fixed on the doorway. The past weeks had shown her a man she had not seen before. Without fail, Matt had treated Sarah with compassion and gentleness despite her inexplicable behavior. There were no orders for her to cheer up, no bitter reminders that he had been right to worry about their dependence upon an elderly woman, no complaints about the additional duties he had been forced to assume. He was so unlike Kevin that Carol wondered how she ever could have seen any similarity between the two men. Instead of manipulating the recent events to his own advantage, to score points in the battle of wills, Matt had set aside the old disagreements for the sake of his wife. His behavior was all Carol could have hoped for.

She had misjudged him.

She sighed and left the room. Someday soon she would make it up to him, to both of them, but for now, she had to see to Sarah.

The library was the most logical place to begin the search. Sarah spent nearly all her time there these days, staring at the computer or at the cold, dark fireplace. Sometimes she left the manor without telling anyone and disappeared for hours. Carol had watched from the window once and saw her daughter cross Elm Creek and vanish into the woods, but where she went from there, no one knew. Everyone needed private time, but Sarah had been spending far too much time alone. Matt was right. It was long past time someone spoke to her about it.

When Carol opened the library door, she saw that the lights were off and the draperies were pulled over the windows. The only illumination came from the computer. Sarah sat motionless before it, leaning toward the screen, her hands flat on the desktop, as if they alone held her upright.

Carol softly closed the door behind her. "Sarah?"

She didn't respond.

"Sarah, honey?" Carol said, raising her voice slightly.

Sarah looked up slowly, and the sight of her wrenched at Carol's heart. She looked as if she hadn't eaten or slept for days, and her face was drawn and haunted. "Oh, sweetie," Carol said, stricken. She swallowed and forced her voice into a nurse's brisk tone. "You're going straight to bed, and when you get up, I'm going to fix you something to eat. What would you like, soup and a sandwich, maybe?"

"I'm not hungry," Sarah said distantly, returning her gaze to the computer screen. "I can't rest. I have work to do."

"Surely it can wait. Nothing is so urgent that it can't wait an hour or two." Or five or six, if Carol had her way.

"This can't wait," Sarah whispered. "This is important. This is urgent."

Carol came closer, near enough to see that Sarah was running an Internet search. "What are you looking for?"

"Information about stroke."

"Oh." Carol hesitated, watching as Sarah highlighted some text on the screen and clicked the mouse. "Are you trying to find something to help Sylvia?"

"Yes." Sarah's voice shook. "I'm also looking for the causes, to see if stress, or a fight—to see if being upset can do it, if it can make someone—"

"Oh, Sarah." Carol ached to see her daughter in such pain. "You didn't make Sylvia have that stroke."

Sarah took a shallow, quavering breath. "I think maybe I did."

"You didn't." Carol put herself between Sarah and the computer screen, shaking her head. "You didn't. That's not how it works. It wasn't your fault. It was never your fault."

Sarah looked up at her mother for a long, silent moment before she began to sob. Carol bent down and embraced her, and Sarah clung to her as she hadn't since she was a child. Carol brought her away from the computer over to the sofa, where she held her and rocked her back and forth, and told her that everything was going to be all right. Everything would be fine.

🏠 🏠 🏠

Sarah felt better after her mother described Sylvia's progress. Sarah had noted some of these improvements from a distance, but she had been too ashamed to visit Sylvia and talk to her about them. That needed to change.

When she felt strong enough, she dried her tears, washed her face, and went downstairs to find Sylvia. She was out on the veranda with Andrew. The rain, though just a gentle shower, had been enough to keep them under shelter. When Andrew saw Sarah hesitate some distance away, he offered to get Sylvia a cup of tea. As he passed Sarah on his way into the manor, he paused long enough to clasp her shoulder and smile encouragingly.

Sylvia's gaze followed Andrew as he went inside, and her eyebrows rose when she spotted Sarah. "Well," she said, straightening in her chair. "Look who it is."

Sarah took a hesitant step forward. "Hi."

"Hi yourself." Sylvia returned her attention to the Broken Star quilt pieces in her lap.

"How are you feeling?"

"Oh, just fine, thank you." She gave Sarah a sidelong glance. "You can come closer. It's not contagious."

Sarah took the chair Andrew had left. "How's the quilt coming along?"

"Slowly but surely. I'll be ready to layer it soon." She let her hands fall to her lap and regarded Sarah over the top of her glasses. "I suppose next you'll be asking me what I think about the weather."

Sarah gave her a wan smile. "How did you know?"

"I know all sorts of things about you, Sarah McClure."

"There are a few things I'd just as soon have you forget."

"Hmph." A smile flickered in the corners of Sylvia's mouth as she resumed her work.

Sarah watched as she pinned a green and a blue diamond together, her movements slow and deliberate, but confident. "Do you want me to thread the needle for you?"

"No, thank you. That would be cheating. My therapist wants me to practice my hand-eye coordination. Michael and Todd offered to let me borrow their video games, but I declined."

Sarah laughed, but then she could think of nothing else to say. How could she explain why she had neglected her friend for so long? How could she ever express how sorry she was for the awful things she had said? How could she even begin to describe the terror she had felt watching Sylvia collapse, and the grief and loneliness she felt every time she thought about losing her?

"Sylvia," she began, "I'm sorry. I wish I could—"

"All is forgiven, dear." Sylvia reached over and patted her hand. "Let's not waste any more time on our silly misunderstandings. I'm going to be fine. Let's be grateful for that and be friends again, shall we?"

Sarah's heart was full. "I'd like that very much."

"Good." Sylvia gave her hand one last brisk pat before she picked up her quilt pieces again. They sat in silence for a long moment, listening to the gentle fall of rain on the veranda roof.

Then Sylvia spoke. "Did I ever tell you that when Andrew first saw you on television, he thought you were my granddaughter?"

"No." Sarah inhaled deeply, then breathed out what felt like a lifetime's worth of grief and regret. "You never told me that."

"Well, it's true. That's what he said."

"I think that's just about the nicest compliment I've ever received."

"I'm sure it's not the nicest one," Sylvia scoffed, but a faint tremor in her voice betrayed her true feelings.

When Andrew returned with Sylvia's tea, Sarah left the two alone and returned inside. She walked through the manor to the back door, intending to go to her secret place beneath the willow on Elm Creek, but then she thought of another place she'd rather be. As soon as she thought of it, the urgency to be there spurred her on, so that she hurried out the back door without bothering to put on her raincoat. She ran across the bridge, along the gravel road past the barn, beyond it to the orchard, where she knew she would find Matt.

She searched the rows until she spotted him. She almost didn't see him, so well did his earth-tone rain poncho blend into the trees around him. He was checking the soil at the base of a newly planted sapling when Sarah called his name.

"Sarah?" he called out in disbelief, rising as she approached. "What are you doing out here without your jacket? You're soaked." Then he grew alarmed. "Is something wrong? Are you all right?"

It was only then that Sarah noticed how the cool rain had soaked her clothing and plastered her hair to her face, and she suddenly felt self-conscious and foolish. "I'm fine," she said. "I just—" She broke off and shrugged. "I missed you."

His expression grew serious. Sarah held very still as he walked through the mud toward her.

"I missed you, too."

Then he wrapped his arms around her and held her close.

🪡 🪡 🪡

As the June days lengthened and the dark nights grew milder, Sylvia finished piecing her Broken Star quilt. She layered and basted it by hand, by ritual, each step performed methodically, patiently. This quilt was not meant for a quilt frame, where her friends would pitch in and help her finish it in a fraction of the time. No, this was one project she could not rush. She would quilt it alone, in a hoop held snugly on her lap. Her friends could support and encourage her in her work, as she knew they would, but this quilt was hers alone to see through to the end.

It was just as well that she decided this, for her friends were already using the quilt frame for a project of their own, one made by many hands and with an abundance of love.

# Chapter Fifteen

Sylvia studied her face in the mirror, then tried to force her features into a smile. One side of her face moved naturally into place; the other did not. Sylvia sighed and pushed back the disobedient flesh with her fingertips. There. Now, if she could just think of some excuse to walk around with her hand on her face all day, she'd be fine.

She turned away from the mirror and reminded herself to focus on the gains she had made in the weeks since the stroke rather than dwell upon the little that had been lost. She had been able to return to her room on the second floor; she could walk with barely a stumble; her speech, though not as crisp as it had once been, was clear. Her quilting abilities had survived the experience virtually intact. She had even managed to finish her Broken Star quilt in time for the brunch the Elm Creek Quilters were having that Sunday morning as a farewell party for Carol and Andrew.

It was a shame they had chosen the same day to leave. Sylvia was thankful that the purpose for Carol's visit had at last been accomplished: Carol and Sarah had finally begun to resolve their differences. They still had more work to do, but the gulf between them had been bridged, and both seemed committed to the healing. Carol promised to return for a visit over the Christmas holidays, so they would be seeing her again soon.

As for Andrew—she did not know when she would see him again. He had stayed so much longer than he had intended, and recently his daughter had been phoning every week to ask when she should expect him. Sylvia understood that he had obligations elsewhere, commitments to fulfill. She knew that he had to leave, but she would miss him.

She sighed again and sat down in a chair by the window. The summer had come to Elm Creek Manor at last. It was hard to remember, sometimes, that those dark green hills had ever been covered with snow, that in the mornings the sound of wind in the bare elms had woken her rather than birdsong. She thought she could still detect the fragrance of apple blossoms on the breeze, though she knew the orchards were past flowering for the year. The trees had grown thick and lush so that she could barely see the barn on the other side of Elm Creek through the leaves.

Except for the newly paved parking lot behind the manor, the scene from her bedroom window was unchanged from the time she was a young girl greeting the days with a heart full of happiness and expectation. An entire summer day would have awaited her, full of promise and fun. If Richard wanted, she would take him riding; together they would head out to the far edge of the estate that Hans Bergstrom had established so many years ago. If Sylvia was in an especially good mood, she might have invited Claudia to join them—if only because Claudia would pack them a picnic lunch. The sisters and brother would spend the whole day outdoors, returning hours later, hungry and happy, just in time for supper. Later that evening, Sylvia would steal off alone to her favorite place on the estate, a large, flat stone beneath a willow on the bank of Elm Creek, where she would listen to the murmur of the water flowing over rocks and watch the fireflies as the stars came out far overhead. And she would dream of her future, and plan, and wish, and promise herself that she would travel and have adventures and fall in love with a handsome man who liked horses—but she would always come back to this place, to Elm Creek Manor, to home.

Would she be able to find that stone again, that willow, if she searched for them? Should she even try? Perhaps it would be better to leave the past in the past and embrace the future that she had almost not been granted. She did not want to seem ungrateful to the fate that had given her so many second chances.

A tap on her door interrupted her reverie. "Are you watching for our friends?" Agnes asked.

Sylvia turned away from the window and smiled. "No, just enjoying the view."

"It's a beautiful day." Agnes crossed the room and peered outside. "A beautiful day for a drive, don't you agree?"

Sylvia said nothing.

Agnes sat down in the opposite chair. "It's a shame Andrew has to leave so soon."

"Hmph. I'm surprised he stayed as long as he did. His daughter in Connecticut has been asking for his visit for weeks now."

Agnes reached over and took her hand. "Sylvia, Andrew will stay if you ask him to."

"I couldn't possibly."

"He wants you to."

For a moment Sylvia was too startled to speak. "I couldn't. I couldn't impose on him like that. I can't have him staying on because he feels sorry for me."

"That isn't how he feels, and that's not why he'd stay."

Sylvia hesitated, then nodded. For several weeks now, she had been unable to ignore her growing affection for Andrew. Ever since he had sat on the edge of her bed and helped her remember how to quilt, she had known his heart as plainly as her own. It was nonsense, she had told herself, for a woman her age to be falling in love—but that was not what had held her back.

When she spoke, her voice was thick with emotion. "He isn't my James."

Agnes's eyes were warm with compassion. "He doesn't have to be."

Sylvia pressed her lips together and nodded. Yes. Of course, Agnes was right. James had loved her too much to begrudge her this. He would not have wanted her to live without love for so long.

Agnes squeezed her hand and smiled. "Let's go downstairs and wait for the others, shall we?"

Arm in arm, the two women went downstairs to the kitchen, where Sarah and Carol were preparing the meal. They offered to help, but the mother and daughter assured them everything was nearly ready. While Agnes sat down at the kitchen table to chat, Sylvia excused herself and went outside.

She spotted Andrew from the back steps. He had raised the hood on his motor home and was peering inside. Sylvia felt a surge of hope as she approached him, for surely engine trouble would require him to postpone his departure. But as she drew closer, her heart sank. He was only putting a quart of oil in the motor.

"All ready to leave, I see," she said briskly, forcing a smile onto her face.

Andrew glanced up from his work. "Not quite ready."

"It was very nice having you with us for so long." Sylvia wished she could retrieve her words. She could have been talking to the meter man for all the warmth in her voice.

"I'm glad I came." He emptied the last of the oil, checked the level with the dipstick, and shut the hood. He set the bottle on the ground and wiped his fingers on a rag, watching her all the while.

"Will it be a long drive?"

"Too long." He tossed the rag onto the empty bottle and smiled. "I've gotten comfortable, staying in one place so long. It won't be easy getting used to the road again."

"I suppose it wouldn't be." She hesitated. "Perhaps you shouldn't. What I mean is, it's a shame for you to make such a long, hard drive when you could, perhaps, just stay here instead."

His eyebrows rose. "Stay here? For good?"

"Well—" Sylvia hesitated. "Well, yes. For good, or for as long as you wish. I wasn't planning to lock you in."

"Does that mean I can have a room?"

"Of course you can have a room. You always could have had a room.

You're the one who insisted on staying in—in—" She gestured toward the motor home. "In this thing. That wasn't my idea."

He folded his arms and leaned back against the grill, studying her. "Would you like me to stay?"

"Of course I would." He was making this very difficult. "Would I have invited you if I didn't want you to stay?"

He shrugged, thoughtful. "No, I suppose not." He rubbed at his chin. "My daughter will be disappointed if I cancel my visit."

Sylvia felt a sharp stab of regret. "Oh. Of course. I understand." She gave him a tight smile and turned so he wouldn't see her expression change. "Well, brunch won't be much longer. I'll see you inside."

"Wait." He caught her by the arm before she could leave. "What I meant was, I can't cancel my visit, but I'll come right back afterward."

"You will?"

"I'll just be gone a week or two." His hands were light and strong on her shoulders. "Why don't you come with me? I'd like for you to meet my daughter and my grandkids. Maybe later this summer we could even head out to the West Coast and I'll introduce you to my son."

Her breath caught in her throat. "Why, that sounds like a fine idea. I'd like to meet your family."

"And I'd like them to meet you."

They held each other's gaze for a moment before Andrew kissed her. She was so startled that for an instant she just stood there, frozen—but then she kissed him back.

Then he offered her his arm and escorted her inside.

When their friends arrived, they gathered in the dining room around the table Sarah and Carol had prepared. For Sylvia, the entire day had been transformed now that she would not have to say good-bye to Andrew. The day she'd thought would be filled with partings and loneliness now marked the beginning of what felt like her next grand adventure.

She looked around the table at the smiling faces of her dear, dear friends and knew with all her heart that no woman had ever been so richly blessed.

When the meal was over, everyone helped clear away the dishes; then, at Sylvia's suggestion, they gathered on the veranda. While her friends seated themselves, Sylvia remained standing. "If you'll excuse me, I have to fetch something."

"Wait," Diane said. "Don't rush off. We have to show you something."

"I have to show you something, too," Sylvia called over her shoulder as she returned inside. She retrieved the bag and the folder from the ballroom, where she had left them earlier that day. She couldn't wait to see her friends' faces when she gave them her news.

When she returned to the veranda, all her friends had arranged their chairs around the one Sylvia usually chose—and on that chair rested a large white box.

"What on earth?" Sylvia exclaimed. She nearly dropped her own burdens she was so surprised. Her friends were beaming at her. "What is going on here?"

Sarah moved the box out of the way so Sylvia could sit down. "It's a surprise."

Sylvia took her seat. "But I have a surprise for you, too." Sarah tried to hand her the box, but Sylvia's arms were full. "Goodness, where should we begin?"

"You go first," Judy urged, and the others agreed.

"Well—" Sylvia composed herself. "Very well. I'll go first." She set the folder aside and opened the bag. "I finished my Broken Star quilt last night." Sarah and Carol came forward to help her unfold the quilt, and then other hands reached out to take a corner or an edge, holding the quilt open so all could admire it.

It was lovely; even Sylvia was not too modest to admit it.

The small blue, purple, and green diamonds had been joined together to form a large, eight-pointed star in the center of the quilt. Framing the star were large diamonds, identical to the eight sections of the star, each pieced from sixteen small diamonds. The arrangement of colors created the illusion that the star glowed, adding depth to the Celtic knotwork patterns quilted into the cloth.

Sylvia had made other quilts like it, but although these points were not as sharp as usual, nor the quilting stitches so fine and straight, she was prouder of this quilt than any other she had ever made. This quilt was a testament not to her skills but to her courage, to her refusal to give up. She had hoped that her friends would understand that, because she wanted them to know what it would mean to her when this quilt hung in the foyer and welcomed their guests to Elm Creek Manor. She hoped her friends did not need her to explain, because what she had put into that quilt she did not think she could put into words.

"It's the most wonderful quilt I've ever seen," Sarah said softly, and when she looked up and met Sylvia's gaze, Sylvia knew that Sarah, at least, understood.

"It's lovely, but I hope you're not planning to hang it in the foyer," Diane said. Judy nudged her.

"That's precisely what I planned to do with it," Sylvia said. "Why do you object? I assure you, no machine touched this quilt."

Diane hesitated. "It's not that I object, not exactly—"

"Just give her the box," Gwen said, laughing.

Sarah handed it to Sylvia. "Here's our surprise for you."

Sylvia let her friends take the Broken Star quilt from her and accepted the box. Her friends drew closer as she removed the lid and moved the tissue paper aside.

Her fingers touched cloth, and Sylvia gasped.

In the box was a quilt almost the same size as the one she had made. Her eyes filled with tears as she unfolded it—oh, it was beautiful, simply beautiful. It was a medallion quilt, with borders in several different patterns: Square in a Square, Pinwheel, Mariner's Compass, and Crazy Patch. In the center was a portrait of Elm Creek Manor in appliqué, so painstaking and perfect that it surely must have been Agnes's handiwork. And the outermost border's whimsy spoke of Gwen, as the Mariner's Compass's precision did of Judy—every inch of that quilt bore signs of her dearest friends.

"You made this for me?" she finally managed to say. "It truly is the loveliest gift I've ever received." She looked around the circle. "Thank you all from the bottom of my heart. I'll cherish this always. Diane's right. This must be the quilt we hang in the foyer."

"No, we'll find another place for it," Bonnie said. "Your quilt should be the first one our campers see when they arrive at Elm Creek Manor. It represents everything we try to teach them about quilting—perseverance, setting goals, overcoming obstacles—"

"But your quilt does the same, only in a different way. Your quilt reminds us of cooperation, and friendship, and—"

"Who says we can only have one quilt on that wall?" Summer broke in. "Why don't we hang them both? There's plenty of room."

Gwen hugged her. "Didn't I tell you guys my daughter's a genius?"

"At least once a week for the past two decades," Diane said.

Everyone laughed, and the sound of their voices warmed Sylvia nearly as much as the beautiful quilt in her arms.

"Why don't we hang them now?" Matt suggested. The others chimed in their agreement and moved toward the door.

"Not just yet, if you please," Sylvia called out above the clamor. "I have a few more surprises for you."

She saw them exchange curious glances as they settled back into their seats. She picked up the folder and opened it on her lap, enjoying every extra moment she kept her friends in suspense.

"My attack gave me much to think about," Sylvia said. And so did that argument she had overheard between Sarah and Matthew, but she wouldn't remind them of that awful time. "I decided that it was time for me to put my affairs in order. I met with my lawyer several times in the past few weeks, and I've made some arrangements which I'm sure you'll find quite interesting."

Diane looked dubious. "Interesting in a good way, I hope."

"Oh, most definitely." Sylvia turned to the first page in the folder and put on her glasses. "I've decided that it's time for me to change my role in Elm Creek Quilts. I won't be teaching any longer or organizing the activities. Instead I plan to supervise, pitch in here and there as I'm needed, work one-on-one with our campers now and again, and just generally enjoy myself. However, I don't expect Sarah to add all my duties to her already substantial workload." She peered over the top of her glasses at Summer. "In other words, dear, that full-time job you wanted is yours, if you're still interested."

"Absolutely," Summer exclaimed.

"Good. Then that's settled."

As the others congratulated Summer, Sylvia moved on to the next item on her list. "Then there's this little matter of demonstrations and skateboards and what have you."

They felt silent as all eyes turned to Diane.

"I'm concerned about the effect of continuous incarceration upon company morale," Sylvia said dryly. "I believe I have a solution. We'll arrange for the construction of a skateboard park—a legal skateboard park."

Diane's eyes were wide with astonishment. "You mean here? On the estate?"

"Heavens no. Far too many of our campers come here to escape teenagers; it wouldn't do to give them another whole crop to contend with. I own a small piece of property adjacent to the Waterford College campus. I plan to donate it to the city with the understanding that they will use it for this purpose. I imagine they could put up a swing set or two as well, something nice for the younger children. My lawyer has been speaking with the city planners, and they've nearly reached an agreement."

"This is wonderful, Sylvia," Diane cried. "My sons will be thrilled."

"Good, because the city of Waterford plans to put them to work. They're going to assemble a planning committee to research construction, costs, insurance, maintenance—countless other matters. Your sons will participate, as will several other children from local schools. I imagine it will be quite educational." She licked a fingertip and turned to the next page in the folder. "If nothing else, it will keep them busy and off the streets, so they won't be mowing down helpless old ladies like myself."

Andrew grinned and shook his head at her. "You're many things, but you're not helpless."

She smiled at him.

"You're too generous, Sylvia," Bonnie said.

"Oh, I'm just getting started." Sylvia checked her list. "Ah, yes. The company. I'm going to divide it all up into shares, which will be distributed among the Elm Creek Quilters." She had to raise her voice to be heard over their exclamations and gasps of astonishment. "Not in equal shares, I'm afraid. Each will receive a ten percent share, except for Sarah, who will receive twenty percent, and, of course, I'm keeping twenty percent for myself. My twenty percent will revert to Sarah after my demise, but don't hold your breath, Sarah, dear, for I plan to live forever. Now, where's Matthew?"

Matt raised his hand to catch her attention. He looked stunned. They all did, which delighted Sylvia beyond measure. "Ah, yes. Matthew. You get the orchard. Let's see, what's next? Oh, yes—"

"The orchard?"

Sylvia raised her eyebrows at him. "Why, yes, Matthew. The orchard. The one on the west side of the estate, where you were working just yesterday. Surely you remember it."

"Yes, but—"

"It's yours. The land, the trees, everything. The deed has been transferred to your name. If you don't want it, you can sell it, but I hope you won't." She paused. "I also hope you'll remain as our caretaker, but I'll understand if you don't. You're an essential part of our operation, Matthew. You're our—our secretary of the interior, as it were. I hope that the orchard will give you the independence you desire and the security any man would want for himself and his family, so that you keep your role in Elm Creek Quilts because you want to, not because you must."

"Thank you, Sylvia. I'm very grateful," he said, and Sylvia knew he spoke from the heart. "But the orchard—what am I supposed to do with it?"

"Do with it?" Sylvia looked around the circle in surprise. "For goodness sake, what does anyone do with an orchard? Grow apples and cherries if you like. Develop your own hybrids. Build a cider mill. Experiment. Learn. Tear everything up and plant a vineyard if you like, but have fun." She snapped the papers and hid a smile. "And here I thought you had a green thumb. What do I do with an orchard, he asks. What a question." She glanced at Andrew, and she could see that he knew how much she was enjoying herself.

Matthew had barely recovered his wits, the poor dear. "Thank you," he said again, sinking back into his chair, amazed. She could already see his mind at work, imagining the possibilities.

"The whole orchard. An actual piece of the Bergstrom estate," Sarah teased him. "You must be the boss's pet."

Sylvia fixed her gaze on her. "You only think that because I haven't given you your present yet."

Sarah looked at her, her smile fading. The others grew silent.

"But you're going to have to wait for it." Sylvia shook her head. "I almost fear telling you this. I know what an impatient young woman you are."

"I don't want anything," Sarah said quickly, clenching her hands together in her lap. "I don't even want you to have a will. I don't want you to *need* a will. I don't want anything if it means that you—that you—" Carol put an arm around her shoulders as Sarah's eyes filled with tears.

Sylvia sighed. And here they had been having such a pleasant time. "Sarah, dear, I survived this recent blow, but I won't survive forever. Recently I've learned that I'm stronger than I ever knew, but no one is that strong."

To her relief, Sarah nodded.

"I need to know that the estate will be cared for when I'm no longer here to see to it myself. I need someone who understands that the true value of Elm Creek Manor doesn't reside in its price per acre. You are that person." Sylvia reached out and stroked Sarah's hair. "Matt gets the orchard, the Elm Creek Quilters get the company, and you, my dear, you get everything else."

Sarah nodded, tears slipping down her face. Suddenly she was at Sylvia's side, embracing her. "I'll take good care of it for you. I promise."

Sylvia's heart was full as she hugged her dear young friend, who would perhaps never understand that no estate in the world could even begin to equal what Sarah had given Sylvia. "I know you will."

🪆 🪆 🪆

By the end of the day, two new quilts hung side by side in the foyer of Elm Creek Manor. The first was a testament to the courage of one remarkable woman who refused to be daunted when confronted with the many faces of tragedy. The other was a reminder of the power of friendship, the awareness that any task could be completed if friends thought creatively, trusted in themselves, and gained strength from each other.

In the years to come, whenever new visitors arrived at Elm Creek Manor, the Broken Star and round robin quilts would welcome them. The visitors would admire the colors, the patterns, the intricate quilting, and perhaps, just perhaps, they would sense the love that had been worked into the fabric with every stitch. They would wonder about the women who had sewn a small measure of their souls into the cloth as they labored with needles and thread, as they sat around the quilting frame or worked alone, driven on by hope and determination. Some visitors would discover the true stories behind the quilts; others would be content to imagine and wonder.

But Sarah McClure knew, and for as long as she lived, she would keep those stories close to her heart. She would never forget the lessons she had learned from the Elm Creek Quilters and from the wise woman who had become her most cherished friend. For Sylvia's greatest bequest was the reminder that true friends are the most precious gift, and that even in the darkest of times love illuminates the way home.

# The Elm Creek Quilts series by
# Jennifer Chiaverini

### "Full of homespun wisdom and the joys and sorrows shared by women everywhere."
### —Earlene Fowler, author of *Seven Sisters*

**Available from Plume**